Intrigues & Fun
Enjoy the ride :)

Bloodlines & Betrayal

J. Harris Anderson

Bloodlines & Betrayal

J. Harris Anderson

Blue Cardinal Press • Rixeyville, Virginia

Published by
Blue Cardinal Press
18601 Bluejay Way
Rixeyville, VA 22737
www.BlueCardinalPress.com

This novel is a work of fiction. Names, characters, places, organizations, business establishments, events, and incidents are either products of the author's imagination or are used in a fictitious context.

No portion of this book was created by artificial intelligence.

Library of Congress Control Number: 2025910909

Trade Paperback
ISBN: 979-8-9990434-0-5

First Edition

Cover design by Carol Gana

Author photo by Douglas Lees

Also by J. Harris Anderson

The Prophet of Paradise
A Paradise Gap Novel

The Foxhunter's Guide to Life & Love
An Inspirational Novel

Paving Paradise
A Paradise Gap Novel

A Funny Thing Happened
On the Way to the Fox Den
Observations From the Hunt Field

For more information:
www.BlueCardinalPress.com

In Memory of William Francis O'Keefe
"The Voice of Virginia Steeplechasing"
for more than 40 years.
May his call of "In Hand and In Command" sound forever.

Cast of Characters
(Alphabetically by Last Name)

Main Characters

Elizabeth Billington: Thumper Billington's daughter, a fourth year student at the University of Virginia, preparing to attend law school in the fall.

Myrna Billington: Thumper's sister, recently returned to Virginia from a failed acting career in California.

Olivia Billington: Diarist, Thumper's great-great-grandmother.

Thumper Billington: Owner of the Montfair estate, senior master of the Montfair Hunt, owner of the racehorse Down the Alley (aka "Bumpers).

Cecelia Broadhurst: Owner of Kimber Farm, Miles Flanagan's contact point in his undercover work.

Tavina Doddridge: Assistant Commonwealth's Attorney for Crutchfield County.

Miles Flanagan: Inventory manager and delivery driver for McKendrick Farm & Home Equipment.

Micah Hairston: Jockey, Tobias Johnson's cousin, Miles Flanagan's racing rival.

Margaret Hendershot: Founder and leader of United Friends of Rockwell (UFR).

PJ Hendershot: Margaret's daughter, devoted member of UFR.

Rocky Hendershot: Margaret's son, HVAC tech and devoted member of UFR.

Muriel Hudkins: Bookkeeper for McKendrick Farm & Home Equipment.

Ben Johnson: Tobias Johnson's father.

Wilma Jean Johnson: Tobias Johnson's mother.

Tobias "Cookie" Johnson: TV reporter, Elizabeth Billington's boyfriend.

Ryman McKendrick: Joint-master of the Montfair Hunt, believes he's been chosen by Saint Hubert to establish The Church of Foxhunting.

Shelton "Sheltie Lou" McKendrick: Ryman's daughter, manager of McKendrick Farm & Home Equipment.

Janey Musgrove: Thumper's significant other, author and professor, an authority on fringe religions and primitive cultures.

Natasha Nutchenko: Thumper Billington's housekeeper.

Voytek Nutchenko: Natasha's husband, Montfair farm manager.

Ned Potts: HVAC tech, devoted member of United Friends of Rockwell.

Barstow "Bar" Reinhardt: Sales manager for McKendrick Farm & Home Equipment.

Minor Characters

Josiah Billington: Thumper's great-great-uncle, Civil War veteran.

Tucker Dickenson: Jockey.

Ansel Hart: Farrier, former Mosby reenactor.

Windy Hendershot: Murdered husband of Margaret, father of PJ and Rocky.

Jack O'Meara: Jockey

Crispian "Crispie" O'Rourke: Professional huntsman for the Montfair Hunt.

Portia: Former slave to the Billingtons, a teacher before and after emancipation.

Mildred Preston: Joint-master of the Montfair Hunt.

Nardell Raithby: Ryman McKendrick's wife, honorary whipper-in to the Montfair Hunt.

Georgia Symansky: Jockey

Teeje: Former slave to the Billingtons, a stonemason after emancipation.

Patti Vestor: Crispie O'Rourke's significant other, professional whipper-in for Montfair Hunt.

Aunt "Tee": Tobias Johnson's great-aunt.

UFR "Board Members": Ted Lindstrom, Fred Cornwall, Maynard Tubbs, Krys Pinny.

Wycroft: A retired foxhound, lives with Ryman and Nardell.

Chapter 1

Thursday
Crutchfield County, Virginia

Margaret Hendershot stood before the portrait of her late husband.

"At 3:33 am," she said, "on a freezing cold February night, Edwin Hendershot was brutally murdered, four years ago to this day. He was a husband, a father, a faithful man of God, a good provider, and a friend to all who knew him. He left his warm house—*this* house—to help someone in need. And a vicious criminal, who should have been in jail, killed him."

After a brief pause, she continued. "So we stand here every year on the anniversary of that night, at 3:33 in the morning, to honor his memory."

Another image hung on the wall next to Edwin's. It showed a man wearing a military uniform. To that image she said, "Inspired by your truth, we shall have our justice."

Her son and daughter, standing behind her, said, "Amen!"

Miles Flanagan's sleep was plagued by memories of "The Incident." He saw himself pointing a pistol at his intended victim. The image of another man's body moved quickly in front of the target. A large hand grabbed Miles' arm. A flash of flame and smoke exploded as the black powder charge ignited. A deafening roar and panicked screams echoed in the small room.

Miles awoke. He tapped his phone screen. It read 3:33 am.

Tavina Doddridge's bed partner rolled over and began to snore. A sharp elbow to the ribs corrected the annoyance. Awake now, she thought of the appointment she had for the coming day. More ambush than appointment. Would the target take the bait? If the plan worked, it would be a new highlight on her impressive résumé, assuring her ascension to the next rung on the ladder. Squinting at the bedside clock through drowsy eyes, she could make out the figures: 3:33.

At mid-day Tavina was waiting for her mark to arrive at Kimber Farm, the second-largest estate in Crutchfield County. Cecelia Broadhurst, the estate's owner, conspired with Tavina in a plan to catch the subject alone and off guard. The chosen spot was a large equipment shed that housed two massive tractors, an array of farm machinery and tools. It was the last place the target would expect to encounter an Assistant Commonwealth's Attorney.

She held a flyer in her hand, a call to a protest rally. The inflammatory tone and emphatic cries for urgent action galvanized her resolve. These people had to be stopped.

Miles Flanagan parked the McKendrick delivery truck by the equipment shed's door. Carrying an ordered part, he stopped short when he entered the building. A young, well-dressed Black woman stood next to a John Deere 7830 tractor.

"Sorry," he said. "I didn't think anyone was here. Just leaving this off."

"I've been waiting for you," she said.

He set the package down and took a moment to assess the incongruity of her presence. Maybe she was Mrs. Broadhurst's accountant. Whoever she was, and why she was there, was no concern of his. He had other deliveries to make.

With a typical Flanagan smirk, he said, "Well, if you're waiting for this carburetor so you can fix the tractor, you might want to change your clothes."

She took a step toward him. "Do you know who I am?"

"Ah, nope, can't say I do."

"I'm Tavina Doddridge."

She took two more steps and hovered over his diminutive frame. Miles squinted as her perfumed scent collided with the shed's odor of oil and grease.

"Nice to meet you," he replied with a sarcastic twist. He took a step back and turned to leave. "Gotta go, more deliveries to make."

"We need to talk."

Her commanding tone halted Miles before his hand reached the doorknob.

"I'm an attorney for Crutchfield County. I need your help."

"My help? Look, lady, I'm just a delivery boy. You've got the wrong guy."

She handed him the flyer. "Are you familiar with this organization?"

Miles gave it a quick glance. "Never heard of them." He handed the flyer back.

She shrugged. "I thought you might have some familiarity with this type of thing. As I understand, you've been part of another group that endorses keeping African-Americans in bondage, glorifying the cause of secession to preserve slavery. Isn't that similar to what this group is promoting?"

Miles felt his short fuse start to sizzle. *No,* he told himself, *be cool. This does not look like a woman you want to mess with.* "You mean the Rangers? That's not what we were doing." He repeated the oft-recited words as politely as he could. "We were helping people understand history. And Mosby's Rangers weren't fighting to preserve slavery. They were patriots trying to protect their homes against an invading force."

"And," Tavina countered, "isn't that what a group like this might say they're doing?" She handed him another piece of paper. "Do you recognize any of the names on this list?"

Two or three names looked vaguely familiar. One stuck out. Hendershot. "No, I don't know any of these people. And I don't ride with the Rangers any more. In fact, that's all over. Completely disbanded. And whatever it is you think I can help you with, I don't have time for that either."

"You might want to make time." She pulled another piece of paper from a manila folder. Miles could see the official letterhead for the Crutchfield County Commonwealth's Attorney. "It seems you attracted the attention of my predecessor, an assault accusation some years ago filed by a woman named Natasha Nutchenko. Ultimately dropped, but it raises questions."

"That was just a misunderstanding," he said with a dismissive wave.

"Perhaps. Actually, Mister Flanagan, it's the possibility of another charge, or charges, far more serious, that you should be concerned about. Assault with a deadly weapon, attempted murder. Does that mean anything to you?"

Tavina saw the color drain from his face.

"I don't know what you're talking about," he half-whispered.

"Oh, I think you do. Your friends all refuse to talk, obviously protecting you. Impressive to have such friends, including one who's considered a leader in the community. You should appreciate their willingness to cover for you. But, well, you know, rumors leak out. The kind of rumors that could lead to an investigation. An investigation that, once the truth is revealed, might result in *decades* of prison time."

Miles tried to rekindle his usual bravado. "You're making all that up. Look, lady, I don't know what your game is here. But I ain't got time to listen to this bullshit. I got work to do." He started toward the door again, hoping his knees wouldn't buckle.

"But," she said, "I'm offering you a chance to make all that go away. No investigation, no charges, no risk of prison time. Like it never happened." She paused. "Even though you and I both know that it did."

When he turned back toward her, the faint glint of interest on his face confirmed the hook had been set.

"And," she continued, "with the resources available to my office, it won't be hard to put the facts together. So I suggest you listen to my offer."

Chapter 2

Thursday
Montfair Estate, Crutchfield County

Thumper Billington pulled a leather-bound book from a shelf in his study, a gift to a young woman nearly two hundred years before. The lined and creased cover spoke of its journey, at times perilous, from that day to the present.

Close to the bookshelf, a wooden plaque on the wall held a brace of pistols, Navy Colt .44 revolvers. A brass nameplate read: "Josiah Billington, Captain, 3rd Tennessee Cavalry, 1862-1865. With utmost respect and appreciation, Lt. Gen. Nathan Bedford Forrest."

Thumper sat down at his desk and opened his great-great-grandmother's diary to a marked page. As he read Olivia Billington's account of a seminal event in their family history, the scene became vivid in his mind. With the eye and training of a historian, he imagined the details and exchanges only hinted at through his ancestor's brief and heartbroken report.

****

Teeje was meticulously placing masonry stones for the new schoolhouse at Montfair when he heard the first shot. He looked up to see Josiah's hand pointing a pistol through the upstairs window.

"Good Lord Almighty, not again." He raced to the house, past his sister Portia in the kitchen, bounded up the spiral staircase, and ran down the hallway to Josiah's room.

"The General's been wounded!" Josiah yelled. "Sherman's men! Cut 'em down, lads! Cut 'em all down!"

He fired another shot.

Then, hearing footsteps behind him, he wheeled about and pointed the pistol at Teeje. A flash of recognition prevented him from pulling the trigger. "Burrell! Where's your sidearm? You need to join in the fight, man!"

"I'm not Burrell, Captain Jo. It's me, Teeje. And there's no fight."

"Of course there is man! Private Buchanan, take my sidearm." He flipped the pistol around and offered the butt end to Teeje. He then reached for his other Navy Colt, wedged in the waistband of his breeches, and turned back to the window.

"Captain Jo," Teeje said softly. "No one's out there. Not Sherman's men, not the General. I'm not Burrell Buchanan and you're not at Fallen Timbers. You're home, at Montfair. You just had a bad dream, that's all. Just a bad dream."

The soothing, familiar voice slowly brought Josiah back to reality. "Just a bad dream," he mumbled. "When will it ever go away?" He turned to Teeje. The desperation in the man's eyes was deeper than his lifelong companion had ever seen. "So much death, so much pain. You don't know what it was like. The blood, the screams, bullets all around us, our horses shot from under us, comrades blown to pieces. And all for what? All lost. All for nothing. Or even all for worse."

He stood facing Teeje, his arms dangling at his sides, the pistol held limply in one hand.

"And Fort Pillow. My god! What we did at Fort Pillow. How can I ever atone for that? All those men, some of them could have been your brothers, your cousins."

"You didn't do any of that. It wasn't your fault."

"No, but I should have stopped them. I just stood there as the men went berserk. They were trying to surrender. It was the honorable thing to do, accept them as prisoners. But they were just shot down. The men couldn't stand to see all those Coloreds in blue uniforms. No honor in that. No honor."

"One of your own men would have shot you if you'd tried to stop them."

"Maybe it would have been better if they had."

"How about you let me have that other pistol. I'll take 'em both downstairs and put 'em away somewhere safe. Then you get some rest. Mister Archie's out with his hounds this morning, but he'll be back soon. Then y'all can have a meal. Portia's putting something real nice together right now. That'll make you feel better."

"Feel better." He looked at the pistol still in his hand. "There's only one thing that will ever make me feel better."

When Portia heard another gunshot, she knew something had gone wrong. Teeje had always been able to talk Josiah down from his traumatic delusions. She left the kitchen and dashed up to Josiah's room. The scene she found there froze her in shock and fear.

Josiah lay on the floor, blood and brains splattered on the wall, a Navy Colt .44 beside him. Teeje, holding the other pistol, stood staring at the body.

"He…he did it," Teeje stuttered. "He finally did it."

"And you better drop that gun and get away from there," Portia ordered. "You don't want to be found over the body of a dead white man, holding a pistol in your hand."

Teeje remained frozen in place. "I was his best friend. He trusted me, everyone knows that."

Portia heard footsteps approaching, the lighter tread of a lady moving rapidly up the stairs.

"You know that, and I know that, but you really think the white folks are gonna let it be known that a Billington took his own life? How's that gonna make the family look? How are they gonna bury him in the family cemetery plot by the church? Not when they got a handy Negro to blame."

"Mister Archie and Miss Olivia would never do that to me."

The footsteps drew close to the door.

Heavier steps, those of a workman's boots, echoed from the staircase.

"No, of course they wouldn't. But plenty others would. So you best drop that damn thing and come stand with me, looking as innocent and grief-stricken as you can."

Teeje did as ordered seconds before Olivia Billington appeared in the doorway.

****

Thumper arose from his chair. He returned to the plaque with the two pistols. More than a hundred years would pass from the time they were last fired before Post Traumatic Stress Disorder became an official diagnosis. The need to soften the sting of loss suffered in the American South had turned the war into celebratory remembrance for many. The Billingtons did not participate in that charade.

Standing in his study, a room occupied by a half dozen ancestors before him, Thumper thought he felt a cool hand brush the back of his neck. It was a sensation that occurred at moments like this. He imagined it was the spectral touch of Archie reaching across the ages to comfort him.

"It's freezing in here!" a voice announced from the doorway.

He turned to see Janey Musgrove wrapped in a blanket.

"The heat's not working again," she said.

Thumper cocked his head and listened. He heard the telltale rattle of the aging furnace, struggling to send even a slight solace of warmth through the old house.

The cool breeze was not Archie's phantom hand.

Thumper shrugged. "Guess I'd better call the Jessup guy, see how soon he can get here."

****

An hour later a van from Jessup Heating & Air Conditioning pulled into the service parking area at Montfair. A young man stepped out of the van. Embroidered on his dark blue work shirt was the name "Rocky Hendershot." He moved with the confident swagger of a man accustomed to working with complex machinery, a technician who could diagnose a malfunctioning component with surgical precision. Heavily bearded and thickly built, he'd be equally at home perched in a deer stand, wearing full camouflage, high-powered rifle in hand.

"This old thing oughta be in a museum," Rocky said as he assessed the ancient furnace. His hands were deep into its guts, searching for the cause of the malfunction.

Voytek Nutchenko, Montfair farm manager and caretaker, stood next to Rocky, Thumper behind him. "What I am always doing to make it be working again is not working now. I am very frustrated." A native of Poland, he still struggled with English syntax and some phonemes, particularly for words beginning in "w" and "v". *What* came out as *vhat* and *working* sounded more like *vorking.*

As Rocky withdrew his arm from the entrails of the furnace and reached into his toolbox, Thumper noticed a tattoo on his forearm. It bore the shadowy face of a man that struck Thumper as vaguely familiar. The image was surrounded by a laurel border with an eagle, a twisted cross, and the letters "UFR" in prominent script.

Thumper tried to peek over Voytek's shoulder as he addressed Rocky. "Do you think it's fixable?"

"Gimme just a minute." Rocky fiddled with mysterious components neither Voytek nor Thumper could see. A twist, a turn, a grunt, and…the furnace rumbled back to life.

"Wonderful!" Thumper exclaimed. "You've saved the day."

"Well," Rocky demurred. "It might not be much more than a day. It's gonna need some new parts and I expect they'll have to be special ordered. No telling how long that might take. But there might be some odds and ends around the shop that could work in the meantime. I'll see what I can find and let you know."

Chapter 3

Thursday
McKendricks' Shop, Paradise Gap

Miles Flanagan stumbled through the back door of McKendrick Farm & Home Equipment. An annoyed Barstow Reinhardt awaited his arrival.

"I just got calls from Frank Worsham and Doc Preston," Bar growled. "You screwed up their deliveries. Have you forgotten how to read a goddamn address?"

At six-four, 280 pounds, Reinhardt towered over Flanagan, a former jockey. Bar's size, intimidating on its own, was secondary compared to the wide, jagged scar where his left eye and ear had once been. A patch covered the damaged socket. The remaining eye swam in a pale blue pool, its opaque lightness a glittering contrast to the black cloth that concealed its absent partner. At this moment, the functioning eye shot a cerulean stream of irritation at Miles.

But when Bar saw the anguished look on Flanagan's face, his ire eased. He expected a typically flippant smart-ass reply. Now, though, the small man remained silent and seemed to get even smaller.

"What the fuck's the matter?" Reinhardt asked.

"Bad day, man."

"Humph. We all have 'em."

"Yeah, maybe. But not like this one."

Bar took a moment to assess the pitiful creature slouching before him. He'd seen Miles in a range of moods, from rage-filled to boyishly giddy. But he'd never sensed this level of despair.

"My office. Now." Reinhardt turned and headed to his work space.

He had recently been promoted from head mechanic, a position he'd held for almost forty years, to sales manager for the business owned by the McKendrick family for several generations. To accommodate his new role, a section of the showroom had been walled off for his use. A glass front allowed him to see the sales area. He ushered Miles inside and closed the door behind him.

"All right," Bar said. "What's going on?"

Miles withdrew the flyer from his pocket and handed it to Bar.

"What the hell is this?" Reinhardt asked, studying the incendiary language on the flyer.

"What does it look like?"

"Like a bunch of assholes with nothing better to do than make a stink about some stupid ass statue."

"It's a monument."

"Monument. Statue. Whatever. Either way, what the hell does this have to do with you?" Bar paused and his one eye widened. "Oh, shit! You haven't gone and joined this crazy ass group, have you?"

"No. But someone wants me to."

"Shit, Flanagan, you know better than to get mixed up in something like this." He tossed the flyer onto his desk.

"Yeah, I know better. But some woman wants me to—what did she call it?—*infiltrate* this group."

"You? Infiltrate? Does she know you're a fucking idiot?"

"Maybe. But I guess she thinks I can be a useful idiot."

"So who is this woman and what makes her think you, of all people, are a good choice for something like that?"

Miles took a deep breath. "Her name's Tavina Doddridge. She says she's an attorney for the county. Says she knows about 'The Incident' in Rhetta's kitchen. You ever heard of her?"

Reinhardt paused. He looked across the showroom to the office shared by Shelton McKendrick and Muriel Hudkins. "Yeah, I've heard of her. But how could she possibly know about that? Everyone who was there has a damn good reason to keep their mouth shut."

"She didn't say how she knows. And I got the feeling it's just a hunch on her part. She was kinda cagey about it but said things like 'attempted murder' and 'assault with a deadly weapon.' She says if I don't play along, she'll launch an official investigation."

"Sounds like she knows *something* at least. So what the hell does this have to do with you joining..." He picked up the flyer and read the name. "...The United Friends of Rockwell?"

"She says they're a white supremacist group, that they're planning some kind of attack against Black people. She wants to get the goods on them before they can cause any harm. And she needs someone on the inside to get the proof for her to bring charges against them."

Bar smirked. "And she thinks you've got the wits to do something like that? She does know who you really are, right?"

Miles looked down and mumbled, "Yeah, she knows who I am. She knows too damn well."

"Did she tell you just how you're supposed to get in with this group of assholes? Doesn't sound like something where you can just show up and say, 'Hi. I'm batshit crazy too. Let's be friends.'"

"She thinks riding with the Rangers gives me some cred. Like we were really trying to glorify the Confederacy and thought slavery was a good thing. You know we were just having fun, playing soldiers, riding horses, and camping out. Besides, now that Mosby's name can't be mentioned, Ansel's dissolved the group."

"Yeah, well, you did get a good bit more into it than just 'playing soldier'. But she may have a point about that giving you some cred."

"She also gave me some names. I told her I didn't know any of the people on her list, but it turns out I do."

"Great way to start the relationship, lying to her right off the bat."

"I was hoping she'd back off, decide I wasn't a good choice and leave me alone. But that didn't work. Besides, between working here, helping Ansel with some shoeing jobs, and riding for Mister Billington, I've got no time to play secret agent for this woman."

"That was the plan after 'The Incident,' keep you as busy as possible so you wouldn't have time to get into trouble again. You already used up your one and only 'Get out of jail free' card. Like Muriel told us, the Bible says 'Idle hands are the devil's workshop.'"

Miles looked down at his hands. "Yeah, well, these hands don't have much idle time. None really."

"So who are these wack jobs you're supposed to rat out?" Bar asked.

"Some people we both know. Like the Hendershots. Also Ned Potts, and a few others I've never heard of."

"Geez, I know Margaret had a rough time after Windy died. But I can't see her being involved in something like this. Not Rocky either. He always seemed like a nice kid. Potts, well, yeah, he's an odd bird. Never quite clicked with him when he and Rocky were here working on the AC."

Miles looked up at Bar with what struck the big man as a helpless childlike gaze. "So what do you think I should do?"

For all the verbal abuse he heaped on Flanagan, Bar couldn't help feeling sorry for him. Miles had his shortcomings, which were obvious to all. But he wasn't evil. He'd been dealt some challenges in life and had rarely made the best choices, just dug himself in deeper to a pattern of failed opportunities. And that pattern had led to this dilemma: either figure out how to worm his way into a potentially violent group of extremists to rat them out or face serious prison time. And take down a few others with him, including Bar Reinhardt and Thumper Billington, who, along with some others, were complicit in covering up his delusional actions that nearly cost someone's life.

Bar picked up the flyer. "I know this monument. It's the one in front of the old courthouse. It shows the names of all the men from Crutchfield County who served in the Confederacy. I read somewhere that the board of supervisors is going to vote on having it removed. I can see how a white supremacist group would get their hackles up about something like that."

Miles shrugged. "Yeah, well, I don't really give a shit about it either way."

"But you have a good reason to give a shit, or at least make it look like you do."

"Huh?"

"I'm pretty sure at least a couple of the names on the monument are men who rode with Mosby. And didn't y'all hold one of your reenactments on the courthouse lawn a few years ago?"

"Yeah, now that you mention it, I guess we did."

Bar sat back and flashed what passed for a grin on his damaged face. "There ya go! Show up at this rally. Say someone left the flyer at the shop. You don't know who. And this looked like something you could get behind. You know Rocky. At least you've seen him a few times here. Mention the Rangers, how pissed y'all were that every reference to Mosby has to be erased, like they're planning to do with this monument. Say something like, 'It's just not right to dishonor all those patriots who gave their lives to protect their homeland against an invading force.' You know how to turn on that kinda bullshit. So that could be your intro."

Miles nodded. "Yeah, that could work."

"But don't look too eager at first. That's more likely to raise suspicions. Let them sell it to you."

"Gotcha. Not too eager."

"And after that, as the preacher said in *Blazing Saddles*, 'Son, you're on your own.'"

Bar added a cautionary note. "But just remember this, shit-for-brains. Don't start believing all that crap again. That's what got your ass into this in the first damn place."

Chapter 4

Friday
Montfair

Rocky Hendershot returned to Montfair the next day with an assortment of parts to nurse the old furnace back to a reasonably reliable level of function. As he stepped out of the van, the sound of hammering struck his ears and the scent of steaming metal filled his nose. A horse stood in cross-ties in the barn aisle. Ansel Hart, wearing his heavy farrier's leather apron, lifted the animal's foot and pressed a red-hot horseshoe against the upturned surface. Smoke billowed upward. The horse showed no reaction.

Miles Flanagan appeared from deeper in the barn. He stopped next to Ansel and said, "Next one's ready for you."

Ansel picked up his hammer and pulled a nail from his rolling toolbox.

As Rocky approached them, he could hear snippets of what Miles was saying between the hammering.

Whack, whack, whack. "…those coloreds are no good…" *Whack, whack, whack.* "...need to send them back…" *Whack, whack, whack.* "...only one race that really matters…" *Whack, whack, whack.* "…you know how I feel about Arabs, got no use for 'em…" *Whack, whack, whack.* "...yeah, BLM, a real pain in the ass…"

Rocky stopped. He quick-marched to his van and grabbed two flyers from a stack on the passenger seat. Stepping up to the two men in the barn, he said, "Mornin' fellas. How ya doin'?"

Ansel looked up from his bent over position. "Fine. You?"

Miles stood motionless and mute. Here was Rocky Hendershot, standing right before him.

Rocky turned to Miles. "Hey, you're the guy from McKendricks', right? The parts guy."

Miles struggled to find his voice. "Um, yeah, that's me."

"You into horseshoeing now?"

"Just helping Ansel out in my spare time."

"Well, if you got some spare time next Tuesday night, you might be interested in this." He handed a flyer to Miles. "And you, too." He offered the other one to Ansel. Another spark of recognition flashed on Rocky's face. "And you're the reenactor guy! Mosby, right? Y'all do the living history thing every year on Paradise Gap Day." He turned back to Miles. "I think I've seen you there, too."

"Yeah," Ansel replied, standing upright. "But we don't do that anymore. Not politically acceptable."

Rocky shook his head. "Damn shame. We shouldn't let those assholes get away with erasing our history. It's just not right."

Ansel shrugged. "Yeah. But what can you do? Just the way things are going."

"Not if me and some of my friends have anything to say about it. The county commissioners want to tear down the memorial in front of the old courthouse, the one with the names of all the men who fought with the Confederacy. They're gonna vote on it Tuesday night." He pointed to the flyers each man held. "A bunch of us will be there to protest. Sounds like something you guys oughta care about. I'm pretty sure some of those men rode with Mosby, right?"

"Yeah, a few," Ansel replied. He glanced at Miles with an expression that read *Don't even think about doing this!*

Miles stood mute, staring down at the flyer then back up at Rocky.

"The meeting's at seven," Rocky continued. "We'll be there about six to get organized. Sure would be great to have you guys there. I mean, shit, Mosby himself!"

"I'm busy that night," Ansel said tersely. "Busy now, too." He turned away and went back to his shoeing work.

"Damn shame," Rocky said. "How 'bout you?" he asked Miles.

"I...I dunno...yeah...maybe." He caught a glimpse of Ansel shaking his head as he lifted the horse's hind foot.

"It's important we have a good turnout," Rocky said. "Gotta send a message that our history matters. So think about it, will ya?"

"Yeah, I will," Miles said.

"Okay. I gotta get to work. Seems the old Montfair heating system needs my loving care."

An hour later, Rocky left the house accompanied by Voytek. Ansel was gone. Miles was still in the barn, sweeping up the hoof shavings and other detritus from Ansel's work.

"Humph," Voytek said with a note of disdain. "Little man is still here."

"You're not a fan?" Rocky asked.

"He has been trouble before. A racist thing. Was big fight between him and my wife, Natasha."

"A racist thing?" Rocky asked, his voice rising in surprise.

"Oh, yes. A few years ago now. Big scene in front of many people. Mister Thumper had to fire him. But now he's back. And doing racist things again."

"Like what?"

"Oh, not my business really. I leave that to Mister Thumper. But is best for little man to stay away from my wife."

Their conversation was distracted by a car coming up the driveway. It turned into the pebbled circle at the front entrance of the house and stopped. A young Black man hopped out and ran around to the passenger side as a twenty-something white woman came down the steps carrying a suitcase. Rocky watched as the man gave the woman a peck on the check and hoisted her suitcase into the car. He then held the passenger door open for her as she got in. He dashed around to the driver's side and they sped away.

"Who was that?" Rocky asked.

"Is Mister Thumper's daughter, Miss Elizabeth, and her boyfriend..." He thought for a moment, trying to remember the man's name. "Um...something like 'Kookie'. I am not knowing. My wife said something about them going away for the weekend. But that is also not my business." He shrugged and walked back to the house.

Rocky stood and collected his thoughts. Thumper Billington's daughter is dating a Black man? Interesting. More importantly, Voytek's comment about Miles confirmed what Rocky overheard earlier. Miles was a perfect candidate to join The Cause. Why wait and hope he shows up at the protest rally? Get him on board now.

He caught up with Miles as he was putting away the broom. "Looks like you're a busy man these days."

"Yeah. Best for me to stay as busy as possible. Keeps me out of trouble."

"I don't suppose you're all booked up on Sunday, too."

"My one day of rest."

"We're having a get-together Sunday morning to talk about plans for the Tuesday night thing. How about you come by and join in."

Miles remembered Bar's warning not to be too eager. "I'll...I'll need to check my schedule. Might have some free time."

"Great! Everyone there will be folks who share your view of things. And Mama Hendershot will be serving her famous fried chicken for lunch after we're done. You won't want to miss that."

"Yeah, okay. I'll let you know."

"Ten o'clock at our place, Off the Grid Cuts and Clips. You know it?"

"Oh, right. I used to go there for haircuts before...well, um...it's been a while."

Rocky laid a hand on Miles' shoulder. "Hope to see you there, *brother*," he said.

****

Thumper was at his desk deep into researching his family history when he heard a tap at the door. He looked up to see Miles standing in the doorway.

"Miles! Come on in."

"Um, I don't want to disturb you if you're busy."

"No, no. I could use a break actually. What's up?" He gestured toward one of the high-backed leather chairs in front of his desk.

"Just wanted to see if you'd heard anything more about the new silks."

"Not yet. I told the customer service rep that the white looked dingy, more gray than white. And the red wasn't sharp enough, didn't catch the eye. Been a long time since they produced the original Montfair racing silks, so maybe the dye formulas have changed. Anyway, I guess these will have to do for now." With a wry grin, he added, "Maybe we can talk Natasha into stitching your old silks back together. She was, after all, the one who ripped them up. You just happened to be wearing them at the time."

Miles blushed and bowed his head. "Yeah, well, not really her fault."

"Ah, too long ago to worry about that."

"Maybe. But she avoids me whenever I'm here. And Voytek won't speak to me."

"Not your concern. You just need to focus on keeping Bumpers in shape, get him ready for his first race." Thumper noticed Miles fidgeting with a folded piece of paper. "What's that you got there?"

"Oh, this? It's nothing. Just something Rocky gave me."

Thumper saw the nervous, embarrassed look as Miles tried to avoid eye contact.

"Rocky, huh." He reached out his hand. "Let me see it."

Miles handed him the flyer.

"I heard about the vote coming up to remove the old monument," Thumper said. The names on the stone included Josiah Billington and three Crutchfield ancestors on Thumper's mother's side. But

Thumper was purely neutral on the question. He had his own way of honoring his family's past. A hunk of stone in front of the county courthouse was of no concern to him.

He studied the flyer in more detail. Overblown, misspelled, poorly composed rhetoric attempting to sound patriotic. Nothing overtly threatening, but an obvious undertone of white supremacy. Prominently displayed at the bottom was the same image he'd seen on Rocky's tattoo, accompanied by the group's title: "United Friends of Rockwell." Now he knew what UFR stood for, and why he recognized the face on the logo. There was no contact info on the flyer, just the date and time and a call for like-minded "patriots" to join them in protesting against the "eraser [sic] of our honorable history."

"Rocky gave you this?" Thumper asked.

"Yeah, just now."

"Rocky Hendershot? Huh. I wouldn't have figured him for something like this. Always seemed like a good guy. A little rough but in an honest, rednecky kind of way. Guess you never know." Thumper set the flyer down. "Are you thinking about going to this?"

"Yeah, maybe. Probably. For some reason, Rocky thinks I'm one of them."

"You think that's a good idea? You're supposed to be keeping a low profile after…well, you know."

Miles' fidgeting increased. "Um, I'm not sure I should tell you this. In fact, she told me not to say anything."

"Who told you not to say anything?"

"Some woman named Doddridge."

"*Tavina* Doddridge?"

"Yeah, that's her."

Thumper's mental radar began to ping. "When were you talking to Tavina Doddridge?"

"Yesterday. She was waiting for me at Miz Broadhurst's. Kinda ambushed me I guess you could say."

Miles filled Thumper in on what Tavina said, the leverage she claimed to have over him, and what she wanted him to do.

Thumper remained silent and considered the situation. Doddridge obviously had some knowledge of, or at least suspicions about, "The Incident." And that would likely include the names of those involved. He and the others had acted in what they considered an honorable manner to help someone in need. If there was a local "tribe", Miles was part of it. A troubled, often annoying, and sometimes downright infuriating part of it. But he still held a place in the tribal circle, if only at the edge.

When Miles finished his recap of the assignment and the consequences that would follow if he refused to cooperate, he asked Thumper, "Do you know this Tavina person?"

"Yeah, I know her. She was in a couple of law school seminars I taught. One smart cookie. And it was obvious even then she had big plans to make a name for herself. She's the county's Assistant Commonwealth's Attorney. The word is she's going to run for the top job. My old friend, Jim Trowbridge, her boss, is going to run for state senate." He picked up the flyer and gave it another scan. "If she can get the goods on a group like this, find something to hang an indictment on, and then a conviction, it would pretty much assure she gets the CA job. And it would also be a nice boost for Trowbridge to have that happen under his watch."

"Oh, shit!" Miles moaned. "So that means not just this Tavina woman but her big boss could be on my ass too? Do you think her offer is on the up-and-up? What if I blow it?"

"First of all, as you were instructed not to tell anyone about this, our conversation here never happened. *Comprende*?"

Miles was surprised by Thumper's stern tone.

"Yeah, right. Never happened." He now regretted telling Bar but decided this would not be a good time to mention that. "Just you and me."

"Good. Now when you go to this rally…"

Miles interrupted. "Actually, there's something before that. Rocky invited me to a meeting they're having this Sunday at his mother's place. Something about final plans for the rally. Oh, and 'Mama' Hendershot's fried chicken afterward."

"Margaret's part of this too?"

Miles shrugged. "I guess. I don't know. Maybe she's just making the chicken."

Thumper considered the implications of this situation. Information about "The Incident" had leaked to the Assistant Commonwealth's Attorney. He, better than anyone, knew those involved were taking a chance protecting Miles; some motivated by a sincere desire to help a troubled soul, others cowed by their own culpability. Either way, there would be consequences if Tavina chose to launch a full blown investigation. And the prospects of avoiding that now rested on the slim and shaky shoulders of Miles Flanagan.

"So here's the deal," Thumper said. "You do what Doddridge wants you to do. I'll do what I can to help, strictly behind the scenes. You keep me filled in on everything that happens. Any doubts about what you should do, check with me first. Any dirt that turns up, you fill me in before you pass it along to Tavina. You good with that?"

Miles stood. He felt like he should salute his commanding officer ordering him on a secret mission. Instead, he just said, "Yeah, I'm good with that."

Chapter 5

Saturday Morning
Montfair Front Lawn

The front lawn of the Billingtons' home had been the meeting site for the foxhunts that marked the beginning and end of the official season since Thumper's great-grandfather, Thaddeus the First, founded the Montfair Hunt in 1888. This early March Saturday morning, cloudy with a faint mist, promised excellent conditions for a chase.

Hunt members, from young children to one octogenarian (Bing Sensabaugh), bustled about their trailers in preparation for the event. Thumper, flanked by Janey Musgrove (his significant other) and Elizabeth (his daughter), sat astride his favorite hunt horse, a tall, dark bay Thoroughbred named Leonard Slye (aka Lenny).

Huntsman Crispian "Crispie" O'Rourke and his partner Patti Vestor, who served as first whipper-in, watched over a pack of thirty-three foxhounds as they milled about. Several of them looked up at their leader with an expectant gaze. *We're ready for the chase! C'mon, boss, let's be off!*

Joining Thumper were Ryman McKendrick and Mildred Preston, Thumper's two joint-masters in the hunt's leadership. Ryman and his wife Nardell Raithby also served as whippers-in.

Mildred Preston, a recent transplant from New England, led the non-jumping second field, Thumper led first field.

"And a grand good morning to you all!" Ryman exclaimed. "All glory to our blessed Saint Hubert! He assures us of another splendid day."

All through the hunting season, from September until this March morning, Ryman had been energized by his belief that Saint Hubert, the patron saint of hunters, was speaking through him, calling him to launch The Ancient and Venerable Church of Ars Venatica (AVCAV for short, aka The Church of Foxhunting). He had stumbled upon a little known text titled "The Foxhunter's Faith." A list of ten commandments phrased in Biblical style, it was attributed to "A North-Country Hunting Parson." Ryman delivered a short sermonette prior to the start of each hunting day, citing one of those commandments and expounding on its enduring relevance.

When he'd exhausted "The Foxhunter's Faith" and needed new material, Thumper's new book appeared. *The Foxhunter's Guide to Life and Love* featured a collection of life stories and lessons using foxhunting as a metaphor for life. Thumper wrote it mostly as a personal diversion from the serious academic work that dominated his résumé.

Ryman, though, saw it as the hand of Saint Hubert working through Thumper. Diversion or not, it provided the inspiration and material needed to continue his AVCAV mission.

Professor Janey Musgrove had only recently discovered foxhunting. An expert on fringe religions, she happened upon the Montfair Hunt as she and Thumper shared the same literary agent. Ryman's mission was in its embryonic form at the time and offered the perfect target for her next book project. Despite initial tension from conflicting objectives, Thumper warmed to her presence as she warmed to the foxhunting lifestyle. By the midpoint of the hunting season, she had taken up residence at Montfair.

Elizabeth Billington was cut from the same cloth as her father. Billingtons had been attending the University of Virginia since Mister Jefferson created his "academical village" in 1819. Elizabeth was two months away from graduating and nearing her final decision on which law school offer to accept.

Miles Flanagan was perched on a young Thoroughbred nicknamed Bumpers. Sired by Bowling For Bucks out of the mare Downstate Dream, his Jockey Club registered name was Down The Alley. In discussions for a suitable barn name, Janey, from a family of avid bowlers in Minnesota, suggested "Bumpers." All agreed it was perfect.

Thumper acquired the horse a year earlier after the gelding's modestly successful flat track career ended. He was now being prepped to compete in timber races, jumping stiff wooden fences over three-mile courses at local point-to-point and steeplechase events. Thumper, licensed as both owner and trainer, a Billington custom spanning multiple generations, hired Miles to exercise the horse, school him as a jumper, and ride him in the races. Part of that included introducing him to foxhunting where he'd have the chance to go in the company of a group of horses over open country, jumping wooden coops, stone walls, and other obstacles along the way.

Not everyone agreed with Thumper's decision to employ Miles Flanagan for that duty. During his earlier days as a jockey, Miles rode for Thumper and others. But, despite his successful record in the saddle, his combative nature with his fellow humans led to a steady stream of firings. His racing career was halted following a particularly nasty exchange with Thumper, a physical confrontation narrowly avoided when Natasha Nutchenko, Montfair's indispensable housekeeper, intervened. Flanagan was no match for the two hundred pound Polish woman in full mama-bear mode. Fortunately, the only physical harm done was to the Montfair jockey silks Miles was wearing when he tried to escape Natasha's grasp. The flimsy material was left in tatters.

But Billington wasn't one to hold a grudge and the concept of *noblesse oblige* had been drilled into him by his patrician parents. Following the more recent "Incident", Thumper had good reason to rule Miles out of his life forever. Instead, along with a few others,

Bar Reinhardt among them, he became complicit in a plan to shield Miles from any consequences of his actions and work to rehabilitate him. Chief among that objective was to keep Miles as busy as possible, thus minimizing any temptation to drift astray.

"So," Thumper asked Ryman, "where does your Saint Humpty-Bump tell us to go this morning?"

"The young vixen awaits our arrival at Blackberry Covert, ready for a lively chase," Ryman replied.

Throughout the season, Ryman's predictions proved accurate. Montfair Hunt had tallied an unbroken string of excellent days. Had Ryman McKendrick really received a miraculous vision and supernatural powers from a little known sixth-century saint? Or had a lifetime spent immersed in mounted sport resulted in a critical blend of knowledge and instinct that created the illusion of a mystical gift?

Only Thumper and Janey knew the truth behind the "vision" that had inspired Ryman to launch his Church of Foxhunting. The physical confirmation of that truth was hidden in what they believed was a safe repository. Although highly skeptical of Ryman's claims to mystical powers, Thumper and Janey decided to let him play out his delusions rather than reveal the truth. Mystical or not, everyone was enjoying the sport. Why risk ruining the streak?

Thumper turned to the assembled field of hunters and unmounted spectators. "Well, another season comes to an end. I think we can all agree it's been one of the best ever."

"Amen!" exclaimed Nardell, Ryman's chief—and only—acolyte.

"As most of you know," Thumper continued, "while today closes out formal hunting, we will continue to take hounds out informally a few more times, mostly as a way to school the young hounds that will be joining the pack next season. Dress is casual, everyone's welcome to attend. We just ask that your horse is steady around hounds. We don't want the youngsters having any unpleasant experiences on their first hunting days. So now…" He turned to Crispie. "…Mister O'Rourke, let's go hunting!

In keeping with his pronouncements throughout the season, Ryman's prediction proved accurate. A young vixen was roused from Blackberry Covert, a high spot on the backside of neighboring Fair Enough Farm, the McKendricks' home, and the hunters enjoyed a spirited chase.

As hounds and hunters returned to the meet, the Montfair foursome peeled off toward the home barn, untacked their horses, and turned them out.

"Bumpers looked good back there this morning," Thumper said to Miles as they watched the young Thoroughbred peacefully munching hay in the pasture.

"Seems like he really enjoys hunting," Miles replied. "We were out—what?—two and a half hours? Lots of running and jumping. And he came in with plenty of steam left. Nothing better than hunting for getting a horse ready for the races."

"That was always the old school way," Billington replied, "from the time my grandfather got us into it." Noticing Janey and Elizabeth strolling out from the barn, Thumper added, "I expect the ladies are eager to get to the breakfast."

"And I need to get to the shop," Miles replied.

The hunt breakfast was an elaborate spread of tempting fare and tasty delicacies, much of it prepared by Natasha. She was confident that her culinary skills were the equal of any professional caterer and superior to many. A few trusted hunt members were allowed to bring something for the tables, but most was prepared by Natasha's talented hands.

The members milled about, all in good spirits, discussing what a wonderful season of hunting they'd all enjoyed and speculating on how much of that was due to Ryman's seemingly mystical powers.

Janey took the opportunity to speak with Elizabeth out of Thumper's hearing. "Have you made a decision about your law school choice yet?" she asked.

"Pretty close," Elizabeth replied. "Leaning heavily toward Georgetown."

Janey was surprised. "Not UVA? I would have thought…y'know…family heritage and all. Why Georgetown?"

"For one thing, it's close enough to get home to Montfair on the weekends."

"Um…isn't Charlottesville closer?"

"Yeah, but Georgetown has other advantages. It's close to Capitol Hill and the Supreme Court, which is what I plan to focus on. And, to be honest, I've always felt some people thought I had an unfair advantage at UVA because of that family heritage, that I was a legacy admission."

"Well, your performance certainly should have squashed any of those thoughts. Graduating with honors? Really?"

"Yeah, but if I stayed on for law school, it would be even worse with my father's role there, his visiting professor thing, seminars, guest lecturing. I won't have to deal with any of that at Georgetown."

Janey cocked her head and asked, "I don't suppose the fact that a certain handsome young reporter lives and works in DC has anything to do with that, does it?"

Elizabeth showed a faintly guilty smile and replied in a comic Southern Belle voice. "Why Miz Musgrove, what evah do you mean?"

Chapter 6

Saturday
Off the Grid Cuts & Clips

Rocky Hendershot pulled up to the entrance of Off the Grid Cuts & Clips. He hit the button on his remote and the security gate swung open. To the left was the rambling log house his father built. On the right was what had served as the office and warehouse for the once-thriving Hendershot Heating and Air Conditioning business, founded by his grandfather. A section of the front area had been arranged for Margaret "Mama" Hendershot's hairstyling business. The single barber chair and attendant tools remained, but customers were rare. Only a few loyal locals were willing to ignore the incendiary slogans and images that covered the walls to enjoy the benefits of Mama's coiffure skills. Some also found the ever-present 9mm Luger strapped to her side disconcerting.

Rocky knew where his mother would be on this Saturday morning: sitting in her barber chair watching cable news.

"I believe I've found us a new recruit!" he announced.

She cast a skeptical eye. "I hope it ain't another girlfriend like that last one. What did she call us? 'Crazy-ass hate-filled rednecks'?"

"No, not a girlfriend. This is a guy. Miles Flanagan. He works at McKendrick's. And he just might be a perfect member to join The Cause."

Her suspicious nature held. "Perfect how?"

"Well, for one thing, he used to be a member of Ansel Hart's Mosby's Rangers. Y'know, those reenactors who played Southern patriots."

"Used to be? If he's so perfect, why is he a used-to-be-member'? How come he ain't a still-doing-it member?"

"Because the group's been disbanded. All this crap about erasing Southern history has made Mosby's name a bad thing."

"Yeah, well, maybe he's pissed about that, maybe not."

"Oh, that's just part of it. I overheard him saying some things that really show he's one of us."

"Like what?"

"Like how Coloreds should be sent back, only one race matters. He even got in a couple of digs about Arabs and BLM."

"And you just happened to hear him say these things?"

"Yep. I was at Montfair working on their old furnace, and he was there helping Ansel shoe horses. They didn't know I was listening, but I heard him say all that stuff."

"So how about Ansel? What did he have to say? Maybe you should be recruiting both of them."

"I couldn't hear anything Ansel said. He was bent over nailing on a horseshoe. I gave them both the flyer for the rally. Miles seemed interested, but Ansel not so much. Kinda standoffish."

Margaret considered her son's suggestion. Maybe this fellow was a good prospect. But she always had her radar on full alert. There was no end to the crap the government might try to pull to take down honest patriots like her and her small band of loyal followers.

"But here's the kicker," Rocky said. "The old Polish guy who works for the Billingtons had something to say about Miles. Are you ready for this? He actually used the R-word. It was obvious he doesn't like Miles. Said the 'little man' is a *racist*. What more evidence do we need than that?"

"Well, first of all, we're *not racist*, damn it! We're *patriots*! To our country and to *our* race. Lots of Black people feel that kind of loyalty to their race. But, boy, don't ever call *them* racists." She paused and her tone softened. "But it sounds like his heart might be in the right place. Maybe you should bring him by sometime."

"How about tomorrow?"

"Damn, boy! You really are hot on this guy. Okay, fine. Maybe after the board meeting."

In addition to the three Hendershots—mother, son, and daughter—the official United Friends of Rockwell membership consisted of just five others who embraced the UFR doctrine. To create a sense of formal structure, the eight adherents considered themselves a "board of directors," despite the absence of any other followers to direct.

"I was thinking *for* the meeting," Rocky replied. "You know Fred's probably going to drop off. Wouldn't hurt to start looking for a candidate to take his place."

"Now hold on! You know we gotta be careful about letting someone we don't know well into our circle." She pushed herself out of the barber chair and stood before a framed photo mounted on the wall. It was a duplicate of the one in the house next to her late husband's image. "*He* never had many followers. But even with a tight knit crew, it was one of his own men who betrayed him." She turned back to her son. "Sure, we could use a few more people. But better to have just a few we can trust than end up with troublemakers who ain't truly committed to The Cause. Or, worse than that, somebody who turns against us, maybe even tries to bring down our glorious and sanctified mission."

"Look," Rocky countered, "tomorrow's meeting is just about plans for Tuesday's rally. And this has a special meaning for Miles, what with his Civil War reenacting stuff. I think this'll be a really good chance for the key people to check him out. You, PJ, Ned, and the others. If any of y'all see something that ain't right, we'll know not to let him in too far."

"Okay, then. But make sure everyone knows not to mention anything other than this one rally. Nothing about any other plans."

Chapter 7

Saturday Evening
Montfair

Myrna Billington, Thumper's younger sister, returned to the family home after spending most of her adult life pursuing an acting career on the West Coast. The pursuit never amounted to more than a few bit parts in B-movies. Realizing her chances of ever being a success on the big screen were over, she thought she might have better prospects working behind the camera. Her idea for a documentary about pioneering women in the film industry—directors, writers, producers, editors, and others—was sure to be a hit. Every studio exec that she approached agreed the concept had merit. But putting the project in the hands of a woman with zero directorial experience—whose most notable film credit was "Hooker #3" in *Van Nuys Valentino*—did not.

Convinced she would prove them all wrong, she accepted funding from an "alternative financing" source. When the project folded before the first scene was shot—proving all the naysayers right—that source demanded immediate repayment at usurious interest. The demands were conveyed through a large man with a shady past and an unsettling Eastern European accent.

Desperate for relief, Myrna fled to Virginia where she concocted a plan to sell her share of Montfair to a developer. That plan also failed. Ultimately, Thumper agreed to bail her out on the condition that she remain at Montfair and work off the debt over time as resident barn manager. Both knew it would take more than two lifetimes for her to repay the full amount. But she was, after all, family. And family unity was a hallmark of the Billington legacy.

Sitting at the dinner table that evening with Myrna, Janey, and Elizabeth, Thumper sensed that legacy would soon be challenged by spirits from the past.

"You two are coming to Wilma Jean's birthday party, right?" Elizabeth said, pointing toward Thumper and Janey. "Nothing elaborate, mostly just the family."

"Of course," Thumper replied, trying to sound upbeat. "Wouldn't miss it."

"Wilma Jean?" Myrna asked.

"Cookie's mother," Elizabeth answered.

"Aaannnd…" Myrna said, dragging the word out, "Cookie?"

Elizabeth realized Myrna wasn't up to speed on this budding relationship. "Sorry. Tobias. You've met him. He's a reporter. Cookie is his nickname."

"So was he, like, a short order cook before he got into reporting?"

Elizabeth chuckled. "No, not that. The way his mother tells it, he loved Cookie Monster when he was a kid, used to run through the house yelling 'Cooookie!' trying to sound like the Muppet. So everyone started calling him 'Cookie' and it stuck."

"That's adorable."

Elizabeth turned to her father. "May I be excused? I promised him I'd come up with ideas for a birthday gift. Gotta do some browsing and get a few choices for him."

"What are you going to search on?" Thumper asked. "'Gift ideas for a Black woman turning 60?'"

Elizabeth scowled. "Other than the Black part, yes, I guess that's exactly what I'll search on."

Feeling scolded, Thumper mumbled, "You're excused."

When Elizabeth had left the room, Myrna said, "Nice to see the family tradition of old fashioned manners still holds. She looked at you the same way we did when asking for permission to leave the table."

"I reckon there are still a few of us who think manners matter. Damn few unfortunately."

Myrna folded her napkin and said to Thumper, "You still haven't told her, have you?"

"I don't see the need at this point."

"Really?" Myrna said. "'Just the family'? And out of all her law school choices, it looks like she's going to pick the one that's in DC? Purely coincidence that 'Cookie' happens to live and work in that town?"

"What haven't you told her?" Janey asked.

Myrna flashed her a look that said *I'll tell you later*.

"I'll know when the time is right," Thumper said, trying to muster an aura of authority.

The ladies were unimpressed, but opted to let him continue in his state of denial.

Seeing the opening, Myrna announced, "I'm thinking about getting back into riding."

"That's great!" Janey said.

"Yeah, well," Myrna continued, "it's been a long time. Very long time. Like decades. But, y'know, being back here at Montfair, working with the horses…hell, living right above them in the barn apartment, watching you guys riding every day. I loved it all when I was a kid. I just felt like I had to rebel against something and the only thing I had to rebel against was my family."

"And now you're back," Thumper said, his mood softening. "The stuff Elizabeth's outgrown is stored in the attic. It's all about your size. Grab what you need and we'll get you back in the saddle."

Chapter 8

Sunday Morning
Montfair

Thumper was up early Sunday morning. On his way to the kitchen for a cup of coffee, he stopped on the staircase of his ancestral home and studied the portrait of Olivia Billington. According to family records, it was painted in 1850, when she was twenty. Her dark brown hair, neatly parted down the middle, was gathered into a thick bundle behind her neck. She wore an off-white gown with a low-cut neckline and billowing sleeves. A gold chain held a locket that hung just above a corsage of carnations and roses pinned between her breasts. Flawless pale skin highlighted the red coloring applied to her cheeks and lips. Steady brown eyes held the viewer's attention. Her mouth, neutral to the observer, appeared to be at the ready to assume whatever reaction a situation demanded: a polite smile, a gentle frown, a bemused smirk?

Coffee in hand, he went to his study and withdrew a book from the shelf. His mother had composed a history of the women in the Crutchfield and Billington families: *Ladies Led the Way. A History of Virginia Women In Times of Struggle*. It was not intended for broad publication, but as a resource for future generations. Thumper was glad to have that resource as a means to deepen his insights into the life of his great-great-grandmother.

Olivia Bauer Billington (1830-1902) was born into a Quaker family. Her father died when she was in her early teens, and an uncle became her guardian. He did not adhere to the Society of Friends' anti-slavery position. He arranged to marry off his niece to the wealthy and powerful (and slave-owning) 32-year-old widower Archibald Billington (1815-1892).

Archie's first wife, Deborah, gave him three daughters but died in childbirth in 1842. The child, a boy, also died. Archie grieved for the next five years before he agreed to a friend's urging to marry Olivia. She then bore him three more daughters before finally providing a male heir, Thaddeus the First, in 1855.

The tenets of Quakerism, particularly those that encouraged frugality and opposed slavery, were deeply seated in Olivia from early childhood. Given the limited rights women were allowed in her time, including white women of privileged birth, she could not refuse her uncle's marriage arrangement. She could, though, use her gentle persuasion to influence Archie in desired directions.

Immediate emancipation for all those held in bondage to the Billington family was not an option. The best she could do initially was assume responsibility for their care and working conditions. There was no avoiding the harsh demands imposed by fieldwork in those times, regardless of the workers' skin color and legal status. She trod a delicate balance between limiting the burdens on those responsible for the estate's income while assuring the revenues did not suffer. As long as the latter did not occur, Archie was willing to indulge her in the former.

Her ultimate desire to convert the agricultural workforce to paid laborers was aided by the creation of Liberia. Supported by fellow Virginian and Billington family friend President James Monroe, the movement to send freed slaves to a newly created nation on the west coast of Africa attracted adherents with varying motivations. Some saw it as a solution to the potential problem of free Blacks encouraging those still in bondage to violently revolt against their oppressors. Others were less concerned about a bloody uprising but felt the white and Black races were not intended to live together as equals. And some, such as Olivia, saw the colonization movement as a benevolent, if imperfect, option to gradually reduce the cohort of those held in bondage.

At best, she was only able to achieve a slight reduction in the number of enslaved field workers prior to full emancipation that would eventually be mandated by force.

The house staff was a different matter. With seven children and the responsibilities imposed on the wife of a member of Virginia's landed aristocracy, Olivia needed help. It was, though, possible for her to assure working and living conditions for the household staff were little different than would have been the case for paid hirelings. There was just one major exception—education.

Fearing the power that literacy might serve to make those held in bondage more aware of their oppressed conditions and better able to organize among themselves, Southern legislatures enacted laws that forbade teaching slaves to read and write. To overcome that obstacle, Olivia needed every ounce of her persuasive abilities to convince Archie to turn a blind eye to her creation of a clandestine school. A compromise was struck that allowed her to provide basic literacy instruction for the house staff and their children. He agreed to her efforts to improve life for the field workers, but drew the line at teaching them to read and write. His position among the state's power base, prominent thanks to the Billingtons' extensive landholdings, could only allow him to circumvent Virginia law to a limited extent.

By the late-1850s, talk of secession was rumbling throughout the South. As a state senator, Archie was privy to the leanings of those in leadership positions empowered to decide which way Virginia would go. He opposed secession but feared he could not stop the growing sentiments that favored it.

Part of his opposition stemmed from his concerns over what impact secession would have on his own family's financial security. No one could then foresee the coming upheaval and the long term impact a lengthy and destructive war would have on Virginia. But Archie was financially savvy enough to know that, even without the

North moving to force the rebel states back into the Union, trying to form a new government, with its own currency and banking system, was sure to be a messy, uncertain process. He was only two generations removed from the formation of the United States, a process his grandfather witnessed firsthand. His father lived through the early years of independence as the infant nation struggled to find the right path. Sorting out the monetary details had been especially tumultuous in those fledgling times.

The solution came through Olivia's family connections. The Bauers where prominent members of the business and banking community in Philadelphia. Through that channel, a sizable portion of Billington assets were transferred there for safekeeping should the worst happen. When it did, many prominent Virginia families were left with little, if any, of their former wealth. The Billingtons' fortunes were diminished. But, thanks to Archie's foresight and Olivia's relations, enough remained to ease the postwar recovery.

Then there was the matter of participating in the armed conflict itself. Archie could not claim advanced age as an excuse to refuse an officer's commission in the Confederate military. (He was eight years younger than Robert E. Lee.) That required the complicity of others in powerful positions. He was owed many favors thanks to his artful handling of political compromises over his years in the legislature. His claim of infirmity was accepted with a wink.

His younger brother, however, was eager to serve. Had Josiah fought with a local militia unit, or ridden with Mosby's Partisan Rangers, the fortunes of Montfair might have fared far worse when the Confederacy fell and the Union imposed martial law. Knowing the risk, Archie agreed to let Josiah join Nathan Bedford Forrest's Tennessee regiment where he'd be kept clear of combat on his home territory.

Mosby was another matter. The local populace was largely supportive of the 43rd Battalion's guerrilla tactics and provided support for shelter and supplies. Tales abounded of the Rangers' exploits that caused havoc among the invading Union forces. The reports, at times embellished, elevated the band of cavaliers and their young leader to heroic status. Olivia herself could not dismiss a flutter at the sight of Mosby—wispy thin and courtly mannered—when he dined at Montfair. She confided to her diary that his demeanor at the table was relaxed and good humored. Yet there was an aura about him suggesting in an instant he could spring from his chair, leap onto his horse, and be away in a storm of blazing pistols.

She did not object to Archie's covert efforts to provide aid when needed. This included constructing a hidden space in an upstairs bedroom with access to the attic and an escape route down the trellis along the back of the house. The room, situated at the building's corner, offered a sweeping view of the countryside to the north and east, the directions from which Union forces would most likely approach. The view also included the crest of a hill where the private graveyard lay.

Many years later it came to serve as Elizabeth Billington's bedroom.

Chapter 9

Sunday
Montfair

Immersed in Olivia's story, Thumper was oblivious to the approach of a vehicle pulling up to the house. The sound of voices in the hallway slowly drew him back to the present. Janey, Ryman McKendrick, and Nardell Raithby appeared at the door of his study. A glance at his watch reminded him that he'd agreed to meet with them. The agenda focused on the progress of Janey's book about Ryman's campaign to create The Ancient and Venerable Church of Ars Venatica.

With everyone seated, Janey began. "The latest update from my agent is that it's down to two hot prospects for cutting a publishing deal. They're both fairly small shops but with a good track record for books similar to this. There's still a possible deal with a larger house but that's lukewarm at best."

"I have faith," Ryman said with the confidence of a true believer, "that Saint Hubert's hand is at work and he will guide us to the right path."

Thumper tried to muffle a snort at his old friend's statement. "And I have faith," he said, "that Janey's excellent skills as an expert on fringe religions and cults will result in a suitable publishing arrangement."

"AVCAV is not a *cult*," Ryman protested. "And with Saint Hubert's guidance, the good word will continue to be spread. Did he not work through you to produce *The Foxhunter's Guide to Life & Love*? You may have thought it was all your own doing. But Nardell and I know where the inspiration really came from."

"Amen!" Nardell added.

"Actually," Janey interjected, "the prospects for this current book depend in part on what happens next. If you do keep the mission going, in one form or another, that opens up the possibility for a follow-up. Publishers prefer an ongoing series over a one-time splash." She turned to Thumper. "I know you were just having fun with 'The Foxhunter's Guide' piece. But Ryman has a point that it could mesh well with his AVCAV mission."

"I did 'The Guide' mostly for my own amusement," Thumper said. "Or at most for a very limited audience. Didn't see it becoming part of the scriptural canon for a new religion."

"It's not a *new* religion," Ryman exclaimed. "Hunting-based belief systems are one of the oldest forms of religion known to man. Isn't that right, Janey? You're the expert on that sorta thing."

"He does have a point," Janey conceded.

"There. You see," Ryman said with a hint of triumph. "It all fits together. Saint Hubert sent me the vision of the stag. Three times it appeared to me. Then he led me to 'The Foxhunter's Faith'. When that was done—Boom!—here comes your Seven Principles of the Foxhunter Model. And, maybe best of all, he brought Doctor Janey Musgrove into our world to chronicle it all so the message can reach a wider audience. Maybe the whole world!"

Ryman glowed with apostolic energy as he thought of the AVCAV mission extending to all corners of the globe.

"But none of this would have happened," he continued, "if Saint Hubert hadn't arranged for me to fall off that horse and arise to see The Stag!" He spread his arms wide to emphasize the foundational significance of that event. "And the glorious image of that amazing cross shining above his noble head."

As Ryman sat gazing upward in beatific thrall, the study door opened. Myrna appeared cradling what appeared to be a bundle of junk in her arms.

"I…I was looking through the trunks in the attic for some of Elizabeth's riding kit," she said. "I didn't know which trunk was hers, so I was just going through each one till I found her things. One of them turned out to be Uncle Josiah's. I was kind of curious. I remember childhood stories about how he had a secret compartment built into the trunk to keep the Yankees from finding things, like his pistols. When I looked, the pistols weren't there…but this stuff was."

Thumper and Janey knew what she was carrying. They looked at each other and nodded.

He arose and moved toward Myrna. "Oh, that's nothing. Just some old junk that must have gotten in there by mistake. Here. I'll take it and toss it out."

As he reached for it, Ryman stood up and stopped him. "Hold on a second. Let me see that."

He saw two pieces of wood joined together as a cross. The horizontal piece was square at both ends. The vertical piece was adorned with a rounded top. They had been painted white but were now faded to a dull gray and showed several scrapes as if they'd been rubbed against something. Affixed to the wooden cross was a bundle of wires. Ryman grabbed the wires and lifted them from Myrna's arms.

Thumper cast a helpless glance at Janey. There was no point trying to stop Ryman now.

Ryman spread his arms with his hands as far apart as the width of an alpha buck's antlers. A perfectly shaped crucifix hung at the center, just above where the crown of the deer's head would be.

"Son-of-a-bitch," he muttered. "It's a fucking fence." A flash of recognition shone on his face. "The spot that was missing from Patti's garden fence, that she was ragging on Crispie to fix. The buck musta tried breaking through the fence and got this shit stuck in his rack." He looked at Thumper. "You found this, when the stag appeared at The Cabin, got tangled up in those vines, and you got to him before I did. Am I right?"

Thumper shrugged in helpless concession.

Ryman's shoulders sagged. "Jesus. I really did just imagine the whole thing. It wasn't a miraculous sign from Saint Hubert. It was a bunch of broken crap from a fucking fence."

Nardell leaped up and went to his side. "No, sweetheart. You're wrong. Okay, so it wasn't an actual miracle. But surely Saint Hubert arranged for the deer to get it stuck in his antlers, so it looked just like what he saw all those centuries ago. And what about everything else? Your ability to communicate with horses and hounds, to always know where a fox would be found? And finding the Ten Commandments of 'The Foxhunter's Faith'? Then there was Thumper working on his 'Guide' thing without realizing it was Saint Hubert's hand leading him."

"I dunno," Ryman replied. "A lot of that could just be coincidence. Like Thumper kept saying it was. Or maybe because I believed I'd been sent a special message, I also believed I had those other powers." He turned to Janey. "That sorta thing happens, right?"

"A strong faith can sometimes make seemingly miraculous things occur," she replied. "Or at least the true believers think they're miracles."

"But now that it turns out my 'faith' was just based on a couple sticks of wood and some wire, maybe those other things weren't as miraculous as I thought."

Janey considered her extensive knowledge of fringe religions. "I have seen instances where, once the foundational miracle turns out to be bogus, the faith soon fades."

"I'm so sorry," Myrna said. "I should have left that stuff where it was. It was just, well, so odd to find it like that, hidden in Josiah's trunk. I wanted to find out why it was there."

Ryman slumped back down into the chair. "S'okay. You couldn't have known."

"Ryman," Nardell said, "you need to be strong. Saint Hubert is just testing you. Our mission is still to spread his blessed word to the masses. People need to hear..."

He raised a hand to silence her and addressed Thumper. "You knew this, and I reckon Janey did too, but you decided to keep it from me. Why did you do that?"

Thumper thought for a moment, then said, "As annoying as it could be at times, this Church of Foxhunting thing had you more energized than you've been in years. In an odd kind of way, you were finally getting your act together. Maybe it was something to distract you from your father's death. Or the likelihood the shop was going to go under. When I saw that buck caught in those vines and realized what you'd been seeing, I made a split second decision to cut it loose and hide the evidence before you got there." He looked over at Janey. "And, well, there was this book project in the works and, y'know, I didn't want to mess that up."

"Oh shit!" Ryman exclaimed. "Janey's book! You can't publish that now. It'll make me look like a damn fool. The whole 'miracle' thing has turned out to be nothing but bullshit." He held up the remnants of the fence. "'Exciting new religion turns out to be inspired by discarded junk.' Big whoop."

"Look," Thumper countered, "this was just going to be about your church up to this point. It's already written, and nothing revealed about where your visions really came from. So maybe there won't be a second book now." He turned to Janey for confirmation.

"I guess not," she agreed. The disappointment in her reply was clear.

"Not good enough," Ryman said, "Shit leaks. Y'all know how this works. Everyone in this room can make a vow of silence and we can toss this crap in the fire. But somehow, some way, the real story will eventually get out. And who's gonna believe me then? Half the foxhunting world already thinks I'm bat shit crazy. Nope. You gotta pull the plug on that damn book now. And I gotta rethink my priorities."

"Now Ryman," Thumper pleaded, "Janey's worked her butt off on this book. And she's so close to getting a publishing contract signed. You can't deny her that."

"Thumper," Janey said, "it's okay. I don't want to cause Ryman any more stress than he's already feeling. I'll find something else to write about."

"No!" Thumper insisted, his anger rising. "We've put up with Ryman's Saint Hubert antics long enough. I've fended off efforts from the North American Foxchasers Association to shut him down. I've stood up for him when others were attacking him. He can't tell you now what to do with your year's worth of work."

Ryman stood up. "My Saint Hubert *antics*, huh? Is that what you think? And when you had the chance to tell me the truth, you chose to hide it from me. Like I was some kinda kid who believed in Santa Claus and you didn't want to disappoint poor little me." Clutching the wood and wire to his chest, he continued. "C'mon, Nardell. We're going home. I need to sort this out. But I'll say one thing. If you do go ahead and publish that book, I'll sue you for…for…declaration of character!"

It was all Nardell could do to keep from whispering "defamation." But she kept quiet, put on a stern, disapproving face, and accompanied him as they stomped out the door.

Chapter 10

Sunday Morning
Off the Grid Cuts & Clips

Miles had visited Off the Grid Cuts & Clips for the occasional haircut. But he'd been there only once since Windy Hendershot was murdered and, soon thereafter, Margaret began espousing radically racist opinions. Before that, the name was a mildly amusing play on the oddly remote location for a hair styling business. Margaret once had a loyal clientele willing to make the drive through the woods and down a rough country road. Her skill was renowned and the privacy allowed for an unending flow of local gossip.

Now, though, a chain link fence, six feet high and topped with razor wire, surrounded the small compound. A callbox mounted by the gated entrance was fitted with a sign ordering visitors to announce their presence and state their business. A notice beneath it declared "All Transactions Cash Only!"

A variety of warnings, most of them featuring images of guns, decorated the fence:

- No Trespassing…We're Tired of Hiding the Bodies.
- You Are No Longer Trespassing. You Are A Target.
- Prayer Is The Best Way To Meet God…Trespassing Is The Fastest.

- Due To The Increase In Ammo Prices, Do Not Expect A Warning Shot.
- We Don't Call 911.
- No Trespassing…Violators Will Be Shot. Survivors Will Be Shot Again.

Miles pressed the button on the callbox.

A youthful female voice announced, "State your name and business!"

"Um, Miles Flanagan. Rocky invited me."

A whir, a click, and the gate swung open.

Miles drove his Ford Ranger into the yard and parked at the end of a row of vehicles; three pick-up trucks and two jacked-up Jeeps. Each was decorated with a variety of affinity identifiers—window decals, bumper stickers, and license plate frames:

- Redneck Lives Matter.
- Pure White Trash.
- It's Not Gun Control. It's Freedom Control.
- Proud To Be Deplorable.
- Don't Blame Me. I Voted For Jefferson Davis.
- Vegetarian: Ancient Word For Bad Hunter.

A slender young woman opened the door when Miles knocked. The family resemblance to Rocky was obvious. Her dark brown hair cascaded several inches past her shoulders. Thick eyebrows accentuated her pale skin and chestnut eyes. She stood three inches taller than Miles.

Her welcoming smile served as a counter to the threatening messages at the gate and the mocking slogans on the vehicles. "Hi! I'm PJ, Rocky's sister. C'mon in. You can toss your coat over there."

She pointed toward a pile of well-worn coats—Carhartt, Cabela's, Mossy Oak; two in neutral brown, three in camouflage; all well-worn, some tattered and stained. Even from a slight distance, Miles could detect the scent of decaying leaves, scraped tree bark, gun oil, and grease.

PJ ushered him into the dining room where "Mama," Rocky, and five others sat around a long table. He noticed two photo portraits on the wall, one of which he recognized as Windy. The other appeared to be an older black-and-white photo of a man in military uniform, although he couldn't tell which service branch. He thought it might be an ancestor of the Hendershots, maybe a grandfather.

A stack of hand-drawn signs affixed to wooden supports leaned against the wall in the corner of the room. Only the one at the front was readable: "We're the Good People on the Other Side."

Rocky stood up and took the hand-off from his sister. "Glad you could make it, Miles. Hey everyone, this is Miles Flanagan. I think he's here mostly for Mama's fried chicken," he said with a teasing grin. "But I told him he'd have to sit through our meeting first. Miles rode with Mosby's Rangers so he has a special interest in what we're planning to do this Tuesday. And, well, he shares our views on certain other topics. Isn't that right, Miles? You can be honest with us. We're all friends here."

Miles was baffled by Rocky's assumption that he shared their White Supremacist views. He understood the Rangers connection. But portraying a Confederate cavalryman in living history events hardly suggests that he, personally, was a modern day racist.

He recalled Bar's counsel not to sound too eager at first. "Yeah, well, I'm sure we all have a few things in common."

A man Miles guessed to be 50-ish—hefty but not flabby, a pleasant face with full cheeks and cheerful eyes, his mustache and chin beard flecked with gray—stood and extended his hand. His baseball cap bore the image of a tattered American flag, a screeching eagle with the phrase "We The People" above and "Are Pissed Off" below.

He extended his hand. "Nice to meet you. Ted Lindstrom. Folks call me Lindy." He then said something that sounded to Miles like "Day-oh vin-DEE-chay, brother."

The others all said in unison, "Day-oh vin-DEE-chay!"

As Lindy sat back down, Rocky continued the introductions:

Fred Cornwall: Mid-40s, broad shouldered, with a thin black mustache and neatly trimmed dark hair. His stony expression suggested an aloof superiority. He simply nodded at Miles.

Maynard Tubbs: "Tubby," he offered, with a jovial tone. One light blue eye was noticeably smaller than the other, creating the impression he was halfway into or out of a wink.

Krys Pinny: A bespectacled, clean-shaven, boyish fellow with close cropped ginger hair and skin so white it seemed he'd not been touched by sunlight in months.

Ned Potts: Seated at the end of the table, Miles recognized Ned from his HVAC service calls to the McKendricks' shop. As it was a chilly early March morning, the other men all wore long-sleeve shirts. If any of them had tattoos, they weren't visible. But Ned wore a black tee shirt that exposed intricate full sleeve tattoos on both arms with images of skulls, daggers, snakes, and some odd emblems Miles couldn't quite make out. A scraggly goatee grew below his thin lips and his pinched, pockmarked face was framed by oversized ears, creating the look of a malevolent elf. A pair of sunglasses hung from the front collar of his shirt. He wore a faded blue cap with the American flag and the letters "NRA" on the side, the image of an AR-15 rifle on the front above the words "Come And Take It."

"And, of course," Rocky said when he'd finished going around the table, "you know Mama."

Margaret gave Miles a searing stare. "I remember you. You used to come to me for your haircuts. Wanted it to look like it was done in the 1860s. I remember you brought a photo. Said it was some guy you were pretending to be. Haven't seen you lately though. Didn't I do a good enough job?"

"No, ma'am," Miles mumbled. "You did it just right."

"So what happened?"

"We're not doing that anymore."

"Yeah, well, looks like you still need a decent haircut." She cocked her head from side-to-side and assessed the unruly tufts poking out from under his McKendricks Farm & Home Equipment cap. “Looks like someone’s been cutting your hair with a dull weedwhacker. You’d best come back to me for a decent trim.”

“Yes, ma’am.”

“So,” she said, “Rocky tells me y’all had to quit being Mosby’s Rangers.”

“Yes, ma’am. The name ‘Mosby’ is a bad thing now. Y’know, erasing history and all.”

“Yeah, well, some of us are going to put up a fight about that kinda crap. Can’t let the history deniers get away with it. At least not without us having our say first. Day-oh vin-DEE-chay, right?”

“Um, yes, ma’am. Right.”

“Okay,” Rocky said, “Now you’ve all met Miles, let’s get things going.”

The next hour was spent discussing plans for the Tuesday evening rally. It was agreed that only Margaret would address the council in the administration building’s meeting room. Everyone else would remain on the lawn in front of the courthouse displaying their signs and expressing their opposition to removing the Confederate monument.

The board members had been handing out flyers. A special focus was targeted on those who, like Miles, might be moved by the historical significance of the monument separate from any direct racial connotation. On that basis, the initial response had been mildly favorable. But once the prospective attendee read the flyer in detail, the interest quickly cooled

As the final details were being wrapped up, Rocky delivered a warning. “Now, we want to see a good turnout, but make sure everyone you invite knows that UFR is strictly about *peaceful* protest. We don’t want anyone doing something stupid so the media has an excuse to twist it around and make it look like we’re all a bunch of lunatics. And, of course, as always, keep your radar tuned for anyone you suspect might be a government plant. Got it?”

A chorus of “Got it!” replied.

No one noticed the quiver in Miles’ voice or the nervous shifting in his eyes as he joined the response.

"Now," Margaret said, "We need to decide what else we can do to express our opposition, the types of things where the Commander would have made an appearance. Y'all have had some time to work on this, so let's hear your ideas."

There was no shortage of suggestions. The opportunities included:

- Multiple school boards planning to remove the names of Confederate generals: Robert E. Lee, Stonewall Jackson, J.E.B. Stuart, and others. Some would be replaced with the names of African-Americans. (It was noted that this should be of particular interest to Miles, even if Mosby's name wasn't on the list.)
- A magnet school for science and technology that announced plans to lower admission standards to admit more Black students. (At least for now, the fact that the school was named for a slave-owning Founding Father was not on the docket.)
- Statues of Confederate "heroes" located in neighboring towns that were on the list to be removed. (Another nod toward Miles.)
- And, while not a race-based topic, holding Drag Queen Story Hour at the Crutchfield County library was surely something the Commander would have decried. So that made the list too.

When the schedule was completed, Miles said, "I might not be able to make some of these. Evenings are okay, but Saturdays, like for the statues, are a problem."

"Oh, right," Rocky said. "The McKendricks' place is open on Saturdays. But…wait. Y'all close at one o'clock, right? The statue protests will be sometime in the afternoon."

"It's not about the shop," Miles countered. "Racing season is starting. That'll take up a good bit of my day."

"Racing season?" Ned asked. "You mean like drag racing? You into that?"

"No, horse racing," Miles replied. "Steeplechase and point-to-points. I'm riding for Mister Billington."

Ned scoffed. "Aren't you a bit old for that? I thought being a jockey was a young man's game."

"Guys older than me are still doing it," Miles countered.

PJ perked up. "Ooo! Can we come and watch?"

"Sure," Miles replied. "Lots of folks come and have tailgate parties. It's not like flat track racing with viewing stands and all that stuff. More of a local thing for country folks and horse people. The season started last weekend but Mister Billington didn't like the ground conditions, too soft and muddy. The next races are this coming Saturday."

PJ turned to her mother. "We don't have anything on the schedule that day. Can we go?"

Margaret thought for a moment, then shrugged. "I don't see why not. Might be good for us to get out and have some fun. I think the Commander would approve."

"Great!" PJ exclaimed. "Will I get to pet the horses?" she asked Miles.

"Um, it's not like a petting zoo kinda thing. These are Thoroughbred racehorses. They can be kinda…amped up…highstrung."

That image fueled PJ's excitement. "And you *ride* them like that?"

"Yeah, well, one of them anyway. I used to do that a lot, several a day. Now I'm just riding the one horse for Mister Billington."

"Wow. That's so cool," she said, impressed with Miles' nonchalant bravado.

"Enough of this horseshit," Ned growled. "It's time for chicken."

As the UFR members split up into smaller subgroups, PJ took a seat next to Miles.

"How's the chicken?" she asked.

"I gotta admit, it's about the best I've ever had. What's her secret?"

She swept her hair over her shoulder and smiled coyly. "Well, if I told you, it wouldn't be a secret anymore, would it?"

"No, I guess not. But maybe you can tell me something else, unless it's a secret too."

"What's that?"

"Something y'all kept saying. Sounded kinda like 'Day-oh vin-DEE-chay."

"Oh, that. Deo Vindice was the motto of the Confederate government. It means 'God Is Our Protector.' We've adopted it as the United Friends of Rockwell motto."

"And the Rockwell part? Is that your brother?"

"Well, no, not him. But the name, yes. It's our mother's maiden name. And there's some history behind it that we found out about recently. Fits right in with our cause."

Miles was tempted to ask her to explain what that cause was, but thought it best to simply nod as if he already knew. He looked across the room at the portrait of her father. "I'm so sorry about your dad. I met him a few times when he and Rocky came to work on the AC at the shop. Really nice guy. Must have been tough losing him like that."

Her smile faded. "Yeah, it was tough. On all of us, especially Mama."

"Y'all are doing okay now?"

"Okay? Um, better maybe. Not all the way to okay, but we're working on it."

Miles noticed Rocky and Ned engaged in an intense conversation, their heads down and voices low.

"So Rocky went to work for Jessup after your dad died?" Miles asked.

"He'd been working with our father as an apprentice. The plan was for him to work his way up to qualify as a master tradesman and contractor, like our dad was, so he could take over the business one day. But that dream vanished when…when…well, y'know."

She needed a moment.

Continuing, she explained, "Mister Jessup offered to take over dad's accounts, along with all the parts and equipment he had in the warehouse. It meant a really nice compensation package, enough to take care of Mama. He also agreed to take on Rocky as a trainee, help him get his full license."

Miles looked over at the two portraits, this time pointing toward the unfamiliar one. "That other guy, was he, like, a family ancestor?"

"Yeah, he kinda was. You don't recognize him?"

"No. Should I? Is he somebody famous?"

"He is to some folks." Her smile returned and she flung her hair again with a toss of her head. She patted him on the leg and said, "Don't worry, you'll find out soon enough."

When lunch was over, PJ escorted Miles to the door. She reached toward a stack of pamphlets on a table in the hallway and handed one to him. "Here. You should read this before Tuesday night. It'll give you a better idea of just what we're all about."

The front page showed a glowing cross above the phrase "Deo Vindice." The heading read "One Nation Under God." A caret wedged between "One" and "Nation" pointed to the inserted word "White."

Chapter 11

Monday
Kimber Farm

There was nothing scheduled for delivery at Kimber Farm on Monday. But no one who saw the McKendrick delivery truck pulling in would suspect anything out of the ordinary. Instead of the equipment shed, Miles parked at the barn where Cecelia Broadhurst waited in the tack room.

Just in case, he carried an empty box to complete the ruse.

Direct communication with Tavina Doddridge was too risky. Phone calls, emails, and text messages would leave an electronic trail. Cecelia was the perfect go-between and Kimber Farm the ideal location.

Miles handed Cecelia a sheet of paper. "Here are the names of who was at the meeting. I can't guarantee they're all spelled right. Not like they were wearing name tags."

He then handed her the pamphlet PJ gave him.

Cecelia *humphed* at the front page title but her eyes widened as she turned to the inside pages.

"Can you believe this?" she said. "What century are these people living in? This is straight out of the days of George Wallace, Bull Connor, Orval Faubus."

Those names meant nothing to Miles. Cecelia, old enough to be his mother, had lived through the civil rights turmoil of the '60s. She'd seen the images on TV and in the papers of Black protestors in the deep South being beaten by police, blasted by fire hoses, and set upon by attack dogs.

She flipped back to the front page. "United Friends of Rockwell. Rockwell…," she muttered. "That sounds familiar. Did they say anything about that name?"

"Rocky's sister said it was their mother's maiden name. There was a photo hanging on the wall next to the one of her father. Some guy I didn't recognize, but it kinda sounded like he might have something to do with it."

"What did he look like?"

"Geez, I dunno. White guy, wearing some kinda military uniform."

"Did you see any swastikas?"

"Any what"

"You know, the twisted cross thing the Nazis used as their symbol."

"No, nothing like that."

Cecelia thought for a moment, trying to recall a sliver of memory from her youth. "Was he holding a corncob pipe?"

"Yeah, he was!" Miles replied, surprised that she would pull up that seemingly odd detail.

"Lincoln Rockwell! George Lincoln Rockwell! The American Nazi Party. Gotta be him. That explains all this," she said, pointing to the pamphlet. "These quotes sound like they're straight out of his mouth. '*White Man, stand with us and fight. We will do anything to ensure the survival and happiness of White, Western People. The color of your skin is your uniform in this ultimate battle for the survival of the West. Let us stand together to secure the survival of our people, the beloved, miraculous, wonderful, blessed and masterful white race!*' She shook her head in disgust. "I doubt Margaret and her kids came up with this kind of crap on their own."

"And," Miles said, "for some stupid ass reason, they think I agree with that shit. I guess it's just the Mosby thing. I've never said, or even thought, anything like that."

"Well, we can assume they're not the brightest bulbs in the box. I just can't imagine what's motivating them. I mean, Margaret and her kids never came off as overt racists. Certainly not Edwin when he was alive. He was a wonderful guy. Everyone liked him. They were all known to be pretty strong fundamental Christians, but they never pushed that on anyone. So where's this rabid racism coming from?"

"Beats me. I may not know much about the law and stuff, but I guess being a racist ain't illegal. Y'know, free speech and all. As long as they're just talking stupid shit like this, where's the crime? How am I gonna get your pal Tavina off my ass if it turns out there's nothing she can use to go after them?"

"You have to be patient. You've just been to one meeting. They may think you're one of them, but if they *are* up to something more serious than this..." She waved the pamphlet. "...they probably won't let you too far inside right away."

"Rocky did say something about being careful who they invite to the rally. Like the feds might be trying to get a plant inside. And there I sat, just like he was saying. Only difference is it ain't 'the feds,' it's just some small time government lawyer trying to make a name for herself. And using my ass as the bait."

"Don't sell Tavina short. She's a very smart, capable woman. If she thinks there's something worth investigating here, I trust her on that."

"Well, better than her investigating me."

"Yeah, um, you did kinda put yourself in that position, didn't you?"

Her remark surprised him. Only a small group of people were supposed to know about "The Incident", and Cecelia Broadhurst wasn't one of them. He regretted making the "investigating me" remark.

She caught his embarrassed look. "Yes, I have some idea about what happened. Enough to know that Tavina's not bluffing."

"So…so how did she, and you, find out?" He also wanted to ask *And just how much do you know?*

"Shelton."

"Shelton? She wasn't there. She was at the shop."

"Right. But when she got home, she noticed what looked like a bullet hole in the kitchen ceiling. And it still smelled like gunpowder in there. Her grandmother is known more for her blunt honesty than for fabricating stories. So Rhetta told her what happened."

"But how would that have gotten back to this Doddridge woman?"

"You don't know?"

"Know what? I'm just the delivery boy. Nobody tells me shit."

"That Tavina and Shelton are 'an item'."

"What? Sheltie Lou's dating the woman who's trying to nail my ass if I don't become a rat for her?"

"I guess you could put it that way," Cecelia said with a light chuckle. "And more than dating. They're living together now."

Miles rolled his eyes. "So it's really my boss at the shop who's set me up?"

"Shelton doesn't know anything about that. This is all Tavina's idea. She's only taken me into her confidence because she knows I can be trusted and she needed someone to be the contact person, a buffer between you and her. She thought it best for that to be someone other than your boss at the shop. That could have been…well…awkward." Cecelia opted not to mention that she's also the main funder of Tavina's campaign to become the Commonwealth's Attorney now that the current holder of that job has announced his plans to run for higher office.

"Shelton may not know what Tavina's got on me," Miles said. "But now I gotta go into work every day wondering if she's looking at me funny, thinking I may go off the deep end again."

Cecelia dismissed his concerns. "I wouldn't worry about that. Shelton's got enough on her hands trying to keep the business afloat.

And her father's no help as long as he keeps spending all his time on his Church of Foxhunting foolishness. If it wasn't for her, along with Bar and Muriel, the business would have folded by now. And you'd be out of a job."

"Yeah, well, if I screw this up, or even if I get the dirt your pal Tavina wants and she doesn't hold up her end of the deal, I'll be out a helluva lot more than my parts manager and delivery boy job."

"Tavina won't go back on her word."

"So you say."

Cecelia placed a bejeweled hand on his shoulder. "Look, I know this isn't exactly your lane. But that's what makes you such a perfect candidate." She looked at the pamphlet. "How do you feel about what these people are saying?"

"It's total bullshit."

"Of course. But it could be more than that. Anyone with such outlandish beliefs is likely, at some point, to move beyond just words. And then things can get really ugly. And dangerous."

She put her other hand on his shoulder and turned him to face her. He looked up at the aristocratic woman, several inches taller, and saw a patient, motherly expression.

"You," she said, "of all people, should understand how that can happen."

Yes, he knew better than most how radical beliefs can morph into dangerous, potentially deadly action.

He nodded in agreement.

She lifted her hands and said, "Look, you just do what you can to help Tavina. You've got a good start getting inside, better than expected really. If there's nothing for her to act on, if it's all just a bunch of bluff and bluster...*grotesquely offensive* bluff and bluster...but with no action behind it, then you'll have done your job. And I'm sure Tavina will honor that. And if there *is* more than just a bunch of outlandish words, if there might be something brewing that could lead to people getting hurt, or worse, then you'll have done a service for the whole community."

"Yeah, from zero to hero. Unless it's me who ends up in the 'something worse' category. I might need a little Deo Vindice myself."

"Deo what?"

His customary smart-ass nature returned. "It's Latin for 'God will cover your ass.'"

On the way to his next delivery stop, his phone sounded with Thumper's ringtone.

"Hey, boss, what's up?"

"I've been thinking you're going to need a backstory, something to strengthen your cover. It's likely, at some point, someone will ask you about your supposed racist views, how you came to believe the same things they do. You'll need a plausible answer and I've got some ideas. How about you swing by after work and we kick that around?"

"Yeah, okay, I'll be there."

Christ, this shit is getting deep. A 'backstory'? Who the hell does he think I am? James Fucking Bond? Flanagan, Miles Flanagan, secret agent. Jesus!

Chapter 12

Monday Evening
Montfair, Thumper's Study

Miles took a seat in front of Thumper's desk.

"How'd the meeting go?" Thumper asked.

"The fried chicken was great," Miles replied.

Thumper's raised eyebrow chased away Miles' cavalier attitude.

"Well, I met a bunch of guys, found out what 'Deo Vindice' means."

"So they're using the old Confederate motto?"

"You know about that?"

Another raised eyebrow answered the question.

"Oh, yeah," Miles said. "Of course you do." He reached into his coat pocket and pulled out a copy of UFR's latest pamphlet. "You might find this interesting."

Thumper gave it a quick scan. "Holy crap. They really have gone off the deep end. Did you pick up any hints about what's behind this? The Hendershots never struck me as extreme racists. Not any kind of racists really."

"No, nothing that came up then. Cecelia said it looks like they're following some guy named Rockwell, maybe someone from

Margaret's family. There's a picture of him hanging on the wall next to Windy's."

Thumper looked up from his perusal of the pamphlet.

Miles flinched at the annoyed look on Thumper's face. He realized he's stepped in it again.

"Cecelia?" Thumper asked. "You talked to Cecelia about this?"

"Oh, right, I guess I shoulda mentioned that. That's how I'm supposed to get my reports to Tavina. I can meet Cecelia at Kimber Farm like I'm making deliveries and no one would be suspicious." He pointed toward the walls in the study, bedecked with dozens of foxhunting and horse racing photos. "Kinda like how I can do that with you here, since I'm working for you."

With a shrug Thumper said, "Yeah, I can see how that makes sense." He then added in a stern tone, "But Cecelia is not to know you're also reporting to me. Nor is anyone else. You got that?"

"Yes sir! I haven't told anyone about you helping me, not Cecelia or anyone else. No one will know, just you and me."

"Good. Okay, so let's kick around some ideas for your cover story. First of all, tell me about your parents. Did they ever express any racist remarks?"

"No. Well, not anything like what these people are saying. I mean, sure, I heard my old man tell some jokes around his buddies when they were drinking and stuff. But, y'know, just old boys kidding around. Never calling Black people the N-word or saying they oughta be sent back to Africa, none of that crazy shit."

"And your mother?"

"Oh, even less from her. In fact, if she heard my father or one of his buddies telling a joke like that, she'd give him shit for it."

"And your grandparents? Aunts or uncles? Cousins?"

"What? You think there's a Flanagan somewhere who thinks like these Rockwell assholes? Look, we may be white trash, but we're not *racist* white trash. We think everyone has the right to be crapped on just as much as anyone else."

Thumper leaned back and smiled. "That's good. That's the kind of indignation you'll need to convince those people you're for real, that you're one of them. You'll just need to change the wording to match their beliefs."

Miles calmed down and nodded. "Yeah, okay. I get it."

"What about your involvement with Ansel and the Rangers? Mosby and his men really were fighting for the Southern Cause. And, like it or not, that did suggest at least some pro-slavery sentiments. How'd you get into that?"

"Ansel was always looking for new recruits. He had a spare horse he let me use and loaned me most of the gear. I think he wanted me to join because I looked the part and he knew I could ride. Most of the other guys looked more like the fathers, or even grandfathers, of the real Rangers. Too old and, um, too fat. But it turned out to be a lot of fun. And it gave me something to do after things went to shit with my racing career."

Thumper nodded and grunted at that recollection.

"But," Miles continued, "it wasn't like we were shouting 'The South shall rise again! Keep all the slaves in chains!' We tried to avoid that kinda thing, just focused on the military actions and what it was like to be a Partisan Ranger. Anyway, that's all over now."

Thumper cocked his head as a thought occurred to him. "And why is that?"

"Well, y'know, political correctness and all that bullshit."

"And how did that make you feel?"

Miles chuckled. He'd been asked that question countless times in anger management sessions, starting in his teen years and continuing on through his expulsion from the racing community. "Resentful," he said, parroting the response he'd heard others say in group meetings.

Thumper caught the mocking tone. "No, really. You were deep into the reenacting thing, right?"

"Yeah. Too deep, as you know better than anyone."

"True. But the UFR people don't know about that. So let's say the Rangers had been coming under fire for some time, protesters showing up at your events, holding up signs calling y'all racists. Equating you to living embodiments of the statues they want removed. Didn't the Mosby Area Heritage Association have to change its name?"

"Now that you mention it, yeah, I guess they did."

Thumper leaned back and spread his hands out. "Okay, so here you are, up to your ears in reenacting. It's the only thing in your life that gives you some sense of purpose, that you're part of a group, your 'tribe' so to speak. Y'all aren't hurting anyone, just trying to give other people some sense of what life was like during that time and place, a way to step out of the history books and make it a living scene. And then..." He slammed his hands down on the desk. "...Wham! Along comes this self-righteous, virtue-signaling bunch of assholes who say y'all are glorifying racism, trying to make heroes out of people who were so bent on keeping Black people in bondage that they were willing to tear the nation apart and kill anyone who tried to stop them!"

Thumper was now in full oratorical mode. His voice rose as he continued his tirade. "So no more Rangers, no more Mosby, no more glorifying the Southern Cause! Get off those horses, burn those uniforms, and become obedient, compliant servants to the greater cause of racial justice!"

He sat back and caught his breath.

Miles grinned. "Shit, maybe you're the one who oughta be working for Doddridge. You got the fire!"

"Yes, and you need to get it, too." He paused and considered this option. "Yep, that's gonna be your backstory. Stick with me here. Being a Ranger was what gave your life purpose. You poured your all into it. Getting every detail just right. Studying the history, all the fine points and nuances, from the national politics of the time to the individual life of the actual Ranger you portrayed. And because some stupid 'justice warriors' thought you were glorifying slavery and making light of that terrible sin, you were forced to give all that up."

Thumper paused to let Miles process this.

"And," he continued, "did that make you see the error of your ways and join hands with them in the spirit of racial harmony?"

Before Miles could answer, Thumper's hand slammed down on his desk again. "No! It had the exact opposite effect. It filled you with resentment that you'd had this important part of your life ripped away. So, while you'd never really given much thought to whether or not you were a racist, you now decided that, by damn, if that's what these people think I am, then I'll show 'em! I'll become a *real* racist, a full-fledged 'send 'em all back to Africa' kinda racist."

They sat in silence for a long moment while Miles considered this.

He then nodded, smiled, and said, "Yeah, I can see this working. I mean, of course, I don't really feel that way. Well, okay, maybe a little, for Ansel's sake and the other guys. But you and I know I had to give it all up anyway for my own reasons."

"Yes, you and I know that. And just a few others. But the UFR folks don't. So…what do you think? Could you pull this off if one of them asks what led you to embrace their extreme racist beliefs?"

"Who me? Sound angry, frustrated, like I've been mistreated and want to strike out against someone or something?" Miles folded his arms and grinned. "Yeah, I think I could pull that off."

"Good! The question now is what led the Hendershots down this road. Maybe you can dig up that info while you're sharing your story."

Chapter 13

Tuesday Morning
Montfair Kennels

A small group of dedicated members showed up for Tuesday morning's "informal" hunt from the Montfair kennels. The purpose was to take half a dozen young hounds out for their first experience as part of the full pack. If all went as planned, it would be a short outing, confined to a limited area. This would allow Crispie to evaluate how well the youngsters performed under circumstances more controlled than a full on chase over an expansive amount of territory.

"This'll be Bumper's last hunt for the season," Thumper said to Miles as they awaited the release of hounds. "Keep it light. And then some easy work between now and Saturday, a bit more schooling over the timber jumps we set up."

"Gotcha," Miles said.

"The overnights show four others in the Maiden Timber," Thumper continued, "all good prospects. I'm not worried about winning or losing, I just want to see how he does in competition. If he does win, fine. But only if he's going well. Don't push him too hard."

"Yes, sir."

"Voytek and Myrna will bring him, Janey and I will meet you there."

Miles smiled broadly. "Just like old times."

Thumper nodded. "Yeah. I gotta admit, I missed being in the game."

"By the way," Miles said, "I've invited the Hendershots to come. And Ned, too."

Thumper hesitated. "Really? You think that's a good idea? Doesn't seem like their kinda thing."

"What? You mean partying with a bunch of white people who drive pick-up trucks? I mean, this ain't exactly Churchill Downs or Saratoga, is it?"

"Well, when you put it that way…"

"It just sorta came up at the meeting on Sunday when they were making plans for more protests. I said I was busy on Saturdays and when I told them why, PJ got all excited about seeing horses, asked if they could come and watch. I figured it would be a good way to help get me in tighter with them, a chance to kick back and have some fun. Y'know, a kinda bonding thing."

Thumper considered Miles' point. "Yeah, I can see that." He then added, "You do know that Tavina's going to be there, right?"

"What? I don't remember ever seeing her at a race."

"That's because she wasn't campaigning for office. She was hired as Assistant Commonwealth's Attorney, but she has to be elected to the top job. With Cecelia as her campaign chair, she'll bc at the Kimber Farm tailgate spot, complete with posters and flyers to hand out."

"Well," Miles said, "the Hendershots have no idea what she's up to, what she's forced me into doing. They probably don't even know who she is. So that shouldn't be a problem."

Voytek opened the kennel door and two dozen exuberant hounds came flooding out.

Ryman, silent and sullen, remained off to the side. He felt obligated to be there as both a joint-master and honorary whipper-in. But his enthusiasm for the sport had evaporated since the truth behind his "vision" was revealed. Maybe it had served its purpose to get the ball rolling, that Saint Hubert had used the broken fence pieces to convey his message and now it was up to Ryman and Nardell to carry that message forward. Surely, Saint Hubert's hand was at work, regardless of just what had actually been between that stag's antlers.

Or maybe it really was just all pointless coincidence and he'd been fooling himself into believing he'd received a mystical message and been endowed with special powers.

For now, though, he and Nardell would do their jobs as whips, if only for the sake of the hounds who depended on them for safety and guidance.

The outing went as planned. The youngsters stayed with the pack, eagerly searched for a hot line to follow, and responded to Crispie's signals with voice and horn.

As Thumper and Janey rode back to the Montfair barn, he asked if she'd made a decision about her book.

"Do I have a choice?" she replied. "It's a lose-lose situation. If I drop it, it'll mean more than a year's work down the toilet. And Danella's not going to be happy after all the effort she's made as my agent to get it so close to a publishing deal. But if I go ahead with it, it'll cause a huge rift between you and your oldest friend. Not to mention that he's your neighbor and joint-master. And not just between the two of you but others around here as well. He's built up some loyal followers since this began."

With a joking tone, Thumper added, "And then there's the 'declaration of character' thing."

Janey chuckled lightly. "Yeah, that. Seriously, though, I don't think he can do anything legally to stop it. But there's always the risk of a nuisance suit, even if it gets tossed out. And that would just drive a further wedge between people. No, I need to drop it. At least for now."

"Got any ideas of what to tackle next?"

"No, nothing. Fringe religions don't just pop up every day. I pretty much covered every one of them that I could find in my first two books. That's why Danella couldn't get any bites on a third one that wouldn't be a rehash of the first two." She turned to Thumper. "And then I met you, discovered this whole foxhunting world just as Ryman received his 'visions,' and it all fell into my lap. And then Myrna found what was really behind it and, well, here we are."

"Damn me for not just tossing that crap out before anyone could find it. I guess I have some passion for relics. Lord knows, much of my life's history consists of relics of some kind or other."

"I'm glad you saved it. If the truth were ever to come out, it would have been better after the book was published. Then it could have served as a follow up piece."

"You know," Thumper said, "my oldest friend has been known to be somewhat mercurial, even before he started to believe in messages from an ancient saint. Today's objection could turn into tomorrow's approval. Maybe if we just give him some time, he'll come around."

She brightened slightly at that thought. "You think so? Maybe just ask Danella to hold off for a bit? Not pull the plug completely?"

"I think it's worth considering. And maybe start kicking around some ideas for the next project."

"But, like I said, I've played out the whole fringe religion thing. If anything new was brewing, I'd have heard about it by now."

"Maybe it depends on how you define 'religion.'"

"What do you mean?"

"Well, if there's a group of people who hold up a specific deceased figure for their inspiration, adopt this person's teachings as their doctrine, believe they have a righteous cause, are willing to take extreme actions, and consist of just a small number of devoted adherents, would that qualify as something worthy of your focus?"

"Yeah, I suppose so. That pretty much describes the typical fringe religion. But like I said…"

"Maybe you just need to broaden that definition. They may not think of themselves as 'religious adherents,' but there are some other groups among us who fit that profile."

"And they are?"

"White supremacists."

Janey's head jerked at that. She then considered the suggestion. She had only a rough awareness of that movement. As she thought through Thumper's description, she could see the relevance.

"Yes, there's a strong similarity. But, like the other groups I've studied, you can't just show up at the door and say, 'Hi! I'd like to do an exposé on your wacky beliefs.' So do you have another old friend who just happens to be into white supremacy?"

"I wouldn't call him an old friend exactly. But, yes, there is someone we both know who might be able to get the inside scoop on one such group."

"Really? Tell me more."

Chapter 14

Tuesday
Ryman's Cottage

Ryman trudged through the post-hunt necessities. He turned out the horses, put away the tack, then shuffled into the cottage he shared with Nardell and Wycroft, their retired foxhound. Shoulders hunched and head down, he slumped into his tattered lounge chair.

Nardell went to the bedroom to change out of her hunting attire.

Wycroft, sensing his pack leader's despair, slid off the couch. He went to Ryman and placed his chin on his old friend's knee. Ryman looked down into the hound's soulful eyes. A weak smile formed and his spirits lifted half a notch.

Placing his hand on Wycroft's head, he said, "You understand, dontcha boy? We thought we really had a special gift, didn't we? But it was all a load of bullshit. Smoke and mirrors. Just an illusion."

The hound's eyes widened into a pleading message and he wiggled his chin against Ryman's thigh.

An image formed in Ryman's mind. He was looking at a blurry image. As it came into clearer focus, he could see the lowered head of a deer, its nose just above the ground. A large rack of antlers tilted forward at a threatening angle. A cross-shaped object, scratched and weathered to a mottled gray, hung above the buck's head.

Ryman jerked back. "Don't do that!"

His outburst startled the hound and the image melted away.

Nardell, half undressed, came out from the bedroom. "Are you okay?"

"Yeah, sorta." He reached out and stroked Wycroft's head. "Sorry, old boy. We gotta stop doing that."

"Doing what?" she asked.

Ryman sat back and sighed. "Those visions. He keeps sending me these…these…I dunno…like, psychic messages where I can see things through his eyes. Things I thought were messages from Saint Hubert. But now I know it was all bullshit."

"Maybe it wasn't all bullshit."

"Of course it was!" he shot back. "You saw that shit Myrna found. It wasn't a vision from Saint Hubert. It was just a bunch of wire and a piece of broken fence."

Nardell plopped down on the couch. "Okay, so maybe it wasn't an actual vision. But it still could have been a message from the universe. Or even from Saint Hubert, just in a different way, and a different message, than what we'd thought."

With a sarcastic tone, Ryman asked, "So if it wasn't a message about launching 'the Ancient and Venerable Church of Ars Venatica,' what do you think it was?"

"I think you need to ask that question to someone else."

"And who would that be?"

"Wycroft," she replied.

The hound made a muffled *woof* as if concurring with Nardell.

"Look," she said, "you clearly haven't lost your talent for connecting with animals. Not just hounds, but horses too. Even foxes. We know they all communicate among themselves through a psychic connection, not with words like humans, but more like images. You've spent so much of your life working with hounds and horses, and chasing foxes, that you've managed to find a portal into that world. Maybe that's what Saint Hubert's message was trying to tell you."

Ryman scratched the stubble on his chin and considered Nardell's suggestion.

"Look," she continued. "You know the whole Saint Hubert story. He actually *stopped* hunting after he had his vision. And he became the patron saint of hunters and hounds. I mean, the whole 'Blessing of the Hounds' thing is done in his name, right? That's what he really cared about…the hounds. And other animals as well, including the horses and whatever it is the hunters are chasing."

She reached down and rubbed Wycroft's head. "This old guy knows you have that special gift, that he can send you the images in his mind and you'll see them just as clearly as another hound would. That's obviously Saint Hubert's way of really blessing the animals through you. What could be a better gift than that?"

Through all their years together, Ryman had watched Nardell flit from one belief system to another, never finding something that brought her peace and assurance. She had bought into the Church of Foxhunting concept as fully as he had, at times even more so. Now, though, her counsel wasn't about some ethereal doctrine of strictures and ordered behaviors. It rang with a truth Ryman could not deny.

He bent down and cupped Wycroft's head in both hands. "She's right, ain't she? You, me, all your hound buddies, our horses, and even all those wily foxes we follow for our sport. Our good Saint Hubert has anointed me as your spokesman. I'm honored to accept that duty. Whatcha think?"

Woof!

Chapter 15

Tuesday Evening
Crutchfield County Administrative Complex

Ned Potts picked up Margaret and PJ at Off the Grid late Tuesday afternoon. With the placards loaded into his truck, they headed toward town to meet the others.

The winter sun was already setting and the crisp afternoon air took on a sharp chill when they arrived at the courthouse parking lot. Rocky and Miles were there waiting for them, along with the UFR board members, all except Fred Cornwall.

About a dozen others opposed to removing the monument were milling around, cautious to distance themselves from the UFR members. They had their reasons for wanting to leave the monument in place, but they didn't want to be seen as supporting the overtly racist agenda of this small band of radicals.

Catching the question on Margaret's face, Rocky said, "Fred called me. He won't be coming. And, as we expected, he's dropping off the board. Says his business commitments need his full attention."

"Yeah, right," she said. "A lame excuse. Well, better to have him completely out if he ain't gonna be completely in." She looked over at Miles as Ned was handing out signs. "Let's see how your little buddy does tonight. Then we'll talk."

Ned reached into the truck bed, pulled out a sign, and handed it to Miles.

"Here you go," he said with a sly grin. "This should suit you just fine."

Miles wasn't sure how to interpret Ned's expression. Was Ned about to test him with some outrageously offensive slogan? See how he'd react? He took the sign and read the message: "Learn From History, Don't Erase It." Relieved, he nodded and said, "Perfect."

"This one's mine!" PJ proclaimed as she pulled out the one that said "We're the Good People on the Other Side."

Rocky's choice was "That's My Family Name You Want to Erase." There was, indeed, a Hiram Hendershot among the list of names on the plaque. But the records were unclear if there was a direct lineage between Hiram and the modern day Hendershots.

The others armed themselves with a variety of messages: "White History Matters; Honor the Past; Proud to be a Rebel."

Rocky gathered the small group around him. "Okay, y'all. This is a big moment for us. The first official public action by UFR. You know we're gonna get called a bunch of ugly names. And there's gonna be a lot more people against us than for us. So we gotta stay cool. We put one foot wrong, and the media's gonna be all over us, taking our words out of context, doing whatever they can to make us look like fools."

"Shit, Rocky," Ned said. "They're gonna do that no matter what we do. We can go out there and act like fucking choir boys and they'll still make us out to be ignorant, racist rednecks. So I say we might as well embrace that and tell it like it is."

"Tell it, yes," Rocky replied. "That's why we're here, to tell our side, tell the truth. What I'm saying is no matter what others try to do to egg us on, don't take the bait." He turned to the small group of followers, with a separate nod to Miles. "Y'all got that?"

The mumbled chorus of "Yeah" was sufficient.

"Okay, then. Let's go."

Signs held high, they marched from the parking lot to the front lawn of the courthouse chanting "Deo Vindice! Deo Vindice!"

Margaret would join them later. For now her task was to address the board of supervisors and make a plea for the monument to remain in place. The likelihood of achieving that goal was about equal to Jefferson Davis himself rising from the grave and giving the stone his personal blessing.

The memorial, a roughhewn granite boulder with a large bronze plaque, was erected by the Daughters of the American Confederacy (DAC) in 1903. The names of 54 men from Crutchfield County who had fought for the South were listed on the plaque. Near the top in the alphabetical listing was Josiah Billington. Not far below were the names of three Crutchfields, ancestors of Thumper's mother, members of one of the earliest families that settled in the area. The Billingtons arrived first but a Crutchfield outmaneuvered them to secure his family's name for the newly ordained county. Both families predated independence and their men fought in that rebellion to form a new nation. That was the good rebellion. The one several of their grandsons and great-grandsons fought in was the bad one.

Much of Virginia was still struggling to recover from the war's devastation as the twentieth century dawned. Finding some sliver of honor in the Lost Cause was one way to ease that pain. Larger-than-life statues became a popular form of expression. The Crutchfield County chapter of the DAC was unable to raise enough support for such an extravagance. The Billington and Crutchfield families both opposed the plan and refused to donate. With limited funds, the DAC ladies were only able to secure an unfinished hunk of granite fitted with a bronze plaque.

****

The original county courthouse was built in 1755. The current structure, built over the old site, opened its doors in 1902. The county administration building, erected in the 1960s, sat to the left of the courthouse, facing the lawn from the side. A drab, three-story brick structure, it served as a testament to governmental conformity.

The Commonwealth Attorney's division occupied the second floor. The prime offices, including Tavina Doddridge's, looked out over the courthouse lawn.

The board of supervisors held their sessions in the public meeting room on the first floor. Margaret took her seat among the attendees and awaited her turn to address the board. Given the number of people who had signed up to speak, the board chose to limit individual comments to one minute each.

It was widely assumed that the fix was in. One or two supervisors—those from the most rural districts—might make a pointless gesture to vote in favor of leaving the monument in place. They knew they'd be soundly outvoted but could tell their constituents they tried to prevent this reactionary erasure of local history.

By Margaret's rough count, the majority of speakers before her wanted the monument removed. Regardless of the speaker's position, the supervisors were mostly inattentive; reading unrelated documents or whispering among themselves.

They did, however, become more focused when a woman Margaret knew well stepped up to the speaker's lectern.

"My name is Ethel Loudermilk, president of the local chapter of the Daughters of the American Confederacy. Our group sponsored the monument's installation in 1903. My great-grandmother was the chapter's president at the time and spearheaded the project. So I think I can say if anyone has a personal interest in the fate of this monument, I do. And I stand before you tonight as the representative of the DAC to say our group supports its removal."

Vocal expressions, mostly in favor of and a few opposed to what she said, rumbled from the crowd.

The board's chair banged her gavel and called for order.

Ethel continued. "That does not mean we want the monument destroyed. Our position is it should be relocated somewhere other than on public land. We recognize that such spaces should not display objects or images that some might find offensive, regardless of how misguided such feelings might be. We will be happy to contribute to the cost of its removal from the public space to private land where it can continue to serve as a meaningful element of local history, whether considered good or bad, for the benefit of all."

If there were still any doubters, Ethel's endorsement assured the outcome was set. No matter what argument Margaret offered, the monument cause was lost. But she had to state UFR's position, if only for the public record and her own peace of mind.

"Y'all think this monument is offensive to Black people?" she began. "That every one of the men named on that plaque owned slaves, kept 'em in chains, whipped 'em, raped their women, and did all sorts of terrible things to 'em? Well, I'll tell you who most of those men were. They were honest, hardworking folks, farmers and tradesmen mostly. They were trying to stop an invading army from destroying everything they'd worked for and held dear. Can anyone of y'all here tell me which of those men owned slaves and which ones didn't? I'll bet you can't. Y'all have been fed the lie that 'freeing the slaves' was what the war was all about. And anyone who fought for the South was the worst kinda racist, slave-owning, Black-hating type there could be. But I can tell you three names on that plaque who *were* big time slave owners. And all three of those names are 'Crutchfield.'" She pointed toward the wall above the supervisors. "Y'all see that? The official symbol of *Crutchfield County*? So if y'all think that monument is offensive, maybe we need to change the name of the whole damn county!"

As she saw the gavel lifted to signal the end of her speaking time, Margaret leaned into the microphone to be heard over the calls of "Time! Time please!" and declared, "Ethel Loudermilk may be caving in to this BS, but the United Friends of Rockwell stand strong! Deo Vindice, y'all!"

Head held high, she spun around and returned to her seat as a discordant chorus of jeers filled the room.

****

On the lawn outside, Miles stood with the others facing off an opposing group. There were at least four times as many on the opposition's side. Unlike the hand-drawn signs the UFR members held, most placards displayed by their opponents were professionally printed. They included the ubiquitous "Black Lives Matter" in black and yellow. Others read: "The Confederacy Is Dead; Smash White Supremacy; Virginia Is For Lovers, Not Haters; A Heritage of Hate Is Nothing to Celebrate."

A brick walkway ran from the street curb to the monument, formed a circle around it, and continued on to the courthouse steps. The demonstrating groups had agreed to the sheriff's rules to remain on opposite sides of the walkway. Several deputies stood watch around the edges, ready to intercede if there was any hint of disruptive behavior.

PJ noticed a Black woman among the protestors calling for the monument's removal. The woman looked familiar, and the memory was somehow connected to the courthouse. Inside? Outside? The mental image focused on the courtroom, the audience seated as a case was being tried. Gradually, among the amorphous gallery of faces, one came into focus.

"Her!" she whispered to herself.

She poked Rocky, pointed to the woman, and said, "Look! Over there! Can you believe this?"

Rocky followed her finger. "Huh! She's got a lotta damn nerve." He thought for a moment and then added, "We'd better make sure Mama doesn't see her. I'm not sure I could hold her back."

"Hold her back? Shit! I'd like to go over there right now and shove this sign up her ass! She's partly to blame for what happened! If she hadn't given that big sob story in front of the judge, 'Oh, poor me, I'm just a struggling single mother trying to do the best I can for my children…my boy has a good heart, he didn't mean to hurt anyone, he just got mixed up with the wrong crowd.' All bullshit!"

"Yeah, I know. But we need to stick to the plan."

They were distracted by the sound of their mother's voice.

"You're a goddamn hypocrite!" Margaret shouted.

Ethel Loudermilk tried to ignore her and get to the parking lot.

Margaret raced forward, got in front of her, and blocked her path. "How can you represent the Daughters when you're siding with the goddamn assholes who want to erase our history?"

"*You're* the one hurting our image," Ethel replied. "The last thing we need is someone like you spreading your hateful racist ideas."

"Yeah, well, I finally saw the light. And I was about to resign anyway before y'all kicked me out."

Ethel tried to step around Margaret. "Look," she said, hoping to diffuse the confrontation, "this isn't really the time or place."

Margaret continued to block her path. "All you self-righteous bitches think about is the dead from a long lost past. Maybe you oughta think more about what you can do to help people today. You think I got hateful racist ideas? No, I see the truth of what's happening. Maybe if you lost…lost someone…been left a…a widow…"

The encounter caught the attention of protestors from both sides. When Rocky and PJ ran to their mother, the other UFR members, Miles included, followed.

Rocky and PJ stepped between the two women.

"You'd best leave," Rocky said to Ethel.

PJ turned to her mother and said quietly, "Let it go, Mama. Our fight's not with her. We gotta stay focused."

"She had me kicked out. Called me 'an ignorant redneck'. You want me to take that kinda shit?"

Ethel was already taking Rocky's advice and marching double time toward the parking lot.

Hearing the commotion, several pro-removal demonstrators tried to breach the walkway dividing line. Four sheriff's deputies stepped in and blocked them.

One of the protestors, a middle-aged white man carrying a "Virginia Is For Lovers, Not Haters" placard looked between the deputies and noticed Miles.

"Miles?" he asked. "Miles Flanagan?"

Miles' first thought was to hide his face. But he remembered he had a job to do and here was a chance to play the part required of him. He turned toward the man, thrust his chin forward, and said, "Yeah, it's me!"

"You can't seriously be part of this bullshit, can you?"

"It ain't bullshit, and I'm proud to be part of it!" He made sure all three Hendershots heard him. "The United Friends of Rockwell believes history shouldn't be erased just because it makes some people *uncomfortable*." He spat out that last word. "History is truth. Erasing it is a lie."

The man shook his head. "Do the McKendricks know you're doing this? That they've got a white supremacist on the payroll?"

"I got my freedom of speech, don't I?" Miles felt a surge of relief that he'd told Bar the truth. At least his job wasn't in jeopardy as long as Bar protected him.

When the crowd settled down and the protest ended, the UFR members convened at Ned's truck.

PJ slipped to Miles's side and said, "You sure set that asshole straight." She placed a hand on his arm and added, "I'm so glad you've joined us. We need true believers like you to carry our message." To his surprise, she pecked him on the cheek, flashed a smile, and half-whispered "Deo Vindice."

The touch of her lips on his cheek was still smoldering when Rocky's hand came down hard on his shoulder.

"Good job!" he said, nearly knocking Miles over as his paw shook the smaller man. Then in a softer voice he said, "Hey, look, I'd like to talk to you some more about what we're doing, how you can help us. Are you free for lunch tomorrow?"

"Yeah, I get a short lunch break."

"How about meeting me at the general store. We can grab some chow and have a chat in my van." He looked around the dark parking lot. "Y'know, we gotta be careful," he said in a conspiratorial tone. "You never know who might be listening."

Back at Off the Grid, as the Hendershots were putting the protest signs away, Margaret said to Rocky, "Your little buddy did good.

But we gotta be more sure than just from tonight before offering him a spot on the board."

"I got a plan for that," Rocky said, "something that'll either show he's as serious as we are, or he's just a bunch of talk and no action."

"Yeah? So what's this plan?"

When Rocky was done explaining his idea, Margaret said, "Brilliant! When are you gonna hit him with that?"

"I already made a lunch date with him for tomorrow."

Chapter 16

The Diary of Olivia Bauer Billington
Montfair, Crutchfield County, Virginia
May 4, 1866

I received a letter today from my friend and fellow Pennsylvanian, Jacob Yoder, who is serving as a teacher in Lynchburg. His report is most troubling. He states that "It is too plain that the people here still love Slavery with some blind madness. They have only accepted the result of this war, because they must. Many hate every measure that is intended to elevate the Coloreds. Education is their only passport to distinction. Therefore the whites so bitterly oppose it. Since I am acquainted with the treacherousness of the people, I don't like to go out at night."

We are ever watchful here at Montfair as similar sentiments abound. We are afforded some solace as most locals respect Archibald for the protection he provided during the War and the support he now gives to those in dire need. It troubles my soul to see our neighbors struggling. Many husbands and sons were lost. Others survived but with grave injuries. Farmsteads were destroyed. The pride that led many to resist the invasion has now turned to pain in the face of defeat and occupation. Seeking solace, our Coloreds have become the target of their hatred. And that hatred is often expressed through opposition to educating them.

The Freedmen's Bureau is aiding in the establishment of schools in Virginia and throughout the South. Many aid societies in the North are contributing to the cost of supplies and textbooks. The state's Constitutional Convention approved the formation of a state school system.

Sadly, though laudable, these steps are serving to further inflame the hatred directed at both our Coloreds and those who seek to elevate them through education.

As we already have the start of a school at Montfair, albeit necessarily kept clandestine until now, widening our outreach to the broader community seems only natural. When the students were but those among the house staff, lessons could be conducted in relative secrecy. This limited the risk that our then-illegal activity would be discovered. But as we can now offer this service to any child within reach of Montfair, a structure dedicated to its function is needed. Archibald has agreed to fund the expense and has left it to me to determine the requirements.

I have yet to broach this with him, but I'm inclined to suggest the construction of a stone building. I realize this will cost more than wood or even brick. But there have been reports of school buildings being set on fire by marauding bands. To reduce the risk of total destruction, it is my desire to have our schoolhouse built from local stone. It must also be positioned close to the main house where not even the boldest marauder would dare venture, torch in hand.

Happily, we have a skilled craftsman among the Montfair family who has shown great aptitude for such an undertaking. Moreover, I have a budding protégé who desires to help with what I foresee will soon be a classroom filled with faces, both white and Colored, eager to achieve, as my friend Jacob said, their "passport to distinction."

****

Thumper knew who the people were that would help his great-great-grandmother achieve her goals. And he knew where the paths launched by those tasks would ultimately lead. He also knew that Olivia's vision of Black and white children learning together in the same classroom would be forestalled for nearly one hundred years. While the state legislature, which then included two dozen African-American delegates, created a school system open to all, its passage required one notable compromise: the schools must be segregated by race. That policy stood in Virginia and throughout the South until the Supreme Court's *Brown v. Board of Education* decision in 1954. Even then it would be several more years before full integration was realized. The court's wording called for segregation to be ended "with all deliberate speed." Given the definition of "deliberate" as "slow and measured", this allowed the states to drag out the process. In Virginia's case, it would be another ten years before state-sanctioned segregation ended in all parts of the Old Dominion.

He closed Olivia's diary and thought about how life must have been for her and others living through those times. What would she think of how things are today? She'd no doubt be disappointed in the racial division that still exists, a century and a half since her crusade to help correct the wrongs done by her own people. He was sure she'd be horrified by the existence of a group like the United Friends of Rockwell.

What motivated people like that? His knowledge and understanding of the factors that led to secession, through both his academic work and his family's history, equipped him with a finely nuanced appreciation for the turmoil of that time. Nathan Bedford Forrest, Josiah's commanding officer, is widely remembered as "the founder of the Ku Klux Klan." But few bother with details beyond that damning, and incorrect, appellation. In truth, he joined the group two years after its founding. He did hold the distinction of serving as the first Grand Wizard when that position was created.

However, after just two years into his participation, he became disillusioned with the Klan's actions and called for its dissolution, including the destruction of those distinctive costumes. Disturbed by anti-Black violence, he went on to disavow his connection to the Klan and made statements in support of racial harmony and Black dignity.

Whether or not he knew about Olivia's efforts to educate Black children remains unknown. Nor did he travel from his home in Tennessee to attend Josiah's funeral (an occasion the family chose to keep private). Forrest himself succumbed to acute diabetes and died in 1877 at the age of 56. Just a few months before his death, he attended a barbecue in Memphis hosted by African-Americans. Addressing the group, he encouraged the attendees to "work, be industrious, live honestly and act truly." He added, "When you are oppressed, I'll come to your relief."

If someone like Forrest could have had such a dramatic change of heart, a man who had been a paragon of the Southern Cause, what could motivate people today to harbor the abhorrent views expressed in those crude UFR pamphlets?

He'd only known Edwin Hendershot through occasional visits to service the HVAC systems in the Montfair house and dependent buildings. Windy, as he liked to be called, always seemed to be an affable fellow, no hint of anything that would suggest racial bigotry. The same could be said of Rocky, at least until now. Was there some clue suggested by the name "Rockwell"? Perhaps a dormant strain of virulent racism linked to the infamous American Nazi Party leader? A familial infection held in check for decades but now erupting into a pestilential sickness of the spirit?

Maybe Miles would uncover the motivations behind this mindset. He was not the vessel Thumper would have chosen for the mission. But, for now at least, it was all he and Janey had to work with.

Chapter 17

Wednesday Mid-Day
Paradise Gap General Store

Situated at the opposite end of town from the McKendricks' shop, The Paradise Gap General Store featured two main attractions: an extensive selection of Virginia wines and a well-stocked deli counter. The former appealed to day trippers out to experience a taste of rusticity while the latter served up homemade fare for the local crowd.

Rocky and Miles exited the store with their lunches in hand and climbed into the Jessup van.

"We're really happy to have you as part our group," Rocky began. "On the one hand, we need more people to help with our mission. But we have to be careful about who we let inside. So…well…I need to ask how serious you are about becoming a full-fledged member. Maybe even joining our board." He didn't think it was necessary to explain that those two positions were essentially one and the same.

"Gee, I dunno. I mean…like…do I have to pay dues? Is there some initiation thing I have to go through?"

"Not dues exactly. Mama's paying for everything out of her own pocket. Not like there's a lot of overhead. So far just materials for the protest signs. She puts the stuff together for the pamphlets and

PJ prints them out. We might have to ask for contributions at some point, but for now no one else is chipping in."

He took a bite of his sandwich, a swig of Mountain Dew, and continued. "But…um…there is something I need to ask you. How much do you know about George Lincoln Rockwell?"

"Not much," Miles replied. "Well, to be honest, not a damn thing. Never heard of him." He thought it best not to mention what Cecelia had told him about Rockwell and the American Nazi Party.

"Yeah, you and most people these days. But we're going to change that. He was a visionary, like, sixty years ago. He saw what was needed to put America back on the right track. To stop the way the country was becoming mongrelized by race mixing. But everyone hated him for trying to tell the truth, made him out to be the bad guy, really evil. And then he died a martyr, murdered by one his own disciples. Just like Jesus was."

Although Miles' biblical knowledge was scant, there was something about that analogy that seemed misplaced.

Rocky went on. "So, you see, if you want to be a real member of the United Friends of Rockwell, you need to know who it is you're being a friend of."

"A *real* member?" Miles asked. "Are there, like, different levels of membership? Real and unreal?"

Rocky chuckled at the question. "I hadn't really thought about it like that. Maybe membership isn't the best way to put it. It's more like commitment." His tone turned serious. "Look, this is a hard road we're going down. No point in sugarcoating it. You think you guys got some crap for pretending to be Rebel soldiers? Shit, that's nothing compared to what we're likely to be hit with. We're just getting started, so we're not much of a blip on anyone's radar screen yet. But that will change the more we get rolling and start making our voices heard. A lot of people aren't going to like that, and some of them have the power to come after us with full force." He took another swig of Mountain Dew. "I know you share our core beliefs. And that's a good start. But it's one thing to believe, another thing to be willing to act on those beliefs. So I gotta ask you…how willing are you to put your beliefs into action? Even if that comes at a price?"

Miles thought about the price he'd pay if he didn't come through for Tavina. Whatever difficulties might lie ahead for pretending to be a white supremacist would only be temporary. If his undercover mission succeeded, he might even be seen as a hero for his role in busting these wackos. If he failed…well, anyone with the taint of white supremacy, real or fake, probably wasn't among the most popular group in the prison population.

He turned to Rocky, mustered what he hoped was a convincingly serious expression, and said, "Whatever the price, I'm in. Like you said, we need to put this country back on the right track."

A hand slammed down on his shoulder and Miles almost dropped his sandwich.

"That's what I was hoping to hear, brother!" Rocky said. "Now then, we need to get you up the curve about Commander Rockwell. I've got something for you." He reached into the driver's door pocket, pulled up a tattered paperback, and handed it to Miles. The title on the faded cover said *White Power*. "This'll get you started."

Miles was hoping Rocky would give him something short, maybe a booklet or just a pamphlet. His optimism faded when he saw the book ran to nearly five hundred pages…in small print.

"Commander Rockwell wrote several books," Rocky explained. "This one's the best."

Miles flipped through random pages and said, "Might take me a while to get through this. I'm kinda more of a visual learner. At least that's what the school guidance counselors always told me. Will there be, like, a test I gotta pass? I'm not good at tests."

Rocky chuckled again. "I hear ya, bro. Tests ain't really my thing either. Getting through the exam for my license was a nightmare. My father was tutoring me on it, but, then…well…" He took a deep breath and looked out the window. Regaining his composure, he turned back to Miles. "If it hadn't been for Ned's help, I'd have never passed it. So, no, not like a written test. But, um, we would like you to do something as kind of an initiation. Y'know, to show that commitment thing."

"Initiation? Are we talking guys in hoods in a dark room with paddles, that kinda shit?"

Rocky grimaced and shook his head. "Ooo…hoods. Ah…probably best we don't do the hoods thing. But, no, nothing like that."

"So what then?"

"I have an idea, something that would serve multiple purposes. It'll give you a chance to start learning about Commander Rockwell's teachings, at least on one subject anyway. And it would fit in with a special occasion we'll be observing soon."

"Special occasion?"

"Yeah. The Commander's birthday is coming up in a couple of weeks. We've been marking that with an observance the past few years. This year we want to make it extra special. Ned's going to invite a bunch of folks, people who share our views, and we want to put on a kind of…sort of…*performance* type thing I guess you could call it. A way to remind people what we're fighting for, what Commander Rockwell stood for and why his message is still so important today."

"So how do I figure into this?" Miles asked. "I'm not much of a performance kinda guy either."

"I disagree. You're an excellent performance guy. I saw you at some of the reenactments you guys did. You, like, *became* one of Mosby's men. People would toss questions at you and you were always, like, '*I* did this' and '*We* did that' and 'when the Yankees were chasing *us*'. What do you call that? First person stuff? You even had a name for the guy you were supposed to be."

"Well, he was a real guy. Lieutenant Palmer. I just learned as much about him as I could find and then said what I thought he would have said."

"Exactly! And that's why we think you'd be the perfect person to represent our hero for our guests."

"Geez, Rocky. I dunno. I put a lot of time into learning about Palmer. And all the details about the battles he was in. I don't know shit about Rock…er…the Commander. If people start asking questions, like they did at our reenactments, I'd be screwed."

"Not a problem. This wouldn't be that kinda role playing thing. You can work up a script and there won't be any questions from the audience. And this would also be a way to get you up the curve to really understand what we're doing and why we're doing it."

"How can I come up with a script when I don't know anything about the guy?" He held up the book. "Gonna take me a long damn time to get through this."

"Don't worry about that. You just need to focus on one topic. And there's plenty of stuff online to work with. You do have a computer, right?"

"Yeah, of course."

"So all you have to do is look up stuff on what the Commander had to say about one subject…mixed marriages."

"You mean like Blacks and whites marrying?"

"No," Rocky said mockingly. "Humans and dogs." With a huff he added, "Of course Blacks and whites. That was one of his major points, about how mongrelization was happening, destroying the purity of the white race. All you need to do is look up some stuff on that, what the Commander had to say about it, and then give a short presentation. It'll give you a quick boost to learning about the Commander's teachings, show the others how committed you are to the cause, and, most of all, make Mama happy. And," he added with a grin, "you know ain't no one happy if Mama ain't happy."

Both men sat silent while Miles considered his options.

"Couple of weeks, huh?" He shot Rocky a mischievous grin, nodded, and said, "Guess I'd better get rolling on the research."

Over dinner that evening, Rocky filled in Margaret and PJ on his talk with Miles.

"Good choice on the mixed marriage thing," Margaret said. "The Commander tried to warn people about that. But no one listened and look where we are now. The 'browning' of America."

"Yeah," Rocky agreed, "like Mister Billington's daughter dating some Black guy, whoever he was. Can you believe it? An old, respectable family like that?"

"Old, yeah," Margaret said. "Respectable? Shit, you remember the Billington's wouldn't contribute to the monument fund. Not the Crutchfields either. The DAC coulda had a really beautiful statue made if they'd chipped in. They had plenty of money, even back then when most others were still struggling. But, no! 'Gotta put it all behind us' they said. 'Move forward to a new world.' Well, they've moved all right. But more backward than forward if you ask me."

"He doesn't look much like the Commander," PJ mused.

"That ain't the point," Rocky replied. "Like we figured, he'd never heard of our leader. No surprise there. We need to see how he feels about our cause, how serious he is about joining us. This will force him to start getting up the curve, get a better handle on our mission. If he balks at this, blows the job, then we'll know not to let him in any closer."

"Well, even if he doesn't look like the Commander, he is kinda cute," PJ said.

"Shit," Rocky replied. "He's old enough to be your father."

"So what? And he rides horses. Now *that's* sexy."

"You mind your mouth, young lady," Margaret chided. She turned back to Rocky. "He could be useful, down the road anyway. We'll see how he does with this and then decide where things go after that."

Chapter 18

Thursday Morning
Fair Enough Farm

The second, and final, informal hunting session called for hounds to be hacked over from the kennels to the front lawn of Fair Enough Farm.

Thumper was tacking up Lenny in the Montfair barn aisle when his phone rang. The screen showed Miles' name.

"S'up?"

"Um, could I stop by after work this evening? Like around six? Something I need to talk to you about."

Thumper caught a shaky note in Miles' voice. "Sure. Everything okay?"

"Yeah. Maybe. Geez, I dunno. I'll explain when I get there."

Janey noticed the troubled look on Thumper's face as he clicked off his phone. "Who was that?" she asked.

"Oh, just Miles. Coming by this evening. Probably no big deal." He glanced at his watch. "You about ready?"

"Whenever you are."

They led their horses out to the mounting block, climbed aboard, and headed over to the McKendricks'.

At the same time, Ryman and Nardell rode to the kennels where they awaited the hounds' release. Crispie called the pack to order and trotted off with all hounds following obediently, Patti to one side, Nardell on the other, Ryman to the rear.

When they arrived at Fair Enough, an ebullient Ryman McKendrick called out, "A grand and glorious good morning to you all!"

Shocked by this joyous outburst, Thumper rode up next to Ryman. "Well, you certainly are in a good mood. Nardell put something special in your cereal?"

"Ah, I do have my lovely wife to thank for helping me see the light. Her and old Wycroft." He turned his attention to the hounds. "Ain't that right, lads and lasses? Ryman has seen the light!" Every hound in the pack looked up at him and replied with a chorus of *woofs!*

Turning back to Thumper, he explained, "Saint Hubert has also worked through you, with some help from Myrna, to show me where my true purpose lies. My mission to the human members of the hunt has been fulfilled. I must now focus on the good saint's true purpose, the care of his beloved hounds, not just on Blessing Day but every day, hunt season and off season."

"Whatever's caused your latest epiphany," Thumper said, "whether Saint Hubert's spirit or something in your cereal, it's good have you back. So are you still getting a message about where Crispie should take hounds?"

Ryman brushed off the question. "Doesn't matter. Just leave it to them to do their job. Their ability to know where the fox is and how to get one up for a chase is ten thousand times greater than mine. They've been the ones giving us such great runs all season. Just let them do what they're good at doing and all we have to do is follow along and enjoy the ride."

"Fine," Thumper replied. He turned to Crispie. "Mister O'Rourke, the morning is yours. Take hounds wherever you will."

With a well-bred, highly trained pack of hounds, aided by an expert staff—two professionals and two volunteers—the morning's outing once again went as planned.

With all hounds on afterward, they hacked back to kennels. The few members who had shown up loaded their horses onto trailers and pulled away. Thumper and Janey rode off at a leisurely pace back to the Montfair barn.

"Maybe the 'declaration of character' thing is no longer a threat," Thumper said. "You just might be okay moving ahead on the 'Church of Foxhunting' book with no objection from the prime figure in your story."

"That's certainly a relief," Janey replied. "Any idea what's caused this sudden turnaround?"

"Did I mention my oldest, bestest friend can be a bit mercurial? Who the hell knows what wacky shit goes on in that addled brain. But, hey, if he's found a new diversion, for whatever reason, that's good news for us."

"I did mention to Danella that there might be a problem, but I didn't go into any detail. Figured I'd give it a few days to see what happened. Sure glad I did! I'll let her know it's full steam ahead."

"Great! And then you can start thinking about your next project. Y'know, that white supremacy thing."

"It's still a mystery to me how you'd know someone with a connection into that world."

"Well, no one else is supposed to know what's going on. I'm not even supposed to know. But I reckon it's okay if I bring you in on it. Just don't say anything to Danella or anyone else just yet. Okay?"

"Yeah, sure. So…?"

"All right, here's the scoop. It starts with that incident in Rhetta's kitchen."

Janey's eyes widened. "You have my full attention."

Chapter 19

Thursday Evening
Montfair

Miles found Thumper in his study that evening.

"Thanks for seeing me, boss. Kind of a major development in UFR stuff I need to talk to you about."

Before Thumper could reply, Janey walked in, followed by Myrna.

Miles clammed up. To Thumper's eye, Miles looked like a teenager whose mother had just caught him in his bedroom at an inopportune moment.

"S'okay," Thumper said. "Janey already knows what's going on. And we might as well tell my sister too."

"But…but she said I wasn't supposed to let anyone else know."

"Yeah, well, you already botched that by telling me," Thumper replied. "Look, once word starts to get out that you're involved with this group, and you know that'll happen at some point, people are going to wonder why I don't fire you. I can fend them off, for the most part. But it'd be kinda tough doing that with these two ladies." He gestured toward Myrna, who was bursting with curiosity. "I think we can trust them to keep the secret. And, really, they have a stake in this too. So, for my own household harmony, we have to let them in on this."

Thumper gave Myrna a quick rundown on Miles' predicament. She and Janey had been present at "The Incident" and understood the implications for all involved if the truth came out. When Thumper finished explaining what Tavina was forcing Miles to do, Janey and Myrna each gave him a hug and expressed their full support.

Janey said, "We'll certainly help you any way we can." She then added, "I hope this doesn't cause you any problems at the shop."

Thumper caught the flicker in Miles' eyes. "Ah, jeez. You told them, didn't you?"

"Just Bar! And, well, he's kinda involved in this too. Right?"

Thumper sighed. "Yeah, I reckon he is. As much, maybe even more, than the rest of us. But if there's anyone who can keep a secret, under any circumstances, it's gotta be Bar." He shot a stern, fatherly stare at Miles. "Just don't tell anyone else. All we need is for some word of this to get to Luella and we're all screwed."

Luella Starrett, proprietor of the general store, was known as the Gossip Queen of Paradise Gap. The local expression was, if you wanted to spread information through the local community, "Don't telephone, tell Luella."

Miles flashed to his meeting with Rocky the day before, the two of them taking their sandwiches from Luella's hand. She'd no doubt seen them getting into the Jessup van together. It wouldn't take her long to put two-and-two together. That would be fine as long as she believed Miles was truly becoming a member of UFR. It might even help boost his credibility with the group. He just hoped her uncanny radar wouldn't detect the real reason behind his mission.

"So," Thumper said to Miles, "what was it you wanted to talk about."

Miles filled them in on his conversation with Rocky and his assignment to do a role playing performance about mixed marriages.

His three listeners exchanged uncomfortable glances when the topic was revealed.

Thumper thought for a moment, then said, "*Loving versus Virginia.*"

"What?" Janey asked.

"The landmark case about mixed marriages," he explained. "It started in the late 1950s. A white man and a Black woman were married in Washington, DC, where it was legal. But they were from Virginia and when they moved back to their home county, that's when the trouble began. Miscegenation—mixed marriage—was illegal here and in several other southern states. The appellate court in Virginia upheld the local circuit court's ruling against them. The case eventually made its way to the US Supreme Court in…" He gazed up at the ceiling and scanned his memory files. "…'67 when Virginia's law was unanimously overturned. And that voided the miscegenation laws in all other states as well."

Myrna looked at Janey and said with a shrug, "You can take the professor out of the classroom, but, well…y'know."

"Hey!" Thumper said, "It was a pretty major event in constitutional law but doesn't get much attention these days. Everyone knows about *Brown versus Board of Education.* But mention *Loving versus Virginia* and you're likely to get little more than 'a soft wound of silence', to borrow an old Norman Mailer line." He turned to Miles, who looked more confused than encouraged. "It's perfect, don't you see? I'll need to brush up on Rockwell, but I'm pretty sure it's the kind of thing that would have set him off. As it would anyone in the racial purity camp."

"So," Miles asked, "I'm supposed to pretend to be, like, a lawyer or a law professor giving a lecture about some legal case from the '60s?"

Myrna had a sense of where her brother was going with this. Her theatrical background kicked in. "No," she said. "You'll be playing the *part* of Rockwell ranting about what he thought of it."

Thumper's enthusiasm shot up three notches. "Perfect! Hang on. Let me check something." He did a quick search on his computer. "Let's see…the court's ruling was in '67…" A few scrolls. "June. The decision was announced in June of that year. Now, Rockwell….Rockwell…George Lincoln Rockwell…" More scrolling. "Ah! He died in '67…August! Yes, perfect!"

Miles began to see what Thumper and Myrna had in mind but didn't share their enthusiasm. "So I'm supposed to pretend I'm this Rockwell guy and do a rant about mixed marriages?"

Thumper thought for a moment. He scrolled through a series of photos on his phone. The images showed that Rockwell was more than a head taller than Miles and, to Thumper's eye, conveyed a blend of prep school elitism and military bearing. A few images of him holding a corncob pipe, à la General Douglas MacArthur, struck Thumper as a silly prop. He looked at Miles, who was a poor casting choice for the role. But he was all they had to work with.

"Maybe not a rant exactly," Thumper said. "We'll need to study this guy, get a better feel for how he would have handled this. Hell, maybe he wrote about it before he died."

"'We'?" Miles asked.

"Hey," Thumper replied, "I reckon we're all in this together now." He turned to Janey. "What do you think?"

"Well," she said, "I don't know anything about Rockwell or mixed marriage laws. The only time we had a mixed marriage back in Clara City, Minnesota, was if a Lutheran married a Catholic. That might have raised a few eyebrows but nobody got arrested for it. However, some form of initiation, or a test of worthiness, is pretty common among cults. I've described it as the 'take-away sales method' in my books. A prospective new member is encouraged to learn more about their beliefs, all in a very non-threatening way. No hard sales pressure. Full membership is held out as something only the true believers can achieve. When they see the prospect is eager to join, they hold back. 'No, no. You have to prove yourself worthy.' Which serves to make full membership even more desirous. What's required can range anywhere from something fairly harmless, like, say baptism by immersion, to something more challenging, like walking across hot coals, to the really extreme. You don't want to know the kind of things a violent gang like MS13, which is pretty much a cult, requires for full membership."

Thumper shuddered at the thought. "No, I don't suppose we do." He turned to Miles. "So this shouldn't be too bad. No hot coals at least. Not literally anyway."

Miles shrugged in submission. "Okay. I mean, what else can I do?"

"What you can do," Myrna said, glowing with enthusiasm, "is make this an award-winning performance!" Here was her chance to finally be a director, small time though it was, to mold the raw material of Miles Flanagan into a celebrated star. She turned to Thumper. "Your job is to work up a script. I'll handle the staging." Then to Janey, "And you…you can be our cult consultant."

Hands on hips and head held high, she said, "Let's do this!"

Thumper turned to Miles. "So, Flanagan, you good with this?"

"I don't really have a choice, do I?"

"No, I reckon not. But, hey, you've got a great team backing you up now. We'll make this a win-win for everyone."

Miles was only slightly reassured by Thumper's encouragement.

Chapter 20

Friday Evening
Kimber Farm

A spark had been flickering between Shelton McKendrick and Tavina Doddridge since childhood. But, aside from a tenuous connection to Tavina's aunt, they spent their girlhoods in two different worlds. Tavina was the academic star, high school debate team captain, and class valedictorian. Shelton grew up as a rough-around-the-edges farm girl, into 4H and Pony Club, a decent student but not Honor Society material. She spent much of her free time hanging out at the family's agricultural equipment shop, wearing grease-stained coveralls and helping Bar Reinhardt work on tractors and other farm gear.

Following college and law school, Tavina returned to Crutchfield County where she began her career as an assistant prosecutor. There had been a stutter or two—one fairly significant—in her early days there. But that was behind her now and she was clearly on the path to higher office.

Shelton's CV consisted of a degree in Animal Sciences followed by an MBA from a second tier school, which led to a position as a veterinary pharmaceuticals rep covering the northern West Coast. That career was interrupted by the death of her grandfather, which required her to return home to salvage the failing family business.

Now, as independent women, Tavina's aunt again served as the contact point for them to reconnect.

"I think that went quite well," Cecelia Broadhurst said as the last prospective donor left her house late Friday evening.

"I can't thank you enough for serving as my campaign chair," Tavina said.

"We need more strong women like you in these positions," Cecelia replied. "Breaking up the 'Old Boys' network is my mission. Having you as the county's first female Commonwealth's Attorney will be a big step in that direction."

Shelton remained silent but she knew what Cecelia was thinking. Not just a "female" but a woman of color and part of the LGBTQ community. With a triple threat like that, Tavina would win in a walkover if they were in a more progressive urban area. But Crutchfield County was still heavily rural and conservative. For some voters, those qualities worked against her. So best to focus on her strengths as a prosecutor, her tough-on-crime record, as an appeal to that group. The other two attributes—skin color and sexual preference—could still be conveyed with a wink and a nod.

"I'm already hearing rumbles," Shelton said, "that our opponent plans to use the Rolfe case in his attacks."

"Ah, that was four years ago," Cecelia said with a dismissive wave of her hand, "Tavina's first year on the job. And there were a lot of mitigating circumstances."

"No, no," Tavina countered. "It's a perfectly legitimate campaign point. The best way to diffuse something like that, rather than sounding defensive or striking back, is to deflect the attack with humility and wisdom. My response would be that I have always strived to see the better potential in people, to believe that no one's future is solely defined by their past mistakes. As a young prosecutor, I soon found out that such idealism is better suited to social work than to the criminal courtroom. It was a critical, if painful, experience to strengthen my mission to protect the law-abiding citizens of Crutchfield County. And I believe my record since then clearly supports that."

Shelton and Cecelia both sat silently processing Tavina's remarks.

Tavina had been expecting immediate endorsement, if not a standing ovation, for her sagacity.

After a long moment, Cecelia said, "Well, not exactly a bumper sticker quote. But it should play well with the more literate voters."

"Yeah," Shelton added, "kinda admitting you botched the case without actually saying you botched the case."

Tavina's deflation was evident. "So what should I say?" she asked, revealing a hint of the defensive tone she'd just disavowed. "'Gee, yeah, I let some asshole off who then went and did something much worse. But, hey, I've been one tough-ass bitch ever since. So vote for me!'"

Cecelia opted to be the voice of reason. "I think the way you presented it is an excellent way to respond when the situation calls for it. Like, say, in a debate or a press conference or interview with a reporter. As for what we post on the campaign website and put in our outreach materials, probably best to just pretend it never happened. In terms of the modern news cycle, this is pretty much ancient history."

Tavina accepted her benefactor's counsel with a nod.

Chapter 21

Saturday Morning
Montfair

"You've outdone yourself," Thumper said, "if that's even possible. Enough to feed the entire audience."

Natasha pointed to the platters of food on the kitchen table. "These are for tailgate," she replied, her English syntax and placement of articles forever hampered by her native Polish. She then turned to a similar number of dishes on the countertops. "And these are for officials' tent."

"Really good of you to do all this for our racing guests and the officials crew."

"Bah! Is what I most love to do. And good of you to pay for it all."

Thumper heard footsteps on the main stairway. The steps stopped at the midpoint landing.

Tobias Johnson stood gazing at the portrait of Olivia Billington. He wore a neatly pressed blue pinstripe shirt, yellow checkered bowtie, and Nantucket red trousers. Six years out of college, his sartorial choices remained heavily influenced by his days at UVA. He'd been in the same fraternity every Billington "gentleman" had been a member of since the club's founding in 1869.

Thumper looked up from the foot of the staircase. "You'll be the best-dressed fellow at the races today," he said.

Tobias pointed toward the portrait. "A Billington ancestor, I assume."

"My great-great grandmother," Thumper explained.

"Which makes her Elizabeth's great-great-*great*-grandmother," Tobias observed.

"See any resemblance?" Thumper asked, half-jokingly.

Tobias paused. He cocked his head and studied the painting. "Yes, I do. A similar balance of femininity and rock-solid determination. She's neither smiling nor frowning, as if either would reveal too much emotion. And those brown eyes! Those inscrutable, unfathomable brown eyes. What is she thinking? Is she tacitly approving some comment you've made, brilliant in your mind? Or has she just deflated any shred of profundity you may have assumed?"

Thumper chuckled. "The words of an English major. And of someone who knows my daughter well. Look, I've got to check in with Voytek on something. Natasha has the coffee on if you want to grab some before the others come down."

"I was thinking I might take a walk first, stroll around the grounds."

"Well, Voytek's doing some work up at the old graveyard. That's where I'm heading. Want to come with me?"

"Sure."

As they walked along, Thumper asked, "Did you sleep well?"

"Like a rock. So peaceful and quiet out here. I think Elizabeth was teasing me, some story about a ghost who still haunts the guest room. A relative who died there. But I slept just fine, didn't hear any rattling chains or phantom moans."

Thumper paused and looked back at the sprawling old mansion. "Lots of people have died in this house. As have countless others in homes everywhere. That's just how it was for much of human existence. Most of our Billington ancestors have passed here."

With a gesture toward the hilltop, Tobias asked, "Are they now buried in that graveyard?"

Thumper turned and resumed walking toward their destination. "Um, well, no. The Billingtons are all buried in the cemetery next to the church in the village."

"Then who's in the graveyard up there?"

"Some special people. Not family members exactly, but each one an essential figure in Montfair history."

"'*Essential figure*'," Tobias repeated. "A convenient euphemism for 'slave'?"

Thumper shrugged and continued walking.

The old graveyard was enclosed by a wrought iron fence, four feet high. It held a dozen tombstones, most of them thin and plain. Some leaned at a slight angle, others tilted sharply, close to toppling over. Three graves were marked by simple stones on the ground. Where inscriptions were still visible, they were faint at best. The carvings had not been deep when first made and had since worn down from a century and a half of exposure to the elements. A large oak tree along the back of the enclosure provided some shade but little shelter.

Voytek knelt by the fence, a wire brush in his hand. He scraped a few flakes of loose paint from one of the pickets to reveal a few spots of rust.

"We are needing to remove old paint," he said, "treat for rust, and repaint whole fence."

"Looks like it," Thumper agreed.

"When are you expecting to have new project ready?" Voytek asked.

"Looks like late April if all goes well. Can you get the fence work done by then?"

"Is not a problem."

An up-and-coming investigative reporter, Johnson's radar kicked in. "What's the new project?"

Thumper waved the question away. "Something that's long overdue. A family thing."

Sensing his host's dismissive tone, Tobias opted to leave further inquiries for later. Perhaps Elizabeth could fill him in.

Scanning the enclosure, he tried to read some of the inscriptions. He could discern a few letters but not enough to make out any names or full dates. That would require much closer examination, perhaps using tracing paper and a block of wax. He had no such items handy, nor was he inclined to kneel in the damp grass wearing his cherished Nantucket reds.

Thumper patted Voytek on the shoulder. "Sounds good. Your wife has outdone herself with food prep for the races."

Rising with a groan, Voytek replied, "Is not surprising."

"You might need to haul some of it in the trailer with Bumpers," Thumper said jokingly. "Not sure it will all fit in the car."

"She will make fit. Will all be set up and ready when you get there."

Thumper nodded, looked at his watch, and turned to Tobias. "Elizabeth and Janey should be up by now. Let's get to breakfast!"

As they walked briskly back to the house, Tobias considered various ways to uncover the secret of Thumper's graveyard project.

Chapter 22

Saturday
Point-to-Point Racecourse

Hosting a local hunt point-to-point race in March is a risky endeavor, given the mercurial whims of Virginia weather. It could be cold and snowy, sunny and warm, windy and cold, rainy, foggy, or a panoply of conditions that can change gradually or in an unforeseen instant. One minute you're in shirtsleeves and the next you're reaching for gloves, scarf, and a parka.

This March day found the racing gods disposed to allow pleasant conditions: partly cloudy with mild temps and a light wind, only the occasional gust that blew unsecured paper plates and napkins from tailgate tables. Ground conditions were acceptable for mounted sport: slightly damp but not deep.

When Miles arrived at noon for the pre-race meeting, the viewing area was already abuzz with tailgate parties. Many were centered on actual truck tailgates laid out with store-bought snacks and a cooler or two of beer in the truck bed. Others boasted tables crammed with a lavish variety of gourmet treats, expensive bottles of wine, and decorated with elaborate floral arrangements. The adjoining Kimber Farm and Montfair spots, positioned for the best view of the rolling racecourse, displayed the high point of the latter category. Even so, they were somewhat modest compared to how the elegance would ramp up as the season went along and the events moved from the hunt-sponsored point-to-points to the larger, big money meets sanctioned by the National Steeplechase Association.

Miles and Bumpers would be vying today for a paltry $1000 payout if they won. Purses in the sanctioned races started at $15,000 and rose steadily to where the top prize at the Virginia Gold Cup hit $150,000. And the size of the crowd at the season's finale, along with the elegance of the party spots and the extravagance of the costumery, rose to an equivalent level of excess.

The pre-race meeting for this early racing day was held in the officials' area, where the jockeys declare their rides and weights for the day to the clerk of the scales. Of the six men and two women who assembled there, seven had multiple rides lined up for the day. Only Miles was slated for a single ride.

The others were already assembled when Miles arrived. They all knew about the altercation he'd had with Thumper and Natasha in the past and that he'd narrowly avoided losing his license, thanks in large part to Thumper's influence with the stewards. But they also knew he'd become a pariah among the racing community. No owners or trainers would hire him. They were, then, surprised to see his name listed in the program, once again riding a Billington horse.

He was met with cautious greetings.

"Well, look who's here," said a veteran who'd been in many finish line battles with Miles. "My old nemesis."

"So you're back, Flanagan," another said. Then added with an Irish lilt, "Got that hot head o' yours cooled off, did ya?"

A young woman who had only recently begun riding as a pro, and had already scored some impressive wins, had never met Miles. But she'd heard about him and his hot temper. She extended a hand cautiously and introduced herself, but offered nothing more.

Micah Hairston, a lanky young man, stood back from the others and eyed Miles with a narrowed glare. He and Miles had always been adversaries, both on and off the racecourse. Although Hairston never said so, Miles wondered if some of that had been because he rode with Mosby's Rangers. As one of the few Black jockeys in the game, Micah might have felt less than friendly toward someone who appeared to be glorifying the Confederate Cause. The question now was if Hairston knew about Miles' budding involvement with UFR. Did he know about the monument demonstration at the courthouse? Far worse than pretending to be a Rebel soldier from a long ago past would be aligning himself with a band of actual present day white supremacists.

Miles simply nodded in neutral response toward the other jockeys, said nothing, and tried to blend in with the scenery.

When the meeting was over and his duty there complete, he made his way to the hill above the tented tailgate area where he found the Hendershots and Ned. They had hauled in camp chairs, two large coolers with wheels, and a small folding table.

"Looks like y'all have this under control," Miles said.

"Not our first rodeo for setting up a campsite," Rocky replied. "The scenery's a little different, but the function's about the same."

PJ held up the racing program. "We bought one of these. I had to flip through a lot of pages to find you. But here you are. 'Maiden Timber. For Five-Year-Olds and Up which have never won over timber. 165 pounds.' I get the age, but what does the other stuff mean?"

"'Maiden' means the horse hasn't won before," Miles explained, "at least not in that type of race. Once a horse scores its first win, it's said that it 'broke its maiden.'"

She raised an eyebrow.

"Yeah, that," he said, then shrugged and continued. "'Timber' means the type of fences we'll be jumping. Wooden fences about four feet high. And the 165 is the amount of weight each horse has to carry to make it fair."

She looked him up and down. "You can't weigh near that much. So what do you do? Put rocks in your pocket?"

"In a way, yeah, sorta like that. It's done with weights that go into pockets on the saddle cloth. We have to weigh out before we mount up and ride onto the racecourse, then get weighed again when we come in to make sure the weight hasn't changed. Since none of the horses in this race have won before, they're all considered about equal, so we'll all carry the same weight. When you get into races with horses that have different records, the weights can vary. Like, the horse considered the best one in the group may have to carry more weight than some of the others to make the competition more level. That's what handicapping is all about."

"Gosh, I never knew all that. I figured you guys just hopped on and saw who could go the fastest."

"A lot more to it than that. Don't even get me started on some of the other stuff. Like what kind of whip we have to carry, how many times we can use it, medical exams, license requirements, lots of crap like that."

She read from the program again. "You're riding 'Down the Alley.' How'd he get that name?"

"Thoroughbreds are usually named with some reference to their lineage. His sire was Bowling for Bucks and his dam was Downstate Dream. So…he's Down the Alley. But we call him Bumpers. Y'know, like those things at a bowling alley that keep the balls from going into the gutters."

"Ah, that's really cute."

Her attention suddenly switched to the area below.

"Oh, look! Are those ponies?" she asked, pointing toward the paddock, her voice rising in excitement.

"Oh, right," Miles said. "The pony races. They go on before the real races start. Something for the kids to do, a way to help bring on the next batch of jockeys. And the crowd loves it."

"Wow! I wish I could see them better. It's so hard from up here."

"Well, we can go down to the paddock and get a better look. And watch the races from there."

"Really? We can do that?"

"Hey, sure we can. I got connections."

She turned to the others. "Y'all wanna come?"

"That's okay," her mother replied. "You two go on."

PJ grabbed Miles' hand and pulled him along. "C'mon! I wanna see the ponies!"

They scrambled down the hill and took a spot by the paddock where four ponies were being walked in a circle, awaiting their young riders to hop aboard.

"They're so cute!" PJ said. "And so little."

"There are three classes," Miles explained. "They start with the small ponies. The next race will be medium ponies, a little bigger, and then the large ponies, just a hair beneath official horse size."

"Did you do this when you were a kid?"

"Nah, I went straight into horses. I hated the ponies. Nasty little bastards if you ask me."

"Oh, I think they're adorable."

"Yeah, to look at. But looks can be deceiving."

He immediately wished he hadn't said that.

As the first official race was now just an hour away, a steady stream of spectators strolled in from the parking area, heading toward the rows of tailgate spots. PJ remained happily fixated on the ponies and the young jockeys when a faintly familiar voice caught Miles' ear.

"It's such a pleasure to see you!" he heard Tavina Doddridge say.

He turned to see her shaking hands with a lady he didn't recognize.

"I'll certainly be voting for you," the lady said.

"Thank you so much! Here." She handed the woman a stack of flyers. "If you can pass these along to your friends, neighbors, relatives, I'd sure appreciate it. And if you'd be willing to put out a yard sign, come to our tailgate along the rail. We have a bunch of them there."

"I will!"

Miles watched as Tavina greeted another well-wisher. He was relieved that as long as her focus was on them, she'd be unlikely to notice him.

PJ saw his attention was elsewhere. When she turned from the ponies to see what he was looking at, she gasped and said, "Her! What's *she* doing here?"

This took Miles by surprise. "You know her?"

PJ tried to regain her composure. “Oh, um, no, not really. Just someone I…well, it wasn’t really…” With a wave she said, “It’s nothing.”

“So who is she?” Miles asked. He now saw this as an opportunity rather than a threat to his cover. “Looks like she’s running for some kinda office. I don’t follow that sorta thing much.”

“Me neither,” PJ said. “It’s not important.”

As Tavina moved along, PJ’s attention was drawn back to the ponies. “Hey, look!” She smacked Miles on the arm. “They’re getting on!”

They watched the small pony race from along the snow fence boundary between the racecourse and tailgate spots. PJ hollered and threw her arms up as the two leaders dashed toward the finish line neck-and-neck. “Wow! That was so cool!”

Miles turned to see the Montfair trailer pulling into the horsemen’s area. “Look,” he said, “I gotta go. Need to check on the horse and stuff.”

“Yeah, okay. Can I stay here and watch the other pony races?”

“Sure. And if you want to see us off, y’all can come back down here when we’re in the paddock. Get a closer look at the real horses, not these shit ponies.”

She grabbed his arm as he started to leave. “Here, in case I don’t get to do this later when you’re busy.” She leaned over and kissed him full on the mouth. “That’s for luck.” She turned him around, gave him a push on the back, and said, “Now go get ready to win that race!”

He stumbled away, confused and lightheaded.

When the pony races were done, PJ returned to the Hendershots’ spot.

Looking down from the hill and pointing toward the Kimber Farm spot, she said to the others, “Did you see who’s here?”

“Yeah,” Margaret said, “we saw her. Kinda hard to miss with all those signs they got plastered around.” She waggled her hands in the air. ‘Doddridge for Commonwealth’s Attorney.’ Thinks she’s heading for the big time. And here I thought we were gonna have a pleasant day in the country, some R&R we all need. Then *she* shows up!"

"It's okay, Mama," Rocky said. "Let her have her delusions of grandeur. She won't be enjoying them much longer."

Ned took a long pull on his beer and then said, "You got that right!" He then added, "Hey, Rocky, did you see who's at the spot beside that one? Ain't that the Billington girl and the boyfriend you were telling us about?"

"Yep," Rocky replied, "that's them."

Ned took another swig of beer, shook his head, and said, "Damn shame. Sure would break the Commander's heart, wouldn't it?"

"It sure would."

"Think there's any way we can score one for the Commander on this?"

"I'm thinking about it," Rocky said. "Got a couple of ideas."

"Good man." Ned reached into the cooler. "Here, have another beer."

Chapter 23

Saturday
Point-to-Point Racecourse

When the announcer called "Horses to the paddock for the third race!", the Hendershots, along with Ned, made their way down the hill. PJ and Margaret wedged their way into the crowd along the fence while Rocky and Ned stood behind them. Five young, eager, well-muscled Thoroughbreds were being led in a circle inside the paddock. Each was guided by a groom holding a lead shank. The jockeys stood off to the side, each wearing the "silks" with the owners' distinctive pattern of colors. Below the flimsy long-sleeved shirt, they wore white breeches and black boots. A gaggle of officials and owners, including Thumper and Janey, stood with them.

"Remember the plan," Thumper said to Miles. "Don't push him too hard. Let him have some fun. If he wants to make it a race, fine. But it's more important that he have a good schooling. There's a long season ahead, plenty of time to get serious."

"Yes, sir," Miles said. His gaze drifted from his boss to the small group of admirers watching from the fence, then over toward Micah Hairston having the same chat with his mount's trainer. Hairston was the picture of calm assurance. He'd already ridden a winner in the day's first race, and looked set to notch another victory in this one.

Thumper caught the hesitant look in his jockey's eyes. Miles had always been a nerves-of-steel guy, no matter what horse he was riding, however stiff the competition, or however hefty the purse. Today he looked more like a novice about to ride his first real race.

"You can do this," Thumper said reassuringly. He put a hand on Miles' shoulder. "The old Miles is back, right?"

"Yeah, I'm back." He squared his shoulders and took a deep breath. "Right!"

The paddock judge hollered, "Riders up!" and the jockeys headed toward their mounts. Voytek gave Miles a leg up, tossing him with such force that Miles had to grab mane to keep from flying off on the other side. Miles took up the reins and pointed Bumpers toward the paddock gate. He looked back toward the crowd along the fence just in time to see PJ blow him a kiss.

The riders assembled their mounts at the designated point, awaiting the signal for the race to start. A dozen sturdy timber fences awaited their two circuits around the rolling course.

The starter dropped the flag and five horses surged forward. Miles settled Bumpers in at the middle of the pack, just behind Hairston, riding Signs of Life. With two-and-a-half miles to go and twelve fences to jump, an experienced jockey knew it was rare for a horse to go wire-to-wire—start off in the lead and hold it all the way to the finish line. Better to let someone else set the pace and hope your horse has plenty of gas left when the lead horse tires.

It took only a few strides for Miles to settle in and realize that, yes, he *was* back! Back to what he was born to do, what he loved more than anything in the world. He was fully in synch with the twelve-hundred pound animal beneath him, blended into an unspoken partnership, a steady flow of communication through muscle and bone. They'd formed a solid working relationship in the hunt field and on schooling rides. Most of all, they'd built a bond of trust. Bumpers would do whatever Miles asked because he knew Miles would only ask what he knew the horse could do.

They were over the first fence before Miles had a second to think about it. He couldn't begin to tally the number of fences he'd been over on a countless string of horses. His muscle memory was so ingrained, he could have lapsed into a coma and still stayed in the saddle.

The pace remained steady, all five horses in a tight pack. Across the Seas, a chestnut gelding, was in the lead, no more than three lengths ahead of the last. Miles kept Bumpers just behind and slightly to the side of Signs of Life. Bumpers felt comfortable there, easing along as if cruising in the other horse's slipstream. Hairston kept his focus ahead, aware of Miles' position and unthreatened by it.

With the first loop around the course completed, the tension began to rise. Which of these youngsters showed promise for a successful career? This is where those prospects would begin to show—or not. Miles remembered Thumper's counsel: *Don't push him too hard. Let him have some fun.* Well, wouldn't it be fun if he and Bumpers won their first race together? Especially against Micah Hairston.

By the tenth fence, Across the Seas remained in front, but the other jockeys could tell he was beginning to lose action. Hairston and Miles were right behind him over that fence. The other two had dropped back and were clearly out of contention, now more of a schooling exercise for them than a racing pace.

With the final two fences to go, it was time to make a move. The announcer's voice rose as the dash to the finish began.

"Across the Seas is still in front but Signs of Life and Down the Alley are starting to make their moves. Across the Seas is over the eleventh, barely inches ahead of his two challengers, who now are kicking into high gear. Across The Seas drops back to third as Signs of Life and Down the Alley head toward the final fence neck-and-neck. They're over the fence as if joined at the shoulders and here they come! Micah Hairston urges Signs of Life on, but Miles Flanagan and Down the Alley stay with him as they sprint to the finish. Signs of Life pulls ahead by half a neck. Down the Alley digs in and cuts the lead to barely a nose!"

Miles Flanagan was in his happy place. The cheering crowd was sweet music. Pounding hooves sent a frantic percussive beat through every fiber of his body. Hairston's face was contorted into a strained grimace as he went to the whip. No way he was going to let this little shit beat him. Certainly not on the little shit's first time back in the game. Miles saw Hairston's panic and that was all the victory he needed. *Let him have some fun*, Thumper said. And that's exactly what they were doing.

With one tap of the whip, Bumpers responded and took the lead by a nose for himself.

Miles looked over at Hairston, smiled, and winked.

It had the desired effect.

Hairston was furious. He dug his heels in, raised his whip, and gave his horse two solid whacks.

"This could be a photo finish!" the announcer declared as the battling duo neared the finish line. "And Signs of Life makes a final surge to take the lead by a neck. And…it's Signs of Life! Down the Alley a close second."

As the horses slowed to a canter and then down to a trot, Hairston's anger morphed into relief. Yes, he'd beaten the little shit. But it was too damn close. Billington had found a good prospect in that horse. And, his personality faults aside, Flanagan knew what he was doing when it came to racing. There was a long season ahead, and Hairston knew he'd see this pair again.

Miles hopped off and strolled over to Hairston as Voytek clipped a lead shank to Bumpers and led him back to the paddock.

"Congratulations, Micah," Miles said with a friendly tone. "Good race."

Hairston was confused. In the past, if Flanagan had lost in such a close finish, he'd be spitting bullets, accusing the winning jockey of cutting him off, bumping him, using his whip too many times, swearing he was going to file a complaint with the stewards. Being gracious in defeat was not Miles Flanagan's style.

"Um, ah, yeah," Micah replied haltingly. "You too."

"See ya at the next one!" Miles said, then strolled away to complete his weigh in duty.

PJ was waiting for him at the paddock gate.

"Wow! That was amazing! You came so close!"

"Yeah, well, that was just sort of a warm up. We'll get more serious next time."

"Look, for tomorrow, Mama, Rocky, and I always get together for breakfast before the guys arrive. We were kinda thinking it would be nice if you could join us."

"Really? Are you sure that's okay? I mean, I don't wanna intrude on your family ritual."

"Not a problem. We'd love to have you."

"Well, if you're sure it's okay, I'll see you then."

Chapter 24

Sunday Morning
Off the Grid

Margaret and PJ were preparing breakfast Sunday morning when they heard the front gate intercom crackle.

"Margaret," a woman's voice called in a friendly lilt. "It's Betty. Carl and I thought we'd stop by to see you."

"What the hell," PJ said. "Were you expecting them?"

"Shit, no. I thought they'd sworn off the three of us."

"Should I tell them to go away?"

"No. Buzz 'em in. Let's see what they got to say."

A minute later PJ opened the door to her aunt and uncle. A third person she did not recognize—a woman wearing a clerical collar—stood with them. They were ushered into the living room where Margaret stood waiting.

With a defiant smirk on her face, she asked, "To what do we owe this surprise visit?"

"We've been worried about you," Betty replied. "Carl and I wanted to talk to you, see how you're doing."

"I'm doing just fine. Couldn't be better." Looking over Betty's shoulder at the other woman, she asked, "And who's this?"

Carl spoke up. "This is Reverend Eloise Gunther. She's the associate pastor at our church."

Margaret harrumphed. "Figured you'd need some spiritual help to deal with me, did you?"

Eloise stepped forward. "Betty and Carl have been worried about you since their brother died. And their niece and nephew as well. They asked me to come along as a neutral party."

"Neutral, huh?" Margaret said. "Like you're gonna referee a boxing match?"

"No, no," the Reverend protested. "Just a chat, that's all."

"Fine," Margaret conceded. "We'll have a chat. Why don't y'all sit down, make yourselves comfortable."

As they were taking seats, Margaret added, "But don't get *too* comfortable. We got a bunch of folks coming over soon."

"Is Rocky here?" Betty asked

"No," Margaret replied. "He got a call early this morning from dispatch. Someone's heat went out. He's on duty this weekend. You remember late night emergency calls, don't you? They can be a life-changing event. Or life-ending."

"Look," Carl said, "we know how devastating Edwin's loss was to you. And to the kids. It hit us all hard. But, well, we're concerned that it's affected your perspective. Y'know, with this United Friends thing. We just don't want to see you, or the kids, getting hurt."

"Getting hurt?" Margaret shot back. "What do you know about getting hurt? Y'all just keep cruising along in your comfortable lives. You refuse to see the truth of what's really going on. Losing my husband—the *way* I lost my husband—opened my eyes to the truth."

"And what truth is that?" Reverend Eloise Gunther asked.

"That America was founded by and for white people and should stay that way. Or, more like, get back to that way. Just about everything that's going wrong with this country is because of trying to mix the races."

"Now Margaret," Betty said, "you can't truly believe that."

"The hell I can't! Just look around, watch the news! The country's getting taken over more and more every day by degenerates who don't believe in the American Way. Blacks, Jews,

A-Rabs, queers. They're all trying to tear down every good thing in this country, the things white Christian people built and have worked hard for. They even got drag queens teaching little children that girls can become boys and boys can become girls."

Reverend Gunther kept quiet but couldn't suppress the line from the Kinks' "Lola" running through her mind.

"And, oh my!" Margaret continued, waving her hands. "Don't let white people say or do anything to oppose what's happening. Seems we got 'white privilege' and that's a bad thing. Like we've been taking advantage of them others all these years. Shit, I ain't never taken advantage of nobody. I've had to struggle to get what little I got. Rocky's daddy worked hard, tried to help people in need. And where did that get him? Into an early grave, that's where. And left his kids fatherless." Her angry stare eased as she looked at PJ. "They've turned out okay, thank the Lord. The Bible says, 'Raise up a child in the way that he should go, and when he is old he won't depart from it.' Well, Edwin and I raised them up right and they know the way to go."

Her maternal warmth faded and the irate fervor returned. "And the word 'racism' has got completely turned around. It's okay to be as racist as you want if you're talking about how terrible white people are. But try to criticize a 'person of color' and the whole system will come down on you. Doesn't matter how true the criticism is. A Black person can kill a cop and somehow it's the system's fault." With a mocking tone she said, "'The poor child was disadvantaged. Didn't have the opportunities others had. That's why he turned to drugs and crime.' Bullshit!"

She cocked her head and asked Eloise, "So, *Reverend* Gunther, did you know the Bible clearly says the races should not be mixed?"

"Oh," Eloise replied with a dismissive tone, "I believe that's a misinterpretation of a minor Old Testament passage about the Israelites and their pagan neighbors. Hardly relevant to today's world."

"Old Testament misinterpretation, huh?" Margaret leaned forward and fixed the woman with a challenging stare. "Are you familiar with Acts 17, verse 26?"

Eloise suddenly regretted not bringing a Bible with her. She thought that might create the wrong impression, as if they were coming to perform an exorcism, splash holy water on Margaret, and command the racist demon begone. She tried to recall that verse from memory. But, while other lines from the Acts of the Apostles rolled through her mind, nothing about mixing the races popped up.

Margaret didn't need to hear a reply. The look of confused surrender on Eloise's face was all the answer she needed. "Ha! And you call yourself a 'Reverend.' What that verse says is 'From one man he made all the nations, that they should inhabit the whole earth; and he marked out their appointed times in history and the boundaries of their lands.' Did you get that? *Boundaries of their lands*. God intended the nations, which means the races, to stay within their boundaries. And this, *Reverend* Gunther, is the *New* Testament. Sure, like you said, there's all kinda passages in the Old Testament about the same thing, for the Israelites to not mix with other people. But folks who don't know their Bible, like it seems you don't, can scoff at that and say, 'Oh, that's all Old Testament stuff. It don't apply anymore.' Well, the *New* Testament says people oughta stay within their boundaries. That's why Commander Rockwell preached that the Blacks should all be sent back to Africa where they belong. That's *God's* plan."

Margaret thought of the man who inspired her beliefs. A reverent glow lightened her face. "Commander Rockwell saw it all perfectly clear decades ago. He called it 'White Self-Hate' and said it was the 'Master-Stroke of the Enemy.' Everyone wrote him off as a wack-job back then. But he was truly a prophet and we see the wisdom of his vision now. At least some of us do."

She slid to the front of her chair, looked in turn at her three visitors, and then said, "And now they got white women thinking they shouldn't have kids but should have a career instead. Meanwhile, the lesser races are breeding like rabbits. If they get their way, we'll just end up a tiny minority and Lord knows how much worse things will get once they got no one left to stand up to 'em. That's why we gotta act now. And act big!"

The three visitors all wondered what she meant by "act big." But none had the nerve to ask.

With her focus back to Eloise, she pressed on. "How 'bout you? Got any kids?"

"Well, no, I don't," she stammered in response. She now deeply regretted her willingness to accompany Betty and Carl, realizing she was ill-prepared for this type of verbal assault.

"Y'see?" Margaret said to Betty and Carl while pointing at Eloise. "Been too busy with her 'career' I bet. Gettin' that 'Reverend' in front of her name. But it's the natural purpose of women to procreate, keep the family lineage going. The Blacks and Hispanics got that down pretty tight. The Asians too. It's only whites that have bought into this zero population growth bullshit. The population's gonna keep growing. It's growing all over the world. But it's all the inferior races that are growing while the white population keeps shrinking. Seems like the plan is working out just fine for those who want to take over. And they got most white people going right along without any idea that they're being manipulated. But not us." She turned to PJ. "Ain't that right, darlin'?"

"That's right, Mama," she replied with a triumphant smile.

Betty and Carl saw their hope was dashed that Eloise would deliver a well-reasoned, persuasive argument to dissuade Margaret from her racist lunacy. Reverend Gunther had always seemed so eloquent and erudite when she filled in for the head pastor on Sunday services. But, absent the benefit of a carefully prepared sermon and an agreeable audience, she was clearly out of her depth.

If they were going to persuade their sister-in-law to abandon her insane path, they would have to do it themselves.

"Margaret," Betty said, "I don't know the Bible as well you do. But surely it doesn't teach that some races are superior to others. Didn't Jesus come to save everyone, whatever their skin color?"

"You're right," Margaret replied with a smirk. "Totally right…that you don't know as much about the Bible as I do. But you may know more than the Reverend here, who apparently don't know shit. Two things. First, Jesus coming to save everyone doesn't mean all those 'everyones' are equal. He came to save the lesser races as well as the superior race. But that doesn't mean they're not still lesser. And, two, that has nothing to do with what the Bible clearly says about 'the boundaries of their lands.' Get saved, fine. But stay in the boundaries of your lands where you belong. Commander Rockwell saw clearly that the Blacks don't belong here. It was a big mistake bringing them here as slaves. This country woulda got along just fine without them. And they've been bitching and moaning about how bad things are for them ever since they got here, even after all the special benefits they've been getting. So, the best way to undo the mistake of bringing them here is to pack 'em up and send 'em back. Why can't you see how much sense that makes?"

"Because," Betty said, "the Black folks who are here today are as much Americans as you and I are. Actually, most of them a lot more American given how far back their ancestry goes. Four hundred years for some of them." She paused, reached out, and placed a hand on Margaret's knee. With a soothing, sympathetic tone, she said, "Look, I know how devastating Windy's death was for you. Especially the way it happened. And I understand why you'd need to channel your grief into…"

Margaret knocked Betty's hand away and leapt to her feet. "Channel my grief! What do you know about channeling grief? You think I'm in some delusional state, that this is all just some coping mechanism?"

PJ sprang to her mother's side as the three visitors also got to their feet.

Margaret took a step towards Betty who backed away.

Carl inserted himself between the two women. "Let's all calm down," he urged. "We didn't come here for this. We just wanted to have a reasonable talk."

"Like hell you did!" Margaret shot back. "You wanted to gang up on me and make me change my mind." She pointed at Eloise. "And you brought this poor excuse for a reverend to do your dirty work for you. Well, it ain't gonna work. And I'm asking you to leave my house. The house my Edwin built for me and our kids. The house he'll never get to be in anymore because…because…"

They were all distracted by the crackle of the gate intercom.

"Hey, y'all," a male voice said. "It's me. Miles."

"I'll get it!" PJ said.

She sprinted to the front hallway and pressed the gate button.

When Miles came through the door, she grabbed him and said, "Thank goodness you're here!"

She dragged him into the living room where he found an odd tableau—four middle-aged white people looking like they were about to pull knives and have at it.

PJ whispered to Miles, "These people have to leave before Mama completely loses it. Do something!"

It took him a moment to collect his wits. Realizing this was a chance to make an impression on the right people, he sprang to Margaret's side and said, "Are you okay, Missus H? Want me to toss these assholes out?"

"Who the hell are you?" Carl asked.

"None of your damn business!" Miles shot back. "But I'm someone who'll toss you out of this house on your goddamn ass if you don't leave right now!"

The visitors—ill-suited to physical confrontation—were in no position to argue.

"You heard the man," Margaret said. "And if he don't toss you out, I will!" She turned to Miles and grinned. "Which one you want first? How about you take the old man and I'll grab this so-called reverend lady. See if a bolt of lightning comes down and fries my ass when I hurl her down the front steps."

The threesome collected their coats and hustled out the door as PJ held it open.

"Bye, y'all. *Don't* come again," she called out with a mockingly sweet tone. She then turned to Miles and said, "You were great!" Taking a damsel-in-distress pose, she added, "My hero!"

"Aw, shucks, ma'am. T'weren't nothin'," he replied with a shuffle, and then asked, "Who were those people? And why did you want them kicked out?"

"Oh, some irritating relatives who refuse to see the light," Margaret replied. "What matters is you came through for us when we needed you. Just like you did at the rally the other night." She patted him on the arm and with a beaming smile added, "Looks like Rocky found us a real gem."

PJ leaned over and gave him a peck on the cheek. "C'mon. We were just getting breakfast ready. Let's eat!"

Rocky, Ned, and the remaining four board members arrived at their usual meeting time.

As they took their seats in the dining room, Ned said, "As y'all know, the Commander's birthday is in two weeks. Miles here will be giving us all a presentation honoring our leader. Ain't that right, Flanagan?"

"You betcha, Mister Potts!" Miles shot back.

Ned nodded. "I've heard back from all but one of those I've invited. They all think it's a great idea and most of them will be able to attend. I have a solid number on how many chairs we'll need to rent and Rocky and I will get the warehouse cleaned up to make room for everyone." He turned to Margaret. "We're gonna need a lot more chicken."

Need to rent chairs? Miles thought. *Make room for everyone*? Jesus! He was hoping this would be just the UFR board members and maybe a few extra followers. His stomach tightened at the image of a sea of faces watching him, certain that would cause him to bomb miserably.

Ned's voice returned him to the moment. "You gonna be ready to wow the crowd, Flanagan? Or are you too busy doing your horsey thing?"

Miles fought his natural instinct to strike back against Ned's insult, the mocking way Ned said "horsey thing," as if it were some silly childish hobby. Instead, despite his fear of making a fool of himself in front of an audience he needed to impress, he did his best to sound confident and in control as he replied, "I'll be ready. Y'all be prepared to get wowed!"

Chapter 25

Monday Afternoon
Kimber Farm

"So that Rockwell guy we were talking about last week," Miles said, "you were spot on. That's what the 'R' in UFR stands for."

"Other than the name coincidence," Cecelia replied, "it just seems like such a strange connection for them to make."

"Well, it gets even stranger."

"How's that?"

"So the guy's birthday is coming up. They want to make a big deal of it and guess who gets dumped with the job to make that happen."

"Get to the damn point!" Cecelia shot back.

"Okay, right. They want to make a presentation to a bunch of friends they're inviting to be there—obviously fellow white supremacists. I'm supposed to do something about mixed marriages, how Rockwell would have felt about that." Miles added with a smirk, "Pretty sure he wouldn't have approved."

"You can bet he wouldn't have," Cecelia agreed. "So what's your plan to pull this off? I mean, up until a week ago you'd never even heard of him."

"True that. But, y'know, we got this internet thing now."

Cecelia shook her head. Miles could not resist being a smart-ass. Sometimes best to let him be his true self.

"When does this happen?" she asked.

"Sunday after next."

"Will two weeks be enough for you to pull this together? I can certainly pitch in if you need some help."

He was confident Thumper, Janey, and Myrna would come up with something that would do the job in fine style. Anything Cecelia tried to add would only muddy things up.

"I think I'm good at this point," he replied. "Gotta sort through all the online stuff I've found. I'll let you know if I need any help. I also found the technical word for mixed marriages. Miscega…miscanega…"

"Miscegenation," Cecelia corrected.

"Yeah, that."

"What do you know about these friends they're inviting? Any idea how many will be there?"

"No, Ned didn't give a number. But he did say he knows how many chairs he needs to rent. When I heard that, I guess I kinda blanked out on anything else. I'm fine with having a thousand people watching me in a horse race. But on my own feet, face to face with even a small audience…" He shuddered at the thought. "…not so much."

Cecelia considered this scenario. "We'll need a list of who's there."

"What? How am I supposed to do that?"

"Just get whatever you can. Names, the groups they're with, whatever you can remember. If there are multiple groups involved, working together, and they're plotting something, this could turn into a RICO case." She thought of the impact something like that could have on Tavina's career—*Local Assistant Commonwealth's Attorney Brings Down White Supremacist National Network.*

Miles broke her reverie. "Who's Rico?"

"Not a who, a what. It's a federal law used mostly against organized crime groups, like the Mafia. But it can apply to pretty much any group that collaborates on criminal activity."

"Hell, we don't even know if any crime's been committed, or ever will be. Getting a little ahead of ourselves, maybe?"

"Doesn't hurt to consider different angles, round up some resources. Might be useful, might not. Either way, I'm sure providing Tavina with a list of attendees, whatever you can put together, will score some points for you. And the more points on your side the better. Right?"

Miles wasn't sure how he'd be able to pull that off. But if it would help him get out of this situation, he'd figure some way to get it done.

"Yeah, right," he replied. "Let's score some points for good ol' Rico!"

Chapter 26

Wednesday
Montfair Tack Room

"If I was a casting director, you wouldn't get this part," Myrna said.

"And if I was an actor, I wouldn't be trying out for it," Miles replied.

Myrna shrugged. "But we'll make it work…somehow. Here, try this on." She handed him a light brown, long-sleeved shirt with epaulets on the shoulders and a buttoned flap over the breast pocket.

As Miles removed his shirt, Thumper said, "I've been reading up on the details of the *Loving* case. I couldn't find any record that Rockwell made a direct comment about it, but I think it's safe to assume he would have opposed the court's ruling. He had plenty of other things to say about what he called 'the mongrelization of the white race.' So this should fit in nicely with the plan."

Miles buttoned up the brown shirt and said, "A little big, isn't it?"

Myrna tugged at the material billowing out around Miles' trim waist. "Smallest I could find that looks anything like what he's wearing in the photos. If you'd prefer, I could call my old friend who does period wardrobes in Hollywood, see if she can put her hands on a Nazi uniform, swastika armband and all."

"That's all right," Miles demurred. "I can live with this."

"Good. You'll need to wear this, too." She handed him a thin black tie. "You do know how to tie one of these, right?"

"Yeah, of course," he replied in an assured voice, while wondering who he knew that could help him do it.

"And," she continued, "you do own something other than jeans and riding breeches, like a pair of normal pants?"

This time she had him stumped. "Um, well, maybe…I'll have to look…"

"Fine," she snapped. "I'll hit the thrift shop in town again. They probably have something that'll work. Maybe in the children's section."

Janey offered Miles an escape from Myrna's wardrobe lecture. "I ordered this online." She handed him a corncob pipe. "Seems our hero imagined himself to be a General MacArthur-like figure."

Miles studied the pipe. "I don't have to smoke this stupid thing, do I?"

"Nah," Thumper assured him. "Just hold it, maybe clamp it in your teeth once or twice just for show. You can set it down when you're writing."

"Writing?" Miles asked. "I'm supposed to write something?"

"Not actually writing, just pretending that you are."

Miles smiled nervously. "I guess I'm okay at *pretending* to write. Writing for real, not so much."

"Myrna came up with a brilliant idea for the staging," Thumper said. "You won't have to memorize anything, except some stage directions, but it won't look like you're reading your lines either." He smiled at his sister. "Pretty ingenious, actually."

"It's an old stage trick," she said. "But to make it work, we're going to need something for you to sit at. Like a table or a desk. Is that going to be doable?"

"Ah, damn," Miles replied. "I have no idea. Ned said something about renting chairs, and clearing out space in the old warehouse. But I've never been in there."

"Well," Thumper said, "you're going to need to find out. Maybe ask Rocky or Ned, tell them you're working on the presentation, need to know the 'lay of the land' sorta thing."

"I'll be back at Off the Grid on Sunday for another meeting. I expect I can get the info we need then."

"Good. Janey and I will keep chipping away at the script. Once we have a decent draft worked up, we'll do some rehearsing, make sure you're comfortable with it."

"I ain't sure 'comfort's' gonna have much to do with this." He paused, looked at each of his three helpers—saviors, really. "You guys are the best," he said humbly. "I know it was me that got y'all into this. And helping me get my life back together after that stupid-ass thing I did has now put y'all in a difficult situation too. So I owe you doubly. Triply even."

Thumper nodded. "Yeah, you're right about getting us all into this. But in a weird way, I'm kinda glad you did. I mean, while using you as an unwilling mole may not have been my preferred method, I think Tavina's on the right track to stop these people before they do some real damage. The kind of outlandish crap they're spewing is unlikely to go no farther than handing out ridiculous, absurdly racist pamphlets and protesting over Civil War monuments. Stir up enough people, both for and against them, and some serious shit's gonna happen sooner or later. So if we can help Tavina defang them before that happens, it's a win-win for all of us. Even if she doesn't know we're all secretly helping the cause."

"Man," Miles said with a tone of relieved appreciation, "that makes me feel a shitload better. I just hope I can come through with the goods and not let everyone down."

"You just keep playing along," Thumper advised. "You've already got them believing you're one of them. So sooner or later, if they're really up to something, you're gonna find the evidence Tavina needs." He gestured toward Janey and Myrna. "We'll all do what we can to help." He put a hand on Miles' shoulder. "And then, son, you're on your own."

"Yeah," Miles mumbled, "not the first time I've heard that line."

Chapter 27

Saturday Afternoon
The Johnsons' House

Wilma Jean Johnson's birthday was a milestone event—her sixtieth.

Thumper followed the directions Tobias provided. The route took him and Janey into the neighboring county northeast of Paradise Gap. They pulled up to a simple but substantial brick residence; two stories with a double front door and a row of white Corinthian columns along the front. Thumper had to park a block and a half away as the street was already lined with cars.

As they strolled up the neatly arranged cobblestone walkway, Thumper detected a few design elements that seemed familiar in some way.

He pressed the doorbell and a tall man with a bright smile greeted them. The sleeves of his golf shirt strained around his biceps and the open collar revealed a patch of short, curly gray hair against the dark skin of his chest. His chiseled upper torso drifted into a softer, more expansive mid-section.

There was no mistaking him as the father of Tobias Johnson.

"You must be Mister Billington," he said warmly, reaching out for Thumper's hand. "And Miss…Musgrove is it?

Janey nodded.

"I'm Ben Johnson. C'mon in!"

They entered the home to find more than two dozen people milling about. Ages ranged from a newborn infant to a woman who looked to be at least ninety, possibly closer to a hundred. A few more were in the backyard, where a small group gathered around a massive barbecue grill.

One wall of the home's living room was filled with photographs and bits of memorabilia. A quick comparison of the youthful framed images with the adult faces in the room led to an easy match of Tobias and his five siblings; two brothers and three sisters.

The doorbell sounded again, although Thumper couldn't imagine cramming still more people into the house.

"Dad!" Elizabeth called in greeting and wedged her way through the crowd. "You made it."

He leaned closely to his daughter and whispered, "I thought you said this was just a family thing."

"Well, it's a *big* family," she replied with a playful twinkle. "Anyway, the Johnsons were thrilled that you two agreed to come. Everyone's looking forward to meeting you." She saw who Ben was greeting at the front door and her bright mood faded.

Thumper and Janey followed her gaze. Ben was giving a slender Black man a hug. The young man introduced Ben to a tall white woman who appeared to be a few years older than Elizabeth. Her grooming and attire, combined with the assured way she accepted Ben's offered hand, were those of someone who conducted her work in conference rooms and at cocktail parties.

"Hey," Thumper said, "I know him. That's Micah Hairston, the jockey. He should be at the races today."

"He's Cookie's cousin," Elizabeth replied. "*He's* a good guy. But I can't believe he brought *her*."

"You know her?" Janey asked.

"That's Charlotte Reynolds. She and Cookie used to date. When they broke up, she started dating Micah. She's Nate Plummer's comms director. I guess you could say there's some history between us."

The Billingtons and Plummers had been close friends, both families cut from the same Old Virginia cloth. Nate was a protégé of Thumper's father and took over his seat in the House of Representatives when the senior Billington died. After being reelected to several succeeding terms, all with help from Thumper as his campaign strategist, he was now gearing up for a Senate run. This, though, would be without Billington's help. The relationship unraveled over an international resort company's attempt to build an expansive facility in Crutchfield County, partially on Montfair property. Nate aligned himself with the developer and employed underhanded tactics to counter Thumper's opposition.

Elizabeth had interned several times in "Uncle" Nate's congressional office during school breaks. But that ended when she discovered what he'd tried to do.

Charlotte looked over at Elizabeth with a challenging, triumphant smile.

Elizabeth shot back a *screw-you* grin and said under her breath, "The bitch only started dating Micah out of spite after she and Cookie broke up. She'll drop him as soon as a better target comes along."

Janey placed a hand on Elizabeth's arm. "Looks like you're the winner here."

"Yes, I am. C'mon, let me introduce you around."

She began guiding Janey and Thumper through the crowd. An hour later they had met every guest at the party. The ancient lady, introduced as Aunt Tee, was a bit cool but Thumper wrote that off to her advanced age.

Noticing Micah Hairston in the next room, Thumper excused himself and squeezed his way through the crowd. "Micah! What are you doing here? I thought you'd be at the races."

"I was gonna ask you the same question," he replied. "I saw your horse listed in the overnights. Did you scratch? Is the horse okay?"

"Yeah, he's running. With Miles aboard. But I was required to be *here*. Ryman is filling in for me with the owner's duties. But what about you?"

Micah grinned broadly. "I, too, was *required* to be here. My uncle can be very persuasive, especially when it comes to keeping his wife happy. Had to be the whole family for her birthday. No excuses, no exceptions."

"I hear you," Thumper replied. "My daughter can also be very persuasive. Especially when it comes to…well…to keeping herself happy."

Both men shrugged and smiled sheepishly.

Thumper caught Elizabeth signaling him.

"Cookie's parents would like to talk to you," she called out.

Thumper and Janey were led out to the backyard where they were seated at a small garden table set on an intricately detailed stone patio. Ben and Wilma Jean took the seats across from them. Tobias and Elizabeth stood at the barbecue grill with Tobias's two brothers, joking and laughing as they kept the food coming for the ravenous crowd.

Wilma Jean Johnson was considerably shorter than her husband. Her dark hair showed only a hint of gray and her cocoa-brown skin, dotted with a constellation of freckles, retained a youthful smoothness. She spoke with a crisp, pleasant zephyr of Southern lilt, her words perfectly pronounced, properly arranged. The gentle, assured tone and Old Virginia diction reminded Thumper of his own mother's voice. But Cyril Celeste's coolly judgmental timbre was replaced by Wilma Jean's gracious warmth.

"Cookie and Elizabeth have told us so much about you," she said.

"He's a fine young man," Thumper replied. "Elizabeth tells me you're a teacher."

"That's right. Sixth grade. Thirty-eight years. Hardly seems that long. I suppose I should think about retiring. But I believe I have a few more good years in me."

"I'm sure you do," Janey said.

"I still love going to work every day. Not many people can say that, especially after they've been doing the same thing for so long."

Thumper looked down at the patio. "The pattern in this stonework is amazing. Whoever did this is truly an artist."

"I've been telling him that for years," Wilma Jean said, beaming at her husband.

Ben smiled sheepishly.

"You did this?" Janey asked.

"Ben's a mason by trade," his wife explained. "He's been doing that work longer than I've been teaching sixth graders. Learned it from his daddy, and his daddy's daddy before that. For about the past twenty years or so he's been specializing in architectural brick and stonework, intricate designs and such. Many of them he designs himself, like this patio."

"I built most of this house," Ben said. "The exterior and the structural support that is. Designed it too. It's here to stay for a long time."

"Mama!" one of Tobias's sisters called from the sliding doorway. "C'mon. It's time for the cake!"

The backyard revelers streamed inside to join those already jostling for position around the dining room table. The crowd parted to let Wilma Jean and Ben through. Elizabeth and Tobias grabbed Thumper and Janey and pulled them toward the front.

An enormous birthday cake was laid out on the dining room table, awaiting the celebration's zenith moment when Wilma Jean would blow out the candles to welcome in the start of her seventh decade. She was positioned in the place of honor and her daughters began to light the sixty candles. Bathed in a blinding glow from the cake, she said, "My, my! I'd better blow these out quickly before the smoke alarm goes off. Then I've got some things to say."

She drew in a deep breath, bent over, and started blowing out candles. It took three breaths before all sixty were extinguished.

Straightening up, her eyes wide, she placed a hand on her chest and regained her composure. "I can't tell you how much it means to me for you all to be here. My six children, grandchildren, cousins, special friends, so many dear people, and, of course, Aunt Tee." Everyone looked over at the thin, frail old woman and nodded their respect.

"Oh!" Wilma Jean exclaimed. "Did I forget to mention my husband, Ben?"

She turned around to accept Ben's embrace as everyone laughed.

"And," she continued, "I'm so happy to have some new friends here too. You've all met Cookie's friend Elizabeth." She waved a hand toward the young couple. "And I'm so pleased her father and his friend have joined us today. So now, it's time for cake!"

Pieces of cake were passed around, partiers mingled, and the chatter ramped up. Elizabeth, standing close to where Aunt Tee was seated, turned from a conversation with one of the Johnsons' neighbors to find herself facing Charlotte Reynolds. Micah Hairston stood a step behind her.

"So I hear you won't be helping out in Congressman Plummer's office this summer," Charlotte said.

"I have more important things to do," Elizabeth replied.

A croaking voice sounded beside them. "Plummer? Did I hear the name Plummer?"

They turned to see Aunt Tee staring up at them.

"Yes," Elizabeth replied. "We were talking about Congressman Plummer. Charlotte works for him. Do you know him?"

"Know him? I wish I'd never heard the name. What he and his daddy did to us! He shouldn't be in Congress. He should be in jail!"

A sudden silence fell among those crammed into the dining room.

Wilma Jean stood motionless, holding her fork above a piece of cake. "Aunt Tee," she said, as if speaking to a disruptive child in her classroom, "this is no time for such unfriendly talk. These people are my guests…in my house."

"Your house!" the old woman replied, her agitation rising. "That's right, *your* house. You're lucky you've got this house. I had a house once. Ben's momma and daddy had a house too."

She pushed her way up from the chair and shuffled forward until she was right in front of her nephew. She wore an ill-fitting wig and her Sunday church dress was two sizes too big for her emaciated body. Deep ebony skin hung from her bones in loose wrinkles.

"You remember?" she asked Ben. "Then some white men showed up one day. Said they were gonna do us all a favor." She shook her head and added mockingly, "All us poor Colored folk. They said maybe we didn't really own the land. Maybe we'd just been squatting on it. It's been about fifty years or so since they showed up. But I remember. Told us some stuff about 'titles.' One of them said he was a lawyer. Something about the records not being too clear. If we tried to sell the land, it might come out that we don't really own it. Then we got nothing."

Her murky brown eyes grew larger and she waved her stick-like arms in a wide arc. "But 'Oooohhhh' he says! They're gonna help us out. They're gonna do us a *big* favor. They'd like to buy the land anyway. Said they were willing to take the chance, because they were such nice men and all." She looked like she wanted to spit. "And they offered us what they said was *lots* of money. Thirty thousand dollars a parcel as I recall. We hadn't ever seen that kind of money. Not likely to ever see it again." She turned her attention to Ben. "So my man—your Uncle Horace—and your momma and daddy, we all talked it over and we decided to take the money. Thirty thousand for me and Horace, thirty thousand for your folks. You remember that?"

Ben bowed his head and said softly, "I remember. I was just a boy, but I remember."

"So those 'nice' men," she continued, "turned around and sold that land just a few years later for ten times what they paid us for it. They made a killing. And we got what Black folks have always gotten…the shaft!"

She stood silently for a moment, then cocked her head to get a better angle on her nephew's downcast eyes. "And do you remember who those men were?"

Ben mumbled a response that was inaudible to everyone.

"Who?" she demanded.

"Their name was Plummer," Ben said, this time loudly enough for all to hear.

The old woman stood as erect as her shriveled body would allow and announced to all, "That's right, the Plummers, father and son. The old man did most of the talking. But the son handled the paper work, told us where to sign." She snorted in disdain. "Didn't look old enough to be some lawyer. Barely a boy at the time. But now he's a big time member…" She finished the rest of the statement with exaggerated emphasis on each syllable. "…of the U.S. House of Representatives."

She focused her anger on Charlotte next. "And I heard on the news that now he wants to be a Senator. You're going to help him do that, are you?"

"I…I…didn't know anything about that." Charlotte moved closer to Micah for protection. "I mean, he's always seemed like such an honorable man to me."

"Oh, he's honorable all right," the old lady shot back. "So long as you're the right color and got lots of money. I doubt you know what he did with the school boundaries either."

Thumper noticed Wilma Jean flinch at that remark.

"School boundaries?" Charlotte asked. "What school boundaries?"

"Back when he was on the county school board," Aunt Tee explained. "He made sure that only a few token Black kids went to the same school as his lily white daughter. Kids like Ben and Wilma Jean had to keep going to that old, rundown junk heap of a school, even though the new one was much closer to where they lived. It's…what do they call it?...jerseymandering?"

Thumper couldn't help himself. "Gerrymandering."

"Yeah, that's right." She nodded in his direction.

He was impressed, and a little surprised, by her knowledge of Plummer's career. But he was hoping she was not aware of the role he'd played in getting Plummer elected multiple times as he moved up the ladder. It was always Thumper's preference to work behind the scene and stay out of the spotlight. That strategy appeared to be serving him well now.

Aunt Tee's expression brightened as she looked toward Ben and Wilma Jean. "These two still turned out all right, thank the Lord. It's a shame how things went for the Plummer girl. But I expect it wasn't easy growing up with a father like that."

Charlotte may not have known about the land swindles or the school boundaries. But the struggles of Plummer's daughter—drug addiction and multiple brushes with the law—were common knowledge, at least among the political cognoscenti if not the general public.

The venom returned to the old woman's face as she focused on Micah, her great-nephew. "And here you are now with this white gal, someone who's working for a man who did all those things. Swindled money from your family, made sure Black kids had to go to rundown old schools. God only knows what else he's done that I haven't heard about. Bad enough a Black girl's not good enough for you. But if you gotta have a white woman, at least try to find one not working for someone who's against us."

Elizabeth was waiting for her to be the next target. Did Aunt Tee know that she'd also worked for Plummer as an intern? Did she know that he'd written her a reference for law school, or about the mostly white private school she'd attended? She held the same hope as her father did that none of this had been detected by Aunt Tee's perceptive radar.

The energy seemed to ebb from the ancient body. With all eyes still on the family matriarch, her posture sagged and she shook her head. She turned to another young man standing nearby. "Juney, take me home. I've had enough of this."

Everyone remained silent as she crept toward the door, escorted by an obedient great-grandson.

Charlotte tried to avoid eye contact with anyone. Her confident aura melted into a puddle of embarrassment. "I'm sorry," she said to no one in particular. "I had no idea." Then to Micah, "I think we should go now."

The festive atmosphere was replaced with awkward discomfort. Wilma Jean stood holding a plate of half-eaten cake.

Elizabeth whispered to Thumper, "Did you know about this?"

"No. We always brainstormed what might come up in opposition research, but these things never did. And Nate never volunteered the info."

"I can see why," she replied.

"I think Janey and I should be going," Thumper said. "I don't want to impose on the Johnsons."

He stepped over to Wilma Jean. "Thank you so much for your hospitality. It's been a pleasure meeting you and all your family. I'm sure we'll see each other again soon."

She tried to force a smile. "Yes, of course. Thank you so much for coming." Her gaze drifted over to Tobias and Elizabeth. Aunt Tee's words to Micah, *Bad enough a Black girl's not good enough for you*, ran through her mind. Was her own son being disloyal to his people? What did "his people" even mean?

She caught Thumper's arm as he started to turn away. "No. Don't leave yet. C'mon, let's visit some more."

She pulled Ben away from a conversation with one of his golfing buddies and the foursome returned to the patio.

"My aunt—great-aunt actually—is known for speaking her mind," Wilma Jean said. "She's always been like that. But now, at her age, she's even more inclined to just blurt out whatever she wants to say."

"That's a pretty common trait among the elders in many groups," Janey offered.

"Janey specializes in studying that sort of thing," Thumper added.

"And where are you from?" Ben asked.

"Minnesota. A little place called Clara City."

Wilma Jean studied Thumper's companion. "And does that differ much from what you've found here in Virginia?"

"In some ways. But in many ways not so much. I've studied small group dynamics all over the world. Prejudice against 'others,' however that gets defined, is pretty common across the planet."

"Even in little Clara City?" Wilma Jean asked.

"Certainly."

"I've never been to Minnesota. But I've always imagined it being almost all white people."

"Prejudice takes many forms: Church affiliation, social status, and to an increasing degree, political leanings. And the racial make-up is changing there as well."

"A changing racial make-up," Wilma Jean mused. "I suppose we here in Virginia have more history of racial make-up than most other states. More than four hundred years of it now. A very wide chasm for much of that time. It may have narrowed, but there are still some messy aspects from that past that continue to haunt us today." Her eyes settled on Thumper. "In light of Aunt Tee's remarks, I feel I must ask you an uncomfortable question."

He spread his hands and nodded as a gesture of concession.

"How do you feel about your daughter dating my son?"

"Well, given your great-aunt's comments, I suppose I could ask the same question of you about your son dating my daughter."

She smiled and nodded. "Touché."

"I think," Thumper said, "we shouldn't get ahead of ourselves. At their age, relationships ebb and flow. Tobias is just starting to build his career. Elizabeth has even farther to go. It's a bit early for either of them to be making lifetime commitments."

"Yes, you're right," Wilma Jean replied.

With that settled, the conversation wandered toward more comfortable topics. As Ben was describing a difficult, and ultimately successful, stonework job, Thumper studied the patio design more closely. A hint of why it looked familiar began to form.

Chapter 28

Sunday Morning
Thumper's Study

"I'm sorry I wasn't there to see his first win," Thumper said when Ryman wrapped up his account of the previous day's racing action.

"You'd have been really proud of them both. Looks like you made a good choice taking on that horse." He paused for two beats. "And letting Miles back into the game. I'd say that pair were made for each other."

"Well, thanks for standing in for me. There was no way I could miss this social function to be at a horse race. I'm sure the Johnsons already think of me as an over-privileged white guy. It would have made that even worse if I said I couldn't attend Wilma Jean's birthday bash because I thought watching my racehorse run was more important."

"Yeah, well, you *are* an over-privileged white guy. But most of us peasants still love ya in spite of that."

They clicked off and Thumper turned his attention to the book laid open before him.

****

The Diary of Olivia Bauer Billington
Montfair, Crutchfield County, Virginia
September 14, 1869

The years of planning and labor have today come to fruition as we welcomed our first class of students into the Montfair Schoolhouse. It is every bit the noble structure I envisioned more than three years ago. As I have chronicled here, the project was not without its challenges, particularly in locating, acquiring, and transporting the stone I insisted on using for its construction. But the result of that effort, and the labor to then craft the building to my design, has resulted in what will surely stand for decades, perhaps centuries, as a lighthouse for the education of all who will pass through its door.

Sadly, our beloved brother Josiah will not see the shining faces of the children who gathered here today to continue the journey toward their passport to distinction, as my friend Jacob expressed it some years ago. (I am also saddened by the news that he has found it necessary to abandon his mission in Lynchburg and, fearing for his life, has fled back to Pennsylvania.)

The loss of Josiah and departure of Jacob are, though, softened by my pride in the efforts of Teeje and Portia without whom today would not have been possible. The former has shown himself to be particularly adept at stonework, meticulously placing each element to create what now stands as a seamless edifice, a testament to his eye for detail and insistence on perfection. The latter has embraced her role as teacher with evangelical fervor. Her devotion to crafting lessons and imparting knowledge to our students has allowed me to focus on all the details necessary to complete the construction of our new schoolhouse. Now, rather than gathering in a spare room in the house or outside on the lawn, our students have a fully equipped building dedicated solely to their education.

May the light from the Montfair Schoolhouse shine for generations to come. May it help lead our community to a better future where all can learn and grow in the spirit of brotherhood.

****

Thumper knew what the years ahead would bring. The spirit of brotherhood Olivia prayed for would see only an occasional flicker for most of the coming decades. Even now, a century and a half later, her desire had yet to be fully realized.

He left the diary on his desk, went outside through the mudroom door, and walked around to what now served as the Nutchenkos cottage behind the main house. The front half of the schoolhouse had been converted into a living room with a kitchen and utility area at the back. An addition had been constructed to one side with a small dining area, two bedrooms, and a full bath.

Thumper stood outside facing the front door. A decorative symbol—a quartet of four-point stars—had been carved into the lintel. It had been there for as long as Thumper could remember, surely etched into the stone when the schoolhouse was built. The forces of nature had buffed away the once-sharp edges but the image was still clearly visible. He'd never paid much attention to it, had always assumed it was just a design element someone thought would make a nice decorative touch. And he rarely had occasion to visit the Nutchenkos cottage, felt it best to not invade their private space, a policy his father had adopted soon after Natasha and Voytek arrived.

He was staring at the symbol, wondering why the same design was part of the Johnson's patio stonework, when the door opened and Natasha rushed out, almost knocking him over.

"Oh, my goodness!" she said, halting her charge just in time. "Mister Thumper! I am not knowing you are standing there!"

Regaining his balance, he said, "Sorry, my bad. I was just…just…" He wasn't sure how to explain his presence.

"Is there something I can be helping you with?" She gasped and her face turned ashen. "You are bringing bad news, yes?" Why else would her employer be standing at her front door, a place she'd rarely seen him. He must have come to tell them something that could only be conveyed in person.

"No, no! Nothing bad. No news at all really. I was just admiring…this…this lovely design above the door."

She turned to look where he was pointing, then back to him with a quizzical gaze. "That? You are admiring that? Has always been there, no?"

"No. I mean yes. Always been there." He started backing away, turning awkwardly to leave. "I'll just…get back to the house…sorry if I bothered you."

"Is no bother. We are just leaving for church. Voytek is always being late."

"Right. Well, don't let me hold you up."

He returned to his study where Olivia's diary awaited further reading.

Chapter 29

Sunday Morning
Off the Grid Cuts & Clips

Miles pushed his chair back from the table and placed his hands on this stomach. “That was the best breakfast I’ve had since…well, since I can’t remember since! But this had better not become a habit or I won’t be able to make weight on race days.”

“You’re welcome any time,” Margaret said. “You could use a bit more meat on your bones.”

Miles shook his head. “Maybe when racing season’s over. Till then, I don’t think Mister Billington would be happy if I showed up overweight. I owe him a lot for letting me get back in the game.”

“So why’d you decide to quit?” Rocky asked.

Miles flinched. “Didn’t quit, exactly. More like…well…there were some complications. But I’m trying to put all that behind me now.”

“Looks like you’re doing a fine job,” PJ said as she reached over and squeezed his arm.

“Still workin’ on it.” Miles shrugged. “But making progress.”

“Speaking of progress,” Rocky said, “how’s your speech for next Sunday coming?”

“Chippin’ away at it. I gotta admit studying up on what the Commander stood for has been a real eye-opener. Stuff I’ve believed for years but didn't really have any way to…well…to, like, put into words. I mean words that really made sense of it all, that backed it up with, like, clear thinking. Know what I mean?"

All three Hendershots smiled and nodded.

"Yeah, brother," Rocky said, "we know exactly what you mean."

"I just hope I don't disappoint y'all. I've never been much for public speaking, but I'll do my best."

"I'm sure you will," Margaret said.

"So," Miles asked, "we're doing this in the warehouse, right?"

Rocky nodded. "Right. Looks like Ned's got a good crowd coming. Guys who feel the same way we all do. Most are with other groups from different areas. We all feel it best to work independently, kinda like the way the church we came up in does it."

"How's that?" Miles asked.

Margaret jumped in. "Y'see, the way the first churches were set up, like in the Bible, they were all independent. There wasn't some central body governing all the churches, telling them all what to do, how to think, how to worship. They let the Holy Spirit guide them and it all worked just fine. But then some folks thought there needed to be some kinda central control, like an organization that all the churches had to join. And the people who ran that central thing would then tell everyone else what to believe, how to worship, and so on. That's where things started going wrong. But some believers refused to be a part of that. They chose to stay independent. Plenty of fellowship between the individual churches, but each body of believers stayed in control of how they worshipped."

She paused, took a sip of coffee, then continued. "So that's our model for United Friends. And that's how a lot of others who feel the way we do, at least about some things if not everything, are set up. Fellowship between us, but no group telling another what to believe and how to act."

"There's another advantage to that," Rocky added. "The larger a group gets, especially if there are people at some headquarters somewhere making rules and stuff, the higher the risk."

"Risk of what?" Miles asked.

"Three kinds of risk," Rocky replied. "First, like Mama said, the risk that those people will make choices we don't agree with. Y'know, what to believe and what to do. They might, like, say we oughta go out there and do some things that we don't think we oughta do. Or we gotta agree with them about everything even if it's clear from the Commander's teachings that he didn't feel that way. The second kinda risk is that the bigger you get, the more likely it is you'll start setting off the radar of government thugs like the FBI. And, third, the easier it is for some asshole to get inside and cause trouble."

Miles mustered what he hoped was a convincingly innocent look. "Yeah, that all makes a lotta sense."

"So," Rocky continued, "this way we only let in people we know we can trust, who aren't gonna create problems. Worst of all, someone who's working for the feds, maybe trying to plant something they can use against us. It's no secret they hate people like us, who see the truth and aren't afraid to share it. Kinda funny, really. They label us 'hate groups,' say what we're saying is 'hate speech' when, shit, they're the ones filled with hate, hate against *us* because we threaten their power over everyone. And that's what makes us seem dangerous."

Miles decided to take a risk of his own. "But even if the group's small, how can you be sure someone you think you can trust won't turn on you?" He leaned back in his chair, spread his arms out, smiled, and said, "I mean, how do you know I'm not gonna cause you any trouble?"

"Shit, Miles," Rocky replied, "if I hadn't overheard you talking to Ansel, I might have been a little hesitant about inviting you in. But, I mean, c'mon, 'the Coloreds have gotta go back…only one race matters…BLM's a pain in the ass.' You even tossed in a slam on the A-rabs for good measure. I heard it all loud and clear. Oh, and then there was what the old Polish guy said. I didn't tell you about that. But he sorta confirmed what I heard. So it all seemed like a sure sign you were meant to be a UFR member."

Miles had no idea what Voytek might have said to confirm Rocky's impression that he shared UFR's outlandish beliefs. But the realization began to dawn about what Rocky thought he heard versus what Miles had actually said and why Rocky had been so eager to invite him into the group. He saw how he could play that to his further advantage. "Yeah, well, I had no idea you were listening. But I meant every word of it. I'm just happy I found y'all. Now I got a way to do more than just bitch to Ansel but keep my mouth shut around everyone else."

"No need for that around here," Margaret said, beaming with motherly pride.

"So, um, look," Miles said, "back to the plans for next Sunday. I got some ideas about how to make it work, but it kinda depends on some details. It would help to know just how things are gonna be set up."

"Like what?" Rocky asked.

"Well, I'm gonna need something like a table or a desk if that's possible. I might be able to make it work without that, but if there's something available…"

Rocky cut him off. "You're in luck, bro!" He turned to his sister. "How about you show him. We got a bit more time before the guys get here."

"Love to!" She leapt up from her chair, grabbed Miles's hand, and said, "Come with me." She led him out the door and toward the old warehouse.

****

The "Hendershot Heating & Air Conditioning" sign still hung above the entrance to the low, wide metal building. The front area inside contained Margaret's Cuts & Clips shop, now used almost exclusively as her private refuge rather than serving customers. On the other side was Windy's office. It remained locked and untouched since the day he died.

Starting in PJ's early teens, Windy had been tutoring her on the HVAC trade. She showed an aptitude for mechanical drawing and a quick grasp of the technical aspects of airflow and ventilation dynamics. Windy was aware that women made up less than two percent of the HVAC workforce. There had never been any doubt that Rocky was destined to take over the family business at some point. But Windy saw early on that PJ actually had more talent for the trade than her brother had. The work involved less heavy lifting than it once did but required more brain power to deal with the increasingly sophisticated technology. The ever-more complex and demanding codes—local, state, and federal—added a further element to the need for attention to detail.

When other girls her age were focusing on whatever fleeting trends were capturing their attention, PJ was practicing her mechanical skills by designing complex venting system components and then fabricating models from construction paper. When she wasn't doing that, she was memorizing the location and function of every piece of stock in the warehouse.

But her father's murder derailed that career trajectory. She was a high school senior when that happened. In addition to taking over the Hendershot accounts, equipment, and stock for a generous compensation package, Jessup HVAC also agreed to take Rocky on as a trainee apprentice. When PJ asked to be considered for employment, the answer was, "Sure, we could use a bright young woman like you taking phone calls and scheduling appointments for the techs." She begrudgingly accepted the offer, hoping once in the door she could show herself worthy of being moved into the tech training program. Four years later she was still taking phone calls and scheduling appointments for the "real" techs.

She and Miles passed through the door into the back area, a cavernous space with rows of empty metal shelving units. Miles noticed an old wooden desk crammed into a corner.

"This used to be my happy place," PJ said. "Is that, like, too weird?"

"Hell no," Miles replied. "I kinda feel that way about the McKendrick stockroom. It's like, well, I guess like a place where I'm in control." He walked toward the shelves and pointed toward the bare spaces. "I know where everything is, which spots need to be filled, how to pull things together from an order sheet. And when deliveries arrive, it's..." He turned to her with a playful smile. "...it's kinda like...like presents. You get to open the boxes and see what you got. New things to play with. And then you put them all where they need to go and everything's in order. The stock doesn't argue with you, doesn't ask for favors, doesn't care what time you come or go. It just stays in its place, waiting its turn to do its job when you say so."

She stood in stunned silence for several seconds. A broad grin illuminated her pale face. "Holy crap! You nailed it! That's exactly how I felt, but I could never put it into words. You totally understand!"

"Yeah, well," he replied with an aw-shucks shrug, "so much of my life the past few years has been a total mess. I guess I was kinda lost. Out of racing, spending too much time pretending to be a figure from the past, so much that I started to believe I really *was* him, that I was back in the 1860s riding with Mosby." He shook his head. "Didn't end well. Although it coulda gone a lot worse." His mood brightened slightly. "But working in the stockroom has been my one steady thing, where I can be me and things are real. Probably kept me from going completely crazy."

"After my dad died," PJ said, "this is where I'd come to think about him. It was like he was still here, like he might walk in at any minute and say, 'Hey, PJ, get me a Modine draft inducer assembly, 115 volt.' And I'd go right to it. Nothing made me feel better than that look of pride on his face when I handed it to him."

She wiped the corner of her eye, forced a smile and said, "So, anyway, yeah, I know exactly what you mean."

They stood together in silence, both marveling at this shared moment.

Then Miles brightened, pointed to the corner, and said, "That desk! It's just what I'll need!"

He marched over to the desk and examined it. "Perfect. Just need a chair, and I'll be all set." He looked at the narrow space between the front wall and where the shelving units began. "Um, so, we're gonna do this in here? Not a lot of space if Ned's got a bunch of people coming."

"Oh, yeah, right. Well, the plan is for him and Rocky to move all these shelves back, clear out enough space to set up some chairs here." She swung her arms wide to indicate where the open space would be.

Miles noticed a door on the far side of the building. *That'll do the job*, he thought to himself.

"We can't wait to hear your speech…or presentation…" she said, "whatever it is you're gonna do."

"I hope I don't disappoint y'all. Like I told Rocky, I'd never heard of the Commander before. Seems like all I was thinking about was the 1860s and kinda missed learning much about the 1960s. But, man, did he ever have it all figured out. So I assume Rocky's named for him, right? Is there, like, some family connection."

"Well, kinda yes and kinda no. Rockwell is our mother's maiden name. That's where my brother's name came from. 'Rockwell Edwin Hendershot.' To be honest, he and I had never heard of the Commander either. Mama knew a little about him, but not much really. And she never thought about a family link. But after my dad died, she started looking into the kind of things he was all about. And that's when she started to wonder if there was any connection. She did the DNA thing, started researching ancestry stuff, turned out he was a distant cousin, like fifth or something. Mama took that as a sign, and also that she'd chosen that name for her son." She paused for dramatic effect and raised an eyebrow. "Then it got even deeper."

"Go on," Miles said, eager for the story.

"The Commander had a daughter…Phoebe Jean." Another pause. "Like…PJ?"

"Wow! Don't tell me that's also your name."

The theatrical flair deflated. "Well, no. I'm Paula Jane. But, hey! Same initials, right? So it all really fit together…the Commander's teachings, the family connection, the names and everything. And so we became the United Friends of Rockwell. And it's our mission to take up his cause and carry it forward. To restore this nation to its rightful place as a home for white people, the way God Almighty intended it to be!"

A flash of the True Believer flared in her large brown eyes.

"Deo Vindice!" Miles exclaimed.

Her smile almost filled the width of the warehouse. "Exactly! Deo Vindice!"

He thought for a split second that she was going to rush into his arms, plant a torrid kiss on him, and they would collapse together onto the warehouse floor in unspoken passionate communion.

But his reverie was broken as the door behind them swung open with a loud smack.

"What the fuck are you two doing?" Ned demanded. "Everyone's here and the meeting's started."

"Oh, um," PJ replied, "I was just…just showing Miles where he'll be doing his presentation next week. And…ah…he's gonna need…need the old desk. And a chair!" Turning to Miles she said, "Right? A chair?"

"Yeah, right. A chair."

Ned eyed them suspiciously. "Fine. We'll have *lots* of chairs. Now get your asses back to the house. We got plans to discuss."

Chapter 30

Sunday Evening
Bar's Trailer

More than four decades had passed since Barstow Reinhardt showed up at the McKendrick's home, Fair Enough Farm, looking for work. He told Fergus and Rhetta McKendrick that he'd served with their son, Teedy, in Vietnam and had been with him when he died. The surprise assault by the North Vietnamese had cost Bar his left eye and ear. The rest of the platoon had been wiped out by the time the choppers arrived to counter the attack.

Fergus, a former Marine, offered Bar part-time work at the tractor shop and a temporary place to stay—a small, unused hunter's trailer deep in the woods. Over time Bar became the shop's head mechanic and had recently moved up to sales manager. He still lived in the trailer, his personal refuge of peace and privacy, sufficient for his basic needs, and a place where he could enjoy the company of the vultures he considered his pets.

Miles Flanagan had never been to Bar's trailer. But he, too, was in need of some refuge, and a confessor figure on whom he could unload the swirling mass of thoughts spinning in his head.

Dusk was approaching as his Ford Ranger bounced along the rough road through the woods. As he stepped out of the truck, he looked up to see a half dozen large black birds perched in the trees above him. They studied him as if contemplating a piece of flesh at the butcher's counter but decided he wasn't on their menu plan and went back to their evening routine.

Bar stepped out of the trailer. His new role at the shop required him to wear a shirt emblazoned with the McKendrick logo—denim during the winter months, polo the rest of the year—under his customary white bib overalls. He also wore a patch when at the shop to conceal the scarring where his eye had been blown away. But in his off duty hours, the patch and shirt were tossed, and he reverted to his standard habit of just the overalls covering his beefy body. One shoulder strap hung loose and his size 12 Redwing boots were untied.

The big man gestured toward two dilapidated lawn chairs. "Have a seat. I'll get us some beers."

The evening air was turning chilly. Miles was glad he'd worn his woolen Confederate gray artillery coat, one remnant from his reenacting days that was still useful.

Bar emerged with a six pack of Budweiser, dropped into the other chair, set the beer on the ground between them, handed a bottle to Miles, and took one for himself. He drained half the bottle in one gulp and said, "So, you want to have a little chat? Okay, the floor's yours."

Miles handed Bar one of the UFR pamphlets. As Bar browsed through it, repeatedly muttering "Holy shit!", Miles gave him a recap of how things had gone since Tavina forced him to infiltrate the group—the meetings he'd attended, the monument rally, the rapid acceptance of him as part of the group, the Hendershots and Ned attending the races, and his upcoming assignment to play Rockwell in front of an audience of other white supremacists. He neglected to mention that he'd also told Thumper about his mission and that now Janey and Myrna were also in on it.

"Shit, man, this whole thing has gotten fucking weird," Miles said. "But I'm not seeing a damn thing this Doddridge woman could use. Sure, they got some wacky ass ideas, and I got no idea why they feel that way, so full of hate for a whole bunch of people they don't even know. And not just Blacks. They're not too fond of Muslims, Asians, Jews, really anyone other than white Christians. Pretty much in line with all of 'Commander' Rockwell's beliefs."

"They appointed him 'Commander'?"

"Yeah, well, turns out he was in the Navy and that was his rank. So in that sense I guess it's legit. But I think they use it because it sounds…um…*commanding*. The Hendershots themselves, I gotta say, they actually seem okay in some ways, if you ignore the racism stuff. Especially PJ. I'm not so sure about that Ned guy though. Something kinda creepy about him. You know, you've met the guy."

"Yeah," Bar said. "He ain't exactly Mister Warm-and-Friendly. Look, you've only been at this…what?…a couple of weeks? Did you think you were gonna show up on day one and they were gonna let you in on some big scheme to overthrow the government, round up millions of Black people, and somehow ship 'em all to Africa? Shit, I don't think these idiots could overthrow a kindergarten school board. The fact that they somehow think you're also a fucking racist fanatic tells me they ain't the most brilliant operators."

Miles put his head in his hands. "I dunno. Seems like I could end up fucked either way." He lifted his head and turned to Bar with pleading eyes. "If I can't find anything Doddridge can use, is she gonna say, 'Well, you tried. Thanks for the effort. Forget what I said about going after your ass for assault with a deadly weapon and attempted murder. You and all your friends who covered for you just go and have a nice life.' And if they *are* up to some shit that could turn nasty, and they find out I'm a mole, or I can't stop them from doing it…" His voice trailed off, he dropped his head back into his hands, and mumbled, "This ain't gonna turn out well. I'm no fucking spy. And it ain't just me. You, Thumper, all y'all who covered for me." His voice quivered. "I'm sorry. I'm so fucking sorry."

A large, rough hand landed on his shaking shoulder.

"Look, man," Bar said, "I know what it's like to be in a tough situation. Been there too many times myself. You just gotta think about where your advantages are, what assets you got that you can use to your advantage."

"Assets? What do you mean?"

"Like for me, one thing's always been my size. It intimidates a lot of people, which gives me an edge. At least it did till I went to 'Nam. Then it made me an easy target. So I kinda developed an 'I don't give a fuck' attitude. If I make it out alive, fine. If not, no big deal. I wonder sometimes if that's why I was the only one who survived when…when…well, all those other guys, like the McKendricks' boy, had something to live for. Fate figured it would spare the one asshole who didn't give a shit. Fate can be a real bitch like that."

He paused for a moment then took a pull on his second beer.

"Anyway," he continued, "after that, I had a new asset." He pointed to his missing eye and ear.

"That's an asset?" Miles asked.

"For what I was doing back then. I don't talk about it much, not really at all now that I think about it. But, for what it's worth, I got into some crazy shit. Seems my Marine Corps experience didn't provide me with much in the way of gainful post-war employment. My expert rifle badge meant I was the best shot in our unit. But it didn't do shit to impress a job interviewer in the civilian world. And my modified facial features…" He waved a hand over the left side of his face. "…didn't help much." He waggled his hands in the air. "The ads said, 'Don't Forget. Hire A Vet.' Yeah, well, a lotta people forgot."

After another swig and some silent reflection, he went on.

"So I found what work I could, given my *specialized* qualifications."

"What was that?" Miles asked.

"So there was this guy—this was on the West Coast—who had his hands in a few different things. Some legit, some, well, maybe kinda iffy." He shrugged. "The guy needed people who, let's say, were willing to cut some corners to get things done, who were good at convincing others to, um, see things his way. And could back it up with what the consequences might be if they didn't hold up their end of a deal."

"Holy shit!" Miles exclaimed. "You were a fucking enforcer? Breaking kneecaps and shit? Or, like, a hit man? Jesus!"

Bar waved it off. "Nah, not as dramatic as it sounds. It was mostly just about intimidation. Although I did partner with another guy for awhile who really was a fucking psychopath. Fortunately, he's now far away and forever out of action. For me, it was using the assets I had, like I said—my size and my fucked up face. I made up some pretty wacky stories about how that happened and what I could do to make them look like me if I chose. I figured the truth would make me sound too much like a goddamn hero. Y'know, Purple Heart, wounded vet kinda shit. Good for sympathy, not so much for scaring the crap outta someone." A thought occurred to Bar. "Oh, but there was one relic from my Marine time that came in handy in a couple of ways. Wait here."

He pulled himself up from the lawn chair and went into the trailer. Miles could hear him opening drawers and shuffling through the contents.

"Here it is!" he said as he returned to his chair. "Check this out." He handed Miles a medal that showed two rifles crossed over a wreath hanging from a bar with the inscription "Rifle Expert."

"Way cool," Miles said. "But I thought you said no one in civilian life gave a shit about something like this?"

Bar took the medal back and gazed at it. "In *legit* civilian life, no one did. But when you're dangling it in front of some poor asshole's face and saying, 'Listen, motherfucker, see this? "Rifle Expert." You know what that means? It means I can take your worthless ass out with one shot from so fucking far away, it's like I'm in another state. No one would ever know where the bullet came from that's splattered your worthless brains from one end of the street to the other. Just like I did to all those goddamn gooks in 'Nam.'"

Miles thought he saw an eerie glimmer of nostalgic pleasure flash from Bar's remaining pale blue eye.

"Oh!" Bar said, "And then there was this." He undid the pin on the back of the nameplate, and placed it between his index and middle fingers. He made a fist with the pin protruding from his clenched hand and held it in front of Miles's face. "Remember this?" he said with a leering grin.

Miles had a flash of Bar's hand hovering over his face with a truck key in the same position as the pin. A heated dispute in the McKendricks' office several months earlier had resulted in Bar lifting Miles off the ground with one hand, holding him against the wall, and dangling the key in front of his eye, threatening to gouge it out. Miles fully understood what an intimidating presence Bar Reinhardt could be when he unleashed that hidden demon from his long ago past.

Bar pulled his hand away and continued his tale.

"The medal came with two of those little things that you stick on from the back through your uniform. But they were a pain in the ass to use with these fingers." He held up his hands and flared out his thick, calloused, permanently grease-stained digits. "So I had a jeweler replace those with this pin, oversized and a bigger clasp to match."

Miles noticed the end of the pin showed a slight bend. "What happened there?" he asked. "Ram it into some poor sumbitch's skull?"

"Oh, that," Bar said with a chuckle. "Turned out the pin served a secondary purpose I discovered by accident."

"What was that?"

He held the pin up and turned it around, eyeing it carefully. "It's good for picking the lock on handcuffs."

"What? How'd you find that out?"

"I had some rough times when I got home from 'Nam. Like I said, I couldn't find work, veterans weren't well thought of like they are now. Nobody was thanking us for our service. We were called 'Baby Killers' and shit like that. I got into a few scuffles when some asshole in a bar would badmouth the Marines or make fun of my scars. Whoever did that quickly regretted it, but I usually ended up taking a ride in the back of a cop car.

"One time, a cop tossed another guy in the car with me as he and his buddies were busy rounding up a bunch of other jerks for being drunk and disorderly. The other guy and I were both handcuffed. This guy, who had some kinda European-sounding accent, says, 'Hey, man, you got anything sharp on you, like a pin or something?' I thought for a moment, then realized I had this in my pocket." Bar held up the medal. "I carried it as a sorta good luck piece. Didn't really work for shit though. Anyway, I said, 'Yeah, I got something in my pocket.' He said, 'Lemme get it out and we can get these cuffs off.' I said, 'Why bother? The cops will just put 'em back on.' 'Yeah, but it's fun fuckin' with 'em.' I could see his point. I mean, who doesn't love fuckin' with the cops when your ass is gettin' hauled to jail, right? So he got the pin outta my pocket, said it was perfect, and used it to spring the lock on my cuffs. Then he told me how to do it so I could unlock his. If the cuffs are double locked, you need something with an angled end, like an Allen wrench. You stick it in the keyhole on the front, first this way…" He held the pin with the bent angle facing down. "…turn it, then hold it the other way and turn it again. Bingo! If the cuffs aren't double locked, you just stick something straight into the hole in the front and off they come. Of course, if the cop's done his job right, your hands will be behind your back, so it only works if you have someone to help you. Assuming you even have something like this to use.

"Anyway, the cop got back in the car and off we went. The other guy and I spent the ride to the slammer sitting in the back seat looking like we were still cuffed. When we got to the station, we stepped out with our hands free and the cuffs lying on the back seat. The cops were dumbfounded. We were, like, all innocent and said, 'Gee, officers, I guess you forgot to put those on us.'"

"So what happened?"

"Oh, the usual. We spent the night in the slammer in some podunk town in Northern California, got released the next morning with a stern warning from the sheriff to never set foot in his pristine little village again." He held up the medal and examined it. "On the upside, the other guy said he knew someone who was looking for 'muscle'. Thought I might be interested in some side work. Shit, at that point I was willing to take any work. So we became a team. He turned out to be one crazy ass son-of-a-bitch."

Miles shook his head. "Jesus, Bar, I knew about you getting wounded and all that, but I never knew about all that other shit."

"Yeah, well, I don't dwell on that." He waved an arm towards the woods. "Got my little private haven here. Just me and my birds. Nobody fuckin' with us."

They sat in silence for a few minutes. Then Bar turned to Miles, looked him up and down, and said, "So, shit-for-brains, let's think about your assets."

"My assets?"

"Yeah, what can you use to make this deal work? To get Doddridge what she wants and to get your ass, and the asses of the rest of us, off the hook?"

"Shit, Bar, I dunno. I mean, yeah, you had your size and strength. And you even turned your scars into a positive, at least for what you were doing back then. What the hell have I got?"

"Well, let's think about that. What are you good at? Beside being an annoying little smart-ass."

"Yeah, I'm pretty good at that. But I don't think that qualifies as an asset."

"Nah, probably not. So what else?"

"Um, I guess I'm good with horses. Much better with them than I am with people. But I don't see how that's gonna help me any here."

"Hold on. Let's work that a bit. What does it mean to be 'good with horses'?"

Miles thought for a moment. "I guess it means I'm pretty good at sensing where the horse is coming from. Some are high energy and need a calm rider to settle 'em down. Others might be kinda nervous or timid, need their human to make 'em feel safe. I dunno, all kinds of variations really. I guess the bottom line is the horse has to trust you, whether in the saddle or on the ground. You gotta build a partnership and that takes trust to make it work. The horse is still gonna be its natural self, but if you got a good connection, you can sometimes sense things before it all goes to hell and avoid what could be some nasty consequences. I've never really thought about it like that. I've just always felt a connection with horses and most of them sense that and give it back. So, yeah," he said, "I'm good with twelve hundred pound animals with a brain the size of a walnut. Lotta good that's gonna do me dealing with these UFR people."

Bar cocked his head. "What if you thought of each one as a horse?"

"Huh?"

"Y'know, which one is high strung and needs a calming hand. Which one is easy going and just wants a pal. Maybe one of them's kinda timid, or sad, and needs someone to lean on. Y'see where I'm going? You gotta build trust with these wackos so, if they are up to some crazy shit, they'll let you in on it before it all goes to hell."

Miles sat quietly and thought about Bar's suggestion. He could see Margaret as the boss mare, the one who always runs the herd, doesn't put up with any misbehavior from her underlings. PJ's a young filly, full of spunk but at the bottom of the pecking order. Her desire to break out on her own is offset by her need for security from the group. Rocky is an affable draft cross, not overly aggressive, eager to please. And Ned? Oh, yeah, Ned. He's the stallion you can't trust, something in his eye that always has you on alert. It's clear he's been in some battles and he's always on the lookout for anyone who might try to threaten his position in the herd's hierarchy. You don't mess with that kind of horse. And you don't trust them either.

"Yeah, okay," Miles said. "I see what you mean. Read 'em as if each one was a horse. I can try that. Might need a bit of luck, too."

Bar held up his medal and gazed at it. "Y'know, I used to think this thing sucked as a good luck charm. But, in the long run, maybe it did work." He waved an arm around his small, bare yard. "I mean, look where I am now. A shitload better than where I used to be. Might be it just needed some time for the luck to kick in." He handed the medal to Miles. “Here. You take it. Maybe it’s still got some magic in it. Couldn’t hurt, right?”

“Ah, no, man!” Miles protested, holding his hands up. “I couldn’t. I mean, you really deserved that. Wouldn’t be right for me to…”

“Bullshit! Take the goddamn thing. I insist!”

“Yeah, okay,” Miles said in a submissive stutter. He stuck the medal in his coat pocket, picked up a beer, opened it, and raised it toward Bar. “Thanks, man.”

As they clinked beers together, Miles added, “Deo Vindice!”

Bar jerked his head. “What the fuck does that mean?”

Miles grinned and said, “It’s the UFR slogan, the old Confederate motto. It means ‘God is our protector.’ But fuck God. I’d rather have you, and your good luck medal, protecting me. You are one bad-ass son-of-a-bitch.”

Bar chuckled and shook his head. “And you are one pain-in-the-ass little shit. You sure ain’t no master spy. But if you play this right, you can get Doddridge what she needs and get your ass and everyone else’s ass off the hook.” He picked up the pamphlet again and flipped through the pages. “Jesus. Talk about walnut-sized brains.”

Chapter 31

Monday Morning
Montfair, Thumper's Study

The Diary of Olivia Bauer Billington
Montfair, Crutchfield County, Virginia
July 4, 1876

This is a momentous day for our country, or perhaps I should say *<u>some</u>* *of our country. I remember as a child, before my father died, we made family trips in the summer to visit our relatives in Philadelphia. Such trips were timed around Independence Day celebrations, which held particular significance for that city. I recall the processions, picnics, contests, games, military displays, and, of course, fireworks. As members of the Quaker community, we were repulsed by the evils of slavery that persisted in what was to become my home state of Virginia and elsewhere. But we prayed it could soon be brought to an end and, in our innocence, that this could be achieved through reasoned discussion and not with violence.*

It is now the Centennial Anniversary of the Declaration of Independence, one hundred years since Mister Jefferson composed the indictment of King George and provided justification for the Colonists to declare themselves no longer under the Crown's rule. That action ultimately resulted in a glorious outcome, one worthy of celebration. Sadly, there is no such celebratory spirit around the observance of Independence Day here in Virginia. Nor throughout the Southern states, many of which remain under the boot of military control, a lingering legacy of the Confederacy's misguided and ultimately failed attempt at a far less noble statement of independence.

It is a scant six years since the restraints of martial law were lifted from the necks of Virginians. In that same year of 1870, the US Congress declared July 4 to be a national holiday of celebration. While my relatives in Philadelphia are surely enjoying the same festivities that were a highlight of my girlhood, there is no spirit of mirth here in Crutchfield County.

Under martial law, Unionist Republicans conducted an aggressive campaign to enfranchise the newly freed Coloreds. Many were placed in government positions and others elected to public offices. Archibald cited wide complaints among his acquaintances that many of these individuals lacked the knowledge and skills to perform the duties of their office and, in fact, were little more than puppets of the military rulers. It is not without irony that I note how such circumstances might have been different had others shared my mission to provide education to all residents of our state, regardless of race, whether enslaved or free. The very laws that denied education to the Coloreds resulted in a scarcity among the formerly enslaved capable of filling positions that required some level of education.

While I nonetheless applauded the effort, Archibald correctly predicted that, once Congress reinstated Virginia to full statehood, much of this progress, even if of limited immediate merit, would be halted and even reversed.

Although we here at Montfair are not able to exert any influence of significance on the State as a whole, we have continued to make whatever advancements are possible within our purview. The most notable examples of this are the advancements made by Teeje and his sister Portia.

The former has established himself as the preeminent stonemason for all of Crutchfield County and even to areas beyond. He has also trained his son in this noble and much-needed craft. The young man has shown a similar aptitude for the art as his father possesses. I am both happy and not a little saddened that plans are now underway for young Benjamin to leave us and establish his own practice in a neighboring county.

It has now been more than twenty years since we began our underground school, initially for the children of our house staff. Portia asked if she might be allowed to sit in as I conducted the lessons. In her role as mistress of the kitchen, which often entailed managing the preparation of elaborate dinners and luncheons on the front lawn, we had worked out a rudimentary system of written communication, a form of checklist to keep track of the details. From that functional, albeit scant, foundation, she showed her ability to absorb quickly the subject matter and to then assist in teaching others.

I was surprised to find that the children responded to her more readily than they did to me. It was, I must admit, an uncomfortable revelation that, despite my sincere desire to give them the gift of learning, even at the risk of criminal prosecution and the sullying of my husband's standing in the community had we been found out, I was still seen as their mistress...dare I say as their owner. To this day that word leaves a sour taste in my mouth to even think it, let alone commit it to paper or give it voice. But the reality could not be denied. While, legally, they were my husband's property, I still held a certain authority over them. The fact that I suffered, and continue to suffer, under my own restraints as a woman with barely more rights than they had made little difference. Despite those many unjust limitations, I have at least some protection against being summarily sold at the whim of the Master.

Yet, my sincere intentions aside, I noticed a more relaxed and eager demeanor among our small band of pupils when Portia took over while I sat off to the side and observed. Granted, her syntax, pronunciation, and sentence structure retained elements of the distinctive Negro vernacular. But I was happy to overlook those shortcomings for the broader goal that our students would become sufficiently literate to read and write, even if the quality of their compositions fell somewhat short of grand eloquence.

Now, these many years later, it is one of our early pupils who is taking the lead in our schoolhouse. Portia's daughter, Bryna, serves as our instructor while her mother now sits where I once did and observes, offering the occasional suggestion and helping where she can. Bryna revealed early on a bright and inquisitive mind, an eagerness to ask questions and, when the answer seemed unsatisfactory, to press the point and, in many instances, to offer her own logic to reach a more acceptable answer. It was this inquisitive spirit that led to a mispronunciation of her mother's name. This amusing episode then came to serve as a testament to the mental acuity and tenacious desire on the part of both mother and daughter to achieve their own passports to distinction and to then inspire that fervor in others.

Again, though, we face a happy but sad development. Like her cousin Benjamin, Bryna will soon be leaving Montfair as she has agreed to marry a young man from the northern part of our county. He is a fine fellow, a carpenter by trade, and we are optimistic for their future. To her credit, she has delivered one ultimatum on which her acceptance of him is conditioned. He must employ his carpentry skills to build a schoolhouse in their community where she can continue her mission to equip children, Colored and white, with their "passport to distinction."

School is now out of session as we are at the height of summer field work. When classes recommence after harvest, Portia will resume her role as teacher, at least until we can secure a more permanent, and younger, replacement for Bryna. This will be no easy task as we must find someone who is both sufficiently erudite (and thus most likely white) and willing to teach only Colored students. I pray somewhere there is the Golden Apple we seek.

Would that such fruit might have been produced in our own orchard. Although blessed with six daughters, none caught the fire that burns within me to lift the veil of illiteracy that has for so long served only to bolster the vicious circular logic that the Coloreds are incapable of learning.

It was clear that the girls all considered my initial efforts to teach the house staff children to read and write both a fool's errand and a risk to the family's reputation had we been discovered. What self-respecting, honorable gentleman would deign to court and marry a young lady from such a disgraceful family! At their father's stern insistence, they begrudgingly ignored those clandestine sessions. He, of course, also wanted to see each daughter properly married off and did his best to arrange suitable unions for all them as soon as possible. His motivations were both to blend his family lineage with that of other prominent, propertied families and to lessen the burden on his own resources with the upkeep of a half dozen daughters.

So each was soon gone, some to other parts of Virginia, some to more distant regions, leaving Portia and me to carry on the work that consumed us both.

If there is no spirit throughout Virginia now to celebrate the reunified nation's Independence Day, at least we at Montfair have some cause for optimism that the future may hold better promise. Perhaps one day Virginians will be able to again share the enthusiasm of my Philadelphia cousins for this holiday.

Chapter 32

Monday Mid-Day
Kimber Farm

“I’m not sure your pal Rico is going to be much help,” Miles said.

Cecelia lifted a fifty pound sack of horse feed and deftly dumped it into a large metal bin. Pausing before she reached for the next bag, she turned to Miles and asked, “Why’s that?”

“You said that law’s about organized crime, right?”

“Right.”

“Well, it doesn’t look like the white supremacist world is very organized. At least not the way the UFR people are involved in it. They may have friends in other groups who feel kinda the same way, but they’re pretty fierce about keeping their independence.”

“How did you find that out?”

“We were talking yesterday about who’s coming for ‘Rockwell Day’. No names of people or groups were mentioned, but Margaret explained their position about staying totally independent. She said it’s like the way the old churches did it. Each one did its own thing, no higher up group telling them what to do.”

Cecelia nodded. “Yes, I’m familiar with that. My daughter was in that kind of church some years ago. ‘Independent Fundamentalists’ they called themselves. Pretty extreme.”

"Rocky said that kinda thing made sure there weren't other people telling them to do things they didn't want to do. Like things 'The Commander' wouldn't have agreed with."

"Or," Cecelia countered, "maybe not letting them do things they *shouldn't* be doing. Like some of 'The Commander's' more outlandish ravings."

"Yeah, that too. But then things started to get kinda paranoid. And made me kinda nervous. Rocky said staying small and independent made it less risky that they'd draw attention from—how did he put it?—oh, yeah, from 'government thugs'. He mentioned the FBI but I got the feeling that in their minds saying 'FBI' means any kinda law enforcement thing."

"You mean," Cecelia said, "even down to a local county prosecutor?"

"Yeah, that."

"Well, someone would need a pretty vivid imagination to take you for a law enforcement agent, at any level."

"Um, that's where the paranoia really kicked in. He said the third risk for them is that some asshole might get inside their group and make trouble. When you put that together with the FBI thing, that comes down to me, doesn't it?"

Cecelia grabbed another bag of feed, hoisted it with a grunt, and dumped it into the bin. A dozen more bags were stacked and waiting to be put where the rodents couldn't get to them.

Miles stepped toward the bags. "Here, let me help you with that."

A raised hand stopped him. "Thanks, but no. This is part of my healthcare program. I could pay my farm help or the delivery guy do it, then drive forty minutes and pay more to go to a gym." She pointed toward the bags. "Or I can do things like this and get plenty of cardio and strength work."

Miles guessed Cecelia to be at least thirty years his senior, maybe a good bit more. Thanks to fortunate genes and some surgical touches, she retained enough of her youthful beauty to show how she'd landed four husbands, each one wealthier than the last. The final hubby, Mister Broadhurst, had passed a few years earlier and bequeathed the expansive Kimber Farm to her.

Miles stepped back and waited as Cecelia lifted and dumped another bag.

She then turned to him and said, "RICO or no RICO, Tavina's still going to need something to work with. A list of who's there for 'Rockwell Day' could prove helpful. Seems to me you're making progress, getting closer and closer to the inside. Something's bound to turn up eventually." She thought about mentioning the upcoming election and the need to have this done in time to use it as a campaign point. While that was the main impetus behind forcing Miles to infiltrate UFR, better to let him think it was a noble cause to protect his community from these radical nut jobs.

"Yeah, *eventually*," he muttered.

Chapter 33

Monday Afternoon
Johnsons' House

Wilma Jean did not recognize the incoming number on her phone. It showed a local area code, so perhaps not a spam call. She chose to accept it. "Hello?"

"Wilma Jean, Thumper Billington here."

"Oh, Mister Billington. What can I do for you?"

"Please, call me Thumper. Um, look, we're hosting a tailgate spot at the hunt races on Saturday and, well, I know it's kind of short notice, but we'd love to have you and Ben join us. Tobias and Elizabeth are coming. So if you're free that day…"

"Oh, that's so nice of you." A swirl of thoughts spun in her mind. *Should we do this? A joint family event? What does that mean about where things are going with Cookie and Elizabeth? What's the proper etiquette for something like this? Should we take something? What should I wear?* "I'll need to check with Ben, make sure he doesn't have any other commitments that day. He's not home from work yet."

"Oh, sure, right. Well, no pressure if you can't make it. But I hope you can."

"We'll let you know. And, either way, thank you so much for thinking of us."

She spent the next hour considering the pros and cons, the implications, and the logistics implied by this invitation. When Ben arrived, she accosted him when he was halfway through the front door.

"I got an unexpected phone call," she announced.

Ben read the serious timbre in her voice. "Oh, my God! What's happened? Is it Aunt Tee? Has she…?"

Wilma Jean's tone softened. "No, no. Nothing like that. Mister Billington…um, *Thumper…*"—she winced as the sound of that odd nickname passed through her lips—"…called. He invited us to their horse races on Saturday. He said Cookie and Elizabeth will be there."

Ben relaxed. "Oh, well, that was nice of him. But, y'know, that's my golfing day and…"

"This is much more important than your golfing day!" she shot back. "Do you not see what this could mean?"

"Um, I guess I don't," he replied with a sheepish shrug.

"It was one thing for him and Doctor Musgrove to come here for my birthday party. But now he's reciprocating by inviting us into *his* world. Have you ever been to the hunt races?"

"Well, no, but I…"

"Of course you haven't. That's not our world. Is he trying to set us up for a test? What does this say about his thoughts on his daughter dating our son? Does he want to see if we're suitable in-law material?"

Ben tried to be the voice of reason. "Aren't you getting a little ahead of things? Maybe he's thinking about Cookie, that he'd be more comfortable with us there when he's surrounded by all those rich white people."

She dismissed his suggestion. "Cookie can handle himself anywhere and with anyone. White, Black, rich, poor, whatever. He's shown that over and over, strong and self-assured, just like all our children. No, there's something more here."

"I guess I could skip golf. My guys will have to find someone else to make up the foursome."

"Skip golf? Of course you can skip golf! This is much more important than your golf game."

"Really, are you sure you're not over-thinking this?"

"Ben Johnson! Sometimes I wonder about you. These are the Billingtons we're talking about here. The *Billingtons*! Does that mean anything to you?"

Ben sighed and rubbed his forehead. "Yes, yes, of course it does. So what are we supposed to do? Pretend none of that ever happened? We chose not to burden our kids with all that. But we never thought…well…you know…"

Wilma Jean's tone softened. "Yes, I know. Do you think *she* knows?"

"Maybe, maybe not. If she does, it doesn't look like it's making any difference."

"You'd better let your golf buddies know you won't be there next Saturday. We need to do this."

"I'll call 'em right now."

Chapter 34

Wednesday
McKendrick Farm & Home Equipment

Miles and Bar were in the stockroom discussing what to do about a delayed parts order when Bar's attention snapped to something in the shop sales area. Muriel stood halfway between the office and the sales counter. She was frozen in place, her hand on her forehead and her knees wobbling. Shelton came running out from the office and grabbed Muriel just before she collapsed.

Bar dashed from the stockroom with surprising speed for a man his size.

Miles followed, unsure what to do.

With Shelton on one side and Bar on the other, both looming over the petite lady, they guided her back to her desk and gently lowered her into the chair.

Bar turned to Miles. "Get her some water!" he barked. Then to Shelton, "You call 911!"

Muriel waved her hand. "No need for that. I just had a little dizzy spell. It happens sometimes. I'll be fine."

"What?" Bar said. "You've been having spells? And you didn't say anything?"

"I didn't want to bother anyone about it. My closest friends at church are praying and I know the Lord is watching over me."

Muriel Hudkins had been a deaconess in the Paradise Gap African Methodist Episcopal Church for nearly fifty years. She remembered well the time when Blacks and whites in Virginia strictly observed the rule that, while supposedly assembling to worship the same God, each race was required to do so separately. Much had changed from her girlhood days, most of it for the better. But Martin Luther King, Jr.'s lament that "11:00 on Sunday morning is the most segregated hour in America" had seen little variance over the ensuing decades. That was certainly the case in Paradise Gap, if no longer by law then still by custom.

Miles returned with a glass of water. Muriel thanked him and took a sip.

"Have you seen the doctor about this?" Shelton asked.

"Oh, it's nothing to worry the doctor about," Muriel said, dismissing any concerns. "I suppose it's just something that happens when one gets older." She forced a smile. "And I'm older than most now, praise God."

"If you don't want to go to the doctor," Shelton said, "we could get the doctor to come here. I'm sure Doc Preston would be happy to…"

"Absolutely not!" Muriel insisted in a voice contrary to her usual gentle manner. Catching the shocked look on the faces of her three helpers, she said politely, "I do truly appreciate your concern, each of you. Such dear friends. But really, you need not concern yourselves." She looked up at Shelton and Bar. "Thank you both. I assure you, should I find myself in need of assistance, I know I can turn to you." She then addressed Miles. "And you as well, Miles. I believe the Lord still has a plan for you. You just need to open your heart to his calling."

Miles felt the heat rise on his cheeks and knew he was blushing. Religious talk always made him uncomfortable. "Um, yeah, okay," he replied.

"Muriel," Shelton said, "I worry about you being home alone. What if this turns out to be something more than just a dizzy spell and there's no one there to help you?"

“But I’m not alone,” she replied. “The Lord is with me. He knows when my time will come.”

“You really believe that?” Bar asked.

“Oh, yes, indeed I do. In the Book of Job it says, ‘Seeing his days are determined, the number of his months are with thee, thou hast appointed his bounds that he cannot pass.’ And the Psalmist says, ‘All the days ordained for me were written in your book before one of them came to be.’ So fretting over when my time comes is pointless. God will work in his own time.”

“Look,” Shelton said, “you know how much I admire your strong faith. But don’t you think the Lord also wants you to be responsible about your health? And what about us?” She waved her hand toward Bar and Miles. “We love you like family. But we also depend on you as part of our team. We’d be lost without you.”

Muriel sighed and considered Shelton’s point.

“Maybe we could arrange for someone to check in on you,” Shelton offered. “Nothing intrusive, just stop by to see how you’re doing. Like the way Tavina checks on her mother.”

“Oh, well,” Muriel countered. “Tavina’s dear mother is truly in need of assistance. Between her stroke and other issues, there’s an army of family members and health care workers driving back and forth on that torn up old road to her house. It’s sweet of Tavina to check on her, even if just on Wednesday evenings. Of course, she’s so busy with her work and all, I expect that’s the only time she can fit it in. You might think, though, that her position with the county could help get that road fixed, maybe even paved. But, well, you know, when it’s Black folks living at the end of the road, the county always seems to be too busy elsewhere.”

Muriel shook her head, pushed herself up from the chair, and declared, “And now we must get back to work. I believe there are customers at the door waiting to be let in.” She shooed them all out of the office.

Shelton went to open the front door, Bar and Miles headed to their work stations. Along the way, Bar looked down at Miles and said, “Can you believe those Rockwell assholes would like to ship

Muriel off to Africa? This country needs a whole lot more people like her and a shitload less of idiots like them."

"Um, one question," Miles said, "this Tavina person Muriel mentioned. Gotta be Doddridge, right?"

"You know any other 'Tavinas?'" Bar shot back.

"No, of course not. But Tavina's mother…is she, like, Muriel's friend?"

"She's Muriel's sister."

"What? Muriel is Tavina's aunt?"

"Gosh, you figured that out all by yourself? Brilliant."

Bar patted Miles on the shoulder and stepped away to greet a customer.

Chapter 35

Wednesday Evening
Off the Grid Warehouse

Ned backed his truck up to the side door of the warehouse. Rocky dropped the tailgate and they offloaded three dozen folding chairs.

Rocky asked with a sarcastic tone, "Think you got enough?"

Ned smirked. "If your little buddy doesn't come through, makes a mockery of the Commander's birthday, we'll need some extra chairs to throw at him."

"Very funny," Rocky said dismissively. But, from what he'd heard about some of the people on Ned's invitation list, he wasn't sure it was a joke.

"He'll do fine," Rocky countered. "He told me he's been working really hard. And, like I planned, it's helped him learn about the Commander. It may not be, like, an award-winning speech, but I'm sure he won't embarrass us."

"Yeah, well, we'll see about that. I've still got my doubts about him. As a regular UFR member, sure, he's fine. Better than fine, even. Certainly a notch or two above those other losers we call our 'board members'. I wouldn't trust any of them to be part of what's really gonna happen. They talk a big show, but I can tell none of them got the guts to be a Commando."

"I got a good feeling about Miles," Rocky countered. "But, yeah, he'll need to pass a couple more tests before we invite him to join the Commandos."

"You got something in mind for the next one?"

"Kicking around a few ideas. It's gotta be a lot more than just carrying a sign at a rally or giving a speech in front of a friendly audience. Something that shows his true commitment to The Cause."

Ned put a hand on Rocky's shoulder. "Look, I know what all this means to you, your mother, and PJ. We get this done, and y'all will have gotten what you want. But The Cause is much bigger than that. There's a nation to save. We may not be able to do that by ourselves, but we need to be a part of it in any way we can. You see that, right?"

"Yeah, sure I do," Rocky replied. "We're all with you. Whatever it takes."

"Okay!" Ned turned toward the bare warehouse shelf racks. "C'mon. We gotta move some of these, make space for the audience and your little buddy's performance. It's a good thing the Commander's birthday falls on a Sunday this year, makes it easier for lots of these guys to come." He looked at Rocky and, with a grin tinged with a hint of malevolence, added, "Y'know, sometimes the stars align just the way you want them to."

Chapter 36

Thursday Morning
Thumper's Study

The Diary of Olivia Bauer Billington
Montfair, Crutchfield County, Virginia
November 15, 1879

A recent copy of the Richmond Times-Dispatch reached us at Montfair today. Prominently placed was a report on the passing two weeks ago of General Nathan Bedford Forrest at the age of 56. The article focused mainly on his wartime exploits, a recounting that rose to the level of hagiography. There is no doubt that he was a fearless warrior and brilliant tactician. Our dear late brother Josiah revered him, as did virtually all of his serving officers and troops. He will, no doubt, live on in history as an exemplar of the Lost Cause Hero.

Yet I have been privileged to receive personal insights that paint a fuller, and more admirable, portrait of the departed General. The wives, many now widows, of the officers who served in the 3rd Tennessee Cavalry graciously offered to include me in their correspondence as the closest female relation to Josiah, who had remained unmarried. Many, including Nathan's widow, Mary Ann, recounted what could only be considered a remarkable conversion, details not mentioned in the Times-Dispatch obituary.

After a brief flirtation with the pestilent group of hooded cowards who call themselves the Ku Klux Klan, Nathan disavowed himself of the group and set about to atone for his past behavior. The one-time slave trader offered himself as a friend and supporter of the Negro community, a position that elicited furious criticism from multiple corners.

Sadly, his life of conversion ended before he was able to see any meaningful progress in the plight of our Negro brethren. Although freed from the open and abhorrent practice of chattel ownership, they are still restrained by far too many restrictions, both legal and societal.

It is this type of restraint that our dear Bryna is now experiencing in her struggles to provide education for the Colored children in her local area. Her most recent letter arrived in the same bundle that contained the newspaper account of the General's passing. She reports that construction of the schoolhouse is now complete and classes are being held daily. With the combined talents of her husband Timothy's carpentry skills and her cousin Benjamin's masonry talents, she states that the new schoolhouse is both a substantial structure and, in the eyes of many, a work of art.

Unfortunately, the hopes I once held to see all children, white and Colored, gathered together in the same classroom were dashed when, in order to assure passage of the State's postwar constitution, a craven concession was made to require all schools to be segregated by race. This despicable two-tiered system has resulted in woefully inadequate resources for the Negro schools. No little persuasion was required to convince Archie to declare our Montfair school to be for Colored children. There is a perfectly adequate school in the village for the white children.

Portia continues to conduct classes in our little school behind the main house. Archie graciously makes up the difference—a veritable chasm—between what the State provides and what the children truly need. He has also agreed to help supplement Bryna's meager budget at her new school.

It continues to grieve me that others refuse to see the value of equal education as the pathway to a more just and harmonious society. To deny one race access to education and then claim that they are incapable of performing at the same level as another race is the vilest form of circular logic imaginable.

Would that I were not also restrained by the dictates of our male-dominated world. While I am vastly more fortunate than most others to have at least some sway over our small home community, thanks to my husband's largesse, my voice cannot be heard much, if at all, beyond the borders of Montfair.

I am, though, hopeful that I will have many more years to make what efforts I can to improve this inequity. Perhaps one day, if not in my lifetime, at least at some future date, this will be achieved.

****

Thumper marked the passage and closed the diary. Billington children had traditionally been tutored at home, the males then matriculating to university—William & Mary for the earlier generations and then to Mister Jefferson's Academical Village in Charlottesville from 1819 onward. The village schools were strictly for the children of farmers and tradesmen. The practice of home tutoring for the aristocratic families changed to private schooling starting in the early 1900s. The opportunity for higher education had eventually been extended to women but most such institutions in Virginia remained segregated by gender and race for several decades thereafter.

The University of Virginia clung to its reputation as "The Gentleman's University" until 1970 when, after 151 years as an all-male institution, women undergraduates were admitted. The racial exclusions had been removed, at least in theory, some years prior to that but creatively devious methods continued to limit the percentage of non-whites granted admission.

Over time, though, virtually all such barriers were relegated to the trash heap of history. Olivia would no doubt have been immensely proud of her great-great-great-granddaughter's accomplishments and future prospects—perhaps even more so of Tobias Johnson's.

Thumper's gaze drifted over to Josiah's pistols. He knew the history of Nathan Bedford Forrest, the contradictions between his life before the war as one of the most prominent slave-traders in Tennessee, his military exploits in service to the Confederacy, a brief flirtation with the KKK, and then his apparent epiphany to embrace the Black race which he had so sorely mistreated throughout most of his life.

The once feared Klan had now been largely defanged, relegated to little more than an ugly and sad comic satire, easily mocked and disregarded by most. Yet now a remnant of that virulent strain, in the form of the United Friends of Rockwell and similar cells, was festering in Thumper's own community. How heartbreaking that would be to Olivia if she knew such hatred still existed.

Thus far, UFR was nothing more than a small band of demented racists exercising their free speech rights, largely unfettered by the level of disgust to which that speech sunk. There was nothing Tavina could use against them for that alone. Thumper recalled the spirited discussions held in his law school seminars when the Supreme Court's *Brandenburg* case came up. The 1969 decision significantly narrowed the scope of permissible speech restrictions. Tavina displayed impressive mental gymnastics in her arguments to circumvent those limits. But, in Thumper's estimation, her efforts failed to find any viable wiggle room around the high court's ruling.

So there had to be another option, something legally actionable. And if there was, would Miles Flanagan be capable of recognizing it and acting in time? It was a shaky hope at best. But for Thumper and the others complicit in covering up "The Incident", it was the only hope they had.

The next step in that effort was scheduled to take place in just a few days when Miles would perform his Rockwell role-playing act.

The support team—Myrna, Janey, and Thumper—had been hard at work providing Miles with the resources to pull it off in convincing fashion.

Myrna, using her theatrical skills, formulated a staging plan, drilled Miles on how to project his voice, schooled him on mannerisms and movements, and assembled a costume that would approximate Rockwell's typical attire using elements easily found at a discount store. Perhaps most helpful of all, she recalled a ploy sometimes used in live stage performances to spare an actor the burden of memorizing a lengthy soliloquy. That alone assuaged much of Miles' anxiety.

Janey contributed her knowledge of how cult groups recruit and test would-be adherents, the hints that signal a willingness to accept the group's beliefs, no matter how outlandish.

Thumper's task had its own challenges. He needed to craft a script that would hit the mark with this narrowly focused audience while not raising suspicions that someone more talented than Miles had put the words in his mouth. For this, he put himself into a familiar mindset: composing speeches and talking points for political candidates, some of whom were aspiring to high level positions but had difficulty ad libbing a cogent argument unaided by a teleprompter. Fortunately, Myrna's staging ploy provided a device to serve as a similar crutch.

Another helpful advantage was Miles' reenacting skills. Thumper had witnessed his performance on several occasions when Mosby's Partisan Rangers participated in Paradise Gap Day. The annual event was centered on the celebration of a little-known, and ultimately pointless, skirmish between the Rangers and a Union cavalry unit. Miles' interaction with the audience had been impressive. He *became* Lieutenant Ben Palmer in speech and mannerisms, as if he'd just been transported through time from a smoke-filled 1863 battlefield. Granted, he'd had far more time to prepare for those appearances. But, despite the short prep window, if he could morph so convincingly from the rough-edged Miles everyone knew to the eloquent diction of a Confederate cavalry trooper, surely he could pull off his role as Rockwell.

The trio had done all they could, short of standing in the wings and feeding him lines. It was now up to Miles to make it work. A successful performance would move him deeper into the confidence of his targets. A botched job would likely set the effort back several notches. A total disaster might blow his cover and possibly put him in danger.

Thumper kept such imaginings to himself. But Janey noticed he hadn't been sleeping well the past few nights.

Chapter 37

Saturday
Point-to-Point Races

"I want you to have a good time," Margaret said. "But remember, we're still checking him out."

PJ grinned. "Oh, I'll check him out all right. Especially when he's on that horse!"

"You mind yourself," her mother chided. "If he's going to achieve Commando status, we have to be absolutely sure. When the time comes, we'll need everyone fully committed."

"I hear you, Mama. If I see anything suspicious, any hint he might not be Commando material, I'll be on it."

The gate intercom sounded and Miles announced his presence.

"Okay, then," Margaret said. "Go. Enjoy yourself. But just remember…" She looked heavenward. "…your father and the Commander are watching. We can't let 'em down."

The passenger seat in Miles' battered Ford Ranger was usually filled with a jumbled mass of horse tack and fast food trash. The back compartment was even worse. He'd cleaned out the garbage from the front seat and crammed the tack into the back to make room for PJ.

"I'm riding in the fourth race," he said, "but I have to be there early for the officials meeting. We can hang out, watch the other races, mingle a bit. I know most of the people who will be there. Should be some nice tailgates to mooch from."

"More importantly," she said, "are you and Bumpers all psyched up and ready?"

"Yeah, I think so. He's had some really good workouts. Now that we've racked up that first win last week, Mister Billington told me to go for it every time. Too bad he couldn't have been there to see it. Something about a special birthday party he had to go to."

"Um, speaking of Mister Billington, Rocky tells me his daughter is dating a Black guy. Did you know about this?"

"Yeah, I've seen them together a few times." He conjured up his faux-racist persona. "Damn shame! Wish there was something I could do about it. But I reckon it's out of my control."

"What about working for a man who condones that sort of thing? And his own daughter! Are you okay with that?"

Miles pretended to concentrate on his driving as they passed through the race course entrance gate. He showed his pass to the attendant and explained that PJ was his groom. The brief delay gave him a sliver of time to consider a reply.

"Let me ask *you* a question," he began. "If Rocky or Ned go on a service call and it turns out to be the home of a Black family, do they refuse to do the work? Or when you're working the phones, if it's obvious the person calling is Black, do you tell them no one's available and hang up?"

She nodded in concession to his point.

"Look," he said. "I'm all in on the Commander's mission. But until we achieve his goals, we still gotta live in this world. For me it's not just that I'm riding for a man who condones race-mixing. I'm also working for a lesbian who I'm told is in a relationship with a Black woman. If anything, this kinda stuff just shows that the Commander was right and we need to keep pushing to get this country back on the right track."

He pulled into the horsemen's parking area and stopped the truck.

With a charming smile, he said, "What do you say we enjoy this nice day and let that stuff slide for now?"

PJ nodded and looked around at the vehicles parked in the field. Some were massive rigs that could transport a half dozen horses, others more modest two- or three-horse trailers. Horses were held by grooms as trainers and jockeys buzzed about with pre-race prep duties. Her mood brightened. "You're right. Let's enjoy the day."

As he was about to climb out of the truck, she placed a hand on his arm. "And let's kick some horse-racing butt!"

PJ waited along the edges of the stewards' area as Miles attended the officials meeting. With that duty completed, he joined her and they strolled along among the crowd of spectators, many of whom were just setting up their tailgate spots. Others had arrived early and were already in the party spirit well before the first race.

Locking her arm with his as they walked along, she asked, "Seriously, what do you think your chances are of a win today?"

"Well, it's a small field for this one, only two other horses. One of the jocks is gonna be tough to beat. He's from a family of trainers and riders, been racking up some impressive wins the past few seasons. But this might just be a training ride for him, a new horse without much of a record. The other rider is a young woman, kinda new to the racing biz, but she's scored some decent wins."

They reached a place on the hilltop looking down over the crowd and out onto the sweeping racecourse. PJ's attention was drawn to two adjacent spots cordoned off along the fence right at the finish line.

"Will you look at that," she said.

"Look at what?" Miles asked.

She shook her head. "It just keeps getting worse."

"What does?"

She pointed toward the Montfair and Kimber Farm gatherings. "Looks like your boss is getting even deeper into this diversity bullshit."

Miles recognized Tobias standing next to Elizabeth. But he didn't know who the older Black couple were chatting with

Thumper. All the others in the enclosure—Montfair Hunt members, local landowners, personal friends of the Billingtons—were white and most exuded a patrician air in their dress and demeanor.

There was an even greater lack of diversity among the Kimber Farm crowd. One Black woman stood next to a tall, thickly built white woman.

"And *she's* here!" PJ spat out with obvious venom.

Miles knew who she meant, but asked with a convincing tone of innocence, "Who's here?"

"*That* woman. Tavina *Fucking* Doddridge. The one standing with your lesbian boss."

He tried to convey an air of casual curiosity. "So that's the 'Tavina' person I heard mentioned at work the other day."

"What? Why would she have been mentioned at your work?"

"Oh, something about her being the niece of the woman who keeps the shop's books. I don't know anything about her. But," he added with a smirk, "I did hear she's good to her mother."

"What! How would you know that?"

"Seems the mother's in poor health and the daughter visits her every Wednesday evening."

Dripping with sarcasm, PJ replied. "Well, ain't that sweet."

"Sounds like y'all have some baggage. Wanna tell me what's going on?"

PJ took a breath and composed herself. "No, just something from the past." She tried to muster a lighter mood. "Let's not let it spoil our day. Like you said, we're here to have fun, right?"

"Yeah, right."

"And to win that damn race!"

Miles looked over toward the horsemen's area and saw the Montfair rig pulling in. "Looks like Voytek's here. We'd better head over there and start getting ready."

****

At the Montfair tailgate spot, the Johnsons found themselves warmly welcomed among the Billingtons and their legion of friends.

Thumper and Elizabeth took turns filling the new guests in on how a point-to-point race is conducted. Janey, a former adjunct college professor, swapped teaching stories with Wilma Jean. Tavina, accompanied by Shelton, came over from the Kimber Farm spot to encourage everyone there to vote for "Doddridge" in the upcoming election.

Thumper and Ben found no common ground in their respective sports of choice—foxhunting and horse racing for Thumper, golf for Ben.

Nor did their professional pursuits offer any fodder for shared experiences. Ben could no more relate to Thumper's career as a legal scholar, author, and political strategist than Thumper could to Ben's work, impressive though it was, as a mason and architectural stonework designer.

And then, when the subject of football came up, especially centered on the Washington home team, there was no stopping them.

"I never knew Jack Kent Cooke was also into horses," Ben said when Thumper mentioned the many times the legendary owner of what was then the Washington Redskins had been a guest in that tailgate spot.

"Cooke had a large farm near Middleburg where he bred racehorses," Thumper said. "Many of them competed on this same course. He and my father became good friends."

From there it was an animated discussion of the glory years when head coach Joe Gibbs led the team to three Super Bowl wins.

Micah Hairston was scheduled to ride in the second race. As he was riding out onto the course, Thumper said to Wilma Jean, "So Micah is your nephew?"

"Yes," she replied. " He's my brother's boy."

"He's one of the leading jockeys in the game," Thumper said. "When I decided to get back into racing, I approached him about riding for me. Turned out his dance card was already full."

Wilma Jean leaned in and said quietly, "I apologize for my aunt's outburst the other day. I'm sure Micah didn't expect anything like that to happen when he brought that white girl to the party. Aunt Tee has always been the outspoken type. But much more so as she's gotten older."

"No need to apologize. The Plummers and Billingtons have a long history. But I never knew about those things your aunt brought up. Actually, Nate Plummer and I had a falling out recently. The way things went then, I can't say I'm surprised to learn about him and his father pulling something like that. Shameful."

"Hardly the first time something like that's happened," she said. "Bad enough, but there's been so much worse." Her gaze drifted out toward the race course. "So much worse," she repeated quietly, as if only to herself.

In an attempt to lighten the mood before the discussion went too far down that unpleasant road, Thumper asked, "Aunt Tee…is the 'Tee' short for a name that starts with that letter?"

"Not the first letter, but part of a name." Wilma Jean giggled. "The first letter would have made for an awkward nickname."

"How's that?"

"Well, would you want to be known as 'Aunt Pee'?"

Thumper chuckled. "No, I don't suppose I would." He turned to Ben. "Question for you. I noticed a symbol that was part of the stonework on your patio, a grouping of four star-like figures. Is that just an artistic touch or does it have some special significance?"

"I guess you could say it's like a signature," Ben replied. "My father always incorporated it somewhere in his work, and his father before him. Likely goes back much farther than that. To tell you the truth, I'm not really sure how it started, but we've always associated it with the family trade. Why do you ask?"

"Oh, I…I just thought it was a unique element in your design. A nice artistic touch."

"It's more than that," Ben replied. "The Johnson men have always strived to build things that will last. Strong structures that hold up and stand the test of time." He looked Thumper squarely in the eyes and, with a warm smile, added, "Holds true for building families, too."

****

When Miles and PJ reached the trailer in the horseman's area, PJ watched an older, heavy-set man step down from the truck cab. He ignored Miles, who returned the icy sentiment, and went about his duty unloading the horse.

A small, perky woman—a stark contrast to her surly partner—trotted around from the passenger side. She stopped short when she saw PJ standing with Miles.

"Myrna," Miles said, "this is my friend PJ. PJ Hendershot."

Myrna caught the slight but discernible emphasis on the last name. So this was Rocky's sister, a principal member of United Friends of Rockwell. Miles' acceptance into the group appeared to be going well.

"PJ," Miles said, "this is Myrna Billington, Mister Thumper's sister."

Joining in on the ruse, Myrna smiled broadly and said, "Soooo nice to meet you. Are you into horses and racing? Is that how you two know each other?"

"Oh, gosh, no," PJ replied. She waved toward the bustling activity around them. "This is all new to me. Miles and I have another shared interest, but nothing we need to bore you with." She noticed Voytek staring impatiently at Myrna. "Don't let me keep you from…from whatever you need to do here."

PJ watched as Miles, Voytek, and Myrna went about their well-practiced routine of getting the horse ready for running a three mile course jumping stiff timber fences at speed and, hopefully, with his good conditioning and expert piloting from the small man on his back, crossing the finish line first.

Led by their grooms, the horses from the previous race returned to their trailers, a trace of adrenaline still flowing as they pranced along with nostrils flaring and heads high.

The announcer's voice sounded over the PA system: "Horses to the paddock for the fourth race, please. Horses to the paddock for the fourth race."

Among the crowd massed along the spectator side of the paddock fence, Elizabeth delivered a running commentary to the three Johnsons and Tavina Doddridge. Thumper was in the paddock conferring with Miles as Voytek led Bumpers around the circle, awaiting the call for "Riders up!" PJ hung back from the crowd, safely out of Tavina's line of vision.

When the call came, Voytek again launched Miles onto the horse with extra vigor. Miles was prepared this time. He grabbed mane and landed gracefully in the saddle.

As the three horses and riders headed out onto the course, the spectators hustled back to their tailgate spots. PJ hiked up the hillside to an unoccupied spot where she could watch the action.

"And they're off!" the announcer exclaimed. The three horses lurched forward in a small but tight pack. "Throne of Zeus, Tucker Dickenson up, appears to be the early pace-setter, but by only a half-length ahead of Pundit Pride with Georgia Symansky in thc irons and Down the Alley, piloted by Miles Flanagan, in third by a whisker."

Miles could feel the horse's comfort level. He was confidently relaxed, cruising along with the other two horses as if taunting them.

The threesome remained within less than a length of each other as they completed the first lap. Dickenson, a wily pro, began to ramp up the pace after the eighth fence. Symansky responded, pushing Pundit Pride to keep up. Miles read her body language and knew she was asking the horse for more than it could handle. Throne of Zeus felt the pressure from behind and accelerated in response.

Bumpers lowered his head and leaned into the bit. *I can take them*, he said. "Not yet," Miles replied. "Let those two battle it out. Then we'll show 'em what you've got."

Throne of Zeus and Pundit Pride were locked in their own two-horse race, oblivious to the presence of another horse cruising in their slipstream.

At the second-to-last fence, Miles saw a gap on the inside. He gave Bumpers the signal. "Time to go, buddy. Take us home!"

Bumpers sailed over the penultimate jump in sync with the other two, hit the turf in full stride, and was easily three lengths ahead by the final fence. From there it was a breeze to the finish line. As the crowd cheered, the announcer called the finish. "And it's Down the Alley and Miles Flanagan by eight lengths. Throne of Zeus second, and Pundit Pride a close third."

PJ wanted to sprint down the hill and embrace Miles the second he dismounted. But the Montfair and Kimber Farm crews, Tavina Doddridge among them, were already halfway to the paddock.

She waited until the others had returned to their tailgate spots and Voytek was leading Bumpers back to the trailer. Myrna was amused to see this tall, slender woman—at least two decades Miles' junior—almost lift him off the ground with an enthusiastic embrace.

"You did it! You guys did it! I'm so proud of you!"

"Yeah, well, thanks," Miles demurred, embarrassed by her exuberance. "But, y'know, this wasn't exactly the Gold Cup. It's gonna get tougher as the season moves along."

Once at the trailer, Myrna held Bumper's shank as Voytek gave him a rubdown with a burlap sack. PJ stepped over and stroked the horse's neck. "What a good boy," she cooed. "You be sure to take care of Miles, okay? He's a pretty special guy."

Miles interrupted the horsey love fest. "I'm done for the day. But we can hang out, watch the other races. I can introduce you around to some friends."

It was an enticing offer. But when she considered Tavina's presence there, her enthusiasm faded. With a half-smile, she said, "Nah, I guess I've seen enough. We can head out if you'd like."

"Okay. Probably best for me anyway. Got a big day tomorrow. Last thing I want to do is screw up the Commander's birthday celebration."

"You'll do fine," she assured him with a pat on the arm. "I believe the Commander's spirit is in you."

As they walked to Miles' truck, he looked back to see Myrna, with a grin and a raised eyebrow, give him a thumbs up. He wasn't sure if it was for the win or for working his way into the confidence of at least one critical UFR member. Perhaps it was for both.

Chapter 38

Sunday
Off the Grid Warehouse

Miles cracked the warehouse side door and peeked inside.

"Jesus! There's a shitload of people in there."

"Ned has connections," PJ said. "And all those guys are eager to see you do the Commander thing." She put her hands on his shoulders and added, "It's a real honor that you've been asked to do this. I know you're gonna hit it out of the park."

Miles forced a smile and nodded. "I hope so."

Twenty men and four women—all white, of course—filled the seats. There were skin-heads—clean-shaven, dressed like rejects from a Lands End catalog in polo shirts and khaki trousers. Two men, possibly father and son, wore tee-shirts emblazoned with "White Power" over their beefy bodies. The younger man was ornately tattooed while the elder bore what looked like a military insignia on his forearm. A boyish fellow who looked barely old enough to shave sported a replica World War II German helmet. A husband and wife wore matching "White Lives Matter" tee shirts. A slender man, probably mid-thirties, with intense eyes that darted around the room as if he trusted no one, sat alone huddled in an over-sized camouflage jacket. A middle-aged man with a wispy goatee and a serious expression sat next to Ned, the two of them engaged in a private conversation. There was something embroidered on the man's denim shirt but he was too far away for Miles to make it out.

PJ stepped back. "You look great, by the way. The corncob pipe is a nice touch."

Miles held a folded newspaper under his arm. He wore a brown shirt, thin black tie, and olive trousers.

He could hear the audience members settling down as Rocky stood to welcome them.

"I'm gonna get in there," PJ said, "so I can video your big debut." She leaned over, gave Miles a peck on the cheek, said, "Deo Vindice, Tiger!" and trotted around to the front entrance.

"Thank y'all for coming," Rocky said. "I know many of you traveled a good distance to be here and we appreciate you coming to celebrate the Commander on his birthday. We've asked one of our new members to give a presentation in the Commander's honor. I'm sure y'all will find it entertaining and, hopefully, informative. None of us have seen it yet, so we're all eager to get going. With that, I present to you…George Lincoln Rockwell, Commander, National Socialist White People's Party."

Miles reached into his pocket and touched Bar's medal. He then gulped, took a breath, opened the door, and stepped into the warehouse.

He turned back to the opened door and said in a theatrical voice, "Trooper, I have a very important letter to write. I'm not to be disturbed."

He closed the door and stepped into the room. Myrna had counseled him to pretend the audience wasn't there, not make eye contact with anyone, look over their heads at the wall behind them if his gaze turned that way. When he did, he caught a glimpse of PJ standing at the back, phone raised to record his performance. She raised her free hand and gave him a quick thumbs up.

The old desk had been moved from the warehouse corner to the center of what served as the stage area, set at a forty-five degree angle. Earlier that morning, without explaining the purpose to anyone, Miles had set up a row of books, held between two horse head bookends, along the end of the desk facing the audience. The books were part of his collection on Civil War history, most of them vintage leather-bound editions. The prop device served to block the desk's writing surface from the view of the audience. He also placed some sheets of paper and a pen in the desk's middle drawer.

When he reached the halfway point between the door and the desk, he unfolded the newspaper and held it out in front of him. The audience members could see the "Richmond Times-Dispatch" banner on the front page.

"What a travesty," he said, shaking his head.

Holding the paper so the audience could see his face, he read aloud from the sheet of paper Thumper had taped inside.

"Virginia Case Makes History, Richmond Times-Dispatch, June 13, 1967.

"*In Loving v. Virginia, the U.S. Supreme Court unanimously struck down Virginia's law prohibiting interracial marriages as a violation of the Fourteenth Amendment. The appellants, Richard and Mildred Loving, of Caroline County, had married in Washington, D.C., in June 1958 and then returned to Virginia, where they were arrested. After pleading guilty, they were forced to leave the state.*

He lowered the paper slightly and declared, "Leave the state? Humph! They should have been locked up, not set free to continue in this abomination."

His gaze returned to the printed words. "*The American Civil Liberties Union filed motions and appeals on their behalf beginning in 1963, and after the Virginia Supreme Court of Appeals ruled against the Lovings in 1966…*"

Another aside comment: "As they certainly should have done."

"*… the U.S. Supreme Court heard their arguments. The case came after nearly 300 years of legislation in Virginia regulating interracial marriage and carefully defining which citizens could legally claim to be white. In 1924, the Act to Preserve Racial Integrity banned interracial marriage in Virginia while defining a white person as someone who had no discernible nonwhite ancestry.*

It was this law that the U.S. Supreme Court ruling said denied Virginians' 'fundamental freedom' to marry."

Shaking his head, Miles said, "Three hundred years of honored history tossed out just like that!"

Returning his focus to the opened newspaper, he continued. "*Loving v. Virginia is a landmark case, both in the history of race relations in the United States and in the ongoing political and cultural dispute over the proper definition of marriage."*

Miles folded the newspaper carefully so the audience couldn't see the other sheet of paper Thumper had taped on a different page.

"*A landmark case*," he mused, trying to minimize any appearance that he was reading his lines from Thumper's script. "Yes, a landmark for when the destruction of racial purity began in the once-proud Old Dominion." Following Myrna's stage directions, he gazed up toward the ceiling. "*The ongoing political and cultural dispute over the proper definition of marriage*." Looking back at the paper, he continued. "Dispute? What is there to dispute? Reality says like should only marry like." The stage direction called for him to gesture back and forth from left to right as he said, "Whites marry whites, Blacks marry Blacks, yellows marry yellows, reds marry reds. That's how God intended it. If the definition of marriage is changed to allow…or more like *encourage*…the races to intermarry, where does that road lead?" He raised one hand in a questioning gesture. "What will come next? That men can marry men? Women can marry women?"

This sparked a chorus of chuckles from the audience.

He snorted indignantly, thrust a fist forward, and said, "This demands a forceful and immediate response!"

He marched to the desk, sat down, and pulled the sheets of paper and pen from the drawer. The papers contained the rest of Thumper's script, along with Myrna's stage directions.

Pretending to write, he said aloud, "To the editor, Richmond Times Dispatch. Dear Sir, regarding the US Supreme Court's recent ruling in the Loving v. Virginia case, as reported in your paper on

June 13, 1967, I am writing to express my disagreement with this shamefully reached decision."

Miles rubbed his chin as if considering what to write next.

With a nod, he resumed the act, speaking as he appeared to be jotting his words onto the paper. "I have been closely following the progress of this case and feared the court would overturn the fully reasonable and rational decisions the Virginia courts made. The Circuit Court of Caroline County brought a fully valid indictment against these two people, to which they had no choice but to plead guilty. However, the judge, Leon Bazile, was merciful. He told them to return to Washington, DC, which had already descended into the sin of miscegenation."

Miles had stumbled over "miscegenation" during rehearsal sessions. With Myrna's coaching and sufficient practice, he'd learned to pronounce it correctly.

Relieved that he'd passed that hurdle, he continued scribbling away.

"As long as they did not set foot in Virginia again for the next 25 years, they would not be jailed for their obvious crime…a crime against both the duly enacted laws of the sovereign state of Virginia and the law of nature as regards the races."

He picked up a different piece of paper with his left hand, a legal sheet with several lines of handwritten text. He held it just high enough for the audience to see, then lowered it and resumed writing.

"In that ruling, the honorable Judge Bazile stated this wise opinion."

Miles read aloud from the handwritten note as he transcribed the judge's quote into his letter.

"'Almighty God created the races white, black, yellow, malay and red, and he placed them on separate continents. And, but for the interference with his arrangement, there would be no cause for such marriages. The fact that he separated the races shows that he did not intend for the races to mix.'"

He set the reference sheet down and continued writing. "But these two scofflaws were not content to accept the judge's kindness.

Instead, spurred on by the ACLU (known to many as the *Anti-American Civil Liberties Union*), they brazenly returned to Virginia. Once there, the authorities dutifully arrested them. And again they had their day in court, this time before the Supreme Court of Appeals of Virginia. That court relied on a precedent set in 1955 that said the State's legitimate purposes were…" He lifted the legal sheet again, studied it, set it down and transcribed the quotes into his letter. "…'to preserve the racial integrity of its citizens,' and to prevent 'the corruption of blood,' 'a mongrel breed of citizens,' and 'the obliteration of racial pride'.

"Despite the unanimous decision in that case, those who sought to further weaken the racial purity of our great nation continued their misguided fight on to the United States Supreme Court. Sadly, they found there a less stalwart body, as we now see in the announcement of this disastrous decision in the pages of your publication.

"Disastrous? Yes, I say disastrous because of what this bodes for the future."

From this point, Thumper was able to weave in Rockwell's own words found in the historical record. The principle UFR members would likely recognize them as such and appreciate Miles' research and deepening appreciation for what they considered their Commander's prophetic warnings. Rockwell was shot and killed two months after the *Loving* decision was handed down. Thumper could find no direct quotes from him related to it. But given the thoughts he left in earlier writings, Thumper figured similar lines would have found their way into the letter Miles-as-Rockwell was writing.

"What is the primary objection to mixed marriages?" Miles asked as he scribbled away. "It is not solely the marriage itself. It is what that marriage will produce. Evolution shows that in the long run, if the superior mixes with the inferior, the product is halfway between, and inferior to what you started with in the original superior group—in other words, mongrelized.

"Every one of us has a deep need for the warmth and love of his group, of those in his biological family of people, of his 'Tribe'. But because of this ill-conceived notion that all races are 'equal' and there should be no barriers against their indiscriminate intermingling, man has lost that feeling of group warmth, loyalty, and love. And the result is the chaos and spiritual emptiness we see all around us in this disintegrating Western society.

"It is not the death rattle in the throat of Western civilization which is surprising; it is the fact that millions of Americans believe that the death rattle is a beautiful song!

"I do not hesitate to admit that I would do anything, absolutely anything, to ensure the survival and happiness of our White, Western People. Perhaps I will go to hell for doing what must be done. But if I can look up and see White boys and girls once again playing in a decent, safe, and wholesome America, then bring on the Devil with his worst."

The closing lines Thumper composed returned to the specific topic of the letter, Rockwell's imagined summation.

"And for our great nation to once again assure that we provide that life for our precious children, I must strenuously object to the decision this group of nine weak-kneed so-called 'justices' has handed down.

"Sadly, Judge Bazile passed away just three months ago. It may be best that he did not live to see this miscarriage of justice. But if this sorrowful news has reached him in the Great Beyond, I have no doubt he is shedding tears in the hereafter, as I am in the here-and-now."

Miles sat back and considered the sheets of paper on the desk. He then nodded, leaned forward, and added the closing line. "Respectfully, George Lincoln Rockwell, Commander, National Socialist White People's Party."

He then folded the pages—Thumper's script and Myrna's stage directions—and placed them in an envelope. He picked up the newspaper, scanned it briefly, and shook his head. He rose from the desk, adjusted his tie, clamped the corncob pipe between his teeth, and, with his head held high, marched to the door, stepped through, and closed it with a loud smack.

The audience sat silent for a moment, then erupted into furious cheers and applause. Miles reentered and took a sheepish bow as the acclamations intensified into a standing ovation. He looked past the crowd to see PJ at the back, clapping and cheering more loudly than anyone.

Rocky leapt from his seat and quick-stepped to Miles. He grabbed Miles' hand, held it aloft, and announced, "Miles Flanagan everyone! How about that performance?"

The cheers rose to a muscular roar, accompanied by frantic clapping, whistles, hoots, and hollers.

Miles blushed three shades of red and nodded in recognition of the accolades.

The audience members started milling around. Some of them gathered into groups of two or three for personal chats. A few drifted to the staging area to shake Miles' hand and congratulate him. Among them was the man who'd been sitting next to Ned.

"Logan Peters," the man said as he pumped Miles' hand. "Great job. Rockwell was a true prophet. Too bad no one with any sense listened to him. Here we are, all these years later, and everything he warned about has come to pass. And look where this nation has gone as a result."

"You got that right," Miles agreed. "Sad, really sad."

"But we can still make it right, can't we?" Peters said. "Not going to be easy, but at least some of us are committed to The Cause. And willing to do whatever necessary to turn things around."

"You bet we are!" Miles replied. "Whatever necessary."

"Good man," Logan said as he gave Miles a chuck on the shoulder.

Ned stepped to Logan's side. For the first time, Miles saw Ned's dour expression ease into a slight smile. "Not bad, Flanagan, not bad."

PJ wedged herself between Logan and Ned. "Hey, you guys, don't hog the star of the show. Let his biggest fan have a chance."

Ned snorted, grabbed Logan by the arm, and led him away.

PJ took Miles' face in both hands, leaned down, and gave him a kiss full on the lips. As she pulled back, she chuckled at his surprised expression and flushed cheeks. "You deserved that," she said, then added with a wink, "And a lot more."

Margaret elbowed her aside. "Don't hog the star of the show. My, my! That was really something young man! I was praying you'd do a good job for us, help our friends understand what the Commander was all about. I know now that he's looking down on us, especially you, with a huge smile, like maybe all his prophecies weren't for nothing and his dreams for saving this nation can still come true."

She pulled him to her and gave him a forceful hug. Stepping back, she said, "C'mon, there's a big spread set up at the house. All these guys can't wait to dig in. And it'll be a chance for you to get to know them. I mean, we're all kinda working for the same cause, right?"

He put on his brightest smile. "Right!"

The adrenaline rush from the applause and enthusiastic praise, along with the relief of having the performance behind him, began to fade. He remembered the task that still awaited. *Get the list! Gotta get that list!*

Chapter 39

Sunday Evening
Off the Grid

It was late into the evening by the time most of the attendees left. A few remained in the living room with Margaret, Rocky, Ned, and Miles.

Miles checked his watch, stood up, and said, "I've had a really great time. But I gotta be up early to exercise a horse, and then get to my other job. So I'd better head out."

The others offered up a final round of praise for his excellent performance and wished him a good night.

When he reached for his jacket on the hallway coat rack, he saw PJ lugging a heavy stack of dirty plates toward the kitchen. She stumbled and the top plate slid, nearly falling as she juggled the tower to keep it steady.

Miles left his jacket hanging and went to her. "Here, let me help you," he said, reaching for the plates.

"Oh, you don't need to do that," she replied in feigned protest. But she didn't resist.

As they entered the kitchen, Miles assessed the mass of dishes, serving bowls and platters, glasses, empty beer bottles, silverware, and a jumbled array of food prep implements. He found the last remaining open spot, set the plates down, assessed the amount of work ahead, and said, "Geez, gonna take a while to clean all this up. Can you leave it till morning?"

"Not a chance," she replied. "That's not how it's done in this house."

"So is your mother going to help? Rocky and Ned?"

PJ snorted at the second comment. "Rocky and Ned help in the kitchen? Oh my god! Those two wouldn't be caught dead doing 'women's work.' Mama's had a long day. She started really early getting everything ready. Nah, I can handle it. I've had plenty of practice."

Miles made a rough calculation of how long the job would likely take, what time he had to be at Montfair in the morning to exercise Bumpers, then said, "Well, how 'bout I give you a hand? At least just to get things started."

She thought for a moment, surveyed the piles filling the countertops, and said, "Okay. Just so you know, if Rocky or Ned catch you doing this, they're gonna give you some major shit."

"I'll take my chances. But I draw the line at wearing a frilly apron."

She smiled and said, "Deal. I'll wash, you dry."

Miles looked at an appliance built into the counter. "Um, isn't that a dishwasher?"

"Yes, but all this stuff isn't going to fit in there. Cram in a much as you can and then it's hand drying duty, buddy."

Miles nodded and they went to work. As PJ rinsed each piece and passed it to Miles, a sense of domestic harmony, an emotion he had not experienced for many years, embraced him. He flashed back to his parents working together in similar fashion, his mother washing, his father drying. He was into his teens before they were able to afford a dishwasher, but Miles recalled the smooth, efficient rhythm with which they knocked out the chore, more from muscle memory than conscious thought.

"You seem like a natural in the kitchen," PJ said.

"I guess I've had plenty of practice, living alone most of my life."

She glanced over at him. Miles could see the question coming.

"Never married?" she asked.

"Nah. Came close once, but didn't close the deal."

"Girlfriend?"

"Nope on that, too. Had a couple of relationships, but nothing lately." He turned to face her directly. "So what about you? I'd expect a long line of suiters to be hitting that gate button for a date with a catch like you?"

It was the first time he'd seen her blush. "Ah, well, ya see, it's kinda that gate button, and all those signs around it, that…um…I guess…sorta keeps the guys away. We've, ah, gotten a reputation. Not a good one. Most folks around here want nothing to do with us…with me. None of the guys my age want to get involved in our cause. They think we're all nuts." She smiled down at him. "Seems like you get me, though."

It was his turn to blush. "Oh, yeah, well, I get all of you. You, Rocky, your mother. Hell, maybe even Ned." He smiled playfully. "Although that may be a stretch. I was thinking, though, that maybe you and Ned…y'know…might be…a thing."

"Oh, hell no!" she shot back. "I mean, I respect what he's doing for our cause. But…a thing?"

Miles caught a brief shiver in PJ's shoulders.

"I stopped by his house once to drop off some pamphlets," she said. "I asked to use the bathroom and he pointed to where it was, down a hallway. His bedroom door was open and…and…" Another shiver. "There were all these…things…toys I guess you'd call them. Kinky stuff. Like you'd use to tie someone up." She shook her head. "Definitely not for me. So, no, we are not a thing!"

When a few minutes had passed and the discomfort of personal inquiries eased, PJ asked, "Did you grow up around horses? Is that how you became a jockey?"

Miles didn't have to make up a cover story for this. "No, we weren't horse people. My dad's a carpenter, does a lot of odd jobs. My mom works at the farmer's co-op. One summer, when I was fourteen, I was helping my dad with some work at a racehorse trainer's place. They were talking about what needed to be done and I saw a horse standing in a paddock right by the fence. He was kinda looking at us, like he wanted some attention. I walked over and started petting him. He seemed really sweet. The trainer came over and asked if I was some kinda horse whisperer. I had no idea what he was talking about. He said that horse had a bad reputation for being a nasty son-of-a-bitch. Biting, knocking people over, that kinda shit." Miles shrugged. "He seemed just fine to me. The trainer guy said he'd known some people who just had a natural way of communicating with horses. Couldn't explain it, but he knew it when he saw it. He asked how old I was and when I told him he seemed surprised. He said, 'Shit, boy, unless you hit a growth streak, you might have a career as a jockey ahead of you.' He asked if I'd be interested in some part time work. Hell, we always needed extra money and, legally, I was too young for most jobs. But I found out that don't matter in the horse world."

PJ did a final rinse on a large platter and handed it to him. "That's really sweet about how a mean horse took to you, trusted you. It really says something about the kind of person you are."

"Getting along with horses has never been a problem. It's dealing with people that's always been my weak spot."

"Seems like you're getting along just fine with us."

"Yeah, well, y'all are different. More my kinda people." He hesitated, then decided to add, "Especially you."

Shit, Flanagan, he thought, *what are you doing? She's half your age. And she's the freakin' enemy. You're here to get the dirt on her and her family, and all their friends, so Doddridge can nail their asses. And get your butt off the hook. Watch yourself!*

Drying off the platter, he continued. "Anyway, I started cleaning stalls and doing other odd jobs for the guy that summer, then on weekends during the school year. After a while he asked if I'd like to try getting on one his horses. That did it and I've never looked back. Oh, and that growth spurt never hit. Obviously."

"It was so cool watching you galloping to the finish line yesterday. I mean, a handsome man on a beautiful horse...every girl's dream, right? I expect you've never had a problem with the ladies."

He snorted out a muffled laugh. "Um, well, my track record on the actual track is much better than my record with 'the ladies.'" He flashed an impish grin and asked. "So…what do you call a jockey who's had a fight with his girlfriend?"

"I dunno. What?"

"Homeless."

"Oh, that's so sad. You aren't homeless now, are you?"

"No, no. I'm good. I've been bunking in with Ansel, Ansel Hart. He's a farrier. Used to lead Mosby's Rangers. But we had to give all that up. Damn shame!" Miles saw the opportunity this created. He placed his hands on the counter, bowed his head, and muttered, with as much venom as he could muster, "Fucking 'justice warriors'!" He looked up and added, "Oh, sorry! That was rude." He picked up a plate and resumed his drying duty.

PJ's curiosity was piqued. "That's okay. I've heard worse. That must have really bothered you."

He set the plate among the dried items and took the serving bowl she handed him. "Being a Ranger was my life. Things went…well, kinda wrong with my racing career. That's a whole 'nuther story. But riding with Ansel and all the other guys, we were like…a family…a band of brothers sorta thing. For some it was just a part time hobby. But for me it became something that kept me focused." He turned to her and flashed a weak smile. "I have trouble focusing sometimes. Can get a little hotheaded." Working the towel again, he continued. "Anyway, a bunch of assholes started protesting against us. Said we were glorifying the ugly past of slavery. That it was an offense to every Black person and all those calling for racial equality. Just like the people who want the memorial at the courthouse removed. If it's something they don't like, they want to blot it out, or rewrite history to skew it their way. And that covers a whole lotta things for those…those…" He scowled and shook his head. PJ could see his teeth clench.

"Those motherfuckers?" she asked.

"Exactly! I didn't think there was anything racist about what we were doing. But when they managed to get us shut down, put so much pressure on Ansel that he had to call it quits, I got to thinking, 'They want a fight? I'll give 'em a goddamn fight. A fight they never expected.' I…I just didn't know how to do it. And then your brother handed me that flyer, and it seemed like the universe was telling me where I needed to be."

"And so here you are." She reached a soggy hand over and squeezed his arm. "Lucky us."

The look in her eyes—acceptance, approval, even a hint of admiration—left him numb to the soaking wet spot on his sleeve.

He broke away from her gaze, looked past her to the pile of work that still awaited, and half-mumbled, "Looks like we got a good bit more to do. Better keep it comin'."

"Oh, yeah, right."

As she reached for another bowl, Miles said, "I'm sorry about your dad. I met him a few times when he and Rocky came to the McKendricks' shop to work on the AC. Seemed like a really nice guy. There was a lot of talk about what happened."

Her mood darkened. "He was the best, the absolute best. And those people…talk about a bunch of motherfuckers. They're gonna pay for what they did. They've also got a fight coming, a fight they're not expecting." She smiled weakly. "It's so great to have you helping us. Most people don't understand where we're coming from. But I can see you really get it, that you're one of us."

"Well! Would you look at this!"

They turned to see Rocky and Ned in the kitchen doorway.

"Ain't you the perfect little housekeeper," Rocky said with an amused lilt.

Ned said nothing, but his disapproving glare gave Miles a chill.

PJ came to his defense. "Maybe you two macho dickheads could take a tip here. But no! Can't lower your high and mighty selves to do 'women's work'."

"We had other things to do," Rocky shot back. "Important things."

"I thought you had to get going," Ned growled. "Gotta ride your horsey in the morning," he added with a mocking tone.

Miles found a clean towel and vigorously dried his hands. "Just thought I'd help get things started. But, yeah, I gotta get going." He turned to PJ. "Guess you're on your own from here."

"No problem," she said. "You've been a big help." She turned to Rocky and stuck her tongue out in the classic little sister taunt.

Miles squeezed past the two larger men partially blocking the door. Rocky moved a half step aside. Ned did not budge.

PJ returned to her work. The two men stood in place until Miles was out the front door.

Then Rocky stepped to PJ's side, picked up the dish towel, took the plate she handed him, and began drying it off. Ned harrumphed and left the kitchen.

"So," Rocky asked, "find out anything interesting?"

"Yes," she replied. "Yes, I did."

Chapter 40

Monday Morning
Montfair

A mist shrouded the fields of Montfair as Monday morning dawned. The rattle of voices and the swirling montage of faces spun in Miles' head as he led Bumpers to the mounting block. His time in the kitchen with PJ kept playing on a continuous loop in his mind. He needed to clear his thoughts and the best way to do that was in the one place where he felt comfortable and in control—on the back of a horse.

The horse moved smoothly over the dewy ground, his full power held in reserve. He knew the routine. It wasn't a race, just a jog. He rolled along in a graceful, playful canter. For the first time in days, Miles was able to relax. The tension that had plagued him as he prepared for Sunday's performance fell away, like fragments of a full body cast cracking and dropping to the ground with each beat of Bumper's hooves. By the time they'd finished the second lap around the exercise route, Miles' head was clear, his breathing smooth and steady.

As he guided Bumpers down to a trot, he patted the horse's neck lightly and said with a soothing tone, "Good lad, good lad. Whadda ya say we kick some horse racing ass again this Saturday?"

The horse shook his head and snorted in reply.

"Yeah," Miles said, "I agree. C'mon, let's have some fun."

He pressed his heels lightly against the horse's side. The signal was clear. Bumpers rocked back and launched into a powerful stride, happily gliding over the gently rolling ground.

When the pair returned to the barn, Miles was surprised to find Thumper, Janey, and Myrna waiting for him.

"Kinda early for y'all to be up and moving, ain't it?" Miles said.

"We heard you coming in," Thumper replied. "Couldn't wait to get the report on how things went."

Myrna reached for the reins. "Here," she said, as Miles dismounted. "I'll take care of Bumpers." She led the horse into the aisle and began untacking him.

"I guess it went pretty well," Miles began. "At least I didn't mess it up, thanks to everything y'all did. The crowd seemed to enjoy it. Of course, I guess they were hearing the kind of stuff that gets them fired up no matter how it's coming at them."

"That was the idea," Thumper remarked.

Miles pulled out his phone. "The good thing is—at least I guess it's a good thing—PJ caught it all on video and airdropped it to me. You can watch it if you want."

"Hell yeah!" Thumper said.

The threesome gathered together as Miles clicked on the video and held his phone up for them to watch.

When it reached the end, with the audience cheering as Miles took a second bow, the Montfair barn also rang with applause and praise.

Bumpers, who had been standing calmly in the crossties, jerked his head up at the commotion.

Myrna stroked his neck and said, "It's okay. Settle now."

The horse snuffled indignantly and relaxed.

"Wow!" Thumper said. "Great job! You freakin' nailed it."

Myrna chimed in. "If I was a casting director, I'd be making you an offer right now."

Janey nodded. "That had to make a big impression on those people, really prove that you're one of them."

"Yeah, well," Miles demurred, "to be honest, that was kinda the easy part, once I got over the stage fright. I guess all my experience playing the role of a Ranger helped. I mean, it wasn't exactly the same, but I still had to learn a lot about the character I was playing and pretend to be him."

"So...?" Thumper asked, "...if that was the easy part, what happened next?"

"Cecelia gave me an assignment from Tavina," Miles explained. "She wanted me to learn as much as I could about the people who were there. Names, what groups they represented, that sorta thing. Wasn't like I could walk around with a clipboard, ask everyone for their info and write it down. But a conversation PJ and I had in the old warehouse got me thinking about a way I could do this and it helped a lot."

"What was that?" Myrna asked.

"It's like how I keep the shop's inventory in order, knowing where everything is, seeing if something's out of place, remembering stock numbers, that sorta thing. So I decided to think of each person like they were part of the inventory. I saw them on a shelf in the stockroom, labeled with their name and the name of their group. When I left, I made sure I was clear of the place, then pulled over and wrote it all down."

Thumper shook his head and chuckled. "Brilliant! Y'know, I gotta admit I've underestimated you, Miles Flanagan. You just might have a promising future in espionage."

"Hell no!" Miles protested. "This deal is one and done! Get this Doddridge woman off all our asses, then it's strictly the horse world for me!"

Bumpers, growing impatient with standing on the crossties while the silly humans prattled on, stomped his foot on the concrete floor.

Miles stepped over and stroked his neck. "Good boy, good horse," he said soothingly. The horse's eyes softened, his lower lip sagged, and he rested his nose on Miles' shoulder.

Miles looked at his watch. “I gotta get to the shop. Then to Cecelia’s.”

“I’ll take care of Bumpers,” Myrna said. “You get going.”

Miles started to leave but before he reached the barn door he turned and said, “I can’t thank you guys enough for all your help. No way I could have done that on my own. Y’all are the best!”

“We’re all proud of you, Miles,” Janey said. “I know how difficult this job is for you. It’s certainly going well so far, but let’s not get ahead of ourselves. I know we all want you to find something Tavina can use against them, but we don’t want you to get hurt trying to do it. So be careful. Okay?”

Thumper and Myrna nodded in solemn agreement.

Miles’ buoyant mood deflated. “Yeah, okay,” he croaked out. “Careful. I’ll be careful.”

Chapter 41

Monday Afternoon
Kimber Farm

Cecelia skimmed through the list of attendees as Miles awaited her response.

"Good job," she said. "I'm sure Tavina will find this useful."

"Any chance she'll think I've done my job, gotten this information, and we're good now?"

Cecelia smiled and shook her head. "No, not a chance." She held up the sheet of paper. "Nothing here that could be an immediate cause for action. Could it come in handy at some point down the road? Some sort of supportive evidence? I'm not a lawyer, but I've got some idea of how the indictment process works. My second husband…" She paused for a moment, then mused, "…or was it my third? Well, anyway, he was an attorney and I remember him saying a grand jury can indict a ham sandwich. It's heavily skewed to favor the prosecution. But, even so, there has to be some reasonably credible evidence to act on." She looked at the list of names and the notes Miles had added. "Just being a member of one of these groups isn't itself a crime. But who knows? Maybe there's a possible conspiracy brewing. You just need to hang in there and keep digging."

His shoulders sagged.

Trying another approach, he said, "You know Muriel, the lady who keeps the books for the shop?"

"Yes, of course I do. Everyone knows Muriel."

"She gave us a scare last week, had a dizzy spell. She swore she was okay, but she admitted this has been happening lately."

"I'm so sorry to hear that. She's such a wonderful person."

"Yeah, she is. You…um…you do know she's Tavina's aunt, right?"

"Yes, of course. Everyone knows that, too."

"Well, it seems everyone but me. I just found that out."

"So?"

"Well, Christ! She's my coworker. Here I am doing the 'undercover' thing, no one's supposed to know about it but you and Doddridge. Doesn't that seem like a possible conflict?"

"How would it be a conflict? She has her job and you have yours. Nothing to do with your other activity."

"I dunno. I mean…like…what if…if she…"

Cecelia shook her head. "Sorry, but that's not going to work."

"What's not going to work?" Miles asked, trying to sound innocent.

"Using Muriel's family connection to Tavina as a way to get you out of completing your mission." She switched into motherly-mode. "Look, I'm sure it's difficult, a pretty uncomfortable situation. I don't envy you this task." The motherly demeanor vanished and her tone took on a sardonic twist. "But, then, I didn't try to kill someone and then found myself forced into a deal to avoid jail time."

"There's no proof that happened!" Miles declared. "She's bluffing!"

"So would you like to renege on the deal and see what happens?"

"I…I…" *Think, Flanagan! Easy now. Remember what you were taught in anger management. Take a moment. Breathe. Let it go. Let it go.*

Cecelia watched as he took deep breaths and the frustration eased from his face.

"Good," she said. "You need to save that fire for Saturday. We're all going to be there to see you bring Bumpers home a winner again."

Chapter 42

Saturday
Point-to-Point Races

Myrna was leading Bumpers off the trailer when she saw Miles approaching, clad in his Montfair racing silks. "Where's your new friend?" she asked.

"They're over in Duttonville at a protest rally about some statue."

"People can get all worked up over the dumbest things," Myrna said.

Miles shrugged. "I dunno. I'm not a big fan of erasing history. Tear down statues, change the names on buildings. Next thing you know they'll be rewriting the textbooks, making sure everyone who supported the Southern Cause is shown as an evil, whip-carrying—what's the word?—oh, yeah, *oppressor*."

Myrna cocked her head. "Um, are you getting into this UFR thing a little too deep? If it's just us here today, you can drop the playacting."

"This isn't about the Rockwell thing. I mean, yeah, he was way out there, totally nuts. But I know a lot about those times and the people who lived through them more than most folks do. We tried to bring that to life with our Living History presentations. Some of the guys were into it mostly just for the fun. But Ansel and me, well, we got into it with a lot more depth."

"Maybe a little too much depth in your case?" Myrna asked.

That remark hit home. "Yeah, okay, you're right. But that doesn't mean I've forgotten all the background work I did. And then the name 'Mosby' had to be erased. And all my hard work along with it."

She placed a hand on his arm. "You'll get over it. Look at you now! Back in the racing game! Isn't this where you really wanted to be?"

"Yeah, I suppose so." He turned to scan the race course, the tailgate spots along the fence line, and the other trailers parked in the horsemen's area. The viewing crowd and the list of entries were lighter than they were at the other meets. The sponsoring hunt had dropped their races a dozen years before. The attendance just wasn't sufficient to make the effort worthwhile. Now, under new leadership and with support from the broader racing community, the club had resumed hosting a meet. The turnout was trending upward but was still thin compared to other more established fixtures.

To support the effort, Thumper paid the top patron's price for a tailgate spot and entered his horse to compete. But only a few of the Montfair regulars made the trip and, rather than asking Natasha to put in the time and effort required for a full catering job, it was a potluck day.

Miles stepped around Myrna and placed a hand on Bumper's neck. The horse turned his head and rested his muzzle on Miles' shoulder. "How you feeling today, buddy? Ready to kick some butt? Rack up another win?"

Bumpers' nose pressed more heavily into Mile's shoulder.

Miles turned back to Myrna. "You and Voytek gave him a good going over this morning, right?"

"Of course we did," she replied. "Why? Do you think something's wrong?"

"Oh, probably just me overthinking things." He forced a faint grin. "I do that sometimes, y'know."

Voytek lumbered around from the back of the trailer.

Miles' grin vanished.

The call of "Horses to the paddock for the fourth race!" sounded over the PA system.

Miles and Thumper stood in the paddock watching Voytek lead Bumpers in the circle around them. Five other horses were entered in the day's open timber race.

"Two wins for the team so far," Thumper said. "You're doing a great job."

Miles remained silent as he watched the horse move. After a long pause, he said, "Does he look okay to you?"

Thumper studied the horse's movement. "Looks fine to me. Do you see something I don't?"

"I can't see anything either. But…well…I dunno, I just got this feeling, like he's trying to tell me something."

"Maybe it's 'Get your ass up here and let's go win this race!'"

The paddock judge called out, "Riders up!"

Miles shook his head, as if trying to shoo off some annoying insect buzzing at him. "Yeah, okay. Let's go win it." He stepped forward into Voytek's waiting grasp.

The other five horses posed a considerable challenge. Each was a seasoned veteran with multiple wins, ridden by top jockeys, Micah Hairston among them, and trained by some of the best known pros in the game. The racing community rallied to support the effort to get this meet back on the schedule. The trend over the past several years had gone in the opposite direction.

When the flag dropped, Bumpers held his own, never far from the leader. But Miles' radar was on full alert. His words to Bar ran through his mind.

I'm pretty good at sensing where the horse is coming from…the horse has to trust you…if you got a good connection, you can sometimes sense things before it all goes to hell.

Going into the fifth fence, Miles felt a slight hint of hesitation from Bumpers, a signal only a rider with his experience and sensitivity would have detected. It was too late to pull up without risking a collision. So Miles gave the horse an extra squeeze, just enough to assure he'd get over the fence cleanly. Once landed and moving off, Miles' radar went on full alert. It was the left hind. Bumpers was trying to tell him that at the trailer. Not yet lame, but a twinge that signaled a possible problem was brewing. Best to not over stress it. Like any high level athlete, horses know their own bodies. It's most often human failure that leads to disaster.

Bumpers would be listed in the results for that day as "PU"—"Pulled Up." (Which is usually better than "LR"—"Lost Rider.")

The horse wasn't limping as Miles rode him at a slow walk back toward the paddock. The race had one more lap to go and Miles was cautious to not get in the way.

Once through the paddock gate, he leapt off and Voytek took over. Thumper was already there.

"Looks like you were right," Thumper said.

"Might be an abscess just starting to brew," Miles replied. "We can't tell until he's cooled out. But *he* knew something was off." Miles patted the horse's neck. "You gave it a try, buddy. Good for you. You got heart, that's for sure." Turning to Thumper, he said, "Sorry, boss. Just wasn't our day."

"Plenty more to come. Let me know what you find once he's cooled out."

Their attention was caught by the voice of the announcer.

"At the final fence, it's Signs of Life and Micah Hairston with a six length lead. Signs of Life is over the fence and surging toward the finish line in hand and in command."

"Good for Micah," Thumper said. "If it's not us in the winner's circle, I'm happy for him to be there."

"Yeah," Miles said. "Good for him."

Thumper detected the sarcastic tone in Miles' voice. "Oh, right. I remember you two didn't get along very well. Maybe a bit more than friendly professional competition? Something else going on?"

"Nah. Mostly just me being an asshole. I wanted to win every race at any cost. And it often came down to just the two of us. I'm not like that anymore. Sure, I still want to beat him. But only on the fair and square."

"Well, you showed that today, doing the right thing by pulling up and not putting the horse at risk. I appreciate that."

"Look," Miles said, "if does turn out to be an abscess, I'll get that foot soaking, give him a few days off, and see how he does. He might be okay in time for the next race."

"Let's not push it," Thumper replied. "More important that he's sound for the big money later."

As Voytek led the horse back to the trailer, Thumper turned to Miles. "Anything special on the schedule for tomorrow's UFR meeting?"

"Not that I'm aware of. I suppose some of it will be about the statue protest they're all at today, over in Duttonville."

Thumper shook his head. "They didn't succeed in stopping the memorial at the county courthouse from getting hauled away. And I doubt they'll have any better success in Duttonville."

"Yeah," Miles agreed. "If they can't score any wins with that sorta thing, managing to get every Black person in the country shipped to Africa ain't very likely."

Thumper chuckled. "Nope, it sure ain't." His tone then turned serious. "But that doesn't mean they're not capable of doing something, even if on a small scale, that could cause some harm, whether to property or people. So you hang in there. Maybe some of that sixth sense you have with horses can be used to spot whatever it is they're up to before any shit goes down."

"Well, like Bar said, it seems horses and UFR members all have brains about the same size."

"Hey, Flanagan!"

Miles and Thumper turned to see Micah Hairston walking toward them.

"Is the horse okay?" Micah asked.

"Yeah, probably just an abscess starting to brew. Don't worry," Miles added with a playfully challenging tone, "we'll be back out there soon, leaving you in the dust."

Hairston smiled and shot back, "I wouldn't count on it."

As he turned and walked away, Miles thought about the battles he'd had with Micah. It was always Miles who ramped up the heat, pushing too hard, making threats. No wonder the other jockeys hated him back then. It said something about Micah that he made a point to ask about Bumpers and share a friendly, if brief, exchange.

Chapter 43

Sunday
Off the Grid

The Hendershots and Ned sat at the dining room table on Sunday morning, engaged in a private discussion before the others arrived.

"Anything back yet from your people?" Margaret asked Ned.

"They're interested, but need more assurance we're on the level."

"Like what kind of assurance?"

"Like the details of how we're going to pull this off. At this point, I can only give them the general idea. They want specifics, how we plan to deliver the goods. These people don't fool around. They've been through too much to play games."

"This isn't a game!" Margaret said. "You got to let them know we're dead serious about this."

"I've made that clear. But they're not gonna commit to specifics until we have it all worked out on our end. And we've still got some major details to figure out."

PJ spoke up. "I've been thinking about something Miles said at the races. It just might be the answer to one of our problems."

She filled the others in on this and they all agreed it was worth pursuing.

"And," Margaret said, "if that does work out, we're definitely going to need a fifth member of the team." She turned to Rocky. "Where do things stand with your little buddy?"

"I'm kicking around some ideas about one more test for his commitment level. Gotta be something really serious if he's gonna be part of the plan."

"Yeah, well, you need to get something definite soon," she shot back. "He did a good job playing the Commander, showed he can rise to at least some challenge. But, shit, that was nothing compared to what we're planning and what he'll need to do to help us pull it off. Ned needs to assure his people we've got a full team together."

"I'm working on it, Mama!"

Ned grunted. "Y'know, it's possible we could use him for what we need without letting him in on the real plan. Make him think it's more like a prank. And then once the real thing gets rolling, he'll be too stuck to back out."

"I dunno," Rocky mused. "That could be kinda risky. He could end up blowing the whole thing if he, like, freaks out or something."

Ned leaned forward. "Then get him pinned down, if he's in or not. If not, we gotta drop him before he finds out too much. And if that happens, then it's my turn to find us that fifth Commando. And my choice might be…shall we say…a bit more hardcore than your little horsey riding pal."

The gate intercom buzzed with the first arrival for Sunday's meeting.

As everyone assembled at the table, Miles noticed the only other board members present were Maynard Tubbs and Krys Pinney. He asked Rocky, "No Ted today?"

"Not today. Not any more at all actually. Lindstrom's joined Fred Cornwall in the ex-members group."

"Both too busy with other stuff?"

"That's their excuse. But it's been pretty obvious for a while that they were losing interest in The Cause." Rocky looked at the remaining members. "Tell you the truth," he whispered, "I'm not sure how much longer these two losers are gonna hang around. I'm beginning to think they're all here mostly for the free chicken."

Miles grinned and elbowed Rocky's arm. "Well, it *is* mighty damn good chicken!"

Rocky chuckled and shook his head.

PJ addressed the group. "Miles and I have witnessed something at the races that really turned our stomachs. A beautiful white girl, someone who should be carrying our precious race forward, has fallen prey to the race-mixing propaganda. Such a shame!"

Expressions of disgust and agreement rumbled from the group.

Margaret chimed in. "Yes, it is. Another stroke in the browning of America."

"Yeah," Miles said. "A damn shame. I sure wish there was something that could be done about it."

Margaret grunted and shook her head. "Like trying to turn back the ocean. Just another example of how everything abnormal is being turned into the normal in our once-great country. And all these fools who think they're 'enlightened' can't even see the truth of where things like this will lead. We're already becoming a second rate country. Third rate ain't far off. Yeah, sure, if there was some way to at least save this one precious white girl from going that way, I'd be all for it. But I reckon it's already too late. I doubt even a real Commando could pull off something like that."

The meeting achieved little of substance and Miles could easily read the growing lack of enthusiasm among those not part of the core group. Their ardor did, though, perk up considerably when chicken time was announced.

Miles hung around until the others had left. He then took Rocky aside and asked, "Your mother's comment earlier about 'a real Commando,' what did she mean by that? Why is reaching that such a high bar?"

Rocky hesitated, then replied, "We have plans…plans to make a bold statement, to do something not even the Commander himself was ever able to do. Might be just a small part of our overall mission, but, if we can pull it off, it will definitely strike a blow for The Cause."

"So who's achieved Commando rank so far?"

"Just me and Ned. Although Mama and PJ are what I guess you could call 'Commandettes.' They're just as committed as we are."

"Aren't any of the others possible Commando material? Maynard? Krys?"

Rocky chuckled. "Those guys? Shit, they're just posers. If they had any inkling of what we're planning, they'd shit their pants."

"How do you know I wouldn't do the same?"

Rocky studied the smaller man. Then said, "I can tell you're different stock. That once you're committed to something, you see it through, no matter the cost."

That remark took Miles by surprise. "How do you know that about me? I mean, really, I might be just as much bluff and bluster as those other guys."

"So," Rocky explained, "Ned has a friend who does drywall work. Seems old lady McKendrick had a strange hole in her kitchen ceiling. As he was doing the repair, he noticed something odd stuck in a joist. He pulled it out, and found it was the type of ball that would have been used in an old black powder pistol. Y'know, the type a Mosby's Ranger would have carried. How could it have gotten there? Well, rumors get circulating. Now, no one knows for sure just what happened, and who did what. But the word around the back roads is that someone tried to kill someone in that room. And not just any 'someone', but a Black someone who was trying to destroy part of our local culture and, worse yet, was a known abuser of women."

Miles scratched his head and tried to look innocently surprised. "Well, that's all news to me. You know how crazy-ass rumors can get started."

Rocky smiled. "Yeah, I'm sure it's only a bunch of rumors. Maybe you *are* just a load of bluff and bluster. Maybe you need to pass one more test, something only a true Commando could manage, before we confer that special honor on you. And," he added with a wink, "let you in on the *real* plans."

Chapter 44

Sunday Evening
Thumper's Study

The Diary of Olivia Bauer Billington
Montfair, Crutchfield County, Virginia
March 6, 1887

My heart is heavy this night as I reflect on the passing of our dear Portia. The Montfair school, indeed Montfair itself, will forever be indebted to her. If not for her, our initial efforts to begin teaching the children of our house staff to read and write might have ended in failure. No matter how well-intentioned my initial efforts, it soon became apparent that the chasm between our first group of students and myself formed an impassable barrier. The sense of compulsion was obvious. For the educational process to flourish, there must be a sincere desire to learn. That cannot occur when the students see their teacher as someone not of their world, as a figure with absolute power over every aspect of their lives.

It was only when Portia stepped in and, although only slightly more literate at that point than the young pupils, politely usurped my role as mistress. I was shocked—pleasantly I must add—by the way the children quickly relaxed and, by making each lesson a form of game, did the educational process begin to thrive.

It was this playful atmosphere that led to the exchange between Portia and her then young daughter Bryna. In teaching the children how to spell the names of their parents, she saved her own name for last. She wrote "POR-tia" on the chalkboard, held it up, and said, 'POR-sha.' Bryna spoke up immediately. 'But Mama, last week, when you were showing us how to spell Joseph's mother's name, you said "T-I-A" was pronounced "TEE-ah." So shouldn't your name be pronounced "Por-TEE-ah"?'"

I found it necessary to step in and try to explain some of the vagaries of the English language, how it has adopted words from a wide variety of sources, many of which employ different rules of phonics. The blank expressions on the children's faces, as well as Portia's, suggested my brief dissertation had fallen far short of success. Instead, the mood was lightened by Bryna's mischievous insistence that her mother's name should be pronounced "Por-TEE-ah."

This continued into the next generation when Bryna named her first daughter "Portia" but insisted it be pronounced "Por-TEE-Ah."

It is with such sweet thoughts that I choose to remember our sweet Portia.

Chapter 45

Monday Morning
Montfair

As Miles suspected, the cause of Bumper's foot pain was an abscess in his left hind. By Monday morning, the treatment was in its third day. The foot was soaked in a solution of hot water and Epsom salt, gauze was placed over the spot where the abscess had been opened to allow it to drain, and the foot was then covered with vetrap.

With the horse turned out in a small paddock by the barn where he could rest, Miles went to the boss's study.

"How'd yesterday's meeting go?" Thumper asked.

Miles recited PJ's comment about Elizabeth and Tobias, how the entire group thought it was a travesty, and criticized Thumper for condoning a mixed relationship for his own daughter. But at least they conceded there was nothing they could do about it, citing Margaret's comment about how it would take a real Commando to break them up.

Miles then steeled himself for the next part.

"There's a lotta talk about this 'Commando' bullshit. Like it's some secret club with a really high bar to get in. But it got, well, a lot deeper this time."

Miles paused to collect his thoughts.

Thumper, eager to hear the rest, gestured for him to continue.

"Rocky said they have plans for something big, something that will really make a statement. He said not even Commander Rockwell himself ever pulled off anything like they're planning to do."

Thumper perked up at that information. "That's great, Miles! Sounds like they really are up to something that Doddridge could use."

"Yeah, well, I have to be made a Commando to be let in on the real plans. Rocky said I might need one more test before that can happen. But it has to be something big, something, as he put it, only a true Commando could manage."

Thumper ruminated on that comment, *only a true Commando*. And then, with a burst of illumination, it hit him. "Wait! What was it Margaret said about getting Elizabeth and Tobias to break up? That it would take a real Commando?"

"That's what she said," Miles confirmed, surprised by Thumper's sudden animation.

"So what if we could figure out some way to make them think that's happened, and you were the cause of it?"

"Geez, boss, I dunno. That sounds like a real stretch." He took a deep breath and considered Thumper's seemingly outlandish suggestion. "But I reckon if anyone can figure out how to make something that batshit crazy happen, you can." He relaxed slightly and added with a grin, "And maybe with some help from your merry band of co-conspirators like y'all did with the Rockwell skit."

"The hard part," Thumper said, "is going to be figuring out both how to make it look like they're breaking up and, harder still, to convince the UFR folks that you orchestrated it. If we can come up with some way to do that, they'll *have* to confer Commando status on you. And then you're in! Give me a little time to kick around some thoughts on this, see if my 'co-conspirators' have any ideas."

Chapter 46

Monday Afternoon
Kimber Farm

Miles found Cecelia in the Kimber Farm tack room. She wore a pair of yellow rubber dishwashing gloves and was brushing neatsfoot oil onto a leather bridle hanging from a grappling hook.

"The heavy lifting and your own tack cleaning," Miles said, shaking his head.

She replied without turning from her work. "I like to keep my hands in the game, you might say, in many ways. So, what do you have for me?"

"Something might be brewing."

Cecelia stopped the brush in mid-stroke and turned to Miles. "Really?"

"Yeah, well, I don't have any details, not yet anyway. But there's been talk of…how did Rocky say it?…'Making a bold statement.' No idea what that means. And I'm not in deep enough yet to get the inside scoop. But you can tell Miss Doddridge I'm making progress and it's possible there might be something in the works she can use to nail them."

Cecelia nodded and showed a hint of a smile. "So what's your plan to get that inside scoop? We don't have forever to make something happen."

"I'm trying to figure that out. I'm getting pretty close to their inner circle. I just need one more push to make them think I'm for real."

"And that would be…?"

"That's the tough part, ain't it? I'm looking for that wedge. Gonna have to come up with something creative."

Cecelia dipped the brush into the bowl of oil and turned back to her work. "If it helps motivate you, remember what the consequences could be if you fail. Especially if something happens, people get hurt, or worse, and it happens on Tavina's watch. Get the goods on the bad guys before they can carry out their plans, and she's the hero. Get caught by surprise, and…well, not good for her public image."

She studied the bridle, looking for any spot she might have missed. Satisfied with her work, she turned back to Miles and slowly pulled off the rubber gloves.

"Of course, if the worst happens, there would still be a way to distract the public's attention with a different prosecution, something the local media would love to cover. You know, a lurid case of attempted murder and a cover up conspiracy by some prominent citizens." She folded the gloves meticulously over the edge of the utility sink and let that remark marinate in the oiled leather-scented air. "Don't forget there's an election coming up. Either way, I want Miss Doddridge to win. If you want to help make that happen, and not be her fallback option for the PR spin, I suggest you do whatever necessary to get the scoop on that 'bold statement.'"

With a dry mouth, Miles replied, "Yes, ma'am. I'll do whatever's necessary."

"Good." She turned to another bridle hanging on a wall hook and carefully examined its condition.

Miles knew he'd been dismissed.

Chapter 47

Monday Evening
Off the Grid

Margaret held out a key and dangled it in front of PJ.

"I know it's painful, darlin', but you've got to do this. You're the best one to find what we need."

PJ steeled herself, took the key, and went to the warehouse.

She stood at the door to her father's office and held the key in front of the lock. After a long pause, she inserted it, opened the door, and stepped inside.

The once-familiar aromas overwhelmed her. The dominant presence of her father's earthy scent forced her to close her eyes. In her mind she could see him sitting at his cluttered desk, looking up with a welcoming smile, happy to see his budding protégé ready for another tutorial session. Rolled up blueprints reclined in corners and against the wall. Windy was reasonably conversant with AutoCAD, due in large part to guidance from PJ. But he remained more comfortable in the old school world of paper blueprints.

The same applied to his list of contacts. Next to his landline phone, long since disconnected, sat a Rolodex. Hundreds of 4" by 6" cards were jammed into the wheel, their top edges tattered and blackened from the touch of rough, grease-stained fingers spinning them in search of a targeted contact. The names, addresses, phone numbers, and notes were all handwritten, many with outdated information inked over, updated details handwritten wherever space allowed.

During her work shift that day, PJ checked the files at Jessup HVAC. Nothing came up relevant to her search of the company's computerized records. Margaret remembered that when Jessup took on the Hendershot accounts, the deal included a cutoff point for activity. Perhaps the information they were looking for was among those outdated accounts. And the only place to find it was on Windy's old Rolodex.

PJ spun the wheel to the letter most likely to have what she was looking for. She flipped through each card until, about halfway through, her eyes saw a familiar name. She opened the map app on her phone and entered the address. Bingo!

The objective achieved, her joyful memories of time spent here with her father succumbed to the painful reality that he was gone. The anger that arose whenever she thought of why he was gone propelled the pain to a blazing rage.

She stood up, placed her hands flat on her father's desk, and bowed her head. "Don't worry, Daddy," she whispered. "They'll pay for what they did. They'll pay."

She took a moment to absorb her father's spectral presence one last time. Then she lifted her head and marched out of the office.

Chapter 48

Tuesday Evening
Montfair, Thumper's Study

Thumper sat at his desk with Janey, Myrna, and Miles seated before him.

"Before we get into the main subject," he said, "a quick question for you, Miles. What's the latest on Bumpers' foot?"

"I'm still soaking and wrapping it, keeping it clean. But he could be ready to go by this Saturday if you want to give it a try. Your call."

"Nah, I think we should scratch. Not worth the risk with the stiffer races still to come. And it's his first season so he'll have plenty of other opportunities to show his stuff."

Miles was conflicted. As a conscientious horseman, he knew Thumper was right. But he was so glad to be back in to racing that he hated to miss even one contest. It was different when he was at the top of his game, riding for multiple owners. If one horse was scratched, there were still others to ride. Maybe, if his work for Billington continued to go well, other owners might also be willing to hire him again. Best to not taint his chances by putting his one client's only horse at risk.

"Yeah, you're right," he conceded.

"Okay," Thumper said. "So, now to the situation at hand, how to dupe the UFR idiots into believing Miles has managed to cause a breakup between Elizabeth and Tobias. I've been wracking my brains trying to figure out how to pull this off," he said, "and I think I've come up with a plan, but it's going to take some creativity. And we're going to need to bring in two more co-conspirators."

"And who would that be?" Janey asked.

"Elizabeth and Tobias," Thumper replied.

Miles shook his head. "Jesus. Why not just tell the whole county?"

"Hey," Thumper shot back, "you were the one who told Bar. And spilled the beans to me. I had to bring Janey and Myrna in to help pull off your Rockwell skit. Besides, we're all in this together now anyway."

"Your daughter and her boyfriend aren't," Miles countered.

"Just hear me out on this," Thumper said. "We need to get you to Commando status so we can find out what UFR is up to and get us all off the hook." He gave Miles a hard stare. "Especially you, who got us into this in the first place. I've spent the past two days wrangling with a way to pull off this breakup ruse and I think I'm on to something that will do the trick. But it won't work without our two star-crossed lovers' cooperation."

A contrite Miles Flanagan slouched in his chair and acknowledged Thumper's comments with a sideways nod.

"Okay," Thumper continued, "here's the plan."

When he'd finished laying out his idea, the threesome agreed it could work. But it would require careful planning, along with a bit of luck. Mostly, it would require Elizabeth and Tobias to play along.

Thumper reached for his phone, clicked on his daughter's number, and set it to speaker mode.

"I need your help with something, and Tobias's too. We've got a real challenge. But it's for a very good cause. Here's the deal."

Elizabeth listened patiently. She hadn't been present at "The Incident" nor had she been involved in the cover-up. But she knew enough to understand the predicament her father and the others were in.

"Very creative," she said. "I can't speak for Tobias, of course, but I'm pretty sure I can convince him to go along with it."

"Great!" Thumper replied. "Let me know what he says, then we can work out the details. Love ya!"

"Love you, too."

Thumper smiled and sat back. "So, we have a plan." Focusing on Miles, he added, "If all goes well, a Commando thou shalt be!"

Chapter 49

Wednesday Morning
Montfair

Thumper heard Miles pulling in.

"I'll be right back," he said to Janey and Myrna as he rose from the breakfast table.

He intercepted Miles at the front barn entrance.

"Elizabeth and Tobias are good on the plans," he announced. "Myrna stayed up late last night working on a script for them to follow." With a grin he added, "She included stage directions of course."

"Of course she did," Miles said. "Tell you the truth, I was afraid Tobias might not go along with this."

"Well, two enticements were required. One of them was my daughter's powerful persuasive abilities. The other was a promise that, once UFR goes down, Tobias gets an exclusive first on the media coverage. I'm not sure which one was more effective."

Miles snorted. "I'm betting on the first one."

"Yeah, probably. Either way, the plan is a go. Make the call to Rocky, tell him where to be and when. But nothing more. He has to come alone or the deal's off. And not to tell anyone else."

"Gotcha."

Chapter 50

Friday Evening
Montfair Barn

Miles waited on the backside of the barn. Dusk was setting in when he saw Rocky's van coming up the service road.

Rocky parked as Miles directed, with the van out of sight from the main house.

"All right," he said to Miles, "I'm here, like you told me. So what's all this cloak-and-dagger shit about?"

"You'll see. Come with me."

Rocky followed Miles to the loft ladder. Miles scrambled up with simian agility. The larger man moved more slowly. When they were both on the loft floor, Miles put one finger to his lips in the universal "Hush" sign, then waved Rocky forward as they crept to the front of the barn. Miles had stacked two hay bales at the midpoint where the sliding loft doors met. The doors were open just enough for two men to kneel behind the hay bales and peer out over them with a view toward the house.

"This had better be worth it," Rocky snarled.

"Oh, it will be," Miles assured him. He looked at his watch. "Shit should be going down soon. Just be patient. This is gonna make the Commander smile down on us."

Ten minutes later, a car came up the main driveway. Rocky thought it looked familiar. As it pulled into the circular loop in front of the house, he realized it was Tobias's car.

At the same instant Tobias hopped out of the car, Elizabeth burst from the house and ran down the steps.

Rocky expected them to meet in a passionate embrace. Instead, Elizabeth came to an abrupt halt, held up her palm, and shouted, "Stay where you are! You can get back in that car and get the hell out of here!"

"Look," he pleaded, "I can explain. It was just a youthful mistake. I was still in school, had my whole career ahead. She said she was going to take care of it. But she lied."

"*She* lied?" Elizabeth shot back. "What about *your* lie? Your *lies*? You've been lying about it ever since. And your whole family went along with it. Hiding your love child, passing her off as your cousin's kid. Shame on you!"

"How did you even find out about this?"

"Doesn't matter. But whoever it was did me a huge favor, spared me going deeper into a relationship with a man capable of doing something like this. Getting an innocent girl pregnant is one thing." She rolled her eyes. "I've seen enough of what goes on with you frat boys on party weekends. But I thought you were different. Turns out you're no better than any of them. Maybe worse. At least some might have been a man and taken responsibility. Instead, you robbed this poor child of knowing the truth. And I could never forgive you for that."

"Elizabeth, look, I know I should have told you sooner, and I'm sorry for that. But… "

"No! We're done! You can stand there all night if you want. But I suggest you get back in that car and get the hell out of here. And never set foot on Montfair again. Goodbye *Cookie*!" She spat out his nickname, spun around, and marched back into the house.

He slumped back into his car and sped away.

Rocky remained motionless, dumbfounded by what he'd just witnessed.

After several seconds, he said, “How…how did you know…this would happen? And to be here when it did?”

“Because I was the one who tipped her off.”

Rocky’s stunned expression begged for an explanation.

The two of them turned around, sat down, and leaned against the hay bales.

“The racing world is a hotbed of rumors and secrets,” Miles began, “some dark and some, well, not-so-secret. Micah Hairston, the only Black jockey I know on the steeplechase circuit, has a young niece who comes with her parents to some of the races. The parents are both Black, pretty dark skinned. The kid, well, she leans a good bit more toward the white side. A bunch of us were hanging out at a bar in Warrenton one night, came down to just me and Micah. After a few rounds, I asked him about that. Oh, how that liquored-up tongue started wagging. Confessed to the whole sordid deal, how his high-and-mighty cousin Tobias Johnson had knocked up a white girl. She had…what did he call it?…oh, yeah, a ‘crisis of conscience.’ Couldn’t bring herself to have an abortion. Micah’s sister and her husband had been trying to have a kid but it wasn’t going well. So they arranged to adopt the kid.” He made the wiping-hands motion. “Problem solved. Johnson and the girl’s mother are off the hook, and Micah’s sister and hubby get the kid. Perfect, except for that half-white thing. Tell you the truth, I’m pretty sure Micah doesn’t remember telling me any of that, as drunk as he was. I had to call Uber to get him home.” Miles paused and, with an amused chuckle, added, “I heard he threw up in the Uber guy’s car.”

They sat quietly as Rocky took all this in.

He then said, “So, okay, the Johnson guy fathered a kid out of wedlock. No big deal. Hell, that’s just normal shit for those people anyway. Something like…what?…seventy percent of Black kids are born that way now. Helps keep those welfare checks rolling in, right?”

“Yeah, well, this is a little different. First of all, the mother wasn’t black nor on welfare. And the kid now has a good home with two responsible parents. But that ain’t the point. The point is

Johnson kept it from the Billington girl. And that's the kinda thing that will really piss off one of those holier-than-y'all Billingtons."

"So what did you do? Tell all this to…what's-her-name?... Elizabeth?"

"Not directly. She probably would have just blown me off if I tried to tell her face-to-face. So I did it kinda anonymously. I figured if I just planted a seed, she, and probably her old man too, would get curious. And with all their connections, they could easily track it down. So I got one of those burner phones—y'know, the kind that can't be traced—and sent her a message with a tip about looking into this. I found Johnson's contact info on the news outlet he works for and sent him a message. I told him she was on to his illegitimate child thing, and if he wanted to save their relationship, he'd better get his ass out to Montfair Friday evening, around this time, and 'fess up. One more message telling her when he'd be here and there you have it. At least this one terrible case of mixing the races averted. Might not be much, but it's one for our cause. I reckon the Commander would approve, don't you?"

It took a full minute for Rocky to absorb this. "Jesus, Flanagan. I can't believe you pulled this off. If I hadn't seen it with my own eyes…oh, shit!…I should have recorded this." He tapped the phone in his pants pocket. "Guess I was too surprised by what was going on to think about that."

"Damn, you're right. Didn't occur to me either. Well, too late now. But you saw it happen, heard every word. And if I hadn't set the whole thing up, how would I have known to be right here, at the right time, to watch it go down? Right?"

"Yeah, I guess so." He reached over and plopped a hand on Flanagan's shoulder. "Amazing job, little buddy!"

"Amazing enough to qualify for Commando status?"

"Well, it's gotta be a unanimous vote to be official. But once I get this back to the others, I'm sure you'll be a shoe-in. Tell you what, plan on allowing a little extra time on your schedule for Sunday's meeting. There just might be a special ceremony."

Thumper, Janey, and Myrna were seated on the foyer steps, each one grinning broadly, as Elizabeth returned to the house. To assure Rocky wouldn't hear them, they applauded Elizabeth with golf claps.

Elizabeth leaned back against the door and took a deep breath. She then grabbed her phone and hit Tobias's number.

"I think we pulled it off!"

"A good learning experience for me," he replied. "I never want to get on your bad side, whether it's a fake story or not. Now, we're sure this wasn't recorded, right?"

"Miles swore he wouldn't record it and, if the Hendershot guy tried, Miles would figure out some way to stop him. We haven't heard from him yet, but he was to let us know if the guy didn't show up or anything else went wrong. So we're assuming all went well. And no one else will ever be aware of our little performance."

"Okay. Let me know when the guy has left so I can come back to the house." With a joking tone, he added, "You do still want to see me, right?"

She looked at the threesome still seated on the stairs. "Of course. And we have an adoring audience waiting to toast our theatrical success."

Thumbs up from the adoring audience!

Miles marched into the house through the mudroom. (He'd never used the mansion's front door and doubted he'd ever do so.) The others met him in the kitchen and roundly cheered his success. With Tobias's return, the conspirators gathered in Thumper's study where tumblers of Virginia whiskey were passed around.

"So it went as planned?" Thumper asked Miles. "He bought the whole deal?"

"Every bit of it," Miles replied.

"And nothing was recorded?"

"Nope. It all went down too fast for him to think of that. So there's no record that could ever come back to cause a problem for Tobias. And if Rocky ever tried anything, he'd be a…a…what did you call it?"

"An easily impeachable source," Thumper said.

"Yeah, right."

With that settled, Thumper led the toasts. "To our performers, Elizabeth and Tobias; our stage director, my talented sister; our writers,"—this to Janey and himself—"and, of course, the one at the center of it all, the mole extraordinaire, the hero who will soon be a confirmed Commando and will thus deliver well-deserved comeuppance to this scurrilous band of racists, the one and only, Miles Flanagan!"

"Hear, hear!"

Rocky sped home to Off the Grid, burst through the door, and called out, "Mama! PJ! Y'all ain't gonna believe what I just saw!"

Chapter 51

Sunday Morning
Off the Grid

Miles entered the Hendershots' house to rousing applause and cheers from Margaret, Rocky, and PJ. Ned cracked a half smile, his equivalent of full approval.

Margaret stepped forward and gave Miles a powerful hug. The motherly touch was offset by the feel of her 9mm Luger pressing against the front of his hip bone.

"You did it!" she exclaimed. "Rocky told us how you saved that precious white girl from the clutches of that lying Black scum. I bet she'll think twice about letting herself get lured away again from her own kind." She looked heavenward. "I know the Commander is smiling down on us all this fine morning." Then to Miles, "Especially you!"

"And," Rocky said, "you've proven that you're truly Commando-worthy. If you're willing, we'd like to invite you to join our special ranks this morning."

"Well, gee," Miles replied with appropriate humility, "I'm really honored. I mean, I did what I did mostly because it was the right thing for The Cause. I wasn't, like, trying to make it about me."

Ned snorted. "Bullshit! Of course you were making it about you, so you could become a Commando." He held Miles with an icy stare for several seconds.

Was all the effort of the fake breakup for nothing? Rocky said the vote had to be unanimous. Was Ned going to blackball him?

When Ned felt he'd caused a sufficient level of discomfort, he shrugged and said, "So that's what we're gonna to do this morning." He reached out his hand. "Welcome, *brother*." His handshake was firm but his pockmarked face was contorted in his signature sneer.

PJ pushed Ned aside. "Let me get in here!" she demanded.

She threw her arms around Miles and lifted him two inches off the floor.

When she returned Miles to solid footing, he asked, "So is there, like, a ceremony to make this official?" He turned to Rocky. "You said something about that the other night."

"Oh, yeah, that," Rocky said sheepishly. "Well, um, y'see we've never inducted anyone else into Commando status. Ned and me got to be Commandos because, well…mostly because we're founding members. Mama and PJ are sorta Commandos, too. It's about being *really* committed to The Cause."

Miles was half-disappointed and half-relieved. He was hoping for a ceremony in which he'd be highly praised, honored for his devotion and service to The Cause, even if it was all fake. On the other hand, he'd been worried there might be some physical or mental test involved, such as reciting a "Commando Creed" and getting whacked with a paddle if he did it wrong.

"And," Rocky continued, "we all agree you're committed. So…yeah, welcome Commando Flanagan!"

A light round of applause signaled the induction's conclusion.

"C'mon, y'all," Margaret ordered. "Too early for chicken, but there's coffee and a big platter of sweet rolls waiting in the kitchen. Let's eat!"

As they took their seats around the kitchen table, Miles asked, "Are Krys and Maynard coming later for the usual meeting?"

Ned and Margaret exchanged glances. He nodded for her to explain.

"Nope," she said. "Turns out they were all poser assholes." There was a sour note in her voice. She leaned forward and fixed a hard stare on Miles. "Things are about to get serious. *Real serious*. We needed some things to come together for our plan, and that's all finally happened. I asked each of those guys just how committed they were to The Cause, what would they be willing to do to honor the Commander's legacy, pick up the torch, and move his agenda forward in a way that would really strike a blow for what's right." She sat back and shook her head. "Every one of those dipshits backed down." A playful grin lightened her face. "I'll tell you this much, none of them will ever taste my chicken again!"

"So what's the plan?" Miles asked, trying to sound serious, fully committed, anything but a poser asshole. *Could this be the successful conclusion of his mission, he thought? His stomach fluttered. With the plan revealed, he could rush straight to Kimber Farm, pass the info to Cecelia, she'd get it to Tavina who would then do whatever a commonwealth's attorney does to...well, he wasn't sure what she'd do. But that didn't matter. His job would be done and he, along with all the others connected to "The Incident", would be in the clear.*

"Not so fast." At Ned's interjection, Miles' vision of relief melted into haze and drifted away. "There are, um, different levels of Commando status. You start out as, like, Commando Second Class. Kinda like a second lieutenant before you become a first lieutenant, then captain, and so on."

Miles could tell Ned was making this up on the fly.

"You'll be in on the plan when the time's right," Ned continued. "For now, all you need to know is that you be here Wednesday evening, eight o'clock. Wear dark clothes and be ready for action."

"So the plan's going down here then?"

"I didn't say that. You just show up like I said. If you're as committed as you say you are, you don't need to know any more just yet."

PJ pushed the platter toward Miles, smiled, and said, "Another sweet roll?"

Chapter 52

Sunday Afternoon
Montfair

Miles drove straight to Montfair from Off the Grid. He found Thumper in his study intensely focused on what appeared to be a very old book.

Thumper looked up. "So, Commando Flanagan, what's the report?"

Miles plopped down into a chair. He twisted his head to relieve the tension in his neck. "Well, yeah, I'm officially a Commando now. All that's gotten me so far is a couple of sweet rolls and an order to show up at the Hendershots' Wednesday night wearing dark clothes. They wouldn't tell me just what the plans are. I don't know if something's going down at Off the Grid, somewhere else, or, for that matter, if anything's going down then at all. Maybe this will be a test run, something like a practice before the real thing. But at least we know they're up to something, and it could be big, something that Doddridge can use."

Thumper sat back and let out a long breath. "Okay. I reckon the next step is to pass this along to Cecelia, let her get the info to Tavina and see what she wants to do."

"Oh, yeah…um, so here's the thing…how do I tell her I made it into their inner circle, or at least pretty close? No way I can convince her that I pulled off that fake breakup scam all by myself."

"Yeah, good point. How about this? Make it sound like whatever's happening Wednesday night is your final test. You haven't said anything to her about this 'Commando' thing, have you?"

"No, pretty sure I never mentioned that."

"Okay. So just tell her it looks like something might be happening Wednesday night. You don't know what or where. Might just be them testing you to be sure you're on the level before they let you in on the real deal. So you don't want anyone getting trigger happy, riding to the rescue only to blow your cover and end up with nothing to use against them. Tell her you'll get back to her as soon as you have something to report."

"Gotcha."

"One more thing before you go," Thumper said. "What's the latest on Bumpers' foot?"

"All cleared up. No reaction to the hoof testers, no heat. I'll get the shoe back on and he should be good to go for this Saturday."

Thumper grunted. "Sounds good." He signaled they were done with a flip of his hand toward the door, and turned his attention back to the old book.

Chapter 53

Monday Afternoon
Kimber Farm

Miles gave Cecelia essentially the same report he'd given Thumper the day before, minus any reference to his newly approved Commando status.

"Wednesday evening, you say," Cecelia mused. "Any idea why that night?"

"Nope. They all clammed up when I tried to ask for more info. Is there a problem with that? Something I should know about?"

She waved off the question. "No, nothing. Probably just a coincidence. Doesn't matter."

Miles' horse-sense radar bleeped. There was something Cecelia wasn't telling him.

"Just let me know what's happening as soon as you can," she said. "Even if it means calling me. At this point, if they haven't noticed that you just happen to show up here every Monday making a fake delivery, they're probably never going to. Nor would they ever think to somehow get their hands on your phone and see who you've been talking to. Or texting."

"So, like, maybe all this cloak-and-dagger shit wasn't necessary?"

"I think it was better to be safe when all this started. We didn't really know who we were dealing with, what they were capable of."

She thought about the mysterious Wednesday night plans. "Maybe we still don't."

"Look," Miles said, "I gotta get back to the shop. Between my regular deliveries, *real* ones, dealing with this UFR crap, and riding for Mister Billington, my inventory duty is getting behind. Shelton's been ordering heavily for what she hopes will be a spring sales rush. I'm gonna be working late, probably the next couple of nights, catching up on all that. I mean, at some point I'm hoping to wrap up this James Bond shit and get back to normal life. Will be nice to still have my job when that happens."

Chapter 54

Tuesday Evening
McKendricks Shop
Crutchfield County Hospital

Miles wasn't the only one who needed to stay late at the shop and catch up on his workload. The heavy ordering also had Muriel working overtime to keep track of the books. She'd managed to limp along with the old software she and Fergus McKendrick, Shelton's grandfather, had used for the past several years. But with his death the previous year, and Ryman's infatuation with his Church of Foxhunting delusion, Shelton had returned to take the helm and steer the family business away from its potential crash on the rocky shores of bankruptcy.

Shelton brought two new attributes to the long line of McKendricks who ran the shop since its founding in 1885. She was the first woman to do so, and the first ever to hold an MBA.

The former made little difference in how the shop operated. The latter did.

One significant aspect of that was a switch to new accounting software. Muriel trusted Shelton's judgment that a change was needed. But, a few months into the change, and already past the age where most in her position would have retired, Muriel was still struggling through the transition. Her devotion to the McKendricks' business was boundless, her high tech skills limited.

Miles thought he'd found a discrepancy with one of the newer items on his inventory list. Seeing the light was still on in the office, he went to see if Muriel could help him sort it out.

"Oh my, yes," she said. "It does look like these numbers don't line up. Perhaps I didn't enter something right. Let me check the invoice." She rose from her desk. "It should be in the file right over here." She walked toward the metal file cabinets lining the back wall of the office.

Miles noticed she wobbled a little as she walked.

"Should be in…in…this…this one…" She put her hand to her jaw. Her knees crumbled.

With his jockey reflexes, Miles was able to catch her before she hit the floor.

"Muriel! What is it? Are you okay?"

She obviously wasn't okay.

"I…can't…can't breathe. Hurts…my chest…hurts."

"Just stay still. I'm calling for help."

The Paradise Gap fire station was three blocks away from the McKendricks' shop and the rescuers were there in mere minutes.

"I'm going with her," Miles declared. He locked up the shop and climbed into the ambulance.

With Muriel stabilized in the emergency room, Miles remained at her side as arrangements were made for a room in the cardiac unit. He held her hand and distracted her with light banter about the shop. She was giggling at his comical impression of Bar when they both saw a tall, well-dressed woman with an authoritative presence striding toward them.

"Aunt Muriel!" Tavina Doddridge exclaimed. "I got here as quickly as I could! Are you okay?"

"Oh, Tavina," Muriel replied, "Don't you worry. Just a little heart flutter. You know I get those sometime. I'll be just fine."

The attending cardiologist appeared. Addressing Tavina, he asked, "And you are?"

"Tavina Doddridge. I'm Mrs. Hudkins niece, and her emergency contact. I came as soon as I got the call."

"And you?" he asked Miles.

"Oh, me? Coworker. I called 911. Came along just until…until…" He pointed to Tavina. "…this lady arrived." He released Muriel's hand and said, "Guess I can be going now."

Muriel reached out for his hand and pulled him back. "Miles, thank you so much. I do believe you saved my life. If you hadn't been there…well, I guess the Lord knew it wasn't my time quite yet and you were his instrument of mercy. God bless you, Miles. You're my hero."

"I…I'm just glad…glad you're gonna be okay," Miles stammered in response. "Don't know what we'd do without you. You're in good hands now."

The doctor turned back to Tavina. "Our initial tests show your aunt had a significant cardiac episode. Too soon to know the full extent, but we advise admitting her for more detailed tests and observation."

As he was talking, Miles slipped past him and started toward the exit. Realizing he'd left his truck at the shop, he took out his phone to call Ansel for a lift.

"Excuse me," Tavina said to the doctor, "I'll be right back."

She caught Miles in the middle of the bustling ER. Dodging her way through staff rushing by, she guided him over toward the central command center where three nurses sat at work stations, alternately entering data and rising to attend to patients.

"This is…um…awkward," Tavina said. "The last place I expected to run into you. I truly appreciate what you did for my aunt."

"All I did was call 911."

"You did so much more than that. You stayed with her, gave her comfort, made sure she wasn't alone in this scary place until I was able to get here."

"Your aunt's a very special lady. Everyone at the shop loves her. We'd be lost without her."

"And if those United Friends of Rockwell people had their way…well, you know better than anyone what they want to do to Black people. People like my Aunt Muriel."

"From what I've seen so far," Miles said, "those assholes couldn't round up a black cat and send it to Africa let alone millions of Black people."

"Of course not. But they could still cause harm in any number of ways. And that's why you need to help me stop them. Cecelia told me something's happening tomorrow night. Have you found out anything more about that?"

"Nope, just that I'm supposed to be at their place at eight o'clock, wearing dark clothes. No idea what's happening after that."

"I have an appointment around that time. But if you find out something important is going to happen, we can skip the filter system. Call me directly if you need help."

She sent her contact info to Miles' phone.

"Look," she said, "I know this hasn't been easy for you. Pretty much out of your lane. But that's a good part of what's made it work to this point."

"Yeah, well, you didn't give me much choice, did you?"

Tavina smiled. "I played the hand I had to work with. You were my ace in the hole."

"I just hope I'm outta this hole soon. If they find out I'm a mole, things could get ugly. Especially with that Ned guy. He can be a pretty scary dude."

"You'll be okay. If something goes wrong, just hit my number and I'll send in the cavalry."

"Yeah, right. The good guys to the rescue."

Tavina returned to Muriel's side and Miles stepped outside to wait for Ansel.

A nurse buzzed around Muriel's bed, checking on vitals. Muriel noticed her ID badge showed a first name but only the initial letter of her last name.

"Thank you…Jessica," Muriel said, squinting to read the nurse's name.

"Are you comfortable, Mrs. Hudkins? Can I get you anything?"

"No, dear. I'm fine. Bless you for doing this work. Nurses truly are angels."

Jessica smiled, nodded, and moved on to her next patient.

Muriel turned to Tavina. "Why do you think she doesn't have her full name on her badge? Just the letter 'P'?"

"It's common policy these days. There have been cases where patients or family members of patients thought a hospital worker was responsible for a bad outcome, tracked that person down and harassed them. Or worse. So to keep some level of anonymity, they show an initial for the last name."

"My goodness. Who would do such a thing? Especially to someone who dedicates their life to helping others. What is our world coming to?"

Tavina patted Muriel's hand. "You have no idea, sweetheart. But some of us are trying to stop that sort of thing, in places and with people you could never imagine."

Chapter 55

Wednesday Evening
Off the Grid
Crutchfield County Backroad

Margaret, PJ, Rocky, and Ned stood before the portraits of Edwin Hendershot and George Lincoln Rockwell.

"Tonight," Margaret said, "justice will be done to right a terrible *in*justice. And a blow will be struck to honor the Commander's vision of what America should be, how God intended it to be. Deo Vindice!"

"Deo Vindice!" the others shouted.

Turning to Ned, she asked, "You've scoped out the terrain, got the plan for where everyone will be?"

"Thanks to PJ coming up with the address from Windy's old records," he replied, "it was easy to find. It's perfect. Hardly any traffic. No street lights. The house is well back from the road, so we can get set up without drawing any attention."

"And your people are good to go?"

"My people are confirmed," Ned replied. "At my signal, they'll meet us, pick up the package, and take it from there."

"I still think we should let Miles know what the mission's about," Rocky said.

"No way!" Ned shot back. "Yeah, he's shown he's committed to The Cause…to a point. But what we're doing tonight is a whole different level. We can't know for sure what he'll do. He could blow the whole thing. I've worked out a perfect role for him. He'll be the necessary fifth wheel, but no way he can screw things up if he turns out to be a coward."

"He's no coward!" PJ countered. "I'd like to see you get on one of those horses like the one he rides!"

Ned scoffed. "Child's play compared to what we're about to do."

"Knock it off, you two!" Margaret ordered. "I agree with Ned. I think using him as the bait is a great idea. The target might recognize one of us." She gestured toward herself and her children. Poking a finger at Ned, she added, "And you're too scary looking."

This elicited a nervous giggle from the group.

The front gate intercom buzzed.

"He's here," Margaret said. She took a deep breath. "Okay, y'all. We've been waiting a long damn time for this. Justice is about to happen!"

Miles was ushered into the dining room, dressed as ordered. He noticed some of the chairs were missing from their usual places around the table.

"Rocky, Margaret, and me are going in Rocky's van," Ned said. "You follow us in your truck, Flanagan. PJ will ride with you."

"Where are we going?" Miles asked.

"You'll find out when we get there," Ned shot back.

He stretched his hand out and the others placed a hand atop his. "Let's do this! Deo Vindice!" he shouted.

"Deo Vindice!" came the thunderous reply.

****

Miles thought he knew every backroad in Crutchfield County but the van led him down narrow, twisting roads he'd never seen. He tried to squeeze some info from PJ about where they were going and what they were planning to do, but she was unusually tightlipped. All she said was, "Keep driving. You'll find out."

The van stopped along the edge of an unpaved road where thick woods lined both sides. Miles pulled up behind the van. The group assembled between the vehicles.

"Okay," Ned said, "y'all know the plan. Rocky, you and Margaret take the van down that way. There's a logging road on the right just past the driveway to the house on the left. Back the van in there. Miles, turn your truck around here and wait. It's kinda tight, but your little piece of shit can do it." He nodded toward Miles' Ford Ranger. "PJ will let you know what you need to do and when. I'll be in my spot in the woods over here." He reached out a hand toward Miles. "Give me your phone, Flanagan."

"What?" Miles asked. "Why do you need my phone?"

"Call it insurance. Gimme the damn phone!"

Miles looked at PJ, hoping she'd intervene.

Her response was firm. "Give it to him."

"Fine." He handed his phone to Ned.

"Okay," Ned ordered. He looked at his watch. "Get to your places."

Rocky found the logging road entrance and backed the van into place.

Ned disappeared into the woods.

Miles and PJ got back in his truck.

"What the hell is going on?" he asked.

"Are you committed to The Cause?" was her reply.

"Yeah, sure. You know I am."

"Do I? Well, we'll soon find out. A car will be pulling up behind us. When that happens, turn on your flashers, get out, and wave like you need help. Got it?"

"Yeah, I think I can handle that."

"Good." She reached over and put a hand on his arm. "Y'know, if wasn't for you, this wouldn't have been possible. Or it would have been a whole lot harder figuring out how to pull it off."

"Me? What did I have to do with this?"

"Remember the comment you overheard about a certain person being good to her mother? Visiting her every Wednesday evening?"

Holy crap! he thought. *Tavina! This is about Tavina?*

"When I told the others about that," PJ continued, "Mama remembered my father had serviced an old oil heat system for someone named 'Doddridge.' I found the address in his Rolodex and, well, here we are. All thanks to you."

A thousand thoughts tumbled through Miles' mind. How could he have known that one offhand remark would lead to this. Without realizing it, he'd helped them lay their trap. And, of all people, the trap was for Tavina.

After what seemed like the longest ten minutes of his life, Miles saw headlights behind them moving away from a small house set back from the road.

"Flashers on!" PJ ordered. "Now get out and flag her down!"

He climbed out of the truck, stood by its side, and waved his arms.

The car stopped.

A dark figure bolted from the woods and yanked the car door open. Miles could see a raised hand holding what appeared to be a pistol pointed at the driver.

Rocky's van came racing up the rough road and blocked the car from behind.

In the glare of the van's headlights, Miles could see Ned ordering the driver out of the car.

"Undo that goddamn seatbelt!" Ned ordered. "Or I'll shoot your Black ass right here!"

He reached in, grabbed the driver, and yanked her out of the car.

To Miles' dismay, it was indeed Tavina Doddridge.

"Do you know who I am?" Tavina said with an arrogant tone.

"We know too damn well who you are," Ned hissed. "And tonight you start to pay for what you did."

Miles caught the look of shock with a twist of a question on her face just before Ned slapped a strip of tape over her mouth and slipped a cloth sack over her head. He then pulled her hands behind her back and clipped on handcuffs.

Miles stood by his truck, dumbfounded by what he was witnessing.

PJ jumped out from the other side and ran to where Ned held Tavina.

"We got her!" she shouted, leaping up and down. "We got the bitch! Justice will be served!"

Margaret approached from the other side. She put her mouth close to Tavina's head. "If it wasn't for you, my husband would be alive," she hissed. "But he's not. And tonight you'll begin a very long time of paying for it. Verrryyyy long!"

"Flanagan," Ned called out, "get your ass over here." He pointed his pistol to the back door of Tavina's car. "Get in and slide over."

Miles knew he had no choice but to obey. The odds were four to one against him, and at least two of them—Ned and Margaret—were armed. No chance for him to be the hero. He climbed into the car's backseat.

Ned pushed Tavina in after him.

PJ got in the driver's seat.

"All right, y'all," Ned shouted. "Let's roll!"

Margaret got into Miles' truck, Rocky hopped back in his van, and Ned slid into the backseat next to Tavina.

"Watch her from your side," Ned said to Miles. "No telling what this bitch might try to pull. And I don't want to have to shoot her. She's more valuable to us alive. And we've got some serious score settling to do." He leaned into Tavina's shoulder. "You hear that, bitch? You behave yourself and you might at least get out of this alive. Not where anyone will know where you are. But alive…sorta."

The three vehicles sped away.

Chapter 56

Wednesday Evening
Off the Grid

PJ parked Tavina's car in front of the old Hendershot warehouse.

Ned stepped out of the car, reached back in and pulled Tavina out.

"C'mon, Flanagan. You're about to witness something special. The first step in fulfilling The Commander's vision of what America should be."

With a firm grip on Tavina's arm, Ned ushered her into the empty storage area where Miles had performed his Rockwell birthday skit. He unlocked the handcuffs, pushed her against a metal support pole, and then relocked the cuffs behind it. He then yanked the cloth sack from her head, but left the tape over her mouth.

As her eyes adjusted, she saw five wooden chairs lined up facing her.

"All right, y'all," Ned said. "Let the jury be seated."

The five kidnappers took their seats, Margaret at the middle, Rocky on one side, PJ on the other. Ned and Miles took the seats at each end.

"Do you know who we are?" Margaret asked.

Tavina nodded.

"Do you know why you're here?"

She shook her head.

"Think, you bitch! Hendershot. Edwin Hendershot! Sound familiar?"

Tavina closed her eyes and made a slow nod.

"How about Jericho Rolfe? That name ring a bell?"

Another reluctant nod.

Margaret rose and approached Tavina. With their faces almost touching, Margaret continued in a mocking tone. "Oh, that poor boy. So underprivileged. No father in the home. His momma struggling to raise him. He fell in with a bad crowd. Made a mistake. He didn't mean to hurt the Uber driver. He was just desperate because society failed him. But he's on the straight and narrow now. So, your honor, the Commonwealth recommends a year's probation and six months of community service."

Margaret took one step back. "Bullshit!"

Tavina felt flecks of saliva hitting her face.

"Did you even bother to look at his rap sheet?" Margaret asked. "What y'all call his priors? By the time he savagely beat that poor Uber driver he was already a hardened criminal. Probation and community service, my ass! What the fuck were you thinking? Oh, I've heard about your type. It's not the criminal, it's the system. It's out to get Black men. And you think you're gonna fix that. Let 'em off because it ain't their fault."

She stood, hands on hips, staring at Tavina, disgust hardening her face.

"And then what happened? Your precious Jericho, your poster boy for 'Let 'em off lightly'.What did he do not even one month later? You know what he did. He thought he'd steal himself a nice van. Just sitting there, parked along the sidewalk. It was the middle of the night. No one around. What he didn't know was an honest, hardworking man, a man who went out on that freezing cold night to help someone else, was in the back of the van. Maybe he was looking for something he needed for the job, a tool or a part. We'll never know. But what we do know is that when your poor little Jericho realized he was there, he pulled out his gun and shot my husband dead!"

Margaret studied the pleading look in Tavina's eyes, a look that said *I'm sorry*. But she would get no mercy from Margaret Hendershot.

"So my husband, my children's father, is gone. And all because you put a murderous criminal back on the street. So now, you're going to be the one taken *off* the street, so you can't harm any more honest American families. Some place far, far away. A place where your fancy degrees and expensive clothes won't matter. A place where Commander Rockwell thinks you should be. Yes, we're going to make that happen."

Now Miles understood PJ's reaction to seeing Tavina at the races. He wasn't much for following the news. He faintly recalled hearing that Windy Hendershot had died. But whatever happened had little bearing on his life. It simply meant someone different would be handling the HVAC service at the shop. And that had nothing to do with his job there.

Margaret continued. "Commander Rockwell…that name mean anything to you?"

Tavina shrugged and cocked her head to one side. She hoped Margaret would understand that to mean *Maybe*.

"George Lincoln Rockwell," Margaret said. "*Commander* Rockwell, his rank from his service in the US Navy. A true visionary. He saw how our beloved nation was on the road to ruin because of race mixing and abandoning the Christian principles America was founded on. He tried to sound the alert that you and all your kind should be sent back to Africa. Y'all don't belong here. You weren't supposed to be here. And it's time to fix that.

"So far, the United Friends of Rockwell is just the five of us. We may not be able to round up all y'all and ship you back where you belong. But we can at least start with *you*. And here's how that's gonna happen."

She turned, nodded to Ned, and retook her seat as he stepped forward.

****

Ned smiled pleasantly, something Miles had never seen. "Let me first say we appreciate how thoughtful and caring you've been to your mother." The sickly sweet tone gave Miles the shivers. "If it hadn't been for your weekly visits, something that we could rely on like clockwork, we'd have had a much harder time making this happen." He pointed toward Miles. "Happily, we have our newest member, Miles Flanagan, to thank for tipping us off about that."

The question in Tavina's eyes sent a shiver through Miles. How could he have known his offhand remark to PJ would lead to this?

Turning back to Tavina, Ned continued. "I'm sure your mother was grateful for your loving care. Too bad you're never going to see her again."

He paused and let that last remark do its job.

"It's also worth noting," he continued, "that the man whose death you're responsible for helped keep your mother warm on freezing winter nights. Oh, yes, Windy Hendershot went to the little ramshackle house down that beat up old road to service her ancient oil heating system. And…you know what? He never charged her. There was a card in his Rolodex with her name and address, and the word 'Comp' scribbled on it. You know what 'comp' means, right?"

A weak nod.

"So here we are, thanks to Miles tipping us off about you being there every Wednesday evening and that Rolodex card showing us how to find you.

"And now I'd like to tell you a story," he continued. "When I was young, I wanted to help change the world. I thought most Americans were blind to the suffering that goes on in so many places. Especially places like Africa. So I signed up to do relief work over there. Doesn't matter which country. They're all miserable shitholes. You ever been to Africa?"

Tavina shook her head.

"I didn't think so. Well, let me tell you, the place they sent me to could be the poster country for the shithole title. I mean, like, literal shit everywhere. Here's a question for you. Do you support genital mutilation of young girls?"

An emphatic head shake accented with a furrowed brow.

"Well, you'd better not try to tell them that. They'd just think you were an arrogant Westerner trying to undermine their culture. I'm sure that when you were in whatever over-rated, high-priced college you went to—and probably at the taxpayers' expense because, well, y'know—you learned the word 'kleptocracy.' Right?"

She nodded.

"The people over there have that down to an art form. Nothing gets done without the required payoff. Probably the worst part of that is the impact it has on the health care system." His thin lips curled into a feral snarl. "'*Health care.*' Now there's a misguided term. *Poor health* is the norm and nobody *cares*. Even basic meds are hard to come by, the good stuff next to impossible. But I thought I could beat the system, break the agency's rules, go rogue for the right reason. I hooked up with a contact to the black market. Which is pretty much the only market. I doctored the books—which was about the only kind of 'doctoring' going on over there—to pay off the supplier dude. It worked well for a while. And I got in tight with the black market guys, actually became solid friends with one of them. He's since risen to the top of the 'shadow economy' for the whole country."

He held out his arm, his forearm exposed. "See that tattoo?" He pointed to a quartet of four-pointed stars. "It's the symbol in their language for the word 'fence.' It stands for safety and security, things you should care about to protect your family. They're really big on family stuff over there. My contact encouraged me to get this, to let others know I was one of them." He paused, stared at his tattoo, and huffed. "That other use of the word 'fence' in English had no meaning in their language. But I found it amusing."

He rolled his sleeve back down and continued. "Of course, I eventually got busted for violating agency policies. Didn't matter what my motives were. I never pocketed a cent of the money. Every bit of it went to pay for meds and supplies we couldn't get through approved channels. They fired my ass and sent me home. They decided not to charge me with embezzlement because it was clear I didn't keep any of the money. But the firing for cause was a matter of public record. And it didn't explain the whole picture, what the money was being used for. Just that I'd 'misappropriated' agency funds. That's caused me grief ever since, like when I'm applying for a job as an HVAC tech and that comes up. So they're thinking, 'Shit, if this guy did something like that, can we still get him covered under our bonding policy? Like, if he's working in someone's house and something goes missing, is that gonna come back to bite us? Better pass on this guy.'

"But Windy Hendershot was willing to look past that. He took me on as an apprentice, gave me the chance to show I could do the job. And when it was time for Rocky to start learning the trade, Windy gave me a glowing endorsement to Mister Jessup, said I was ready to move up to the big time, better pay and better benefits than what he could offer."

As Ned paused, Miles saw a glimmer of humility he didn't think Ned possessed.

The glimmer quickly faded and Ned's expression returned to that of the hardened misanthrope.

"So now I was back in the good old U.S. of A. And what do I see? Blacks complaining everywhere about how badly they're treated, how most whites in America are terrible racists. Constantly bringing up slavery, something that ended long ago and no one alive today had anything to do with. I got to thinking, if those people could spend a year in a shithole country like I was in, they'd be begging to get back to America and maybe stop screaming about racism all the time, maybe realize there's no better place for a Black person to be than in this country.

"And guess what happened?" he said, his arms waving. "Along comes your boy Jericho and…" He pointed his hand at Tavina with index finger out and thumb up. "Boom! Blows away the most decent man I ever knew." He glanced over at Margaret, then turned back to Tavina. "And then Margaret here…*Mama Hendershot*…introduced me to the Commander's teachings. It all makes so much sense.

"So now we start with you. I've kept in touch with my old friend from the black market days, the guy who now runs the whole operation in that shithole country. And you're gonna get to meet him real soon. He's going to take you on a nice cruise, all the way to the other side of the ocean, to a place where, believe it or not, slavery is still a common practice. Yeah, it's a cultural thing for them, so we can't really criticize them, can we?" He moved close to her, laid his hand on her abdomen, pressed his body against her side, and put his mouth next to her ear. "And you are gonna be one hot commodity in that market. Some obese, smelly, grotesque Black potentate is gonna snatch you right up for his harem. And he has his own private army with guards who will assure no one ever even knows you're there." Ned chuckled when a random thought struck him. "Shit, and you don't even like men anyway. Well, maybe your lady harem-mates will let you do your lesbo thing with them."

He stepped away from her and pulled out his phone. "All I have to do is make a quick call and my old friend will be on his way to pick you up."

Before Ned could enter the number, his phone sounded with an incoming call. The screen showed the name "Jessica Potts."

"Hey, cuz," Ned said. "Kinda tied up right now." He looked over at Tavina and gave her a leering wink. "Can I call you back? What? Some guy named Miles Flanagan? Yeah, I know him." His gaze shot over to Miles, who felt his innards suddenly tighten. "No shit! With who? And they said what? Well, that's interesting. Yeah, thanks for the tip."

His voice calm and icy, he said, "That was my cousin Jessica. She's an ER nurse. Says she was on the command desk last night and overheard a conversation she thought I should know about."

He pulled Miles' phone from his pocket, clicked on contacts, and typed in a name. He looked at Miles, then at Tavina, and back to Miles. "Tell me, Flanagan, why do you have *her* contact info in *your* phone?"

Tavina looked down and shook her head. What a stupid mistake!

Ned blew out a long breath. He then focused a narrow sideways stare on Miles. “We have a mole.”

Chapter 57

Wednesday Evening
Off the Grid

PJ launched from her seat and flew at Miles. "I'll scratch your fucking eyes out! You bastard!"

Rocky caught her in mid-launch just as her fingernails were about to dig into Miles' face.

"How could you!" she cried, her hands scratching the air as her brother lifted her away from her target. "You fucking snake! You led me on, led us all on. You've been a fake from the start! We should have known…should have…" Rocky released her and she crumbled back into her chair.

Margaret was next in line. Unlike her daughter, she remained cool and calm. She stood in front of Miles, a silent, ominous presence, one hand resting on her holstered Luger. "Rocky," she said coolly, "search the little bastard, make sure he ain't wired."

Rocky grabbed Miles by the shirt collar and yanked him up. He ripped his shirt open, buttons flying, and felt all around his front and back for any trace of a device. He then squeezed his hands over Miles' pants. He felt something metallic in one pocket.

"What's this?" Rocky asked.

"Keys," Miles croaked out in response. "I ain't wired."

Rocky pushed the smaller man back into the chair and said, "I guess he's clean."

"He ain't clean!" PJ shouted. "He's a dirty, deceitful, lying son-of-a-bitch! Mama, you should just off him now!"

"Jesus!" Rocky said. "We can't do that! It'd be murder. Bad enough what we're doing with *her*." He pointed toward Tavina.

"So you think that's *bad*?" PJ asked. "You're not getting cold feet are you?"

"No!" Rocky replied in protest. "Of course not. You know I'm totally in on this."

"Knock it off, you two!" Margaret demanded. "The important thing now is to find out if the plan's in jeopardy." She turned to Miles, shirtless and cowering in the chair, and withdrew her pistol. She pointed it at his leg. "Tell me the truth. For every lie you tell, I'm putting a bullet in one of your limbs. First the legs, then the arms. You understand I'm not joking, right?"

"She made me do it!" Miles shouted, pointing at Tavina. He looked around Margaret and said to Rocky, "That thing you said y'all knew about, the bullet in old lady McKendrick's kitchen ceiling. She said she'd charge me with attempted murder, send me to prison for a long damn time, if I didn't cooperate. She thought y'all might be up to something, needed someone to get on the inside to find out. I was hoping that was all just bullshit, that y'all weren't gonna do anything, like, really illegal. Just some protests, passing out pamphlets and stuff. Harmless shit. Then I could tell her we got nothing, she'd drop it, I'd be off the hook, and she'd leave y'all alone." He looked up at Margaret with pleading eyes. "Then no harm done, right? I never thought y'all were gonna do something like this."

Margaret turned to Tavina. "Is that true?"

Tavina remained motionless. She let Miles stew for several seconds. Then she closed her eyes and nodded.

Margaret holstered her Luger.

After letting the Hendershots vent, Ned stepped forward and said, "Now y'all see why I wanted to be cautious with the little shit. My experience in Africa sharpened my ability to sense when someone's trying to fuck with me. Those people are masters of deception. They have to be to survive in that world where life is cheap. I had a feeling that something wasn't right. That's why I insisted we not give him the full plan in advance. And why I took his phone."

He walked over to Miles and calmly said, "So what to do with him now? He'd be no use to the Africans. A scrawny little white man? Not worth shit in the slave market. If we off him here, we'd have to deal with getting rid of the body. And that's a pain in the ass, too risky. But, one way or another, we gotta make him disappear." He rubbed his chin and considered the options. "Maybe we can cut a deal with my pals. Take a few bucks less than what they're paying for her…" A thumb jerk toward Tavina. "…and in exchange take him along and somewhere out in the ocean toss him overboard. Problem solved."

"We can't do that!" Rocky insisted. "This is going too far! Mama, think about it. Selling her to the slavers is one thing. She deserves it. Killing Miles? C'mon, we're not killers. Besides, he's a *white* man!"

"He may be white," his mother shot back, "but he ain't on our side. He was working for *her*, the Black bitch responsible for your father's death. If it hadn't been for Ned's cousin tipping us off, he'd have gone to the police first chance he got and we'd all be screwed."

Rocky collapsed into a chair, put his hands over his face, and began to shake and sob.

"Oh, for Christ's sake," an exasperated PJ said. "I never thought I'd see my big brother act like such a pussy. Pull yourself together. Ned's right. He's gotta disappear. I like the dump-him-at-sea idea. No mess, no trace. Boom, done."

Miles hopped up. "No! Look, we can all get what we want! Y'all can send her off to be a slave somewhere. Yeah, okay, maybe she does deserve something like that. I'm good with it. And that gets her off my ass too. She can't go after me if she's held captive somewhere in Africa, right? So it's a win-win. We all benefit from getting rid of her and y'all don't have to deal with the messy business of getting rid of my scrawny little white ass."

"Nice try," Ned said. "But…nope. Too risky to leave you running loose. How do we know someone else in Doddridge's office won't take up the case and come after you next? You think she was acting strictly solo on this? Shit no. And you've already proven you ain't man enough to stand up and not cave to some government hack lawyer trying to rattle your ass. Sorry, Flanagan. You've screwed the pooch. No one to blame but your sorry ass self."

Rocky bolted up from this chair. "No! We can't do this. Miles really is one of us." He looked at Miles. "Those things I heard you say to Ansel, that coloreds are no good and should all be sent back, that only one race matters, and BLM's a pain in the ass. You even tossed in a hit on A-Rabs for good measure. And the old Polack guy even said you're a racist, and wants nothing to do with you." Turning to Ned with a pleading look, he continued. "All that's gotta mean something, right? He had no idea I heard what he said, or who I was other than the HVAC repair guy. Sure sounded to me like he's on our side and this goddamn bitch forced him into being a mole. He didn't balk tonight, right? Did just what he was told, didn't miss a step."

"All right," Ned said. "Maybe we can figure out another way. Tell you what, go out to my truck, there's a gym bag in the back with some stuff in it. Grab two sets of handcuffs and bring them to me."

Rocky raised an eyebrow.

"Go!" Ned commanded.

The instant Rocky was through the door, Ned gestured to Margaret and PJ. They formed a tight huddle and Ned whispered instructions. The two women smiled and nodded.

They moved apart as Rocky returned with the handcuffs.

Ned saw the disgust on PJ's face.

"You never know when you might meet someone," he said, "who…well, y'know…is into certain kinds of stuff. And I like to be prepared."

"Stuff?" Margaret asked. "What kinda stuff?"

"You don't want to know, Mama," PJ said.

Ned took the cuffs from Rocky and turned to Miles. "C'mere, Flanagan," he ordered.

Miles, thinking he just might survive this ordeal, obeyed.

Ned slapped the end of one set of cuffs on Miles' left wrist, the other set on his right. With a nod of his head, he said to Rocky, "Help me get him over to this other pole."

The two larger men marched Miles over to a support pole several feet away from the one that held Tavina. Margaret and PJ followed. Ned positioned Miles facing the pole.

"We're gonna do this a little different," Ned said. "Rocky, get hold of your little buddy's right hand."

Rocky was confused about where Ned was going with this but reached out with his left arm and did as he was told.

"Good," Ned said. "Now get his left hand."

At the instant Rocky's left hand touched Miles' right hand, Ned clamped the other end of the cuff over Rocky's left wrist. PJ did the same on the other side securing Rocky's right wrist to Miles' left wrist.

Miles and Rocky stood facing each other, a heavy metal pole between them, handcuffed together, dumbfounded by what had just happened.

"That should hold 'em till we decide what to do," Ned said. "PJ, get your brother's phone. And the keys to the van."

The threesome stepped back and admired their handiwork.

"No offense, Margaret," Ned said, "but your boy has a room temperature IQ."

"Don't I know it," she replied in disgust. "And he's sure shown it tonight."

Ned looked at Miles. "We know the plan for you, Flanagan. I just have to call my contact first to make the deal. As for you, Rockwell, that's a tougher question. You've shown weakness, and we can't have that, family or not. But the family part does complicate things. Whatever we decide, it's best you not participate in the rest of the plan. You might have another weak moment, a crisis of conscience, and screw the whole deal. We can't risk that."

He then stepped over to Tavina. "You, at least, are going to live. If you can call where you're going living." To PJ and Margaret he said, "Let's get to the house and discuss our options before I make the call. Let these three have some time together before they're sent their separate ways. Wherever those ways might be."

Chapter 58

Wednesday Evening
Off the Grid

"Shit, Flanagan," Rocky snarled, "I fell for your bullshit right from the start. Now you've screwed us both. I just don't get it. You really seemed to be on the level. I mean, that shit I heard you saying in Billington's barn. You couldn't have known I was listening. And the other stuff, like the Commander's birthday thing. Especially the other night, Billington's daughter and her boyfriend breaking up…I mean…how'd you…how could you have…?" His voice trailed off in a dribble of awed confusion.

Tavina listened with rapt attention. She knew about the Rockwell birthday skit from Miles' report to Cecelia, although nothing about the help he had to make it such a success. But she had no idea what was said in the Billington barn nor about any breakup.

Miles took a deep breath. "I can explain all that. First, what you *thought* you heard me say…I didn't say the '*coloreds*' are no good and should be sent back. I said '*colors*.' I was talking about what I wear when I'm racing. They're called 'jockey silks' and each owner has their own custom design and colors. Mister Billington ordered new silks with the Montfair design, but the *colors* weren't right. So he had to send them back."

Rocky bowed his head and whispered, "Christ. How stupid."

Miles continued. "The only race that matters? The really big money and bragging rights come at the end of the season…the Gold Cup. That's the one we all shoot for, the race that really matters."

Rocky groaned.

"BLM? A pain in the ass? For a lot of us around here, those letters stand for 'Bureau of Land Management.' Ansel has a section of pasture that the government is trying to have declared wetlands, which would mean he can't fence it off or do anything with it. It's *that* BLM that's giving him shit about it."

Rocky blew out a long, slow breath. "So, what have you got against A-rabs?" he asked.

"Oh, that. We'd just come from shoeing a couple of Arabian horses…*Arabs* for short. Some folks love 'em. Personally, I got no use for 'em."

"Yeah," Rocky said, a sliver of hope in his voice, "but what about the old Polish guy telling me you're a racist. How do you explain that?"

"I got no idea why he'd say that. He doesn't much care for me, probably would prefer I not be around. But that's because of something else, nothing to do with racism."

"So that other stuff that made us believe you were on the level?" Rocky asked. "We all bought your performance about the mixed marriage thing. But, Jesus, what I saw the other night, those two breaking up. Was that all a set up too? How'd you do it?"

Miles glanced over at Tavina. "Um, well, I had help. Mostly from Mister Billington. And Miss Musgrove, also his sister Myrna. And, um, Miss Elizabeth and her boyfriend."

Tavina rolled her eyes and shook her head.

"Also a little help from Bar, pep talk kinda stuff," Miles added.

She leaned her head against the metal pole and gazed up at the ceiling. The little shit wasn't supposed to tell anyone, especially not those people!

"And Bar…he gave me…" Miles' head jerked back and his eyes opened wide. "Holy shit! His medal! His lucky charm! It's in my pocket, under my keys. It's our way outta this, if we can do it in time."

"Do what?"

"Get these cuffs off and get the fuck outta here before they come back." He reached down into the right pocket of his jeans, tugging Rocky's left hand along with it. It took some effort but he managed to get his fingers on Bar's medal and pull it out. Using his thumb, he unhooked the pin.

"Work with me here," he said.

With their hands cuffed together around the pole, Rocky had to squeeze hard against it so Miles could reach his right hand over to the cuff on his left wrist.

"I'm pretty sure Ned didn't double lock these. If I remember…Bar said…stick the pin in the hole…and…"

Click! The cuff on Miles' left hand opened. Switching the medal to his left hand, he reached over and unlocked the cuff on this right wrist, freeing him from Rocky.

"Holy shit!" Rocky said. "Fucking brilliant! Let's roll."

Rocky started toward the side door. "My dad's old truck's parked out here. Keys are in the visor."

Miles shot him a questioning look.

"Like anyone's gonna try to steal something from this place," Rocky said.

Miles turned his attention to Tavina. She pulled against her restraints, eyes wide and pleading. Muffled sounds of distress struggled to be heard through the tape over her mouth.

"What about her?" Miles asked.

"Fuck her! This is all her fault. Let the slavers take her!"

"Can't do it," Miles replied.

He stepped in front of her, reached up, and took hold of one corner of the tape. "If I let you loose, do you promise to forget about any charges against me?"

She responded with a stream of emphatic nods and more muffled sounds.

"Jesus, Flanagan! Leave her. They could come back any second."

Miles ignored his pleas. "This is gonna hurt," he said. "Sorry."

He yanked the tape from her mouth in one quick motion.

She wanted to cry out but kept quiet.

Miles unlocked the handcuffs.

Her knees buckled and she started to collapse.

He grabbed her arm and together they headed to the side door where Rocky waited.

The trio climbed into the truck, a classic Silverado that had been his father's pride and joy. With only a bench front seat, Miles boosted Tavina into the cab and then hopped in next to her.

With the headlights off, Rocky drove up to the front gates and pressed the exit button. As soon as the gates opened, he switched on the headlights and stomped the accelerator.

"Hang on!" he hollered. "I'm takin' the shortcut!"

Miles and Tavina were slammed back as the truck launched forward.

****

"All right," Ned said into his phone, "you'll take the little problem off our hands along with the main package. You're good with the directions, right? Yeah, it's an unmarked road. I set an orange cone on one side. Turn in there and it'll take you to the gates. We'll be waiting in the warehouse."

Turning to Margaret and PJ, he said, "My old African buddy is on the way, should be here soon. He agreed to take Miles along with…"

His words were cut short by the sound of a roaring truck engine. He ran to the front window just in time to see Rocky's truck passing through the gate. He caught a glimpse of three heads in the vehicle. "Holy shit! They've gotten loose!"

With PJ and Margaret close behind, Ned sprinted through the front door, leapt down the porch stairs, and vaulted into his truck, a

Ram 1500 quad cab. Margaret barely had time to climb into the passenger seat, with PJ in the back, before Ned backed out, threw the truck in drive, and took off in pursuit.

The gates, set on a short timer, started to close. Ned almost made it through cleanly. He grimaced as he heard the teeth-jarring sound of metal scraping metal as the gate latches dug into the sides of his truck.

Rocky saw headlights closing in from behind.

Ned's truck, with a 395 horsepower engine, could easily outrun the vintage Silverado.

The crack of a gunshot sounded.

Miles and Tavina looked behind them to see Margaret hanging precariously out the window, her Luger raised and ready for another shot. They both ducked as a second bullet whizzed by.

"Miles!" Rocky shouted. "My dad's pistol is in the glove box. Get it and shoot back!"

Miles hesitated.

"C'mon, Flanagan! This ain't your pretend acting shit! This is the real fucking thing! You wanna live or not?"

Miles flipped the glove box open, reached in, and pulled out a rare 1980 Smith & Wesson 520 revolver, .357 magnum.

Another shot from Margaret hit the truck's tailgate. That spurred Miles to action. He twisted around and leaned out the window. The only way he could draw a straight beam on Ned's truck was to shoot with his left hand and hold on to the window frame with his right hand. He'd carried two replica 1861 Navy Colt revolvers in the Rangers' reenacting battles, one in each hand, blasting away with his reins loose on a well-trained horse. That skill served him well. He took aim and fired. The recoil, much stronger than his Navy Colts, knocked him back against the window frame.

The passenger side headlight of Ned's truck exploded in a shower of shattered glass. The light went dark.

Ned reflexively swerved hard to his left. The sudden move launched Margaret halfway through the window.

PJ reached over from the back seat to grab her. "Be careful, dammit!" she shouted at Ned.

Margaret held on and righted herself. "That motherfucker is shooting at us with Windy's pistol! I'll nail his ass! Hold the goddamn truck steady!"

She took slow, careful aim at Miles. As she was about to pull the trigger, she was distracted by headlights turning in from the state road just ahead. At the same moment, Ned's truck hit another bump, impossible to avoid on the rarely used road. Margaret's shot sailed harmlessly into the night sky.

The approaching vehicle stopped, then reversed back onto the state road. The move left just enough room for Rocky to steer between the van and the woods. With the tires now on smooth pavement, he floored the old truck's pedal and took off at full speed.

The driver of the vehicle, a van, and his three passengers caught a glimpse of three people in the truck—two white men, a Black woman between them.

At a command from the man in the passenger seat, the driver pulled the van forward and blocked access to the paved road.

Ned slammed on the brakes to avoid crashing into the van.

Its passenger door opened and a tall Black man stepped out. His commanding presence conveyed the impression that he could have stopped the truck with a simple lift of his hand.

Ned, Margaret, and PJ tumbled out of the truck.

At the tall man's signal, two other Black men—expressionless faces perched on massive physiques—emerged from the van and flanked their leader.

Margaret waved her pistol at them and shouted, "Move that goddamn van! Or I'll shoo…"

Before she could finish the word, one of the bodyguards, with barely perceptible movement, reached out and took the pistol from her hand.

She froze in stunned shock, unable to speak.

"Well, my old friend," the leader said to Ned. "It appears you've encountered a problem delivering the goods. I believe that was 'The

Package' that just went flying by. And perhaps the small man was to be our bonus gift. Yes?"

"We can still catch them!" Ned pleaded. "My truck can outrun that old piece of shit any day. Just move your van and we can…"

The man wagged a finger, tut-tutted, and said, "Ah, that would be very risky now. The agreement was to meet at your—how do you call it?—'Off the Grid' compound, deep in the woods, well-fortified. We did not agree to a high speed pursuit on open roads where law enforcement might be." He gestured toward the men with him. "Should my associates and I be apprehended here in your country, it would not go well for us. I am sorry, but the deal is off. We will not be paying you for goods you have not delivered."

He motioned toward one of the bodyguards who reached back and opened the van's door.

"I wish you success with your endeavors," he said with a comically gracious tone. "Perhaps my country will soon be swarming with millions of those you feel are unfit to live in America." He gazed at each of the remaining three UFR members in turn, shrugged, and added, "Perhaps not."

He climbed into the van. The bodyguards took their places in the back.

The leader took one more look at the sorrowful threesome. He shook his head and, with heavy disgust, said, "White Supremacists. What a joke!" A word from him to the driver and the van rolled away.

As the consequences they were about to face began to set in, PJ broke down in convulsive sobs.

Margaret looked at Ned and said, "That nigger took my gun."

Ned shook his head, then gazed down the dark, tree-lined road as the van's taillights slowly disappeared.

Chapter 59

Friday Evening
Montfair

Thumper, Janey, Myrna, and Elizabeth sat in the Montfair family room watching the Friday evening news.

"We go now," the anchor said, "to Tobias Johnson for his exclusive interview with Tavina Doddridge, Assistant Commonwealth's Attorney for Crutchfield County, who recently survived a horrific kidnapping incident."

"Miss Doddridge," Tobias began, "it's been less than forty-eight hours since you went through this. Thank you for speaking with us. How are you holding up?"

"To be honest, it was quite an ordeal. I was highjacked while leaving my mother's house and taken to a remote location. If you can believe this, the kidnappers' plan was to sell me into slavery in Africa."

"Remarkable! Did they target you specifically or was it just a case of being in the wrong place at the wrong time?"

"I was clearly their target. You see, I'd been monitoring this group, the United Friends of Rockwell, for some time. They base their beliefs on the outlandish rantings of George Lincoln Rockwell, founder of the American Nazi Party. He preached that America was only for white Christians. This was back in the '60s. He and his 'stormtroopers' wanted to round up all Black people in this country and ship them to Africa. I knew his modern day followers needed to be stopped before they caused any real harm. So they must have considered me the main obstacle to their plan, their worst enemy, and they had to get me out of the way first."

"Tell us about your remarkable escape."

"To be honest, I owe my life to one brave, resourceful man, Miles Flanagan. Miles volunteered to work his way into the dangerous group to serve as my informant."

This elicited a chorus of laughter in the Montfair family room.

Tavina went on to describe the events at Off the Grid, emphasizing her steely resolve, Miles' unfailing courage and his MacGyver-like ability to free them and make their escape. She omitted any reference to Jericho Rolfe and her well-intended if misguided naivety as a young prosecutor to allow him back on the streets, which led to the murder of Edwin Hendershot. Rocky was also written out of her narrative. For all the viewers knew, only she and Miles escaped, thanks to his NASCAR-level driving skills.

The screen then split. Tobias appeared on one side. On the other was the image of three people—two women and one man—shackled and surrounded by law enforcement, being frog-marched into a detention facility.

"Three arrests have been made in this case," Tobias said. "The suspects are considered flight risks and are being held without bond. Expectations are that this will be considered a hate crime, which carries stiffer penalties. Reporting from Crutchfield County, Virginia, I'm Tobias Johnson."

Myrna harrumphed. "I don't suppose we'll get any credit for all the work we did to help the ultimate hero, the 'brave and resourceful' Miles Flanagan."

"Nah," Thumper replied. "That would weaken the emphasis on Tavina as the central figure."

"I will say," Janey added, "she's pretty damn good at this public image thing."

"A brilliant political career surely awaits her," Thumper said. "She'll be dining out on this ordeal for decades."

"What about the other guy?" Elizabeth asked. "What's his name? Rocky?"

"Let's just say," Thumper explained, "Rockwell Hendershot no longer exists as we knew him."

"Witness protection?"

"Yep."

Thumper excused himself, went to his study, and placed a call to Miles.

"How are you holding up?" he asked.

"Doin' okay. Just watched the news report. Looks like I've gone from zero to hero."

"Well, Mister Hero, look, if you want to scratch tomorrow, that's fine with me. Bumpers can have a bit more rest. Or I could see if another jockey…"

"Hell no! Bumpers is ready to go! But only if I'm riding him. Besides, I gotta be there to sign autographs, right?"

"Okay, then, if you're good with it. See you tomorrow at Glenwood Park. Get some rest."

Chapter 60

Saturday
Glenwood Park, Middleburg

Miles stepped into the officials' area for the pre-race meeting to a round of applause from the other jockeys. A few of the stewards added their acknowledgement.

Micah Hairston approached and extended a hand. With a wide grin, he said, "I still think you're a crazy-ass little shit, Flanagan. But you got more guts than the rest of us put together. Good job!"

Miles returned the playfully teasing tone. "We'll see how you feel after this crazy-ass little shit beats you today."

The meeting concluded, Miles walked to the horsemen's parking area where Voytek and Myrna waited with Bumpers.

Voytek flashed an uncharacteristically friendly smile and said, "I am hearing you did very good thing in very bad situation. Natasha said to tell you all is forgiven from before."

Miles put a hand on Voytek's shoulder. "Y'know, I think that means more to me than any of this other 'hero' crap. Tell her I really appreciate that." He paused, then said, "But there's something I need to ask you. Rocky said you told him I'm a racist. Where would you ever get such an idea?"

"What?" he replied, shocked by the question. "Of course you are racist." He waved an arm around the horsemen's area. "We are all racists, are we not? Mister Thumper used to be big racist, but after fight with you, he quit. Now he is back, and you too, doing racist things."

"Jesus, Voytek!" Miles exclaimed. "It's '*racing*', not '*racist*'! Totally different things."

Voytek's brow furrowed. "I am not understanding. So, person who does art is artist, person who draws cartoons is cartoonist, plays piano…pianist, goes touring…tourist, has hobby…hobbyist. But if someone does racing, they are *not* racist?"

"No, they are *not*."

Voytek sighed and shook his head. "I am still not understanding your American language."

With an easy laugh, Miles said, "That's okay. In this case, calling me a racist actually turned out to be a good thing. But probably best you don't refer to anyone in the racing community that way in the future."

Voytek nodded in resigned agreement and returned to prepping Bumpers for the upcoming race.

Tavina was the center of attention in Cecelia's tailgate spot. Her campaign posters served as a draw for a steady stream of supporters. Many were new devotees, some not aware until now that an election for commonwealth's attorney was coming up. Shelton hovered beside her, more bodyguard than lover, tall and alert, scanning for any sign of possible threat, highly unlikely though that might be. Thumper watched from the adjoining spot, hoping for a lull that would allow him to have an uninterrupted moment with Tavina.

The Montfair tailgate had its own new celebrity. Several people strolling by noticed Tobias. Some simply caught his eye, nodded, gave him a half-raised hand in acknowledgement, and continued on. Celebrities of a grander scale—famous authors, award-winning film stars, high-ranking government officials—are often in attendance at upper level race meets. Local custom discourages fawning intrusion. Tobias, ranking in the lower echelon of celebrity, was more a target for encouragement than awe.

Thumper noticed a brief ebb in the flow of well-wishers around Tavina. He double-timed his dash to the Kimber spot.

"Ah, Mister Billington!" she declared, "my behind-the-scenes benefactor."

"First of all," Thumper began, "we're all so glad you're safe and unharmed. That must have been a horrendous experience you went through."

"Yes, it was. But the Doddridges have been facing similar challenges for generations. The Hendershots are only the most recent to attack us, whether in Crutchfield County or elsewhere. We've always survived, and always will."

"Um, look," he said apologetically, "I just want you to know it wasn't our intention to go behind your back. As you've found out, Miles Flanagan can't be counted on to follow instructions. So once he'd spilled the beans to me, I felt it was in everyone's best interest to help however I could."

"I admit," she replied, "I wasn't happy when I learned he'd violated my orders. But, well, it worked out fine in the end, didn't it?"

"Yes, yes it did. But, um, there remains the matter of how you persuaded…well…*forced* him, into doing your bidding. Y'know, those unpleasant, and surely unfounded, rumors about a certain incident…"

Tavina leaned in toward Thumper, nodded, and said with a wink, "You mean what happened in Rhetta McKendrick's kitchen? Where Miles tried to shoot Smith Bondurant, the developer?"

"You…you know about that?" Thumper asked in shock.

"Every detail. That you, Doctor Musgrove, your sister, and Bondurant's personal secretary surprised Bondurant and your cousin, Cuyler Corley, when they were trying to convince your Rhetta to sell her land for their resort project…right next to Montfair. And then Miles Flanagan shows up, wearing his Ranger uniform, pistol in hand." She shook her head. "Poor Miles, so lost in his delusions that he believed he really was one of Mosby's Rangers. He saw Bondurant not only as the worst kind of 'carpetbagger' but also someone who took advantage of young women." Adopting a genteel Southern accent, she added, "Now, he couldn't allow such ungentlemanly behavior here in the Old Dominion, could he?"

"But…how?" Thumper asked. "We all swore to keep what happened quiet." Thumper thought for a moment. "Corley! It had to be my snake of a cousin who spilled the…"

Doddridge cut him off. "Nope, not him. Someone much closer to us all."

"Who then?"

"Well…" she drawled out, teasing her reply, "there was this hole in Rhetta's kitchen ceiling, bits of drywall scattered around, and an odd, acrid odor in the room. Shelton was still living with her grandmother and, as you might expect, questioned her about that. Rhetta, who's known for her 'I don't give a rat's ass' attitude, told Shelton the whole story, about how Bar Reinhardt had seen Miles sneaking into the house, followed him, and got the pistol away from Miles just in time to save Bondurant's life." She paused and asked, "How am I doing so far?"

Thumper shrugged and returned a weak smile.

"But then," Tavina continued, "Miles managed to get to his second pistol, pointed it at Bondurant, and…" She leaned in closer. "…a *true* gentleman stepped in front of the target just as Miles pulled the trigger."

Thumper shivered as he recalled the sight of that pistol pointed at him, the ear-shattering report as the hammer hit the firing pin and black powder smoke flashed from the barrel. Then the relief when he realized Miles had only loaded one pistol with live rounds. The other still held the blank loads used in reenactments.

"So," Tavina continued, "late one night, after Shelton moved in with me, she told me all about it." With a mischievous grin, she added, "There might have been some wine involved."

At that point, Thumper figured everyone involved on his side was now screwed, despite their efforts to help Miles' mission succeed.

Tavina went on. "She also told me how you all agreed to keep it hush-hush for Miles' sake, that it would be a group project to get his head straight, return him to a sense of reality. After all, no one was actually hurt. Shelton convinced me to let it go, that Miles was an essential part of the shop's team and, with everything else on her trying to keep the place afloat, the last thing she needed was to lose the one person who knew the inventory system like the back of his hand. And you even rehired him to work with your new racehorse, something no one thought you'd ever do."

Thumper let out a long breath. "So…you've known all this for several months and did nothing?"

"Oh, I wouldn't say I've done nothing. I was holding that card and considering how it might be played. And then I started to hear rumblings about these United Friends of Rockwell wackos. I needed to get someone on the inside and, well…let's just say this was my contribution to the Miles Flanagan rehabilitation program."

She read the concern on Thumper's face.

"Oh, don't worry," she assured him. "This will all stay just between us. Miles is definitely off the hook. I mean, the man saved my life. And, in exchange, I promised him no charges would ever be brought. He also made me swear the same about all of you who conspired to protect him. And you and I both know that a true Virginian, especially those of us who attended Mister Jefferson's university, would never go back on our word."

Thumper took a long moment to let all this sink in. He then said, "Would it be unseemly for me to make a contribution to your campaign?"

"Oh, well, that's purely your decision. I would never try to put any pressure on someone to do that."

"And," he continued, "perhaps we could schedule a fundraiser at Montfair."

"Oh, Professor Billington, that would be lovely."

If there remained any doubt that Tavina Doddridge would be the next Commonwealth's Attorney for Crutchfield County, a public endorsement by Thaddeus Augustus Billington the Fourth guaranteed a record landslide.

****

"Horses to the paddock for the third race!" boomed over the PA system.

Voytek led Bumpers to the paddock. Myrna slipped off to watch the race from the Montfair tailgate spot. Miles joined the other jockeys waiting their turn to mount up for the contest, eighteen timber fences over three and a quarter miles. Four other horses were entered. Micah Hairston was riding Signs of Life, who had bested Miles and Down the Alley by a neck in their first outing. Savvy pro Tucker Dickenson on Throne of Zeus and newcomer Georgia Symansky on Pundit Pride had both been left behind when Bumpers romped to an eight length win in their previous contest. Also vying for the win was Jack O'Meara riding Family Dynasty. Miles and Bumpers faced that duo, along with a few others, on the day Thumper attended Wilma Jean's birthday party. The others in the field had been no threat. Only O'Meara and Family Dynasty had been a challenge to the end. Bumpers showed he knew what the game was all about and was not going to be denied the victory that day.

With today's $30,000 purse at stake, none of the five entries would be out for a schooling lark. They were all hoping to stand in the winner's circle and pocket their share of the winnings. $18,000 of the thirty grand went to first place, decreasingly smaller amounts for second through fourth. The jockeys typically pocketed ten percent.

"Riders up!" sounded.

As Voytek reached to boost Miles into the saddle, he said, "You are winning for Mister Thumper today." Miles wasn't sure if this was a typical case of poor English syntax or if the old Pole had received the gift of prophecy. It was, though, the first time Voytek had spoken to Miles while giving him a leg up. The lift placed Miles perfectly, no need to grab mane.

The five contestants assembled behind the starting line. The starter dropped the flag. The announcer called, "And they're off!"

Hairston let Signs of Life take the lead with O'Meara and Family Dynasty just off his right hip. Symanksy and Pundit Pride followed by two lengths, Dickenson and Throne of Zeus right behind. Miles and Bumpers settled in last, cruising at a comfortable pace.

Hairston and O'Meara appeared to be making it a two horse race, battling it out from one fence to the next, trading the lead but never by more than half a length. The other three trailed, but always within striking distance.

Miles monitored the energy in Bumper's reserve tank. He knew the horse had a strong finish when asked. He could have beaten Micah Hairston and Signs of Life in their first meeting with just one touch of the whip. But the boss told him not to push it, let him have fun his first time out. So he was content then to tease Micah with a threatening move and a taunting grin. As it was, Hairston just barely squeaked out the win.

While he'd beaten Dickenson handily in their first meeting, Miles knew not to discount the seasoned pro. The third generation from a prominent racing family, Tucker knew all the tricks in the book and his ability to read a horse was every bit as sharp as Miles'.

Flanagan could see that Symansky, albeit a relative newbie, was showing herself to be a savvy competitor.

O'Meara's résumé boasted several major wins on courses up and down the East Coast.

It was clearly anyone's race to win at this point.

Miles carefully monitored the two leaders, waiting for the right moment to kick on and let Bumpers show his stuff.

With four jumps to go, Hairston found Signs of Life's fifth gear and pulled ahead of Family Dynasty by three lengths.

O'Meara had misjudged his horse's stamina over this challenging course, longer than most and with more jumps. As the other horses kicked up the pace, Family Dynasty began to drift toward the rear. Jack O'Meara would not be posing in the winner's circle this day.

Miles knew it was time to make his move. Bumpers landed over the fence ahead of the two remaining competitors and dashed off to challenge the leader.

Symansky and Dickenson were in their own battle for third place.

Hairston still had the lead by two lengths at the final fence but Miles and Bumpers were closing fast.

In the stretch to the finish, Miles urged Bumpers to full throttle. The horse responded with a powerful surge. The Montfair duo wasn't playing now. This was for the win.

Shoulder-to-shoulder with one furlong left to the wire, Bumpers pulled ahead in a devastating burst of speed. The sound of a frustrated Micah Hairston shouting "Son-of-a-bitch!" was sweet music to Miles' ears. The PA system added the final punctuation. "Down the Alley, with Miles Flanagan aboard, takes it by five lengths in an impressive finish! Signs of Life with Micah Hairston second; Pundit's Pride, Georgia Symansky up, third; and Throne of Zeus, Tucker Dickenson up, fourth."

The Montfair entourage gathered in the winner's circle. Miles remained mounted as Voytek led Bumpers into place for the glamor shot. Thumper invited his entire crew, along with a few from the Kimber Farm group, to get in the picture. A wide angle shot was required to fit in all the admirers arrayed around a highly alert Down the Alley and a broadly smiling Miles Flanagan.

The photo op over, Miles vaulted off the horse.

Thumper strode up to him, pumped his hand, and said, "Great job! You played that just right. Brought him home a winner and gave the crowd a thrill. We'll be celebrating at Montfair this evening. You're welcome to join us."

"Tell you the truth, boss, I think I need some quiet time. These past few days have been right much more exciting than I'm used to."

Thumper put his hand on Miles' shoulder. "I understand." He stepped back and remarked, "Those Montfair silks sure look good on you."

Miles gazed down at his racing jersey. With a grin he said, "And they finally got the colors right."

Chapter 61

Saturday Evening
Montfair

The residents of Montfair, plus one weekend guest, gathered in Thumper's study for a celebratory toast.

When the last glass was drained, Thumper said to Elizabeth and Tobias, "Let's take a walk."

Janey and Myrna shared a wink.

They strolled up the sloping field to the old cemetery.

"This is the project I was working on," Thumper said with a sweep of his hand toward the graveyard.

Where there had been a dozen randomly arranged markers—most barely legible, some tilting at sharp angles, a few no more than a small slab laid into the ground—there were now new, expertly carved tombstones. Some showed only a first name and death year, others included a birth year and surname. Common to all, however, was an image chiseled at the top, a quartet of four-pointed stars, the same symbol etched into the lintel above the door to what had once been the Montfair schoolhouse.

At the back of the enclosure, two tombstones stood side-by-side, larger than all the others. Thumper pointed to them and said to Tobias, "Read those."

Tobias read aloud. "Tobias Jefferson Johnson. 'Teeje'. 1825-1901. Portia Johnson Hairston. 'Tee'. 1820-1887."

All three stood silently for a solemn minute.

Elizabeth was the first to speak. "Where have I seen that design before? Those stars? It looks familiar."

"In at least two places," Thumper replied. "Above the door to the Nutchenkos' cottage…" With a gesture toward Tobias, he said, "…and?"

Tobias took the cue. "It's our family's signature, placed somewhere into everything my father designs and builds. Goes back several generations. My older brother's also using it now that he's working with our father."

Thumper turned back to Elizabeth. "I noticed it at Wilma Jean's birthday party, inlaid into the patio design. I knew I'd seen it somewhere. Reading Olivia's diary brought it together."

"Where did it come from?" she asked. "Does it have some special meaning?"

"Very special," Thumper explained. "I did some research and found that it's the symbol for the word 'fence" in the Adrinka language, common to the Bono people of Ghana. It means 'fence' in the sense of security, a safeguard around those you love and care about, a way to protect your family."

He placed his hands on the wrought iron fence, freshly cleaned and repainted by Voytek, and focused on the tombstones. "The people buried here did not have the safety and security they deserved in life. Olivia did what she could to help offset that. Her tool was education and she helped many. But there was only so much she could do during those difficult times."

He stood in silence, his gaze directed to the two larger headstones at the back.

With a nod, he continued. "Anyway, while I couldn't go back in time to offer them safety and security in their lives, to put the family fence around them symbolically, I figured the least I could do was provide it for them now."

"I think it was a lovely gesture," Elizabeth said.

"Is there something specific you want us to take away from this?" Tobias asked.

"Oh, I had it done for my own reasons," Thumper replied offhandedly. "Just thought it might be of interest to you two. Do with it what you will." He shrugged and walked away, back to the house.

Chapter 62

Saturday Evening
Thumper's Study

The Diary of Olivia Bauer Billington
Montfair, Crutchfield County, Virginia
October 21, 1901

Once again, my heart breaks to note the passing of a dear friend and, for many decades, a valued member of the Montfair family. Tobias Jefferson Johnson, affectionately known as "Teeje," a distinctive moniker derived from the initials "TJ," left this world five days ago, October 16.

I consider it no coincidence that we received news today of a seminal event in our nation's history. President Theodore Roosevelt invited noted educator and author Booker T. Washington to dine with him at the White House. This occurred the same day as the passing of our beloved Teeje.

We have received reports from different quarters in which divergent opinions are expressed. Some praise Mister Roosevelt for his progressive views and, perhaps more significantly, his willingness to act upon them. Others consider a Colored man dining in the Executive Mansion as a coequal of the president to signal the end of our Republic as we know it.

Sadly, I hear echoes of the vitriolic debates that raged in our nation nearly fifty years ago. From my earliest girlhood I prayed for the day when I would live in a world where there were no masters and slaves. Those of us who lived in that older time did not create this unjust system but had it thrust upon us by others. Perhaps the only way to start on the path to a more just system was through violent upheaval. I would, of course, have preferred a gentler, more reasonable way. But that seemed to be a distant, remote possibility.

Would the repercussions of that disastrous conflict, that cost the lives of so many and left countless others in a state of destitution and despair, be felt for generations to come? I have already witnessed elements of that in our own community. I can only pray that one day the evils of the past will fade from the collective memory and the spirit of brotherly compassion will prevail. If the Billington name survives, may it prove to be a shining light pointing the way toward that goal.

****

Thumper closed his great-great-grandmother's diary. That was her final entry. She took ill shortly after, a rare occurrence for her. Three months later she was gone.

On his way upstairs, he stopped at the landing where her portrait hung.

"We're still working some things out, Grandmother. We've done our best to live up to your call to be the shining lights this world needs. Sadly, as we've just seen, we still have some challenges to deal with. If only there were more people with your noble spirit. I promise you, though, that as long as our family name survives, we'll keep your light shining."

He studied her face, frozen in time. Or was it? The emotions behind her expression had always been an enigma to him. Was she about to smile? Maybe holding back barely concealed distain? Deep in contemplation? For the first time, he saw the hint of a different sentiment.

Hope.

Chapter 63

Saturday Evening
Bar's Trailer

Miles and Bar kicked back in the rickety lawn chairs outside Bar's trailer, a six pack of Budweiser on the ground between them.

"Here," Miles said, offering the medal to Bar, "looks like this thing really is a lucky charm."

Bar raised a hand. "You'd best keep it. If I know you, you're gonna get your sorry ass into some kind of trouble again. And you'll need all the luck you can get to bail you out a third time."

Miles nodded and slipped the medal into his pocket. "Yeah," he said with a resigned sigh, "you're probably right."

The odd twosome sat and contemplated the peaceful seclusion of Bar's private oasis. As the evening light faded, the vultures in the trees before them settled in for the night.

"Y'know," Bar mused, "I need to think about what will happen to this place when I'm gone. Who's gonna take care of my birds?"

"Shit, Bar," Miles said, "those birds can take care of themselves. Besides, you're gonna outlive all of them, and several more generations."

"Yeah, maybe. But someone's gotta make sure the damn developers don't get hold of this place. Ryman's old lady puts up a pretty good fight, but she ain't gonna be around forever."

He paused in thought for a long moment. Then, with a sweeping gesture toward the tiny open spot, the woods around them, and the mini trailer behind, he said, "If you play your cards right, Flanagan, one day this could all be yours."

Miles grinned and shook his head. He thought this was just another one of Barstow Reinhardt's sarcastic remarks. But when he looked over at the big man, he noticed something in Bar's remaining eye, that eerily luminous blue orb, that he'd never seen before. Sadness? Regret? A sense of his own mortality?

Miles raised his beer and extended it toward the big man. The gesture was returned. They clinked bottles to seal the deal.

The troublesome spirits lifted from Reinhardt. Flanagan sensed a presence he'd never felt before from the aging warrior with a shady past.

Peace.

About the Author

J. Harris Anderson attended the University of Virginia and George Mason University, where he earned BSc and MBA degrees. A member of Mensa, his career as a marketing specialist took him through the banking, hospitality, and construction industries. He has served as a consultant to several organizations and as Senior Writer for a firm specializing in training programs and corporate communications.

He is currently the managing editor of *In & Around Horse Country*, a national quarterly publication covering foxhunting, steeplechasing, and other horse sports.

An avid foxhunter, he has served as a field leader, whipper-in, and racecourse outrider. He lives on a Virginia horse farm with his wife and their critters.

A Rockwell Remembrance

George Lincoln Rockwell based his American Nazi Party in Arlington, Virginia, where I grew up. At one point in the mid-1960s, his headquarters occupied a ramshackle house not far from my high school. One autumn afternoon, two buddies and I thought it would be a fun prank to pay a visit and pretend we were interested in signing up. This was a few months after Alex Haley's interview of Rockwell appeared in the April, 1966, issue of *Playboy*. (Like our fathers, we read it for the articles.)

Rockwell either wasn't there at the time or the "stormtrooper" we encountered was shielding him from unannounced visitors. But the trooper responded eagerly to our claims of sharing the party's views and our feigned interest in joining their cause. He loaded us up with their outlandish propaganda—racist screeds and crude cartoons.

We told him we'd earnestly study those materials and return for more, maybe even have the good fortune to meet The Commander himself.

It was all good for a laugh. And we never went back.

Shortly after our visit, Rockwell moved his HQ to another part of Arlington.

Less than a year later, while preparing to do his laundry at a small strip shopping center, Rockwell was shot and killed by one of his troopers. Not exactly on the same martyrdom scale as other political firebrands who were assassinated during that tumultuous decade.

The Arlington police force went into action. Roadblocks and checkpoints were set up throughout the area as they searched for the shooter. I don't recall where I was going at the time (it was August, school hadn't started yet), but I was stopped at one of the checkpoints. With the inquiring officer satisfied that I—a 17-year-old clean-cut kid who was both intrigued and amused by what was happening—was not the shooter, I was allowed to drive on.

I never did get to meet The Commander himself. And I'm good with that.

JHA

Also by J. Harris Anderson

The Prophet of Paradise

A Paradise Gap Novel

Foxhunting, Faith, and Pheromones

The Foxhunter's Guide to Life & Love

An Inspirational Novel

Humorous, lighthearted, and earnestly practical advice to improve your love life, and your love *of* life.

Paving Paradise

A Paradise Gap Novel

You don't know what you've got till it's gone.

A Funny Thing Happened On the Way to the Fox Den

Humorous Observations from the Hunt Field

For more information, to read/listen to excerpts, and ordering links:

www.BlueCardinalPress.com

Made in the USA
Middletown, DE
17 August 2025

11623697R00186